The Frozen River

ALSO BY ARIEL LAWHON

The Wife, the Maid, and the Mistress

Flight of Dreams

I Was Anastasia

Code Name Hélène

When We Had Wings
(co-written with Susan Meissner and Kristina McMorris)

THE FROZEN RIVER

A Novel

ARIEL LAWHON

Doubleday
NEW YORK

Copyright © 2023 by Ariel Lawhon

All rights reserved. Published in the United States by Doubleday, a division of Penguin Random House LLC, New York, and distributed in Canada by Penguin Random House Canada Limited, Toronto.

www.doubleday.com

DOUBLEDAY and the portrayal of an anchor with a dolphin are registered trademarks of Penguin Random House LLC.

Jacket photograph © Natasza Fiedotjew/Trevillion Images
Jacket design by John Fontana
Map of Hallowell, Maine, by Mapping Specialists, Ltd.
Book design by Soonyoung Kwon

LIBRARY OF CONGRESS CATALOGING-IN-PUBLICATION DATA
Names: Lawhon, Ariel, author.
Title: The frozen river : a novel / Ariel Lawhon.
Description: First edition. | New York : Doubleday, [2023].
Identifiers: LCCN 2022057899 (print) | LCCN 2022057900 (ebook) |
ISBN 9780385546874 (hardcover) | ISBN 9780385546881 (ebook)
Subjects: LCSH: Ballard, Martha, 1735–1812—Fiction. | Midwives—
Maine—Fiction. | Murder—Investigation—Maine—Fiction. | Kennebec
River Valley (Me.)—Social life and customs—18th century—Fiction. |
LCGFT: Detective and mystery fiction. | Historical fiction.
Classification: LCC PS3601.L447 F76 2023 (print) |
LCC PS3601.L447 (ebook) | DDC 813/.6—dc23/eng/20221220
LC record available at https://lccn.loc.gov/2022057899
LC ebook record available at https://lccn.loc.gov/2022057900

MANUFACTURED IN THE UNITED STATES OF AMERICA

5 7 9 10 8 6

First Edition

My mother taught me that midwives are heroes.
My sister let me witness the miracle.
My husband sat beside me and held my hand.
For these reasons, and ten thousand more,
this novel is dedicated to them.

And *She* knows, because She warns him, and Her instincts never fail,
That the Female of Her Species is more deadly than the Male.

—RUDYARD KIPLING, "THE FEMALE OF THE SPECIES"

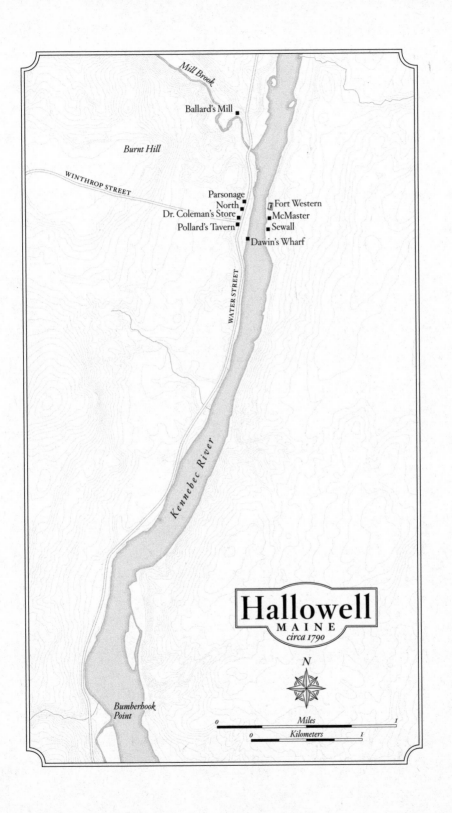

Mill Brook

Ballard's Mill ■

Burnt Hill

WINTHROP STREET

Parsonage ■
North ■   ▧ Fort Western
Dr. Coleman's Store ■   ■ McMaster
Pollard's Tavern ■   ■ Sewall
                ■ Dawin's Wharf

WATER STREET

Kennebec River

Bumberhook
Point

Hallowell
MAINE
circa 1790

N

| 0 | Miles | 1 |
| 0 | Kilometers | 1 |

I

A HANGING

NOVEMBER 1789

Truth will come to light; murder cannot be hid long.

—WILLIAM SHAKESPEARE, *The Merchant of Venice*

WHAT'S PAST IS PROLOGUE

The body floats downstream. But it is late November, and the Kennebec River is starting to freeze, large chunks of ice swirling and
tumbling through the water, collecting in mounds while clear, cold
fingers of ice stretch out from either bank, reaching into the current,
grabbing hold of all that passes by. Already weighted down by soaked
clothing and heavy leather boots, the dead man bobs in the ebbing
current, unseeing eyes staring at the waning crescent moon.

It is a miserable night with bitter wind and numbing frost, and
the slower the river moves, the quicker it freezes, trapping him in its
sluggish grip, as folds of his homespun linen shirt are thrown out like
petals of a wilted brown tulip. Just an hour ago his hair was combed
and pulled back, tied with a strip of lace. He'd taken the lace, of
course, and it is possible—fate is such a fragile thing, after all—that
he *might* still be alive if not for that choice. But it was insult on top of
injury. Wars have been fought over less.

The dead man was in a hurry to leave this place, was in too much
trouble already, and had he taken more care, been patient, he would
have heard his assailants in the forest. Heard. Hidden. Held his
breath. And waited for them to pass. But the dead man was reckless
and impatient. Panting. He'd left tracks in the snow and was not hard
to find. His hair came loose in the struggle, the bit of lace reclaimed

and shoved in a pocket, and now that hair, brown as a muddy river-bank, is a tangled mess, part of it plastered to his forehead, part in his mouth, pulled there during a last startled gasp before he was thrown into the river.

His tangled, broken body is dragged along by the current for another quarter of a mile before the ice congeals and grinds to a halt with a tired moan, trapping him fifteen feet from the shore, face an inch below the surface, lips parted, eyes still widened in surprise.

The great freeze has come a month early to the town of Hallowell, Maine, and—the dead man could not know this, nor could anyone who lives here—the thaw will not arrive for many, many long months. They will call this the Year of the Long Winter. It will become legend, and he, no small part of it. For now, however, they sleep safe and warm in their beds, doors shut tight against an early, savage winter. But there—along the riverbank, if you look closely—something dark and agile moves in the moonlight. A fox. Tentative, she sets one paw onto the ice. Then another. She hesitates, for she knows how fickle the river can be, how it longs to swallow everything and pull it into the churning depths. But the ice holds, and the fox inches forward, toward the dead man. She creeps out to where he lies, entombed in the ice. The clever little beast looks at him, her head tilted to the side, but he does not return the gaze. She lifts her nose to the sky. Sniffs for danger. Inhales the pungent scent of frost and pine along the river and, farther away, the faintest whiff of woodsmoke. Satisfied, the fox begins to howl.

CLARK FORGE

"You need not fear," I tell Betsy Clark. "In all my years attending women in childbirth, I have never lost a mother."

The young woman looks at me, eyes wide, sweat beading on her temples, and nods. But I do not think she believes me. They never do. Every laboring woman suspects that she is, in fact, moments away from death. This is normal. And it does not offend me. A woman is never more vulnerable than while in labor. Nor is she ever stronger. Like a wounded animal, cornered and desperate, she spends her travail alternately curled in upon herself or lashing out. It ought to kill a woman, this process of having her body turned inside out. By rights, no one should survive such a thing. And yet, miraculously, they do, time and again.

John Cowan—the young blacksmith apprenticed to Betsy's husband—came to fetch me two hours ago, and I'd told him there was no time to dally. Betsy's children come roaring into the world at uncommon speed, with volume to match. Shrieking banshees, all slippery and red-faced. But so small that—even full-term—their entire buttocks can fit in the palm of my hand. Wee little things. John took my instructions to heart, setting a pace so fast that my body still aches from our frantic ride through Hallowell.

But now, having barely arrived and situated myself, I find that the baby is already crowning. Betsy's contractions are thirty seconds apart. This child—like her others—is in a hurry to greet its mother. Thankfully, she is built well for birthing.

"It's time," I tell her, setting a warm hand on each of her knees. I gently press them apart and help the young woman shimmy her nightgown higher over her bare belly. It is hard, clenched at the peak of a contraction, and Betsy grinds her teeth together, trying not to sob.

Labor renders every woman a novice. Every time is the first time, and the only expertise comes from those assembled to help. And so Betsy has gathered her women: mother, sisters, cousin, aunt. Birth is a communal act, and all of them spring into action as her resolve slips and she cries out in pain. They know what this means. Even those with no specific job find something to do. Boiling water. Tending the fire. Folding cloths. This is women's work at its most elemental. Men have no place in this room, no *right,* and Betsy's husband has retreated to his forge, impotent, to pour out his fear and frustration upon the anvil, to beat a piece of molten metal into submission.

Betsy's women work in tandem, watching me, responding to every cue. I extend a hand, and a warm, wet cloth is set upon it. No sooner have I wiped the newest surge of blood and water away, than the cloth is plucked from my grip and replaced by one that is fresh. The youngest of Betsy's kin—a cousin, no more than twelve— is charged with cleaning the soiled rags, keeping the kettle at a boil, and replenishing the wash bucket. She applies herself to the task without a flinch or complaint.

"There's your baby," I say, my hand upon the slick, warm head. "Bald as an egg. Just like the others."

Betsy lifts her chin and speaks with a grimace as the contraction loosens its grip. "Does that mean it's another girl?"

"It means nothing." I keep my gaze steady and my hand gentle on the tiny head that is pushing into my palm.

"Charles wants a boy," she pants.

Charles has no say, I think.

Another brutal wave descends upon Betsy, and her sisters move forward to lift her legs and hold them back.

"On my count, push," I tell her. "One. Two. Three." I watch the rise of Betsy's contraction as it tents her abdomen. "*Now.*"

She holds her breath, bears down, and another inch of bald head is revealed, the tips of little ears cresting beyond the confines of her body. She doesn't have a chance to catch her breath before the next wave rolls over her, and then they come, unrelenting, one on top of another, never loosening their grip upon her womb. Betsy pushes. Gasps for air. Pushes again. Again. And again. Someone wipes the sweat from her brow, the tears from her cheeks, but I never look away. Finally, the head pushes through.

I ease my hand forward, cupping a cheek and one small ear in my palm. "Only the shoulders now. Two more pushes ought to do it."

Betsy, however, is ready to be done with this business, and she heaves with the last of her strength, forcing the child right into my hands, then flops back onto the bed as the baby is freed from her body with a *whoosh,* the only remaining connection a slick silver cord.

A tiny, outraged squall fills the room, but Betsy's women neither cheer nor clap. They watch, silent, waiting for my pronouncement.

"Hello little one," I whisper, then hold the baby up for Betsy to see. "You have another daughter."

"Oh," she says, crestfallen, and pushes onto her elbows to see the child.

There is work yet to be done, and I go about it with deliberation. I lay the little girl on the bed between her mother's legs and snip the umbilical cord with my scissors. Once that primordial bond is cut, I tie it off with a piece of string. Then I plunge my hands into a wash bucket, clean them, and swipe my thumb across the roof of the baby's mouth. No cleft palate. Another tiny miracle that I mentally log during any successful birth. I wipe the blood and waxy vernix from the writhing, slippery infant even as I keep an eye on Betsy for excess bleeding. Nothing seems out of the ordinary.

Betsy's women pull back her hair, wash her face, make her sip lukewarm tea. They help her into a sitting position and a clean shift. They ready her to nurse.

"Look how pretty you are," I say to the baby, then add, "Look how *loved* you are."

And I pray to God that it is true.

Charles Clark is so desperate for a son—this is their third child in four years—that his determination might well kill his wife if he isn't careful. As for Betsy, she is desperate to please her husband and will never tell him no.

All appears in order with mother and child, so I wrap her in clean, soft linen and hand her to Betsy. She puts the bundle to her breast and hisses as the baby latches onto her nipple. It makes her abdomen contract once more, ridding itself of the afterbirth. Even this is fascinating to me, and I inspect the remnants of labor for irregularities, making sure it is intact, that nothing has been left behind. It too is normal, and I discard the residue into the bucket at my feet.

"There's one last thing," I warn.

Betsy nods. She's been through this before.

"Bear with me. It will be a few seconds. But it may hurt."

"Go on, then."

I knead Betsy's abdomen, rolling the heel of my hand this way and that, helping it contract. The girl winces but doesn't cry out, and then there is nothing left for her to do but nurse the child.

"What will you call her?" I ask.

"Mary."

A name that means "bitter," I think, but offer the young mother an approving smile because it is expected.

The women work in tandem to clean Betsy and wrap her groin in clean, dry cloths. These will be changed by the after nurses every hour for the next few days.

It is four thirty in the morning—still hours before dawn—and Betsy's women slip away to clean the last of the mess, and then to find what sleep they can. They will come in shifts to care for Betsy and her children over the next week. It will be the only rest the young blacksmith's wife will get.

I remove my soiled apron and wash my hands again, then tie back the pieces of hair that have come loose before I sit on the edge of the bed and drink a cup of tea—now cold—that was brought to me when I arrived. For several moments I observe mother and child.

"Shall I let Charles know that all is well?" I ask.

"Yes," Betsy says, "but don't tell me if he's angry."

"He has no right to be angry. You've given him a beautiful child."

"It means nothing, whether he has a *right* to his anger or not."

I take a deep, calming breath before reassuring her. "Don't worry about Charles. I'll take care of him. You enjoy your daughter."

The Clarks live in a small cabin adjacent to the only forge in three counties. It is a short walk, but I slide into my riding cloak anyway.

The frigid air hits me like a slap, so startling after the near-oppressive heat inside the birthing room. It stings the inside of my nose with each inhale. The night is clear and crisp, the moon proud, and stars bright against an inky blanket of sky.

I don't bother to knock on the forge door—Charles wouldn't hear me with all the hammering anyway—but push it open without announcing myself. Betsy's husband paces, muttering curses and prayers. He is utterly helpless and totally to blame for his wife's recent agony.

Charles lifts his head when I enter his field of vision, and brings a cross peen hammer down on a rod of white-hot iron with such force that I can feel the vibrations through the hard-packed earth beneath me. The room smells of hot metal and baked mud. Of sweat and fear. Charles Clark stands straight, sets his hammer aside, and pushes a wet clump of hair away from his forehead. He's starting to bald—I can see the receding patches at each temple—and it makes him appear older than his thirty years. Dark hair. Dark eyes. Dark beard. Piracy would have been a good option for Charles had he never taken an interest in the smith.

He braves a furtive glance at me, then looks away. "Does my wife live?" he asks, then clears his throat to hide whatever rush of emotion he feels.

"Yes. Of course. She is fine and healthy."

I think this is the closest I will ever come to seeing the man tremble. Relief buckles through his body, and his knees sag, but then he pulls himself together and turns to face me.

"And the child?"

"She has very strong lungs."

His expression doesn't so much crumble, as collapse. I can see the muscle along his jaw work as he clenches, then grinds his teeth. Finally, he swallows hard and asks, "Has Betsy given her a name?"

"Mary."

"I'd hoped for a son."

"I know."

"Because of the forge. I need help. I . . . ." Charles catches himself, embarrassed. "I *do* love my daughters."

"I never said otherwise."

"It's just that I need more hands. There's so much work to do. And I wanted to teach him."

I don't bother to tell Charles that there is no *him,* and that infants are no help in a forge, regardless. That it would be a decade, at least, before a son—if he'd had one—could make even a small contribution to the family business.

"You have John Cowan for help. And you may yet have a son. Betsy is still young. As are you."

Charles nods as though deciding on something important. "We will try harder again next time. I'll make sure of it."

Foolish man.

I step toward the glowing bricks and stretch out my hand until it rests on Charles's forearm. It is muscled and scarred, warm from the fire. Any hair that once grew on it was long ago singed away.

"Not for several months," I tell him. "At the *very* least. If you want a son, you must give her body time to heal. And even then, it is God, not you, who chooses what you will have. Do you understand what I am saying?"

"I'm not cruel," he says.

Just demanding and ungrateful. I do not say this aloud, however. He is the kind of man who will hear the truth, but only when it is spoken indirectly.

"But Betsy needs more than that right now. She needs you to be *gentle.* And patient."

He says nothing, so I give his arm a final squeeze and leave Charles to his work. Having done his job for the evening, John Cowan has retreated into his loft at the other end of the forge. The young man is big, built like an ox, and not much smarter. For now he is lost to a deep and rumbling sleep, oblivious to both the new life that has just entered this world, and the pounding of his master's hammer. John's days are filled with clanging metal, so why should his dreams be any different?

I return to the cabin, find an empty spot beside the hearth, and stretch out on the straw pallet that has been left for me. In a couple of hours, Betsy's women will rise to cook a meal in celebration of this new life. The ritual is commonly observed in Hallowell. A child is born, and a meal is served. Sometimes, it is an elegant feast spread on a linen tablecloth, and at other times a sparse, cold offering thrown together in haste. Sometimes I sleep in a spare bed, and sometimes there is no place for me to sleep at all. I have spent more than one night sitting upright in a chair, jerking awake every time my head lolls. But tonight is typical of most births I attend. A modest home, a normal labor, a simple bed and—in the morning—a hearty breakfast.

I lie curled beneath my riding cloak, staring at the rough-hewn beams of the ceiling, listening to the sounds around me. Little snores and rustles and whispers as Betsy's women bed down for the night. As my eyes grow heavy, the front door opens and Charles walks across the creaky floor toward the bedroom. I listen for the sound of anger, but only hear a man whisper softly to his wife.

*

It feels as though I have barely closed my eyes when I am woken by a large, calloused hand on my shoulder. Charles is there, a lantern in his other hand and urgency in his voice.

"Mistress Ballard," he whispers. "You must get up."

I look to the bedroom where I left mother and child, panicked that something has gone wrong in the night.

"They're fine." He points to the front door. "But someone has come to speak with you. Says it's urgent."

Perhaps an hour has passed, at most, since I fell asleep. It feels as though there are cobwebs in my head and cotton in my eyes, but I wrap my riding cloak a little tighter around my shoulders and follow Charles outside. The blast of cold air is sudden and merciless, and I gasp, then shudder.

Charles lifts the lantern, and I recognize the man sitting astride the horse. He is of middle age and middle height and minor attractiveness, but I can't understand why he is here, and not halfway to Long Reach on a raft with my son.

James Wall looks to be the kind of exhausted that can only happen after being awake all night in the brutal cold. His eyes are red rimmed, hair disheveled, and face unshaved. He licks his chapped lips. "Pardon me, Martha, I don't mean to intrude," he says. "But you're needed in town. *Immediately.*"

"I thought you and Jonathan left on the raft hours ago."

"We did," he says. "But there's been an accident."

WATER STREET

"What happened?" I ask James as soon as we've left the forge.

It took only a moment to check on Betsy and gather my medical bag while James saddled my horse. Brutus didn't make it easy for him, however, and James rubs the sore spot on his shoulder where my horse tried to take a bite out of him.

He takes a shaky breath. "We left Dawin's Wharf late last night when the ice started forming. Me and Sam and Jonathan. There was still an open channel down the middle of the river, about fifty feet wide. We thought we'd have enough time to get the boards to Long Reach, but the ice closed around us an hour ago. I've never seen anything like it, Mistress Ballard. It just swallowed the raft whole. One minute we were moving in the current, and the next we ground to a halt. Sam Dawin fell through trying to get to shore."

"Was he swept under?"

"Almost. But he grabbed the edge when he went down. His toes just reached the bottom. You know how tall he is. Took some effort, but we got him out. Jonathan rode him straight to your house for help."

"Then we'd best hurry back," I say, digging my heels into Brutus's side. He lurches forward into a canter, and it takes a moment for James to catch up.

"Beg your pardon, Mistress Ballard, but we ain't going back to the mill. Amos Pollard sent me to fetch you to the tavern."

"What does Amos have to do with this?"

"When Sam went under the ice, he saw a body." He takes in my look of astonishment and explains, "A man. Dead and frozen. We cut him from the ice. Me and Amos and a few others. That's why we're headed to the tavern. Amos insisted that you see the body first. Before anyone else. Said you would have a particular interest."

I have seen more than my fair share of dead bodies over the years, but never once would I classify attending them as an *interest*. A necessity at times, to be sure, but never something I enjoy.

The sky is turning from ink to pewter, and I tilt my head to study James's profile. The careful set of his mouth. Eyebrows drawn together. Hands tight on the reins.

"What is it that you're not telling me? Who did you cut out of the river?"

After a long pause he says, "It's hard to say."

"Meaning you don't *want* to say?"

"Meaning that I *can't*. I'm not sure anyone can right now." He swallows. "There's been a good bit of injury . . . particularly to his face, I mean."

James Wall is a terrible liar. That skill will take another decade and a good bit more life experience to acquire. So I can see it there in the set of his jaw as he turns back to the road. Not a lie, perhaps, but certainly an omission.

"Fine then," I answer, voice pleasant. "Who do you *think* was cut from the ice?"

The question startles him, and he answers before he has time to think about the consequences. "Joshua Burgess."

Oh.

I am startled at the relief—no, the *joy*—I feel at hearing that name. What a strange miracle. I had hoped to see Burgess swing at the end of a rope for what he did, but dead is dead, and I'm not sad to hear the news. I still don't understand why Amos sent for me, however, and I tell James so.

"There's a lot of"—he pauses, unsure of the appropriate word—"*damage* . . . more than just his face, you see. Someone will have to declare cause of death. So it's official, in case there is an inquiry."

Injury. Damage. Different words, different meanings.

"And Amos Pollard doesn't think Dr. Cony is up to the job?"

"The doctor is known to be good friends with Colonel North."

My mind is quick, connecting dots he's barely had the time to draw with his carefully worded answer. "Then it *is* Joshua Burgess they found? And someone has killed him?"

He doesn't answer. Instead, James's mouth twists as he works up the courage to ask the question he's been holding in reserve.

"Do you think Rebecca Foster is telling the truth? About Colonel North and Joshua Burgess?" He seems embarrassed by his own boldness, and his windblown cheeks redden further. "Do you think they raped her as she claims?"

Even now, months later, the image of Rebecca Foster is clear in my mind. I found the young woman alone, at home with her children, several days after the assault. Husband away, she had been an easy victim. I tended to the split lip, the black eye, the bruised cheekbone. I inspected the dark, purple bruises littered across her torso, arms and thighs, wrists and ankles. Searched for broken bones and cuts, finding little that I could mend. There is no mending the kind of damage they had done. I've seen such bruises before. I knew what they meant. So I bathed the young, pretty pastor's wife and helped her into clean clothes. Wrapped her in a blanket. And then I sat down and let the girl weep into my bosom. I stroked her hair and muttered gentle sounds in her ear. Waited until Rebecca Foster wrung herself dry, then I took that horrible, heartrending confession so that she wouldn't have to carry the burden alone.

Listening is a skill acquired by the doing. By many long years spent sitting at bedsides and in birthing rooms, waiting as women share the secret deeds that bring them to labor. I know these secrets come in waves. The first, horrible admission, and then the smaller, deeper acts that came before. A stolen glance. A secret, erotic touch. Moments of passion and lost control. But sometimes—the worst times—it is a story like the one Rebecca spread before me in that broken, disjointed way four months ago. Sometimes, my job is to sit and listen to the tales of brutality and ravishment. Of women who find themselves confessing sins they did not commit. Or even believe could happen to them. Acts they had fought against. So I had remained still and quiet with Rebecca that afternoon. Encouraging her with the occasional understanding nod of my head, instead of words. No. I couldn't speak. Not then. I knew that the sound of my voice would scare the girl into silence. And whatever else happened afterward, I was certain of two things: Rebecca needed to tell me everything, and I needed to know who must bear the punishment for what had been done to her.

"Yes," I tell James, finally, as I clear the hard knot of rage from my throat. "Rebecca is telling the truth, and I believe every word of what she says. I saw the damage they did to her. But I had hoped Joshua Burgess would hang for it."

James looks at me, mouth set in a grim line. "Don't be so sure he didn't."

POLLARD'S TAVERN

Something is on fire. I can smell it, a quarter mile from town, and I fear, for a moment, that destruction has followed death into Hallowell this morning. But when we round the bend, I see that it is only the tavern heaving thick smoke from both stacked-stone chimneys. Wet wood never burns well, and the smoke settles like a fog, perfuming the air, thick and pungent, making my nose sting.

Pollard's Tavern is a dark hulk against the pre-dawn sky. It sits squarely at the crossroads of Water and Winthrop Streets, a stone's throw from both Coleman's Store and the Kennebec River. The building itself, a two-story rectangle designed in the simple post-and-beam fashion, changes its purpose depending on the public function performed within: tavern, courthouse, lodge, meeting hall—or, in this case, mortuary.

These occurrences are hardly irregular. Last September the tavern served as barracks when the Boston militia marched through Hallowell—the Hook, as locals call our village. They camped here a fortnight, drinking grog and sleeping on the floor, until they could join their regiment in Pittston. The tavern smelled of manure and unwashed male for weeks afterward. Then, exactly nine months after that, I delivered Sarah White's daughter—a rather inconvenient but decidedly permanent reminder of the Boston militia. Still unmarried, the girl has become a favorite topic of gossip among the women, and—unfortunately—of interest among the men. For my part, I pity the girl—pretty faces and misfortune often go hand in hand—but I don't like her any less. Sarah has been a friend to my daughters for many years, and I of all people understand the myriad, unfair ways that women find themselves in childbirth.

"Does anyone else know about the body?" I ask.

"Not that I'm aware."

"How many men did it take to cut him out?"

"Seven. All of them chosen by Amos."

That's a stroke of luck, I think.

A quick glance up and down Water Street reveals that the residents of Hallowell are certainly up, if not about. Curtains are thrown open in homes—revealing the warm light of lanterns within—and children gather wood beneath eaves heavy with snow. More than one industrious housewife is sweeping her front steps even as she stifles a yawn. It is only a matter of time before news of the morning's events makes it to Colonel North—I can see smoke rising from his chimney five houses down—and then across the river to Fort Western and Dr. Cony. I will be lucky if I can examine the body before they interrupt my work or take over altogether.

James helps me down from my perch astride Brutus as best he can—he is a good five inches shorter than I am—and ties both sets of reins to the hitching post. He unbuckles my medical bag from the saddle as I shrug out of my riding cloak and pull off the kid gloves that Ephraim gave me for Christmas. I tuck them through the slits on either side of my riding skirt and into the pockets affixed beneath, then settle my expression into one of trained indifference.

James holds the door open and motions me forward with one thick arm. "After you."

Careful not to make eye contact with anyone on the street, careful to appear as though this is simply an early, *casual* visit, I climb the front steps and cross the threshold. There is an instant uproar. Men spring to their feet and begin shouting. Gesticulating. Pointing toward a door at the back of the tavern. Three of them hold mugs of hard cider. None of them think to greet me. One of them is already drunk. Chandler Robbins sways in his chair with the stupid look of a man who has gone hard and fast into his cups.

"Hush," I snap, setting my fists against my hips. They fall silent as I scan the room, looking each of the seven men directly in the eyes. "An explanation, if you don't mind."

Moses Pollard—a young man of twenty—breaks away from the group and lifts his chin. He is broad shouldered and narrow waisted and has the look of a man who will only grow stronger as he ages. But when he speaks, it is with the soft, kind lilt of his Scottish mother.

"Thank ye for coming, Mistress Ballard," he says. "He's in the back. The man, I mean. The one we cut from the ice." Moses gives me a crooked half smile—also inherited from his mother—but his words are weighted with apology when he adds, "We dinna want to lay him out on one of the tables, ye ken, seeing as we'd be eating off them soon. Apart from issues of cleanliness, my Ma said it would scare off the breakfast crowd to have a dead man staring at them while they eat their porridge."

Amos Pollard drops one heavy arm across his son's shoulders and coughs up a sound that could be either grunt or laughter. His voice—so different from Moses's green, springy cadence—has the guttural baritone of a first-generation German settler. "My vife said she vould wring my neck if I let zem."

The tables in question number about ten, and all—except one where the men have been sitting—are wiped clean with benches tucked beneath and lanterns glowing warmly on top. Each can seat eight and, after decades of use, are worn smooth from plates and elbows. As with most things at Pollard's Tavern—the owners included—the room is solid and rectangular. Open fireplaces—each large enough to roast a spring bull—sit at either end of the room, giving it the look of a Great Hall in an old English manor. The floor is flagstone and swept clean. It smells of candle wax, wood polish, and last night's meal—stew and potatoes, from what I can judge.

The older Pollard is a sturdy man with a square jaw and enormous hands. He runs the tavern as though it were a small city and he the mayor, but his wife, Abigail, is the real heart of the place, beloved in the Hook for her generosity, good humor, and cooking skills. I'm certain that she is keeping her distance from the grim business at hand. Abigail is the sort of woman who can kill, pluck, dress, and roast five geese before lunch but can't stomach the sight of human blood. I have met only a handful of such women in my life, and typically I have no patience for squeamishness, but for Abigail I make an exception because with her it is endearing.

"How can I help?" Moses asks, stepping away from his father.

He's trying to make a good impression. I've seen the way he looks at my daughter Hannah, and I suspect that he's begun to entertain the idea of courting her.

"I'm not sure. I need to see him first."

Amos pops the fingers on his colossal left hand one by one, and I wince at the hard cracking sound. He may as well be snapping tree branches. "It isn't pretty, Martha," he says.

I look him square in the eye and tell him, "Little about my work is."

Amos leads me toward the back room, but as I pass Moses, I give him a sly smile of approval. The more I get to know the boy, the more I like him. He might look as if he'd been spit right out of his father's mouth, but he has his mother's heart and way with people.

I carry my medical bag in the crook of one arm and my riding cloak in the other. The men trail behind, feeling important to be included but keeping in a tight pack. They take turns muttering inanities while trudging across the floor.

"I'd wager the Kennebec is frozen all the way to Bath, or near enough."

"Aye, likely a dozen or more boats locked in till spring."

"My knee is swelt from the cold. Canna straighten it enough to ride."

"Did you hear that Negro woman is back in the Hook?"

That last comment grabs my attention, and I flick a quick glance over my shoulder to look at Seth Parker—meaning to catch his eye, ask if the woman seemed well—but he is looking at the storeroom door and doesn't seem to notice that he's spoken the question aloud. These men may have done the hard work of pulling a body from the river, but their uneasiness crackles in the air as they move closer to it. When the storeroom door gives way with an eerie whine, they draw back collectively.

Good grief. I shake my head. *Men and death: either culprits or cowards.*

A rectangle of light from the main room illuminates the floor and the lower half of a table where the man lies, but the form itself is a dark heap of bent limbs and twisted, frozen clothing.

"A lantern, please," I say, looking over my shoulder at Moses. "Two would be better."

It is only a moment before he returns, a lantern in each hand. The men step aside to let him through, and he sets one at each end of the table. The sudden warm light provides my first good look at the corpse.

Two things are obvious immediately.

It is—without question—Joshua Burgess.

And he has been hanged.

It isn't just the body that is now revealed but the entirety of the storeroom as well. Foodstuffs are stacked against the wall, piled in corners, and strung from the rafters. The contrast of ham hocks dangling from the ceiling and the body sprawled on the table sends a shiver along my spine. It is enough to make one of the men behind me gag.

I ignore the retreating footsteps, the uneasy shuffling, the sudden hush as I step closer to the table. I ignore everything but the slowing of my pulse and the stilling of my mind—a learned form of concentration in which I push aside all commotion and fear and chaos. I take a long breath through my nose, noting scents of lamp oil, onions, and salt—but no blood, no rot, no vomit—and set my medical bag and riding cape on the floor. Then I undo the buttons at each wrist and roll up my sleeves—first the right, then the left—to my elbows. Inside my bag is a clean, tightly rolled linen apron. It is stained from long use and soft from wear. I pull it out and slide it over my head, then tie it behind my back. I do all of this as I make a curious, roving assessment of the body.

"Moses?"

He steps to my side. "Aye?"

"I'll need a wash basin with hot water and clean rags."

He blinks once, confused, then opens his mouth to speak, but I can see him wrestle with the question. He doesn't want to be disrespectful, but he thinks the orders unnecessary. In the end he can utter only a single word before I cut him off. "But—"

"Yes. I know he's dead."

"So why bother cleaning him?"

It is a ruthless question cloaked in simplicity. It marks where his loyalties lie in the scandal that has ripped our community in half. Why clean the body of a criminal? A rapist?

Various grunts and murmurings of assent come from the door-way behind us. Apparently the men chosen by Amos Pollard for this morning's grisly task are all sympathetic to Rebecca Foster.

"I'm not cleaning him. I am examining him," I say, matter-of-factly. "And I do it because it is my job."

A glance over my shoulder proves that the hearth fires are grow-ing, but still, it will be some time before their proffered heat reaches the storeroom. The cold feels damp and malignant, as though it could seep into my clothing. Into my bones. So I rub my hands back and forth across my apron, letting the friction of skin and linen create what little warmth it can.

I decide to put Moses to the test when he returns a few moments later with a small wash basin and a pile of clean rags. It's my right as a mother, after all, and if he intends to marry my daughter, he can't show less mettle than Hannah in a situation like this. I need part of him to be tough as leather, fearless like his father. Having his mother's weak stomach will never do.

"Do you still want to help?" I ask, tilting my chin to the side and giving Moses a look of challenge.

His only sign of uncertainty is a single, hard swallow. "Aye."

"Then you can assist me."

His eyes are wary, but he nods. It is enough to please me though, and I reward him with a full, bright smile. The sight seems to fortify Moses, and he stands a little straighter. My husband is fond of saying that I am not generous with my smiles, that they must be earned, but I think that is unfair. There is usually just so little to smile about.

"What can I do?" he asks.

"There are scissors in my bag. Find them please."

He locates them easily, then stations himself behind me and to the side, ready for additional instructions.

Chunks of ice still cling to Joshua Burgess's hair and torso but have begun to soften and drip, splashing on the stone floor at my feet. I pull the hair from his mouth and lay it back, exposing the oblong strawberry birthmark at his temple. There can be no questioning the identity of the body now. Burgess is the only man in the Hook with such a mark.

Sections of his shirtwaist and trouser legs were cut away when the men of Hallowell hacked at the ice. But it is his neck, snapped and leaning at an unnatural angle, that draws my gaze. There are rope burns below his jaw, and a ghastly white protrusion—windpipe, most likely—from a vertical split in his neck.

But where is the rope?

"Moses?" I ask.

"Aye?"

"You went with the others this morning?"

"Aye."

"Was there a rope around his neck when he came out of the ice?"

"Not that I recall."

"Ask the others please."

He turns on his heel and leaves the storeroom, quiet as a cat.

In my nearly five and a half decades of life, I have seen only one other hanged man, and he'd looked quite different from this—but then again, in that case, the drop hadn't done its job. Performed properly, a hanging breaks the neck and offers a quick—albeit gruesome— death. When done wrong, it is a slow suffocation that causes the face to turn purple and the tongue and eyes to protrude. Joshua Burgess's eyes are open and wide, but the look on his face is one of surprise, not strangulation. His lip is split, however, and several teeth are broken.

But still, there should be a rope. Whether dangling from gallows, trees, or bridges, hanged men must be cut down. The term *deadweight* comes to mind as I run my thumb over the abraded skin at his throat.

"No one saw a rope," Moses says, back again.

Then the killer took it with him.

This troubles me, but I set it aside for now.

Burgess is not married. He lives—*No, he lived*—on a small home-stead, on a third-tier lot, three miles down Winthrop Street. These lots—the smallest, least desirable, and farthest from the river—are typically assigned to single men or former militia with scant means and few connections. Since coming to Hallowell, Burgess has made no secret of the fact that he wants a lot with river frontage so he can join the mill trade. Those lots are hard to come by, however, and, according to Ephraim, have all been leased.

But the fact remains that Burgess *does* have a homestead, and on it are any number of animals that must be tended now that he is dead. I mention this to Moses as I run my fingers along Burgess's scalp, look-ing for wounds that might be hidden in his long, dirty hair.

"I'll go tell Da'," he says, "see if he can send someone to collect them."

Moses is back by the time I've determined that Burgess has no lacerations on his scalp.

"He sent three men to move the animals to the neighbors. They're also going to collect any valuables in the house and bring them here for safekeeping until his family can be found."

I thank him, then steady myself for the next part of the examination. "Scissors," I say, extending my hand to Moses.

He sets them in my palm, then shifts closer. The metal is colder than the air, but the weight grounds me to the task at hand. I cut away what is left of Burgess's shirt and take a half step backward to make sense of what I see. As a student of human anatomy, I am always amazed at the variations it can take. Tall. Short. Round. Straight. Fat. Thin. Burgess is not a big man. Average size, or less, and the kind of wiry that runs to skinny in winter. Yet he is possibly the hairiest man I have ever seen. As is typical this time of year, he's grown a beard, but his chest, arms, and back are carpeted with dark, coarse hair as well. None of it can hide the countless gruesome bruises, or the obvious broken ribs, arm, and fingers. At first glance it looks as though someone has taken a boot to Burgess's entire face and torso. When I cut away his trousers, I see that the damage includes his groin as well.

And that is when the remaining witnesses in the doorway depart en masse, gagging, cursing, and sweating. It would seem that— accusations of rape aside—few men can stomach the sight of another man's crushed genitals.

I look to Moses for signs of distress, but he stands quietly, a muscle twitching along his clenched jaw. He breathes through his nose, and his eyes are unfocused. But at least he hasn't fled. Or vomited.

"Deserved it, he did," Moses finally whispers. "If it had been my sister he'd hurt, I'd have killed him too. And I wouldna feel bad for it."

I wash away the blood and dirt from the exposed, frozen, twisted body. I let the exclamations and comments out in the tavern fade away. I ignore the men as they say their farewells. I don't startle when a door bangs, or a dog barks, or a man curses. Nor do I cease my meticulous inspection of each bruise and cut and gash as a pair of even footsteps tread across the flagstones behind me. My focus remains entirely on the body, on my work, rendering careful inspection.

After several seconds I can feel Moses shift uncomfortably beside me. "Mistress Ballard . . . ," he says, voice rising on the last syllable.

"Joshua Burgess was beaten, hanged, and thrown in the river." I nod, wipe my hands on my apron, and step back from the table, pleased with my conclusion. But when I turn toward Moses, I find that he is looking to the storeroom door. He spoke my name in warning, not in question.

"I think I'll be the one to determine that."

A young gentleman stands in the doorway wearing a good coat and a smug grin. He holds a leather satchel in one hand and a new felt hat in the other. He is freshly shaven and handsome in the meticulously groomed way that has always irritated me.

"Who are you?" I demand.

"Dr. Benjamin Page."

"Where is Dr. Cony?"

"Away. In Boston. I am here in his stead."

"I don't think—"

"I assure you, Mistress . . . ?"

"Ballard."

"Pleased to make your acquaintance, Mistress Ballard." He dips his head, but his voice is dismissive. "I assure you that, as a licensed physician and a recent graduate of Harvard Medical School, I am more than capable of undertaking this examination."

My grip tightens, but I force myself to loosen my fingers and drop my hands so that they hang my side. "No need, *Doctor* Page. For I have already completed the assessment."

He steps forward with a fake smile. "As interesting as your amateur observations might be, I'm sure you won't mind if I take it from here."

DR. COLEMAN'S STORE

"I have to run an errand," I tell James Wall as we stand outside the tavern. "But would you mind doing something for me in the meantime?"

"What's that?"

"Keep an eye on Dr. Page. I don't trust him."

"Aye, Mistress Ballard. I'll stay until he's gone," James says.

The young, new doctor must only verify my findings, then the men of Hallowell can put Joshua Burgess in the ground to rot. But the ground is frozen, and nothing short of a hatchet will break it in this cold. Regardless, there likely isn't a man in three counties willing to do the job. Which leaves them with a dilemma: what to do with the mangled corpse on their hands? For now, they will have to wrap him in linen, then oiled canvas, and store him in the shed behind the tavern until better arrangements can be made.

It did not escape my attention that Chandler Robbins—in his drunken stupor—had suggested pitching Burgess back into the river. They'd cut a hole, after all, he said. No one had paid Chandler much mind, however, and then they'd all dispersed and gone their separate ways.

I leave James looking more tired than ever and go in search of something that only Samuel Coleman can supply.

Thankfully all I must do is cross the street and turn left.

The sign above the door reads COLEMAN'S GENERAL, and it creaks in the breeze like an old gate on rusted hinges. I worry for a moment that the store is not yet open, but no sooner do I set my hand on the knob than I have to jump back as two trappers—bearded and foul smelling—stomp out.

"Din't give us much for them furs, did 'e?" one grumbles to the other.

I hold my breath as they pass. I doubt either of them has bathed in a month.

"Get that silver fox and 'e will. Them's worth twenty dollars easy. More if'n you can keep the head attached when ye skin it."

"Ain't no silver fox in these woods," the second man argues. He steps off the boardwalk and turns left, toward Pollard's Tavern. "Them's rare as virgins in a brothel."

"And just as expensive. But I saw one, anyways. A pretty little vixen. Upriver. Yesterday. Near that mill run by the Welshman."

I watch as they shuffle across the street, shedding bits of mud and refuse as they go. Soon their voices fade to a hard grumble, and they reach the other side. No doubt to spend whatever coin they've just made at the tavern.

The Welshman they speak of is my husband, and the mill belongs to us. But in the eleven years that we have lived there, I have never seen a silver fox. It bothers me that these men think they can kill something on our property and take it just because they want it.

I pull the door open and step into the general store. The little bell rings above my head, and my eyes settle on the pile of new furs stacked beside the counter. Seven in total, mostly beaver, though that's a stoat near the middle, and there is a single blazing red fox pelt on top. I am struck by sudden concern for the silver fox's mate.

Coleman's General was built before we moved to Hallowell, and Ephraim cannot set foot in the place without muttering about how it wasn't framed square. The roof leaks were fixed last year, however, and the townsfolk no longer need to worry about puddles in the dry goods aisle. For my part, I find the place cheerful. The windows are plentiful, the floorboards creak, and the place smells of lamp oil and dried apples. Coleman is getting older, however, and the store is starting to show signs of neglect. Cobwebs in the corners. Dust piled on every windowsill. It's a lot for one man to manage on his own.

"Good morning, Mistress Ballard," he calls out from his perch at the till.

"To you as well," I answer, then move to join him at the counter.

The store is empty except for the two of us, and he sits on a wooden stool, playing a game of chess by himself, spinning the board around as he takes turns between black and white. I've always thought checkers would be easier if the goal were to outsmart oneself, but he insists on the game of kings.

Once he's taken the white Rook with the black Bishop, he looks up from the board. The iris of his good eye has grown milky in recent years, turning the once soft blue into a muddled kind of gray. It is less disturbing, however, than the sunken void where his other eye used to be. The man refuses to wear a patch.

"It's early yet. What brings ye to the Hook?" he asks.

"A birth and a death, among other things."

He smiles, and—what with his multiple deformities—the effect should be grotesque. But it is charming instead. "Souls passing in the night, I take it? Who's come and gone?"

"Charles and Betsy Clark have another daughter," I tell him, smiling at his raised eyebrow, then add, "And someone has killed Joshua Burgess."

"Ah. That's who they found in the river, then."

"How did you hear?"

"Half the town has heard by now."

"Only half?"

"The rest are late sleepers."

This is why I've taken the time to visit Samuel Coleman before heading home. Nothing happens in the Hook without his knowledge. He is known in town as Dr. Coleman, though no one has ever seen him practice medicine. Nor would any trust him to do so given that he possesses only the one eye and a total of six fingers: two on his left and four on his right. Theories abound as to how he lost them, ranging from reasonable (war injuries) to ridiculous (torture by pirates). For his part, Coleman lets those in the Hook think whatever they wish and never bothers to confirm or deny any of their speculations.

In fact, when he chooses to speak at all it is usually to grouse about the French claim that their literature is superior to that of their English counterparts. Whatever he holds against the French is a grudge he means to keep to himself. It is his ability to listen, however, that makes him valuable to me.

"But are they saying anything about who might have done it?"

"I'd imagine there are several men who have cause. Isaac Foster comes to mind immediately. Not to mention Joseph North. And dozens more who were known to dislike him. I've not heard a specific name if that's what you're asking." He winks. "But the shop ain't been open an hour yet, so give me time."

"You'll tell me though?"

He nods.

Several years ago, Coleman and I formed a trade agreement of sorts. Mostly we barter books and information, but occasionally household goods as well. He holds back any reading material that comes through, and I keep him stocked in candles. The gossip is free.

"I'll check back in a few days," I tell him.

"Is there anything else you need while you're here?"

"Just one thing."

"And what's that?"

"What do you know about this new doctor who's come to town?"

BALLARD'S MILL

It is late morning by the time I return home, and the winter sun is hidden behind a veil of drab clouds. The light feels weak and sickly, as though sifted through old cheesecloth. I ride Brutus through the woods and into the clearing, where I pause at a fork in the drive. Right will take me down to the mill, where I can hear the heavy *whack-whack* of my husband's axe. But left will take me up the rise to the house where my girls are caring for Sam Dawin.

I am debating which path to take when I see the silver fox.

There, on the slope that leads to the south pasture, clear against the snow, is a lithe creature, almost entirely black, with piercing amber eyes. She is stunning. Vicious and proud. And I'd sooner shoot one of those trappers myself than let them turn her into a fur stole. Brutus twitches beneath me, curious and on edge, however. He is no fan of tooth or claw. But the little beast neither moves nor makes a sound.

After a long, lazy yawn in which her pink tongue unfurls into an S, she turns her pointed head to look up the hill toward the house. Then back to me. And back to the drive. Three times she does this, slow and certain. Back and forth. Then—out of nowhere—she yaps at me, sending Brutus into a wild jerk. It is a howling, barking noise. But not like a dog. Nor a wolf. Not the mean yip and snarl of a coyote. It is a sharp-toothed and feral sound. Caterwauling, my husband would say.

Finally, the fox sniffs the air, sits back on her haunches, and licks one tufted paw, as though satisfied.

She wants me to go to the house, I think, and am so startled by the realization that I gasp. The fox lifts her head at the sound, meets my gaze again, then springs to her feet and trots toward the woods.

"Stay safe, little one," I tell her, and urge Brutus up the hill.

Our youngest son, Ephraim—a boy just turned eleven and named for his father—meets me at the garden gate. He reaches for the reins as I dismount Brutus.

"Be careful with him," I say, unbuckling my medical bag from the saddle. "He is in rare form today."

"No matter. He likes me." He shrugs, confident he will come to no harm, then flashes a smile that reveals he has lost his final baby tooth.

"Still"—I bend to kiss the top of his head, then gently nip the side of one ear—"he bites."

Young Ephraim giggles, and I ruffle his shaggy hair as he turns toward the barn to care for my horse.

It is hard to have an oldest child, but harder still to have a youngest. Soon he too will have a beard like Cyrus and an Adam's apple like Jonathan. Soon he will spend half his nights away, and that will be the end of childhood in our home. I am fifty-four years old, and that boy is my last. This knowledge is both a relief and a sadness—I have brought nine children into this world, after all, and only six are still living. Like all mothers, I have long since mastered the art of nursing joy at one breast and grief at the other.

I stand at the door watching his loping, childish gait a moment longer, then I go into the house to check on Sam Dawin.

"How is our patient?" I ask my daughters as soon as I'm through the door. Warm air and the scent of freshly baked bread rush toward me, vanquishing the chill I've felt since leaving home in the middle of the night.

"How did *you* know about him?" Dolly looks up, and I can see curiosity burning in her eyes. They are the same bright blue as her father's.

"Word travels fast."

At twenty and seventeen Hannah and Dolly are women, not girls—all hips and curves—racing toward their own lives and away from home. It won't be long before they outgrow me, before they outgrow their willingness to be only daughters and sisters. Soon the inevitable will happen: they'll want to be someone's wife. Someone's mother.

"Well?" I ask. "How is he?"

"Awake—" Dolly says.

"And hungry," Hannah adds.

"And eager to go home. But we made him stay."

Sam Dawin is not a small man, nor does he seem the type to take instructions from anyone, much less young women half his size. Curious, I lift an eyebrow.

Hannah stands by the fire, running flax fibers through thumb and forefinger and onto a drop spindle that swings gently near her feet. The heavy spindle twists the fibers into a line of newly formed linen thread that, when long enough, she wraps around the bobbin at its base. Given the eight spools of thread that sit neatly on the hearth, it's clear she has been at this work all morning. A smile bobbles on her lips. Unlike her younger sister, Hannah has my eyes—wild and brown, like a dust storm. No wonder Moses Pollard has fallen under her spell.

"I hid his britches," she explains.

In addition to having acquired the exact tone and tenor of my voice, the girls have also learned a way of speaking in which they not only finish each other's sentences but, apparently, their thoughts as well. They begin another rapid-fire exchange, and I glance between them, trying to keep up.

Dolly stands at the kitchen table, dressing a roast for dinner. Her dark, curly hair is tied back, her hands deft. "He was *furious*."

"Wouldn't let us in the room."

"But then he fell asleep."

Hannah also acquired my curls, but hers are flaxen instead, pulled into a braid that hangs over her shoulder. "He's been out for two hours."

"Shattered with exhaustion." Dolly ties off the cut of beef with a piece of string.

"Too much excitement."

Laughing, I slide out of cloak and gloves, then lower my voice. "Where did you put his clothes?"

Hannah nods toward my workroom and mouths "cedar chest."

From the time they were born, the girls have been surrounded by men. Father. Brothers. Countless patients. And while I have never specifically trained them to deal with the more obstinate sex—the way I have trained them to stitch wounds and spin flax and cook for a small army—I am gratified to see that they are already well versed in the fine art of managing recalcitrant patients.

"What time did Jonathan bring him?"

The girls look at each other, silently calculate the time.

"Close to three—" Hannah says.

"Maybe an hour after you left to tend Betsy Clark," Dolly interrupts.

"We were still asleep."

As a midwife and healer, it is not uncommon for me to hear a pounding on the door in the middle of the night, accompanied by a desperate summons. A plea of some sort. I am used to waking at the drop of a pin. And my family has long since grown accustomed to being yanked from sleep to tend the needs of our neighbors. But it must have been a rude awakening this morning because they were out late last night with their older brothers at the autumn Frolic. This dance, held seasonally for the young people in our community, is the highlight of their social calendar. The girls had barely made it home before I was called away by John Cowan. They seem to be taking it all in stride, however. My daughters are more accustomed to blood and injury and mayhem than many physicians twice their age.

"Was Sam bad off?" I ask.

Dolly wipes her hands on her apron. "Bad enough that he couldn't walk. Jonathan had to drag him in."

"It's a wonder he didn't die," I tell them.

"He likely would have. But Jonathan wrapped him in blankets as soon as they got him out of the water."

"We stripped his clothes and put him in our bed." Hannah blushes at this, then shrugs. "It was still warm."

"Dad pulled stones from the hearth and wrapped them in blankets."

"We set them on either side of his head, neck, and feet."

Hannah and Dolly go back and forth telling the story, like they're tossing a hot potato between them, holding on to it just long enough to give a detail or two.

"It took a long time for him to stop shaking." Hannah looks at her sister, eyebrow raised.

"Almost till sunrise," Dolly adds. "Once he did, we spoon-fed him some tea."

"Since he held that down we gave him broth."

"Didn't take long for him to fall asleep after that."

They look at each other and burst out laughing. Hannah bites her bottom lip for a bit, then cackles even louder. "Woke up not long ago to realize he is naked as the day he was born. Now he's steaming like a teapot."

They have seen naked men often enough. My patients, mostly, though occasionally one brother or another shamelessly bathing in the river. Not to mention Young Ephraim, who must be chased down and *forced* to bathe—a job they are none too fond of. Both girls are typically rather sanguine about the bare human form, and I've rarely seen them gawk or blush. But I would imagine that Sam Dawin is a rather more impressive specimen than they are used to.

"Nicely done, girls," I say. Then something occurs to me. "Where's Jonathan?"

"He should be back soon. Dad sent him to tell May Kimble what's happened—seeing as how she and Sam are betrothed."

"What about Cyrus?"

A brief, furtive look passes between the girls. "He was up and out shortly after we got Sam to bed. Said there was work to do."

There is always work to be done at the mill, but I've never known any of our sons to volunteer for it after a mere two hours sleep. Hannah turns back to her spindle, and Dolly wipes down the counter. Both turn curiously silent.

"And what's the thing I need to know but neither of you are telling me?"

Again, that look between them. And this time I see Hannah shake her head. *Don't say it,* she silently orders.

But Dolly has always been a bit bolder than her big sister, and she's not yet learned to keep secrets from me. "There was a fight last night. At the Frolic."

"Between who?"

"Cyrus and Joshua Burgess."

I lift my head sharply at this news. Narrow my eyes. "Over what?"

"It's my fault," Hannah says, and those stormy eyes flash. But in anger, not fear. "Burgess asked me to dance, and I refused."

"He kept after her all night, Mother," Dolly says. "But it wasn't until he grabbed her arm and yanked her toward the dance floor that Cyrus went for him. The scuffle didn't last long, but Burgess landed a couple of good hits, and now Cyrus has a black eye and a split lip. He'll be fine. But I'd wager Burgess will be walking with a limp for a month."

I open my mouth to answer that he won't be walking anywhere, ever again, then snap it closed. The girls don't yet know he's dead, and I can't tell them until I've spoken to Ephraim.

I extend one hand to my elder daughter. "Let me see your arm."

"It's nothing," she says, turning back to her work.

"Hannah." A single word, a definitive order.

She drops her spindle to the basket and unbuttons her blouse before shrugging her left arm free. And there on her smooth, milky skin is a ghastly bruise, all red and blue, and I can see five angry finger marks. Burgess hadn't simply grabbed her. He'd had her arm in a vice. Dug into her with his fingernails. Yanked. It is a *violent* mark, and my stomach sours at the sight.

I run my hand along the swollen skin, furious at what Burgess did to her, but also thankful for whoever broke his fingers.

"What happened after the scuffle?" I ask.

"They kicked him out of the dance," Dolly says. "Cyrus and Jonathan and Sam. Several of the others too. Hauled him out by his arms and legs and pitched him into the snow. He never came back in."

I clear my throat so the girls won't hear the emotion in my voice. "It wasn't your fault, Hannah. You don't owe anyone a dance. Or anything else. You were right to turn Burgess down. And Cyrus was right to thrash him for touching you."

Oh God, oh God. The thought assails me, as I step into my workroom to put my things away. *What else did Cyrus do to Burgess last night?*

Once I have settled myself, I go back to the main hearth where a large cast-iron kettle hangs over the fire. I ladle a bowl of stew for Sam Dawin.

"Bread's ready too." Dolly points at several oblong mounds set on the counter and covered with linen towels.

I add a thick slab of warm bread, covered with three pats of butter, to the tray and go to speak with our patient. I don't knock or announce my presence, and when I push against the door it swings open with a soft groan. Startled, Sam sits bolt upright, mouth open, hair wild, looking much like a drowned man himself. He grips the bedclothes so hard his knuckles turn white. Sam is a bit worse for wear after his plunge into the river. His face and hands are scratched, and his right shoulder is badly bruised.

"Mistress Ballard." He offers a polite nod of greeting.

"It's good to see you alive," I say cheerfully.

Sam settles back against the headboard and pulls the blanket up around his bare chest as though embarrassed, as though half the people in this house hadn't already seen him wearing only the skin God gave him. He could use a shave, a haircut, and a full night's rest, but other than that, Sam is in decent shape. He's a good height with a strong back, and even though his auburn hair would be more becoming on a woman, he usually manages to look ruddy instead of sunburned.

"I did fear for a minute I was dead," he says.

"You were close. Or so I've heard." I set the tray on the end of the bed and step back. "Hungry?"

"Very much. Thank you." Sam bends forward to grab the tray and slides it onto his lap. He must have caught sight of one of the girls through the open door because he glares at something over my shoulder. "May I have my clothes? I'd like to go home."

I have never met a grown man who, when thwarted like a child, doesn't act like one. His pinched eyebrows give him the petulant look of a toddler, and I stifle a laugh.

"Of course. I believe they're dry now," I tell him. Sam plunges his spoon into the stew, but stops with it halfway to his mouth, when I add, "But there's one thing you can help me with. Before you leave. If you don't mind."

"What would that be?"

I shut the door then cross the room and lower myself to the wooden chest that sits below the window. I fold my hands in my lap and give him a reassuring smile. "I'd like to know what exactly you saw under the ice this morning."

He draws back with a flinch, and stew sloshes over the edge of his spoon and back into the bowl with a tiny plop. Some look—horror or fear or maybe disgust—flashes through his eyes, but then Sam lowers his head and studies his food, hiding whatever he feels.

"Why would you want to know a thing like that?"

"I've just come from the tavern." He looks up at me sharply, and I add, "They called me to examine the body. But it would also help to know what *you* saw, under the ice."

"A dead man. But you know that already."

"Yes. But could you tell who it was?"

He hesitates, the muscles along his jaw straining as he clenches his teeth. "Not at first. It was dark. The sun hadn't come up."

"But not so dark that you mistook him for a log or debris. You knew it was a person."

"Well, his face was there, an inch or so below the surface of the ice, staring right at me when they pulled me out. I couldn't see much under the water—just a tangled form of some kind. But out of the river it was obvious enough."

"And did you recognize him then?"

"I've seen Burgess often enough to know his face."

"He was hanged, Sam."

He swallows hard. "Who . . ."

"I can think of a few people who'd like to see him dead."

He studies me for a moment before asking the obvious question. "Like Joseph North?"

I lean forward and rest my elbows on my knees. "That will be hard to prove without the rope. I asked at the tavern, but no one saw a rope when they cut him from the ice. Was there anything in the water? Anything at all that you remember?"

"No." Whatever appetite Sam Dawin might have had evaporates. He drops his spoon back into the bowl and pushes the tray away. "I *am* grateful for your kindness, Mistress Ballard. I truly am. But I'd like to go see May now. She's probably worried half to death."

*

When Jonathan returns from telling May Kimble about the accident, I step outside to speak with him. He has just pulled the wagon up to the garden gate and stepped down from the seat when he sees me.

"I've come to take Sam home," he says.

"What happened last night?"

Like half my children, Jonathan has his father's eyes, and I see the flash of terror in that deep, clear blue. But only for a moment. Only until he shutters the expression and locks me out.

"He fell through the ice."

"I mean at the Frolic. With Cyrus?"

It's been a full day, at least, since Jonathan has slept, and everything about how he pushes through the gate says he's not in the mood to talk, but he knows I won't let him pass without an answer of some sort. "Burgess wasn't invited. But he came and caused a scene, and we handled it."

"Well Burgess is *dead* now, and I'm going to need a better answer than that."

My son is twenty-six years old—a man grown, bearded, and strong—but I am his mother, and I know every expression his face can form. The way he avoids showing emotion by breaking eye contact. The way he sets his jaw when troubled. And cries only in private. I know it all. And in the end, exhausted though he may be, Jonathan's will is no match for mine.

"He touched Hannah."

"I know. She told me." He relaxes a bit then, and I ask, "Everyone saw the fight?"

"Was impossible not to. Happened in the middle of the dance floor and the music stopped and everyone crowded round. But he was *alive* when we kicked him out. You can ask anyone that was there."

"People will ask. You know that, right? So you have to tell me *everything.*"

"There's nothing else to tell."

It's not that I don't believe Jonathan; I just have the sense he's giving me only half the story. But pressing him further will do no good. He needs to get Sam home. He needs a hot meal and a warm bed and a full night's sleep. And perhaps, after those things, he'll be more forthcoming with the details.

Sam Dawin rescues him by stepping out the front door. He is dressed and haggard, but he politely tips his hat in farewell. "Thank ye again, Mistress Ballard. I am in your family's debt."

I pat his cheek. "Nonsense. I am glad you're safe. Please give my regards to May."

*

Once Sam and Jonathan leave, I go back inside and retreat to my workroom. It sits off the kitchen, and the sun slants through the windows, illuminating the rows of dried herbs that hang from the ceiling. Shelves filled with bottles and little linen sacks—each carefully labeled—line one wall. There are boxes and baskets everywhere. A long workbench littered with other concoctions from my garden in various stages of fermentation and dehydration. A mortar and pestle. Rolls of twine. Bits and bobs. Corks. A scale. And there, on the hearth, a small kettle for boiling roots. There is a rectangular wooden box with leather hinges—long since brittle and cracked with age—sitting in the middle of the worktable. Sharp, slender knives; and smooth, round stones. This is my apothecary, my sanctuary, and it smells of lavender and woodsmoke, basil and vetiver. Mint. Catnip. Lemongrass. Situated, just so, on the side of the house—thanks to good planning on Ephraim's part—it catches light from sunrise to sunset.

I make my way to a small wooden desk before the eastern window and settle onto the stool that Ephraim built to accommodate my unusual height. Barefoot, I can almost look my husband in the eye. And though there are many things he loves about me, this is foremost.

What a strange beginning to this new day, I think, then take a long breath through my nose, letting the fragrant herbs settle me. I am certain there will be no retreat from whatever comes next. But at least I have a few moments' peace to record my thoughts on everything that has happened in the last few hours. A large leather-bound journal sits at the corner of my desk, and I pull it closer.

Three times a year my husband orders cakes of ink from a stationery shop in Boston. They come two to a box, pressed into small, round disks, with the word *Larkin* stamped on top. It costs Ephraim five shillings for the ink and one for the postage, but he pays it gladly even though he says Ebenezer Larkin has a foul mouth and a fondness for whores. This is how Ephraim shows his devotion, making sure that I always have something with which to write. On our wedding night, many years ago, he gave me the first leather journal, identical to the one on my desk now. He said it was a place to keep my thoughts together in one place, and his only request was that I not let it sit empty. I have filled a dozen of them since. The books themselves are easier to come by than the ink, and it isn't uncommon for Ephraim to return from a trip to Boston with a new volume filled with blank, stiff pages. I find them on my stool, often with a pressed flower tucked between the pages. Those flowers—now dried—remain exactly where he placed them, while the books themselves reside on a shelf across the room.

I keep up with the journals because I enjoy it, but also because it is my *job*. One of the duties of my profession. As a midwife and healer, I am witness to the details of my neighbors' private lives, along with their fears and secrets, and—when appropriate—I record them for safekeeping. Memory is a wicked thing that warps and twists. But paper and ink receive the truth without emotion, and they read it back without partiality. That, I believe, is why so few women are taught to read and write. God only knows what they would do with the power of pen and ink at their disposal. I am not God—nor do I desire to be—but, being privy to much of what goes on behind closed doors in this town, I have a rather good idea what secrets might be recorded, then later revealed, if more women took up the pen.

I suspect that I will need to remember the events of this morning, so I reach for quill and ink.

The journal is spread open to yesterday's entry. As is my habit, I began with the weather, but left the rest of the entry blank so that I might fill it in later:

Wednesday, November 25—Clear and cold. The ice runs in the river.

I break off a piece of ink cake and mix it with water in a small silver dish, the bottom of which is stamped with an image of a man astride a horse. Below it are engraved the words PAUL REVERE SILVER,

BOSTON. Another gift from Ephraim. Another bit of extravagance, though this one rather personal. My husband and Mr. Revere formed a friendship of sorts during the Revolution, and the silversmith has never forgotten him as a result.

I dip the quill, tap it twice on the edge of the dish to knock off the excess ink, and continue the entry:

Cyrus, Jonathan, Hannah, and Dolly attended a Frolic at the home of May Kimble. Got home late. Then Jonathan set out for Long Reach, with a raft of boards. Sam Dawin and James Wall with him.

I lift the quill from the page, pausing. The room is no longer cold, so I can't account for the shiver that crawls up my spine.

It's only that fox, I think, and look out the window to where I last saw the little beast. She is long gone, and daylight has chased all the menacing shadows from the woods, but I still feel something looming in the distance, a portent of some kind.

"Don't be a fool, Martha Ballard," I mutter, then lower both eyes and quill. Before long the gentle scratching continues.

Thursday, November 26—Clear and very cold. Birth. Charles Clark's third daughter.—I was called by Mr. Cowan to attend Betsy Clark who was in travail, at the second hour this morning. She was safe delivered of a daughter (her third child, all daughters) at the fourth hour. I left her cleverly and was conducted to Mr. Pollard's. I am informed that Jonathan and others were attempting to go down with a raft and were enclosed by the ice at Bumberhook Point. The ice makes very fast. Sam Dawin fell through as he was attempting to go to shore but was saved. . . .

My hand hovers above the page, and I am about to record the death of Joshua Burgess, but something scratches at the back of my mind, like a tiny itch that I can't reach, so I flip backward in the diary, searching for an entry that I made last month.

There are no page numbers in my book, but that never stops me from finding an old entry when I need to. The thing about setting ink to paper is that it allows me to remember which side I've written on and where along the page an entry lies. I remember ink blots and words I have struck through. Errors and misspellings. Even now, I can see the entry in my mind, see that the top left corner of the page has been torn off and that there is a smudge in the margin. Recalling those details, it is easy enough to locate.

Thursday, October 1—Clear except some showers. We had company this afternoon. Mr. Savage here, informs us that Mrs. Foster has sworn a rape on a number of men, among whom is Joseph North. Shocking indeed! I have been at home.

Oh God, I think, sitting upright on my stool. *I have to tell Rebecca before someone else does.*

*

The fact that I refuse to ride sidesaddle or pillion has long since ceased to astonish our neighbors. Such arrangements are neither practical nor timely given how often I am summoned to one emergency or another. There is no use in being ladylike when lives depend on my speedy arrival. Once I have changed back into my riding outfit—a brushed twill skirt with two rows of buttons that, depending on how they are configured, can transform the garment into wide-leg trousers—I go to the barn to saddle Brutus.

Cyrus is there.

For a moment I think it's Ephraim—so alike are they from behind—and then he turns, and I see the beard.

He catches sight of me in his periphery and startles. But in the time it takes me to blink, his unease is replaced by a quick smile that reaches all the way to his hazel eyes. Then he winces and I see the split lip, the bruised eye. Though I know he doesn't want me to, I gently set my hand to his face and turn it this way and that, inspecting him.

Cyrus rolls his eyes. Sighs. But allows my ministrations. Nothing is broken. No need for stitches. So I let him go, and step back. These grown boys of mine will allow mothering only in small doses.

"When did you get home?" I ask.

He shrugs, as though time is a construct of little interest to him. And perhaps it is. We do not own a clock, but each and every Ballard—

myself included—has an instinct for time, a certainty learned by the angle of the sun and the length of shadows. Even in winter. Even with nothing to work by other than heavy cloud cover and opaque light. Time is a thing we *feel,* and our days are ordered accordingly.

Brutus hangs his head over the stall door and snorts as though he knows exactly why I've come, as though he is displeased to see me.

"I have to take him out again," I tell Cyrus, with a frown. "I'm sure he'll be an ass about it."

He looks to where Sterling is grazing happily in his stall, placid as always, and I know what he's thinking.

"No," I say. "Brutus has to get used to me. And riding him is the only way to make that happen."

When I move toward the tack room, Cyrus waves me away. I watch my oldest son grab the bridle and lead Brutus from his stall. I watch him methodically saddle my horse, testing the buckles exactly the way his father taught him. This is a new thing, his desire to coddle me, to protect. I find it irritating and intrusive. He is beginning to think of me as old.

As soon as Brutus is ready, I take the reins.

"I know what happened at the Frolic." Those beautiful hazel eyes narrow. He is wary. "And now Joshua Burgess is dead. Jonathan and Sam found him in the river this morning."

Cyrus stumbles backward as though I've slapped him. He lifts his hands, palms out, as though to say he had nothing to do with that.

"I know. But when I get back, you are going to tell me *everything.*"

THE PARSONAGE

In hindsight, I should have bought a fat, lazy horse who likes apples, sugar cubes, and sleeping in the sun. Instead, I purchased Brutus—a six-year-old buckskin stallion, every bit as charming as his name—from one of the Boston militiamen who camped in Hallowell last year. The man could no longer ride thanks to a broken leg, and I only thought to ask how he had been injured *after* I'd handed over payment. Brutus had thrown the man a week before I bought him, and he has thrown me three times since: twice into a briar patch and once in the river.

"I swear to *God Almighty*," I mutter under my breath as we canter away from the barn, "if you pitch me onto the frozen ground, I will have you turned into glue within a fortnight."

Brutus whickers in response, and from the way his muscles roil beneath my calves I fear he is going to bolt or buck. I give a warning tug at the bit, and he snorts in contempt, then settles beneath me. I answer with a low growl, and we both accept the draw.

I suppose I can't blame him. If I'd been pulled away from a meal, I'd be angry too. But Brutus has a single job—to get me where I need to go—and I will not be ordered about by the whims of a horse who is in fact little more than an adolescent. I've dealt with the likes of him before.

Still, our mission this afternoon is not a happy one. And I hate being the bearer of bad news. Although, in this case, bad might be the wrong word. Disturbing. Tawdry. Barbaric. Crass. Any of those options might fit seeing as how it isn't exactly *bad* news I have come to deliver. I felt nothing but relief when I saw Joshua Burgess on that table earlier today. Rebecca Foster might feel differently, however, and I steel myself for whatever her reaction may be.

The home of Isaac and Rebecca Foster is a simple stone cottage set back from Water Street on a narrow, rhododendron-lined drive. Behind it lies a small barn and a garden. They do not own any of this, however. The parsonage—and all the outbuildings—belong to the town and are leased to them for a pittance as part of Isaac's salary as pastor. The fact that he was dismissed from his position five months ago makes their continued residence a point of contention among their detractors.

A tall young woman with hazel eyes and a lovely, plump figure answers on the third knock and invites me inside.

"Good morning, Sally. Is Rebecca home?"

"Aye, Mistress Ballard. I'll tell her you're here." She turns on her heel and swishes away, leaving me to hang my riding cloak on the hook beside the door.

The girl is back in less than a minute, and I marvel at the way she can avoid eye contact even when looking directly at me. Somehow her gaze seems to float over my shoulder, as though searching for something in the distance.

"This way, Mistress Ballard. She's having tea in the parlor."

Given that the parsonage has only a handful of rooms, *parlor* is a loose term for the only extra sitting area in the home. But it does have a cozy fireplace, a window, and a door of its own. Sally ushers me in, then slips away to continue feeding the Foster boys their lunch. I can hear them in the kitchen, squabbling over the last piece of toast.

Rebecca is not the sort of woman who is comfortable having domestic help, but it is one of the things required of her as the minister's wife. Sally came with the parsonage and is the latest Pierce daughter to fill the position. Two of her sisters had the honor previously. The girl is tolerated, but not exactly welcome. In no small part because she is known to hover around corners and report what she hears back to her mother. Bonnie Pierce prides herself on knowing all that happens in Hallowell. Every town has a gossip, and in ours the title belongs to her.

Rebecca sits in a rocking chair by the fire, a blanket across her lap and a steaming cup of tea in her hands. A long thick golden braid hangs over one shoulder. When I walk in, she takes the pile of knitting from her lap and moves it to a basket beside the hearth.

I kiss her lightly on the brow and take the opposite rocking chair. "It is good to see you."

"And you." Rebecca tips her head to the side and listens as the faint, retreating footsteps of Sally Pierce and her children move upstairs, followed by a burst of laughter. "I am so thankful that girl is only here a few hours each morning."

"Most women would be glad of the help," I say with a teasing smile.

"I shouldn't be so unkind." She sighs. "Sally will repeat what I've said. If not to Isaac himself, then certainly to her mother. Half the town already considers me an ingrate."

I hesitate, unwilling to lie. The truth is that half of Hallowell thinks far worse of her than that. "They will understand you soon enough," I tell her, "and you will have your apologies then."

We are only talking in circles, but a shadow falls over Rebecca's face, and I wish that I were here under different circumstances. But still, pleasantries must be observed.

"Would you like some tea?" Rebecca leans forward toward a small table between the rocking chairs. A tea service is laid out in the middle, and steam rises from the pot.

"That would be lovely."

"I'll go get another cup."

Rebecca glides elegantly from the room, so different from the way she moved three months ago when I found her in this very parlor a few days after Joshua Burgess and Joseph North attacked her. I shake the image from my mind and stand so that I can warm my hands in front of the fire. There is a small tin on the mantle, and I pick it up, admiring the tea roses painted on each side. The lid is off, and a bitter scent rises from inside. I sniff, then draw back with a scowl as the acrid odor floods my nostrils. The disagreeable, turpentine-like smell is unmistakable: savine. A second whiff reveals something cleaner and sweet, almost floral, with a hint of camphor. Tansy.

I set the tin back and return to my chair, then lift the teapot to my nose just to make sure. Black tea, plain and simple.

"It's a bit weak," Rebecca says from the doorway with a note of apology in her voice. "I don't seem to have the stomach for anything strong these days."

"I'm sure it's fine."

We sit in companionable silence while Rebecca prepares the tea. One sugar cube. A splash of milk. Two quick stirs with the spoon. The warmth feels good against my cold fingers when Rebecca hands me the cup. Formalities completed, we can move on to the real purpose of this visit.

She looks at me over the rim of her cup, hesitant. "You were in the Hook early today."

I nod. "I was called to the tavern on business, and I have a bit of news that concerns you."

"Good or bad? I can't tell by the tone of your voice."

"Both, actually." I turn to the parlor door, noting that Rebecca left it half open. Sally and the boys are still occupied. I can hear footsteps in the room above and the creak of a rocking chair. "Where is Isaac?"

"In his study. Writing another letter to the Congregational Church leaders in Boston to contest his dismissal."

"Even after the last two failed to reinstate him?"

A wry smile bends the corner of her mouth. "My husband is an eternal optimist."

I would have said pigheaded had I been the one to describe him. Isaac is currently suing Hallowell for two hundred dollars. His contract with the town as preacher was for five years. And he claims that his firing violated that contract and that he is due the remainder of the money promised. To say that things have grown contentious as a result would be an understatement. He refuses to leave the town, much less the parsonage, until the lawsuit has been resolved. Isaac Foster is a man of books. Of belief. Of rules and fairness. And—for a moment—I consider calling him in to hear this news but decide against it. Rebecca should not have to weigh his reaction when expressing her own.

Despite what happened in August, there is still something in her soft brown eyes—a cheerfulness and curiosity—that reminds me of the daughters I lost so many years ago. It's what drew me to Rebecca in the first place. Every interaction with her since has made me wonder what my daughters would be doing now had they survived that long, horrid summer.

She cups her tea in both hands and holds it to her lips, letting the steam curl around her cheeks, before taking a sip. "So what is this news you have for me?"

Instead of answering Rebecca's question, I once again look to the door, listen for a beat, then ask one of my own. "Do you happen to know where Isaac was last night?"

"I don't. In his study, I suppose. But I wasn't feeling well, and I went to bed early. Why?"

I can remember a time, when my sons were younger, when they loved throwing stones over the bridge into the river. They loved the splash and the noise. Being boys, they loved the *disturbance* that it caused. I study Rebecca's face and take no pleasure in upsetting the still waters of her soul.

"Joshua Burgess is dead. They found his body in the river this morning."

Rebecca shakes her head, as though unable to comprehend. "Was he . . . ? Did . . . ?" Whatever questions she means to ask won't form.

"It was not an accident. He didn't drown," I tell her. "He was hanged."

Rebecca goes completely still, except for her hands, which begin a frantic trembling. I watch the amber liquid slosh back and forth in her delicate teacup—this way and that—and I pluck it from her hands before she can dump the contents into her lap. I wait for her to speak.

The reason I believe her account of what happened in August has as much to do with our longstanding friendship as it does with the small, traumatizing details that make up the bedrock of her story.

"Joshua Burgess has a rasp to his voice. You've heard it?" she finally asks, then looks at me. But her eyes are glassy and unfocused, and it is clear that she is elsewhere, in the past.

An image of that white, waxy windpipe flashes across my mind. "Yes. He did. But not anymore."

Rebecca squeezes her eyes shut, blocking out some memory of

her own. When she speaks again, her voice wavers. "He ripped off the lace hem of my shift before he started. He tied his hair back. Why do I remember that so clearly?"

"He's dead now, Rebecca, that's what I'm trying to tell you. He can't ever hurt you again."

"North can."

I want to deny this. But we both know there are endless ways that Joseph North can continue to wound Rebecca without ever touching her again. Not the least is through his continued denials and subtle attacks on her character and reputation. That has been going on for two months now.

"I'm not going to let that happen. I'm going to Vassalboro next month. I will be right there with you in court. And I *will* give my testimony. Everyone will know what he did. And you will have your justice."

When I found Rebecca, after the attack, it took her almost two hours to explain why her face and arms were battered with fading angry bruises, and why her lip had been split. But she has no such hesitation now. Her words come fast and breathless.

"I'm glad Burgess is dead."

"I am too."

"And I hope Isaac *did* kill him."

It's my turn to be startled, and a glug of warm tea splashes over the rim of my cup, across my thumb, and into the cuff of my sleeve. "*Sshh*. You can't say that."

"Am I not allowed to want vengeance?"

"*Of course*. But his body is still at the tavern. There will be an investigation. And can you imagine what will happen if Isaac is accused? Besides, you do have your vengeance, at least one half of it anyway."

"No," she says. "I will never be free of what they did to me."

I cannot argue this. Nor do I try. Instead, I reach for her hand, and we finish our tea in silence, watching the hypnotic dance of flames in the fireplace. Later, when the shadows have shifted and the coals settle in the hearth, I set down my empty cup, kiss Rebecca on the brow once more, and whisper my goodbyes.

Only when I reach the parlor door does she speak again.

"Martha?"

I look over my shoulder. "Yes?"

"I haven't bled since July."

My lips form an O of surprise and I return to her side, placing my hands on each of her shoulders. I can feel the little knobs of bone beneath each palm. "Are you telling me that you are with child?"

"I've had the boys. I know what it feels like."

"Is there any chance at all it could be Isaac's?"

Rebecca shakes her head. "We haven't gone to bed since before he went to Boston. And he hasn't touched me since. There is no way it can be his."

"When was the last time you bled?"

"The end of July. *After* Isaac left."

Four months. Long enough for a child to take root.

"Have you told him?"

"No. But I think he's guessed."

"I am *so* sorry," I whisper, pulling Rebecca to my chest. Only this time there is no weeping, no anguish. There is only a vacant stillness. A void where the spirit of my friend once resided. I pull away and lower one hand to Rebecca's belly. The small, firm mound is easy to find. I press gently, this way and that, just to make sure, but there is no doubt. Rebecca Foster is a slender woman. Soon there will be no hiding it at all.

"I don't know what to do," she whispers. Her eyes, wide and brown, the color of tea. They are swimming with tears.

"You don't have to. Not today."

BALLARD'S MILL

I go straight to my workroom. My mind is on Rebecca Foster, but when I reach for the diary, I find a note sitting on top and recognize Cyrus's loopy scrawl.

I know you want to talk, but I've gone to the Hook with Moses to get some tallow that Amos saved for us. Not sure when I'll be back.

Here there is an ink blot, as though he let the quill rest against the paper while he thought of what to say next.

About Burgess: I guess you know he put his hands on Hannah. That's why I hit him. But if he's dead, I had nothing to do with it. I brought the girls home and went to bed. On my honor.

— C.

I have only the children that I have. But if I've learned anything about raising young men, it's that some are liars and some are confessors. Cyrus is the latter. A confessor. In all the decades he's lived under our roof, I've never had a reason to doubt him. And I have none now.

So I fold the note and set it to the side. Try to remember why I came in here.

I have lost my train of thought, cannot recall what I meant to find in the diary. This is the trouble faced by any woman who sets pen to paper in a busy household. I am never guaranteed the certainty of quiet, much less a solid length of time to chase my thoughts and bind them together. That is the luxury of men with libraries, butlers, and wives. Mothers find a different way to get their work done.

Ha! There it is! A glimmer. I grab hold of the tail end of the thought as it skitters by, then chase it so that it won't evaporate.

I look at the diary entry again. Flip back through the pages.

Thursday, October 1—Clear except some showers. We had company this afternoon. Mr. Savage here, informs us that Mrs. Foster has sworn a rape on a number of men, among whom is Joseph North. Shocking indeed! I have been at home.

I tap the entry with the pad of one finger. Contrary to my choice of wording, it wasn't the news itself that shocked me—I had attended Rebecca in the middle of August after the assault happened—rather that she had gone public with the accusation without first consulting me. Rape is a capital offense in the States, punishable by hanging. But in all my five decades, I have seen only one man dangle at the end of a rope for that crime. It is nearly impossible to prove, and, until lately, most men caught doing so were dispatched before the courts could be involved. The recent War of Independence and the subsequent ratification of the Constitution has put a basic framework of laws in place to deal with such transgressions. There is more of a deterrent now to keep an aggrieved father or brother from taking justice into his own hands.

I run my finger up the column to an entry from the day before, looking for insight into Rebecca's motives for speaking publicly.

Wednesday, September 30—Clear except a light shower in the afternoon. I was called to Mr. Foster's door and asked some questions. Later, Colonel North interrogated me concerning what conversation Mrs. Foster had with me regarding his conduct.

So perhaps not such strange timing after all? Rumor of the attack had begun to spread through the community, and North had likely gotten wind that people were talking. I flip the pages again, farther back, to August when all of this began.

Wednesday, August 19—Clear. Called at Mrs. Foster's. She complained to me that on August tenth she had received great abuses from Joseph North and Joshua Burgess. After relating those abuses, she said that they could have done nothing worse unless they had killed her. She also said that North had abused her worse than any other person in the world had, but she believed it best to keep her troubles to herself as much as she could until her husband returned which she had hoped would be soon. Came home at 1:00 p.m. Feel fatigued.

Rebecca *had* kept her troubles to herself for almost two months after the attack, confiding only in me. It seemed wise at the time. I wanted Rebecca to have protection when she stepped forward with her allegation, so she told no one else until Isaac returned from Boston. The accused were respected men, and Rebecca might have found herself victimized further if she went forward on her own. In hindsight, however, the best evidence Rebecca had of the attack was the damage done to her body. Had she filed a complaint the day I found her, looking like a battered wreck, no one would have doubted her claims. And good God, it had been *awful.* For nine days Rebecca was so ill and sore that she could barely care for her own children. She couldn't bathe, was hardly able to eat. *That* is the woman that I found huddled in her home on August nineteenth. Yet, by waiting all those weeks until Isaac returned, her outward injuries healed, and doubt was given time to grow roots.

If I could do it differently, I would have taken Rebecca by wagon straight to the magistrates in Vassalboro the day I found her. My own lack of action makes me feel complicit in the way things have transpired. And now I fear that nothing can be done for the wounds Rebecca carries on the inside.

Things have only gotten worse for my friend. Given what I learned this morning, I suspect that Rebecca feared a pregnancy in August.

Saturday, August 22—Clear. I was at Mrs. Foster's. Left her as well as could be expected. Indians there.

Tuesday, August 25—Clear. I went to see Mrs. Foster . . .

I went to see Rebecca three times that week. I'd dressed her wounds, cooked her meals, and tended her children. And all the while, I tried to figure out what to do about the assault. Isaac was in Boston, seeking an intervention from the head of his congregation after being dismissed as minister in Hallowell over a series of theological differences.

Sally Pierce, as it turns out, could not serve as a witness for Rebecca. During the month of August she was tending her older sister and newborn niece at Fort Western. Husband gone, help gone, Rebecca was alone and vulnerable. Easy prey. But *why*? That is the thing I haven't yet been able to figure out. *Why* had North and Burgess committed such an egregious, violent crime? They couldn't have believed she would keep it to herself. Or that they would get away with it.

I flip back to September 30, when I'd been called to the parsonage by Isaac to answer that round of brooding questions concerning what happened to his wife. And then, later that afternoon, to my conversation with North in which he asked for an accounting of every conversation I'd had with Isaac and Rebecca since August. I'd refused, of course. It was none of his business, and I wasn't obligated to tell him anything. But now Joshua Burgess is dead, and though Rebecca seemed relieved to hear the news, it came without any kind of real justice. I can't help but think of Isaac, locked away in his study, writing letters. Has he been plotting revenge as well as professional vindication? And should I expect less from a man whose wife was so horribly violated?

I set down my pen. Push the journal away. Fretting over these questions will do no good. It is time to speak with my husband.

*

In summer, the path down to the mill is worn and wide from years of Ballard feet walking back and forth. But in winter it is little more than a channel between snowbanks, packed hard by heavy-soled boots. It winds through the pasture, into the woods, and toward the creek. Pine and sumac grow along its sides, along with patches of pennyroyal. But the dark, mint-shaped leaves have long since dried and fallen, which is a pity because I nearly ran through my supply delivering the last Prescott girl. Concoction of pennyroyal helps calm excited nerves, and I find it useful when delivering a Prescott. Screamers every one of them. Two of the three girls are expecting in the spring, and I dread attending the births. They learned such hysterics from their mother.

The woods are quiet today, and I miss the melodic, tinkling sound of the waterwheel outside the mill. Locked in the ice, the wheel won't turn again until the thaw, and that makes Ephraim's job more difficult. The wheel helps power the long saws, but now it will be Ephraim and our sons heaving their way through every log. Now that the river has frozen, he and the boys will have to make their deliveries by land instead, an arduous, time-consuming task that will leave them all exhausted and testy.

Lucky me.

I run a fingertip over a bright red burst of sumac berries, reminded how I love this path in winter. The combination of verdant pine boughs and blazing berries is striking against the snow, a well-earned bit of showmanship for outlasting all the other plants and shrubs. I make a mental note to come back later and harvest the sumac. When ripe, the berries make an excellent lemon-tinged spice for meats and vegetables, and I think Dolly might like to add some to the roast we'll be having for dinner tonight. But I won't collect them all as the berries are also a favorite source of winter food for rabbits and foxes.

I pause mid-step on the path. *The fox.* I mustn't forget to tell Ephraim about our unnerving visitor. Was it only a few hours ago? I feel as though a month of Sundays has passed since I arrived home.

This is what it means to age, I think. *The days are long, but the years are short.*

The oddness of my encounter with the fox still feels like a portent of some kind, a lingering in the air, like a fog that doesn't burn away with the midday sun. Ephraim will neither laugh at me nor be alarmed. He will simply nod and think on it, the way he does with most things. If I give him enough time, he might even have an explanation. Some men think in a straight line, like an arrow off the string. They go to logic, to the easy conclusion, and avoid the waterways of the mind. But not Ephraim. His head is all rivers and streams, and with a mind like that a thought could run anywhere.

He will have an answer. He always does.

Our lumber mill is set into the bank of Mill Creek, on stone foundations right where the current is strongest. It is large. Larger than our barn, in fact. The first floor has ample space to store and dry a great deal of cut timber, plus additional workspace for Ephraim. The second floor comprises a loft that runs the length of the mill and looks over the space below. Ephraim has even built a convenient staircase to access it for when we host a large gathering. There are few things more awkward, after all, than sending ladies up a ladder in their skirts.

Several years ago, Ephraim counterbalanced a wide, sturdy deck against the building so that it stretches over the water. No more dragging the boards down to the creek and standing knee-deep in mud while they are bound. Now he sends them straight off the pier and into the current below. They make a terrible splash, but they right easily and begin their journey toward the Kennebec, and then on to Hallowell, Farmingdale, and farther south, through Bath, and on to the shipyards in Boston, then to parts unknown. I like to think that there are vessels sailing the Atlantic made of boards sawn by my husband and sons. I like to think that we have contributed something to the wider world.

On the other side of the mill, out of sight, is a large wooden mews, attached to the exterior wall and accessible only by an inside door. Ephraim built it to house Percy, a peregrine falcon he found as a fledgling five years ago, and I can hear the bird now, calling for his lunch.

My husband looks up and smiles when I slip through the door.

"Hello, love," he says.

Ephraim crosses the floor in three long strides and places a warm kiss in the dip between my eyebrows. In his youth he'd had black hair and eyes the color of a summer sky. A straight Welsh nose. Square jaw. His eyes and jaw are still as strong as the day I first met him. But his hair is streaked with silver, and his nose slightly crooked thanks to a dirty punch he received fourteen years ago.

After a momentary glance in which he inspects me for soundness of life and limb, he asks, "Have you finally come to tell me what in blazes happened this morning?"

"Did Moses not say anything when he came to get Cyrus?"

"No. Why?"

"Then I suppose he had words with you about Hannah?"

Ephraim laughs. "No. He's working up to it, though. It withers a lad, finding the courage for that conversation. But he'll get there. Stayed and talked for a bit, though. And made sure to catch a glimpse of her before driving off."

I think about the body of Joshua Burgess and the assistance that Moses rendered this morning. "And did he mention nothing else while he was here?"

He grins. "Only that *you* would have news for me when you returned. But when I pressed him, he insisted that you would want to give me the details yourself. So I can only conclude one thing."

"Which is?"

"You have done something to earn that boy's loyalty."

"*I've* done something?"

"Charmed him in some way, I suspect. You tend to do that."

"I do no such thing! Most people dislike me, as a matter of fact."

"They respect you. Perhaps occasionally fear you. It's not the same thing."

"And miles away from charm."

"*I* find you charming."

"You are biased." I laugh and am grateful for the lightness it brings to my chest. Good humor stretches out from the corners of Ephraim's eyes in the form of crow's feet, and I realize he has lightened my mood on purpose. I must have come into the mill with a storm cloud hanging above my head. "And Moses wants to court Hannah," I add.

"That's hardly news."

"Well, he now sees me as the door he must go through."

"And here I thought I had the honor?"

I snort. "It seems that the young Pollard and I have *bonded.*"

"Over what?"

"A body."

Outside, the squawking grows louder in the falcon mews, accompanied by the heavy beat of large wings.

"Percy is hungry," I say, looking to the far wall and the door that leads beyond.

"You can't change subjects like that, love. I did hear mention of a body."

"Well, your bird is loud and distracting. Feed him. Then I'll tell you."

Ephraim grins, then strides across the floor to where a large bucket sits beside the woodstove. He plucks out a wriggling blueback trout with his bare hand and opens the door that accesses the mews. Percy hops across the floor and plucks the thing right out of Ephraim's fingers. He's a handsome bird, with pointed wings and a long tail. His feathers are a blue gray above and a speckled brown beneath. Percy puffs his white breast and turns his head so that the black mustache-like markings on his face are visible. He always looks French to me. And pompous.

Task accomplished, Ephraim shuts the door, turns to me again, and crosses his arms over his chest, waiting.

I try to ignore the sound of ripping flesh coming from the mews. Where to start? And how to explain everything? I take a deep breath and let my shoulders settle. Stretch my neck side to side, then begin the best way I know how.

"You know that while I was with Betsy Clark, Jonathan's raft got trapped in the ice at Bumberhook Point, and that Sam Dawin fell through while they were trying to get to shore?"

He nods. "I helped Jonathan get him into the girls' bed."

"Did you know that he saw a body when he went under? Or that Jonathan sent James Wall to get men from the Hook to cut it from the ice?"

"I did not." Ephraim's jaw twitches. "Who is the dead man?"

"I never said it was a man."

"Then who's dead?"

"I'm getting to that."

"Rather slowly, I'd say."

"Hush. I'm trying to sort out the details, so they'll make sense."

The small woodstove spreads what little warmth it can through the mill, and I drift closer, palms outstretched, before continuing.

"Amos Pollard sent James to collect me from the Clarks'. They'd gotten the body out. Taken it to the tavern. Amos wanted me to inspect him before Dr. Cony was summoned."

"Him? So it was a man? Like I said."

"Well, you assumed. But that's beside the point. Women get murdered too, you know?"

"*Murdered*?"

"I'll get to that as well if you won't interrupt."

"Go on then, tell me what man has been murdered in Hallowell," Ephraim says. It's not so much the news he's enjoying, but our banter, and I note the flash of humor in his eyes.

I pause, giving import to the name before I speak it. "Joshua Burgess."

Ephraim looks as shocked as he is capable of. His eyes widen for a moment and his nostrils flare. Beyond that he is as impassive as a stump. "Ah," he says. "Well, that complicates things."

"He'd been beaten and hanged, Ephraim. Someone killed him *before* they threw him in the river."

"Well." He scratches his scalp, contemplating. "There are a number of men in this town who would want to hang him."

This is the hardest thing I must ask him today, but Ephraim and I are not in the habit of shrinking away from difficult subjects. "Is our son one of them?"

And there it is, the stillness that overcomes my husband when he is afraid. "Which son? And what do you mean?"

"Have you not spoken with your daughters this morning?"

His eyes narrow. "Only a quick good morning when Dolly brought my breakfast."

"And she said nothing of Hannah?"

"Hannah is coming up an awful lot just now. And no. Dolly did not mention her sister. Why?"

"Because Burgess hurt her at the Frolic last night." Ephraim stiffens and takes one threatening step forward, and I hold out a hand, palm flat to stop him from combusting. "Everything is fine. Cyrus handled it. Thrashed him soundly from what I hear, but the fact remains that Joshua Burgess tried to force Hannah to dance, and he had to be evicted from the Frolic. Dozens of people witnessed it. And when news of Burgess's death spreads, so will that fact."

"And you think they'll come for Cyrus?"

"Him or Isaac Foster."

"There's another man who would benefit directly from Burgess's death."

"Yes. The fewer people who take the stand in Vassalboro, the better for Joseph North."

Ephraim nods slowly, letting that idea take root. "When did James Wall arrive at the Clarks'?"

I shrug. "About five o'clock."

"Is possible that North already knew?"

"*Perhaps.* There was smoke rising from his chimney when I arrived in the Hook. Someone could have told him. Or he could have heard the commotion. Seen them bringing the body to the tavern."

Again, Ephraim nods. "Or he could have been there when Burgess went into the river. Could have done it himself."

The possibility has occurred to me as well. "We aren't the only ones who will wonder about that."

"Accusing and proving are different things. A cause of death would have to be declared. Evidence brought forth."

A sly grin creeps across my face. "Which is, no doubt, why Amos Pollard summoned me this morning. Tomorrow is the last Friday of the month. The Court of General Sessions is meeting."

"In his tavern no less. Clever bastard."

"And, having examined Joshua Burgess, I can declare cause of death."

Ephraim closes the short distance between us. He pulls me against his chest and buries his face in my neck. I can feel him draw in a long breath through his nose, take in my scent, and then a wave of warm air brushes across my skin as he exhales. As is his habit, Ephraim slides his hand into the mound of hair at the base of my skull and pulls out a single curl. He winds it around his finger then lets it spring free. He does this several times as he ponders the situation.

"It seems you've had quite a morning."

"And you've not even heard the half of it."

He chuckles into my skin. "Dare I ask?"

"Oh, nothing quite so dramatic as a half-drowned man and a dead body. But I did see a fox when I got home."

"I thought I heard one barking."

"The fox was black, not red."

"A silver fox, then. Those are rare indeed. Some call them ghost foxes."

"Well, she didn't look like much of a ghost to me. She was quite real. And she was on the rise leading to the south pasture. Near the live oak." I pause, feeling foolish, but Ephraim presses a hand to the small of my back, urging me to continue. "The thing is, there were two trappers at Coleman's this morning when I stopped in. They were talking about that fox. And there she is, waiting for me when I get home? You must admit that's odd."

He doesn't comment one way or another.

"They know that fox is here," I tell him. "They're hunting it."

"It's called poaching when it's on private land. I'll keep an eye out for them. They'll be back, no doubt."

"They'd run that risk? You can shoot a poacher on sight."

"One silver fox is worth forty beaver skins, love. And trappers aren't known for keeping to a strict moral code."

"There's something different about this one."

"How so?"

"I couldn't shake the feeling that she was here for *me*."

"Why?"

"Because of the way she *looked* at me. I was debating whether to come speak with you or go check on Sam. She kept looking at me, then back to the house. Like Sam was more important." I glance up to see if he's laughing. But he isn't. Those bright blue eyes meet my gaze, and there is no teasing tilt to his mouth.

"I've never seen a silver fox, you know. *Alive,* that is. But if one came to you, it's worth noting. Foxes don't come to people naturally. And if you asked the Wabanaki, they would tell you that it is a *sign*."

"Of what?"

Ephraim keeps his hand on my back but turns his face to the window. Only a rectangle of forest and snowbank can be seen through it, but he peers out intensely. "The native people believe that the fox presents itself only in times of great uncertainty. That it acts as a guide."

"And what about you? Do you believe that?"

"I believe," he says, carefully, "that you have had a strange morning. And that you should not discount anything."

*

Indians there.

I gasp and sit up straight on my stool, as though I've been bitten. And perhaps I have, but only by a thought. Little details connect themselves, reaching for one another, forming a theory in my mind.

It is well known within Hallowell that Rebecca Foster often keeps company with the Wabanaki—she has since childhood, encouraged by her parents at the parochial school they ran in Massachusetts. They'd kept progressive ideals of educating the native population, of building a partnership between the two cultures, and Rebecca has maintained the practice of opening her door to them since moving to this community with her husband a few years ago. It is not uncommon to see them at the parsonage. But, as with most things concerning Rebecca Foster, her neighbors are split in opinion regarding this habit. There seems to be little about her that does not cause division in Hallowell.

"What are you doing?" Ephraim whispers. He stands at the door to my workroom, shirtless, barefoot, wearing only trousers that are unlaced and hang low on his hips.

Until three minutes ago I'd been sitting at the dressing table in our bedroom, brushing my hair, when I'd suddenly grabbed the candle and left the room. I came in here to flip back pages in the diary.

"I went to see Rebecca Foster this morning. I wanted her to hear the news about Joshua Burgess from me."

He leans against the doorframe but says nothing.

"And when I got home, something was bothering me about Burgess and the Foster case, so I went back through my entries to try and remember details. Those two things are braided together. I'm certain of it."

Ephraim comes to stand beside me. He reaches out and runs his hand through my hair. "A braid has three strands, love."

"Which means I'm missing one."

"Or maybe you are tired, reaching for meaning where there is none?"

"I don't think I'm wrong in this. Here." I poke my finger at the diary entry.

Ephraim reads it aloud. "Saturday, August twenty-second. Clear. I was at Mrs. Foster's. Left her well as could be expected. Indians there." He peers at me in the dim light. "Indians?"

"You know that Rebecca has befriended them."

"Aye. That's no secret. Indians are there often, I would guess."

"But you also know that there are many in Hallowell who hate her for it. They think it unbecoming a woman of her station. And an insult given all that happened during the French and Indian War."

He nods, uncertain where I'm headed with this.

"Who do you know that is better with herbs than I am?"

"No one. *Except . . .*"

"The Wabanaki." I can see that I've lost him completely now. "I found a tin that smelled of savine and tansy in Rebecca's parlor. It was empty."

Still that steady gaze, but no questions.

"Tansy brings the menses. But savine induces labor. It's hard to find and harder to harvest. The concoction must be prepared carefully and administered in specific doses."

Now he is curious. "Have you ever used this?"

"Only when a woman has gone past her time. And even then, only twice. It makes for a painful labor and, if you are not careful, can cause uncontrolled bleeding."

"What are you trying to say?"

"Rebecca Foster is pregnant. She told me this morning. The child isn't Isaac's."

Ephraim looks at the entry again, does the math. "Twelve days after she was raped Rebecca took savine to end a possible pregnancy. You think the Wabanaki gave her the herbs?"

"It's only a guess."

He shrugs. "It's not a bad one."

*

It is nearing midnight. I can feel it, the way my muscles seem to hang limp on my bones. The way my eyes have gone dry and my neck aches. But I've resumed my place at the dressing table regardless, running the boar-bristle brush through my hair. I do this every night, two hundred strokes. Brushing, brushing until my hair crackles with static electricity. I love the way my scalp tingles, the way my hair slips smooth through my fingers afterward. It is the only way to tame my curls.

Ephraim is stretched out in bed, watching me. After a moment he sighs. He wears nothing now, waiting for me to come to bed. I turn around, match him leer for leer.

"I'm glad you chose me," he says.

"As I recall, *you* did the choosing."

"No. I did the *courting*. But it wouldn't have mattered a bit if you hadn't wanted me in return. Any man worth his salt knows it's a woman who does the choosing. And anyone who thinks differently is a fool."

A small mirror, chipped and distorted with age, sits on the table. I turn back to it—laughing as I see his grin in the reflection—and move a section of hair above my right ear to inspect a thick streak of silver hidden beneath the part. I lift it, coiling the hair around my finger, marveling at this single patch of silver.

Ephraim shifts on the bed, and I hear the soft pad of feet on the floorboards.

"I like it," he says lifting the streak from my hand. He slides it through his fingers.

"It is one thing to be old," I tell him, "and another to feel old. That makes me *feel* old."

"Well, it makes me feel like a king." He smiles at my curious look. "Only a fool would be upset to find a vein of silver running through his beloved territory."

Well, is it any surprise that we had nine children? Not to me. Not with a man who whispers such things in my ear as he stands an inch away, warm and naked.

Ephraim drops my hair and reaches for my hand. "Come to bed, love."

Some things change in thirty-five years of marriage—the silver hair, the softness of my belly, the lines around my eyes—but some things do not, and I am still eager for the warmth of my husband's touch. I go with him gladly and smile as he blows out the candle.

POLLARD'S TAVERN

A large crowd has gathered in the Hook. The Court of General Sessions draws any number of busybodies eager for distraction and a morsel of gossip to Pollard's Tavern. They sit in clusters, elbows propped on the heavy wooden tables, flagons in hand. Or they lean against the wall, whispering and picking mud from their boots. Ours is a community of first-, second-, and third-generation immigrants, and the conversations reflect this diversity. Those gathered speak primarily in English, with varied accents, but jocular bursts of German, French, and Spanish rise above the din as well.

Abigail Pollard sits perched on a three-legged stool beside the blazing hearth, a kerchief tucked into her cleavage. As the room fills and the temperature rises, she plucks it out, mops it across her brow, and returns it to her bodice. Amos Pollard takes advantage of the uptick in patronage, buzzing through the tavern serving rum and ale, beer, and cider to his customers. He laughs at a joke. Slaps a friend on the shoulder. Greets this patron and that. There is good reason that Amos has never insisted the court hold session elsewhere. Court days increase his monthly profits by a wide margin.

Joseph North—Colonel North on most days—has donned the moniker of judge for this occasion, and he enjoys the power and dignity that come with the role. The state of Massachusetts gave him the title twenty years ago for his service during the war against the French and Indians. And while I have always found him insufferable in court, today has the added complication of being the first time I've come before North since Rebecca Foster went public with her accusation.

As is tradition, the fourth Friday of each month is set aside to deal with petty local issues: complaints of Sabbath-breaking, use of profanity, charges of fornication, small grievances and domestic issues. Twice a year North gathers with the other circuit judges assigned to Lincoln County for the Court of Common Pleas. These sessions take place thirteen miles to the north in Vassalboro and cover more serious crimes such as theft, slander, tax liens, and assault. Likewise, the Supreme Judicial Court also meets twice a year and draws a great deal more attention as it presides over murder trials and any appeals from the Court of Common Pleas. These cases are tried to the south, in Pownalboro—the only town nearby with a proper courthouse and jail—and are presided over by a set of esteemed lawyers who travel from Boston. It is a haphazard and somewhat lax judicial system, but our need is slight, and we are grateful to have whatever justice we can get.

Judge North, however, treats all sessions with the same sense of pomp and pageantry. He wears the required wig and red silk robe, buttoned to the top, and a ruffled collar that has turned yellow with age. It hangs against his throat like a limp rag.

I shift closer to the front of the room, ready to give my testimony and be gone. There is an open spot on a long bench near the fire, and I take a seat. I don't see Ephraim until he removes his hat. He stands, leaning against a column in the shadows by the door, arms crossed over his chest. Anyone else would take the look he gives me as disinterest, possibly boredom, but I know my husband well enough to detect the curious tightening around his eyes and the clenching of his jaw. After so many years together, his every movement, word, and hesitation are as clear to me as the lines drawn on one of his maps. Ephraim is uneasy. He wouldn't be here otherwise.

A smattering of women sit behind me, gossiping, waiting for their men to lodge complaints or defend themselves from the same. William Pierce is at a table with his daughter Sally, whispering intently. I can see three of the men who helped pull Burgess from the ice. They've all found seats near one another, and they pass furtive glances back and forth. Henry Sewall—the town clerk—slides into his seat beside North, ready to take notes and keep account of any fines assigned or paid. Other men drift in and out. A baby cries somewhere, and two children bicker over the last apple on one of the tables.

"The Court of General Sessions is now open," North says with authority, then whacks the table once with his gavel.

I'd planned to wait until the end of the session, give my statement just before the court dismisses. But North has other plans. He saw me enter, has been watching me ever since.

"You have business, Mistress Ballard?" He looks directly at me, challenging.

Then everyone else does as well.

I stand. Clear my throat. "I have evidence to give in a legal cause."

"What manner?"

This is a formality. A show put on for the benefit of those present. There is typically only one reason that I attend court meetings, and the citizens of Hallowell know this quite well. When an unwed woman gives birth, it is my duty before the law to ask and record the name of the father while the woman is in travail. The legal presumption is that, under such physical duress, a woman cannot lie. Clearly the writers of the law know little about women and nothing about childbirth. I could give them endless examples of the lies that have been spoken to me through gritted teeth as women heave their children into the world. Regardless, the law, passed four years ago by the Massachusetts General Assembly, is bluntly titled "An Act for the Punishment of Fornication, and for the Maintenance of Bastard Children." It was designed to make sure that unwed mothers had a means of providing for their children, but in practice it is little more than a ritual of public shaming. Of all the responsibilities required by my profession, this is my least favorite. Should a girl *refuse* to name her child's father, she will be fined and possibly jailed for twenty-four hours. Should she cooperate, the girl will still be fined but will not face the indignity of a night spent in the clink. Repeat offenders find themselves subject to higher fines and longer sentences. Yet the men involved in these cases escape both forms of punishment—there is no law pertaining to *male* fornication—unless one considers being forced to provide for one's own child a punishment.

Had the tavern been empty, North would have gotten directly

to the point, but since he has a large audience, he drags out the proceedings. I indulge his showmanship, knowing the assumption every
other person in this room has already made. Another illegitimate
birth. Another declaration of paternity. A bit of juicy gossip for the
neighborhood to gnaw on for a few days.

I dip my head in feigned respect. "I come before the Court of
General Sessions to deliver testimony regarding a death, as is my duty
before the law and the state of Massachusetts." Well-rehearsed words.
I need to be careful.

A wave of mutterings rises behind me.

"What death?" North asks, his eyes tightening at the corners.

"Joshua Burgess."

Now the wave crashes ashore in a full-blown cacophony. North
bangs his gavel on the table to regain order. When the room is silent
once more, I continue.

"Joshua Burgess was found yesterday morning, caught in the ice
off Bumberhook Point. I was called to this establishment to examine
the body and render my opinion on cause of death."

Ephraim shifts uneasily in my peripheral vision when he hears the
cool note in North's voice.

"And what is your *opinion*, Mistress Ballard, on cause of death?"
North asks.

"Murder."

Gasps. Mutters. Exclamations. These sounds erupt behind me,
along with stools clattering backward, men springing to their feet.
Several tankards tip over, and I hear the steady drip of ale splashing
on the flagstone floor. Deaths are far too common in these parts, but
murder is rare. I remain standing, expression as still and disinterested
as I can manage. I keep my eyes on North, and he holds the gaze, locks
it in place with his own. Beside him Henry Sewall glances between us,
his quill hovering above the record book he keeps for the court.

It takes several seconds of gavel banging before order is restored.
"That is a weighty charge, Mistress Ballard."

"I charge nothing, I only state my findings." I stand straight and
tall and speak with confidence. "Bruises covered his face, torso, and
groin. Several teeth were broken. It was clear he had been beaten
badly while still alive. He had numerous broken bones. His neck was
snapped, windpipe exposed, and rope burns were evident in a com-

plete circle beneath his chin. It was obvious that, after being beaten, Joshua Burgess was hanged. I do not believe he was alive when thrown into the river."

North stares at me, his dark eyes turned to flint, but I can't interpret the expression on his face. His voice sounds impartial when he asks, "How can you be sure that he *was* thrown in?"

Oh you bastard, you have never questioned my testimony before, I think, then carefully say, "It is a deduction based on the evidence."

"And have you ever seen a man hanged, Mistress Ballard?"

"Yes." This astonishes me, coming from him, and I'm not afraid to show it. He of all people should know the answer to that question. "I *have*."

I ignore the disruption behind me, pay no attention to the standing, whispering, muttering crowd at my back. So intent am I on North—eager to identify the fleeting expression that crosses his face—that I don't notice the man who has come to stand beside me until he speaks.

"Your Honor," he says. "If I may address the court? I too have information pertinent to the situation."

Dr. Page.

Dammit. Damn it all to hell.

When Judge North speaks again, I finally recognize the look I hadn't been able to identify: certainty.

"Of course. Please state your name and profession for the court records."

"Dr. Benjamin Page. Licensed physician and Harvard Medical School graduate."

The crowd gathered at Pollard's Tavern is adequately impressed. They murmur and nod their approval. Lean forward. Assess the man with curiosity. Several of the younger women sit up straighter. Watch him with acute interest. They are looking for a wedding ring, any sign that he is spoken for. Despite my irritation, I can't deny that this is an excellent way for a new physician to advertise his services.

"Carry on, Doctor Page," North says, his voice louder, imperious. "The court always respects the word of a trained medical professional."

"I too inspected the body of Joshua Burgess yesterday, but I'm afraid my findings are quite different from those of Mistress Ballard."

North lifts a hand, palm up, and waves it, giving him the floor. "Please, explain."

I curl my fingers inward, stopping just short of making a fist, as I turn my steady gaze to Dr. Page. He steps into the open area before the table but speaks only to North.

"While it is true that the body in question does show some . . . *injury*, . . . I believe this is due to being swept downstream amidst ice and debris. A great deal of damage can happen to a body in churning water. In addition, there was no rope on or *near* the body of Mr. Burgess that would indicate a hanging. It is my professional opinion that he died from drowning—most likely due to intoxication—and that all injuries were incurred in a postmortem state."

Page folds his hands across his stomach as though he has just delivered a lecture on human anatomy—complete with appropriate Latin terminology—to a rapt classroom. *Postmortem.* It doesn't take a linguist to decipher the definition of that word, but Page knows that it makes him sound knowledgeable and qualified before the court.

After a moment North clears his throat. "Mistress Ballard?"

"Yes?"

"When you inspected the body did you find a rope on or near his person?"

"I did not."

"And the men who found him, did they see a rope?"

"No."

"You inquired about this?"

"I did."

"Because you found it curious as well?"

"It was something I noted given the rope *burns* on his *neck*."

I slide my eyes to the left and see the faint flicker of a crooked smile warp the corner of Dr. Page's mouth.

I do not consider myself a scribe of any repute. I am a chronicler of facts, not feelings. However, the knowing look that passes between North and Page inspires a sort of enraged doggerel that Shakespeare himself might salute with his quill.

Thou crusty open-arsed babbling liar!
Thou craven hag-born malt-worm!
Thou dankish prick-faced leprous carrion!

North steeples his fingers beneath his chin. Considers. "Rope burns without a rope? Is it possible you misinterpreted what you saw, Mistress Ballard?"

"It's possible the rope came off in the water. Or was cut away. Or reclaimed."

"I see." North smirks, then scribbles something onto a sheet of paper and hands it to Henry Sewall.

Clearly Page had been sent to Pollard's not only to contradict my assessment, but to follow behind and interrogate the witnesses on all that transpired before his arrival. I curse myself for having left so quickly yesterday. I should have stayed with the body until he left.

The tavern is silent now, all eyes on the three of us and our battle of wills. I stare at the doctor. Page looks only to North. But when North speaks again, his words and gaze are directed at me.

"I thank you both for coming today. And for taking such care to examine the late Mr. Burgess—may he rest in peace—but, after hearing the evidence, it is the court's decision that the death of Joshua Burgess was an accidental drowning—as stated by Dr. Page. This matter is settled. Mr. Sewall, please record these findings in the official record." He looks to the crowd. "Who is next?"

I do not stay to hear some ridiculous complaint one neighbor might have against another for taking the Lord's name in vain. Truth be told, I am more than a little tempted to do so myself. So I turn on my heel and walk away. I have half a mind to request that Amos Pollard drag Joshua Burgess into the tavern so the entire town can see for themselves. There is no possible way the river did that damage to his body. But I am halfway to the door—Ephraim moving to intercept me—when an idea flashes bright through my mind.

"Wait!" I stop. Turn. Take one step back toward North.

I can hear Ephraim curse under his breath directly behind me.

"My decision is *final,* Mistress Ballard." North's composure is broken now, his voice louder than necessary.

"I understand that. And I am not challenging your decision. I simply ask that Mr. Sewall record in the official court documents that there are contradicting views as to the cause of Mr. Burgess's death. One that states accidental drowning." I pause for effect. "And one that states *murder.*"

"I don't think—"

"It is my right before the law and the state of Massachusetts to request this." I give him the smile held in reserve for my enemies. "As a *trained medical professional.*"

I am correct on this point. North knows it. And so do any number of other people in the room. As a midwife I am granted a unique legal status most women do not enjoy. If he publicly refuses me, I will have cause to appeal to a higher court, and—should things grow contentious—North could be stripped of his appointment as judge for failing to uphold established law.

He does not capitulate immediately, however, but rather twists his mouth in calculation for several seconds. Seeing no way out of it, he finally says, "Very well. Mr. Sewall, please note that my verdict lies with Dr. Page's assessment but that there is—as Mistress Ballard has noted—a contradicting *opinion.*"

Henry Sewall bends his head over the ledger, and I turn to leave once more. Ephraim now stands at the door waiting, my riding cloak over his arm and an expression of urgency spread across his face.

I hear Judge North call William Pierce forward. "What is your complaint, Mr. Pierce?"

"I am here with my daughter, Sally, your honor. And she has two charges to make."

Again, I slow. Stop. Turn.

Again Ephraim curses, but audibly this time.

"Miss Pierce, what is your charge?" North asks.

Sally's voice is shaky, and she has to clear her throat to get the words out. "I bring charges of fornication, Your Honor."

Now Ephraim is at my side, fist clenching the back of my dress, whispering, "Don't," in my ear.

No, no, no. Please no, I think.

I rise onto my tiptoes to get a glimpse of Sally over the crowd. The girl is staring at the ground, face crimson, lips pinched together in shame.

William Pierce stands beside his daughter, one hand on her back, and I can see his fingers squeezing the small muscle in the dip between shoulder and neck.

"Against whom do you bring these charges?"

"Against my employer, Mrs. Rebecca Foster."

I have been delivering testimony in this room on the last Friday of each month for a decade. But never, in all of that time, have there been two such scandalous occurrences and certainly not on the same day. The people of Hallowell will be chewing on this bone for *years*.

William Pierce steps in front of his daughter. "I told Sally to give her notice this morning, Your Honor, because it has come to my attention that Mrs. Foster is pregnant by a man not her husband. Sally heard her admit to this yesterday! And I feel that to remain in the Fosters' employ would be a blight upon my daughter's character."

"That doe-eyed little traitor," I hiss, and Ephraim has to loop his arm around my waist to stop me from lunging forward. "Rebecca isn't even here to defend herself."

"We need to go," Ephraim says, the tone of his voice brooking no argument. "Right. Now."

"Mr. Sewall, will you please note in the court records that Mrs. Rebecca Foster, wife of Reverend Isaac Foster, has been formally charged with the gross and immoral sin of fornication."

While Henry Sewall records this charge, North leans forward and rests his elbows on the table. "What is your second charge, Miss Pierce?"

She is terrified, that much is obvious.

"Murder."

There is no outburst this time, only the sound of Sally's feet shuffling across the flagstone floor as her father pushes her closer to the table. "In addition to saying that she was pregnant, I also heard Mistress Foster say that her husband did kill Joshua Burgess."

Now there are gasps of astonishment. Whispers.

Dr. Page takes a step back. Glowers at her. I can see him try to figure out a way to explain his miscalculation.

"No!" I am astonished at the sound of my voice. As is everyone else in the tavern, for the room falls suddenly quiet, and all heads swivel to look at me. "That is not at all what Rebecca said."

"Mistress. Ballard," North growls. "I—"

"The reason Sally heard our conversation is because she was listening at the door while I was there yesterday. Did you hear me? I. Was. There. Go on. Ask her."

No one does. And both she and her father remain silent, though her eyes fill with frightened tears. It is clear Sally did not want to do this. But it is already done. And I feel no mercy for her.

North leans forward. "Mistress Ballard, I will not tolerate such an outburst in my courtroom."

I ignore him. "What Rebecca said is that she *hoped* Isaac had killed the man. And can any of you blame her?" I look around the tavern, then take a step forward and glare at North. "Can *you* blame her?"

Enraged now, he brings his gavel down with a hard *whack*. "This is an obscene disruption!"

"No. It is an obscene miscarriage of justice."

Whack!

"Rebecca is not here to defend herself against these charges."

Whack!

"This foolish little ninny came in on the last half of a sentence and thinks she heard a confession? No. She's nothing more than an eavesdropper."

Whack!

"You should not be presiding over this matter," I tell North. "You are one of the men accused of raping Rebecca Foster."

Whack! Whack!

Henry Sewell sits beside the judge, pen held in midair, mouth open in astonishment.

"And you"—I turn and point my finger directly in Sally's face—"you should be ashamed of yourself. You gossiping little liar. Do you have any idea the harm you've just done?"

Whack! Whack! Whack!

I feel Ephraim's hand on the small of my back. There is a tug, urging me to leave. But no. I am too angry, too full of spitting fury to acknowledge him.

"Mistress Ballard!" North's voice is filled with thunder now, and it is the only thing that breaks through the roar in my mind. "You are in contempt of court. Mr. Ballard, remove your wife from my presence immediately."

*

The air outside the tavern is clean and cold, without the slightest tinge of woodsmoke. I can almost taste the frost on my tongue, the bite of winter settling into my lungs.

"What were you *thinking*?" Ephraim hisses in my ear as he pulls me down the steps and toward the stables.

I don't bother keeping my voice down. "I couldn't let her stand there and lie about Rebecca."

"Hush," Ephraim warns as a crowd of people spill out of the tavern. Their heads are bent low, whispering. Several of them look toward us, then away.

"And that helped? What you just did?"

"I spoke the truth."

"And got kicked out of court. Everything else you accomplished today could well be dismissed."

"He wouldn't dare."

Ephraim leads me through the stable door and toward the stalls where Sterling and Brutus wait for us. He pulls a shilling from his pocket and hands it to young Matthew Pollard, the stable boy. Like Moses, he looks like their father, though at the moment he is only dark and lanky. The big and brooding will take some years yet.

"You just gave him the advantage, Martha. North could do anything now."

I am not a woman given easily to tears. They're useless things that serve only to make your voice waver and your cheeks wet. But they accost me now, and I push them away with the back of my hand.

"I couldn't stand there and do nothing! I couldn't. I won't."

When Matthew Pollard leads the horses away to saddle them, Ephraim sighs. He drops his forehead to mine. "You are too involved in this."

"I never asked to be."

"And I would never ask you to turn away from a friend. But that was reckless, Martha. That was *dangerous*. You called North a rapist in his own courtroom."

"I said nothing that isn't already on the record, that isn't being whispered about in this town."

"Behind closed doors? Yes. But you said it to his face."

"And you think it's better to whisper behind a man's back?"

"I think it's better to be prudent in your speech. Measured."

"Suddenly you're afraid to look a man in the eye and call him what he is?"

My husband flinches. Looks away. "That was a long time ago."

"It was no time at all. Yesterday. Just a moment. It is only ever a breath away for me. And I saw the truth of that when North asked if I'd ever seen a man hanged. He knows I have. He was there when it happened. And so were you."

Thirty-Five Years Ago

OXFORD, MASSACHUSETTS

DECEMBER 19, 1754

Billy Crane jerked at the end of his rope. He'd pissed himself—most likely when the trapdoor fell—and a dark stain ran the length of his right leg. The drop was supposed to break his neck, but he was a tall man, and I could see that the rope hadn't fully done its job. His back was arched and one foot twitched.

I looked away, but Ephraim's hand lay soft against my cheek, gently forcing my gaze back to the gallows. "No," he said, "watch it to the end."

I tried to shake loose, but he leaned closer, insistent, mouth brushing my ear. "This is justice, Martha. You *need* to see it done."

No one needs to see this, I thought, but Ephraim held me still. The crowd gathered in the clearing below was silent, collectively holding its breath until the spasms stopped. I saw my parents before the tree, staring up at the twisting form of Crane, murder in their eyes. Only when the hangman cut the rope and let Crane's body drop to the ground with a heavy thud did Ephraim turn me in to the wide shelter of his chest. And then I was crying, my voice muffled by the sharp December wind and the heavy linen of his shirt. I pummeled him with my fists until they ached, but Ephraim did not defend himself, or hold me, or say a word of comfort.

We stood on a rise above the clearing, hidden beneath a copse of fir trees, the crowd below oblivious to our presence, so intent were they on the scene before them. There hadn't been a public hanging in those parts for almost ten years, and my father had forbid me to attend this one. Private hangings—the ones motivated by revenge—were far more common, however. Grisly. Barbaric. Father used several other words to describe the process, none of them fit for a woman's ears, *but*—I thought—he had forgotten to include *riveting*.

He would lock me away for a year if he knew I'd seen them hang Billy Crane. Father had forced me to lay a hand on the family Bible and swear that I would not set foot out the door until Billy had been put in the ground to rot. And I would have obeyed if it weren't for Ephraim Ballard. He came to fetch me after my parents left, and I could no more refuse him than cease breathing.

Finally, after I exhausted myself, Ephraim pushed my tears away with his thumbs and cupped my face in his hands. He looked at me as though I might shatter. He looked at me as though he was willing to pick up each and every piece if I did. As though he would put them back together with his own bleeding fingers.

Ephraim offered one curt nod. "It's done then. He's dead."

"Good God, Ephraim, is this how you court a girl?" I took a deep breath and it rattled through my lungs, frantic, erratic. "Sneaking off in the middle of the day to see a man *hanged*?"

"The courting is done," Ephraim said, and it took a bit of effort to suppress his smile. "All that's left now is the marrying." I wanted to answer that hidden smile with one of my own but couldn't seem to find one. "Besides," he added, "it didn't take much convincing."

He tensed when I said, "Father told me you testified."

Ephraim was taller, but only by a couple of inches, and his wide, blue eyes looked over the top of my head to rest on the scene below. He shrugged, his voice purposefully devoid of emotion. "I told them what I saw."

Them. Five men. Just a handful of town elders, my father included, who'd met the night before to see what could be done about a man such as Billy Crane.

I shuddered. They hadn't let me in the meeting at all.

The clearing had emptied, and I searched it in a panic for my parents. I couldn't see them. "We have to get back. Or they will know you brought me."

Ephraim seemed unconcerned. "Not yet," he said. "They can wait."

I was about to protest when he nodded toward the base of the hill. A dark-clad figure began climbing toward us. He took the hill in a series of long, purposeful strides, and the moment I recognized him, I tensed.

"What is he doing here?"

Ephraim didn't answer. Instead he stepped between us so that I was partially hidden in the shadows beneath the tree. He grabbed the man's hand. "Joseph. Thank you for coming."

"Of course." Joseph North was young and handsome, and the humble words did nothing to hide the flush of excitement that rose above his collar. He'd given the deciding vote that had sealed Crane's fate. "Do you still need me this evening?"

"Yes." Ephraim peered at the sun, judged its angle in the sky. "Four o'clock? Make sure you bring the documents. I want it official."

"You caught me just in time, then. I leave first thing in the morning to join my regiment. We ride for Fort Beauséjour. Our orders are to force the natives out of Acadia." He gave Ephraim a last thoughtful glance, then tipped his hat to me. "Martha."

Joseph North turned and marched back down the hill. When he was out of earshot I stepped away from Ephraim, suspicion pinching the corners of my eyes. "What was that about?"

"I've asked Joseph to be at your parents' when I take you home—"

"My father will be furious, but I hardly think legal protection is in order—"

"To marry us."

I blinked. "*What?*"

Ephraim took one hand with great care, as though lifting a robin's egg from a nest. "It's been only two weeks since . . ." He wasn't typically one to shy away from comment, but he couldn't seem to find the words for this. He cleared his throat. Blushed. Ran a finger along the base of my thumb.

"I know how long it's been." I tried to yank my hand away, but he clamped it into his own.

"Your cycle," Ephraim finally stammered. "It hasn't come yet. Has it?"

"You can't know that."

"Am I wrong?"

My silence was answer enough.

"Have you considered what will happen if you're with child?"

I heard the strike before I felt the sting in my palm, but it was the pain that brought me to my senses. "How *dare* you!"

He wasn't hurt so much as startled, but he grabbed both of my wrists and pulled them to his chest to prevent me from doing it again. He shook me just a bit, and I felt my teeth rattle.

"What was that for?" he demanded.

"I won't have you marry me out of pity!"

"You don't think I *want* you anymore?"

"How *could* you?"

There. It was the truth. The unspoken tension between us.

Ephraim's entire body trembled with rage. I was afraid he would shake me again. Or kiss me. I couldn't tell which to expect by the look on his face. He did neither, in fact, but rather lowered his face until it was an inch from mine. "Let me be clear," he growled, furious. "My feelings haven't changed. But I need to know if yours have."

I was overwhelmed. Terrified, even. But I shook my head because I *did* want to marry him. I always had.

Ephraim crushed me against his chest, my arms pinned between us, before I could register his immense relief. He buried a hand in my hair, rubbing little circles against my scalp with his thumb.

"Then you must marry me. Tonight. Take my name and they can never question the legitimacy of any child you ever have."

I was neither small nor delicate. I had much of my father's height and most of his stubbornness; and when I stood before Ephraim Ballard, I could almost look him in the eye. So I straightened my spine and leaned my forehead against the bridge of his nose.

"Take me home, then," I said, "so we can be married."

2

TO HOUSEKEEPING

DECEMBER 1789

I'll note you in my book of memory. . . .
Look to it well and say you are well warn'd.

—WILLIAM SHAKESPEARE, *Henry VI*

BALLARD'S MILL

One of the great cedar doors to the mill stands ajar, and a large bay mare is tied to the post outside. I don't hear the expected sounds of saw and hatchet within, but rather the muted strain of conversation, so I stop outside the door and tip my head to one side, listening. The horse whickers, and I set a hand on its nose, urging silence so I can hear what is being said.

"I've already completed that survey," my husband argues. "And I have three lumber orders to fill by next Friday. I don't have time to do it again."

I have been married long enough to catch the nuance in Ephraim's voice—every clipped syllable and strained vowel—and there is no doubt he is struggling to control his temper.

"The Kennebec Proprietors *want* it done again."

Ah.

Joseph North.

I press my lips together and give the horse an accusing stare—*traitor*—then pull my hand away from the soft, warm nose and slide closer to the door.

Ephraim clears his throat. "Doing it again won't change the results."

"They might beg to differ."

"They can beg all they like. But they've not seen the land. It's nothing but bog for miles in every direction. Unsuitable for farming. And besides, right now it's little more than a block of ice."

"They want to assign a lease on the property."

"And doom their tenants to a life of failure and poverty?" A drawer rattles and papers shuffle. I can hear the warning note in my husband's voice grow sharper. "Here. The survey. I was there two months ago. I assume you've filed the last copy I gave you?"

"Not yet." I hear the crinkle of paper as North straightens the map and then folds it again. "I can't."

"Can't? Or *won't?*"

"It's not what they're expecting. And you know they have *expectations,* Ephraim."

"I am not leaving my family in the dead of winter to confirm something I already know." Ephraim's voice is now low and smooth and deceptively calm. "Besides, I know what you're doing, Joseph."

"I am reminding you of your *obligation.*" North lightens the tone of his voice, cajoles. "You like this lease, don't you? You like living here?"

Ephraim doesn't answer, and there is wariness in that stretch of silence.

"This land is leased to you by our *mutual* employers. The Kennebec Proprietors can be quite generous when they're pleased with a tenant. I think you've experienced that yourself over the last eleven years. You have the lease—and the surveying contract—but not the deed to this mill. Not yet."

The Kennebec Proprietors, a part of the Plymouth Company in Boston, acquired vast land holdings along the Kennebec valley one hundred and fifty years ago. They own most of the land along the river, for fifteen miles on either side, and have been leasing it out to encourage settlement in the District of Maine. Our family assumed the lease on Ballard's Mill eleven years ago but do not yet own the deed. That won't happen until next April when we finally meet the third condition. The first two were met within a year of living here: building a home and tilling a minimum of five acres. The last, however, is a matter of time. We must live on this property for twelve consecutive years before it can become legally ours. So we are in breach of nothing. Yet I can feel the threat hanging in the air between North and my husband.

"I remember the terms of our lease well enough. You don't have to remind me."

"Don't I? Because you seem strangely unwilling to see reason. Is one survey worth losing both your home and your income?"

"You want me to falsify my findings? To claim it's habitable land?"

"I want you to understand there are bigger things at stake. Without the mill and your contract, you'd find your family in a dire situation." North pauses for a moment, and I would give anything to see his expression. "It is, as you mentioned, the dead of winter."

He has delivered his orders but won't stand around to watch Ephraim mull over the decision. Boots shift impatiently on the worn plank floor. And since I don't want to be caught eavesdropping, I step around the door and into the mill. I say the first thing that comes to mind.

"Have you seen my ink?" I smile at my husband, then make a show of being startled by North's presence.

At his feet lies a mongrel; half mutt—some indeterminate breed that's been bastardized a dozen times over—and half coyote. He is brown and black and white, with tall, peaked ears, a long snout, and yellow eyes. He sees me and growls.

There is a rustling in the loft, and I tilt my chin to see Percy, perched on the rail, rousing his feathers. His talons pulse like a man flexing his fingers in anticipation. The bird likes neither the dog nor the growl. And from the way those hackles rise in response along the bony ridge of the cur's spine, I can see the feeling is mutual.

"Hush, Cicero," North orders, looking first at the falcon, then at the dog. After a moment his gaze returns to me and he says, "*Sit.*"

Cicero obeys because he must, but keeps his teeth bared. I remain standing, with my arms crossed because I will not be told what to do by the likes of Joseph North.

"Your dog has poor manners," I tell him.

"Or good judgment." He tips his hat, but his voice is cold, and his eyes are slanted, hateful. "Martha."

Ephraim notes the exchange with a narrowed gaze. Joseph North is a genteel man, not typically given to rudeness, and I doubt my husband will tolerate another snide comment. I do not return the greeting. North wants an apology for disrupting his court last week, but he won't get one.

"There," Ephraim says, nodding toward the drafting table where a small wooden box is spread open. "Your ink."

My quill lays flat beside the box, the tip blackened by Ephraim's morning scribbles. Beside the writing paraphernalia is a neatly stacked pile of woodworking tools. Knives and blades of various lengths. One of them—Ephraim's favorite—is a wicked, hook-shaped thing used for stripping small branches off felled trees. A bottle of linseed oil and a polishing rag sit beside it, abandoned. The mill smells of frost and sawdust, oiled metal, and old leather. It smells like Ephraim.

Where two disks of ink are usually nestled, only one remains. Ephraim crosses the floor and slides a protective arm around my waist, and I relax as his thumb strokes my rib cage.

"This is your ink?" North asks, lifting a hand. It is only then that I notice the hardened disk pinched between his thumb and forefinger, the pads of which are now stained black. "Ephraim never told me that you draw."

I open my mouth to answer, but Ephraim grabs the back of my dress in his fist and pulls me closer in warning, so I shrug one shoulder instead.

"I suppose it comes in handy. You must need pictures of your herbs. Speaking of which," North adds, "I believe my wife will stop by for another tonic soon. Her headaches have gotten worse of late."

I have never drawn a picture in my life, and I certainly don't need one to help me remember that Lidia North requires a concoction of dried feverfew, peppermint, and ginger, combined with crushed rosemary and yarrow. It only works when I soak the herbs in brandy for sixty days, however. The result is an effective tincture that I try to keep on hand. But if Lidia's debilitating headaches have gotten worse, I blame North and all he's put her through in recent months. Regardless, his cavalier assumption that I will play nursemaid to his wife has me gnawing on the edge of my tongue.

After a prolonged silence, North turns to my husband. "I'll be expecting your survey at the end of the month." And with that he strides out the door and swings onto his horse. The dog trots after him obediently.

Ephraim lets go of my dress and picks up the hooked blade from his worktable. He taps the flat against his palm as the sound of hooves retreats into the distance. More so than anything else on the workbench, that instrument looks like a thing built to maim.

"The rogue hast lived too long," he mutters under his breath, and brings the blade down onto the drafting table in a neat arc. It lodges there, quivering, and swath of pale wood gleams beneath the cleaved board like an open wound.

I peer at him, skeptical. "You've been reading Shakespeare again."

He shrugs, then yanks the blade free. "I like the way he delivers an insult."

"Then surely you can do better than that for a man such as North."

I love my husband's smile. It transforms his stoic face, revealing two rows of straight teeth and laugh lines around his eyes. "That clay-brained guts, that knotty-pated fool, that whoreson, obscene, greasy tallow-catch."

"Well," I say, "your clay-brained, greasy whoreson took my ink. How do you plan on getting it back?"

He tosses the knife onto the table. "I'll buy you more."

"That thing looks like revenge to me," I tell him.

"What?"

"Your knife."

"That's not a bad name for a blade." He picks it up again. Balances its weight in his palm, then brings it down onto the table once more. "Revenge it is."

After a moment, Ephraim turns back to the wide double doors that North passed through, and frowns.

"Are you going to do it?" I ask. "The survey. I overheard your conversation."

He scratches behind one ear. "I don't think I have much choice."

"You realize he's punishing us for what I did in court?"

"Yes. But I think there's more to it than that."

"How so?"

"North wants me to be hundreds of miles away when it comes time for you to testify."

"Why?"

"Because the law of coverture prevents a woman from testifying in court without her husband present."

"No." I shake my head. "I give testimony in court many times a year without you being present."

"Only because your profession allows you to do so regarding a woman's declaration of paternity during childbirth. Those parameters do not extend to a situation like this."

"But if I'm not able to testify next month—"

"Rebecca Foster will lose her only witness, and her allegations will be dismissed," he says.

MILL CREEK BRIDGE

"Goodbye, love."

Ephraim tucks his face into the crook between my neck and shoulder and presses a kiss into my skin. I can feel the warmth of his breath slide beneath the collar of my dress even as the snow falls around us. I walked with him down the lane, all the way to the bridge over Mill Creek, to say goodbye. This has been our habit through all the long years that we have lived in Hallowell. I do not let him leave without a proper send-off.

Water Street spans Mill Creek by this somewhat precarious bridge. It is made of planks nailed to roughhewn logs that rest on a series of stone foundations. Horses can cross two abreast, but wagons must go single file. There are no rails, and the drop is fifteen feet to the creek below. Only twelve-foot-wide and thirty-foot-long, it often feels as though it's held together by little more than stubbornness and wishful thinking. But the bridge has ferried countless travelers across the creek for many years now, weathering flood and storm alike, and it needs little in the way of maintenance apart from having an occasional plank or log replaced. Ephraim checks the foundations every spring, after the thaw, and reinforces them where needed.

"You will be careful, won't you?" I ask.

"Of course."

"And you will come home to me?"

"Don't I always?"

"Ah, but this would be the time you didn't, when I need you most."

We stand beside Sterling—Ephraim's horse—at the near end of the bridge. My husband pulls away from me and tips my chin up with the edge of one finger so that our eyes meet.

"What is it you're worried about?"

"That you won't make it home in time. That I won't be able to testify, and Rebecca will be left defenseless. That North will get away with everything."

"That won't happen. I *will* make it back."

"But—"

"I will." He looks at the falcon who rests on the saddle swell, waiting to depart. "I've taken precautions. We will be married thirty-five years this month. Don't start doubting me now."

"Doubt and fear are not the same thing," I say, following Ephraim's gaze to Percy. The bird is hooded now, so I cannot see his penetrating burnt-orange eyes, and his jesses—the long, thick leather straps around his talons—are tied to the broad ridge of leather at the front of Ephraim's saddle. He can neither see nor fly.

Sometimes I feel that Percy can understand us. And perhaps he can—in his own way—because his head swivels this way and that, as though listening first to Ephraim, then to me. Percy dislikes the hood, but it is the only way to ride long distances. And only on Sterling. Brutus would never allow those lethal talons to get so close. The saddle is crosscut with sharp, savage gashes where Percy has dug into the leather. Better it than Sterling, however. To date, the bird has never injured horse or rider, and they have all learned to tolerate the arrangement.

"Where will you stay?" I ask.

"Fort Halifax. But only at night. I can't camp in this weather. Riding back and forth to the site every day will eat up half my time. Otherwise, I could be home in a week."

A leather satchel, haversack, and a pack basket are strapped behind the cantle. They hold all of Ephraim's surveying tools and his winter gear and are packed tighter than usual given the weather and the distance he must travel. It will be a long two weeks for all of us.

I look to the bank of clouds moving in from the east. "A storm is coming."

"Yes," he says. "My fingers ache."

"It's a bad time to travel."

"I've done this before. It's only snow."

"And freezing winds."

"Only for a day or two. And then it will just be winter, same as always. I'm not worried, and you shouldn't be either."

"I *hate* North for making you do this."

"I hate him for so many reasons this barely ranks," he says, trying to lighten my mood.

Neither of us discuss the legitimate reasons that I have to fear. But the litany runs through my mind nonetheless, all the things that could happen to him in weather like this.

"Two weeks. That's all. And then I will be home, and we will make sure North is brought to justice," he says.

I step into my husband's arms, soaking up his warmth and scent. We are in the twilight years of a long love affair, and it has recently occurred to me that a day will come when one of us buries the other. But, I remind myself, that is the happy ending to a story like ours. It is a vow made and kept. *Till death do us part.* It is the only acceptable outcome to a long and happy marriage, and I am determined not to fear that day, whenever it arrives. I am equally determined to soak up all the days between.

"Two weeks," I tell him. "No more."

He kisses my brow. The tip of my nose. My mouth, slow and gentle, making his promise with both lips and tongue. "Goodbye, love."

The animals can sense that it is time to leave. Sterling stamps his right foreleg, and Percy rouses on his perch, shaking his feathers in anticipation.

They enjoy this, I think.

And then Ephraim pulls away and swings into the saddle. He offers me one last smile. I stand in the snow and watch until he has crossed the bridge. I watch until he rounds the bend and is out of sight.

"Stop feeling sorry for yourself," I mutter, then take a deep breath and turn back toward the house.

But I do not move. I do not breathe. Because there, not twenty feet away, is the silver fox. She is a beautiful specimen, a coalish kind of black, except for ears, paws, breast, and tail, all of which are white. She is perched on the crest of a snowbank, an ink stain on ivory. But it is her vivid, amber eyes that hold me in thrall. They seem to penetrate me, to *study* me.

"You again," I say, then speak her name, my words a soft exhale, a mist in the frozen air. "Tempest."

To name a thing is a proprietary act. It is a commitment. Of ownership or care or loyalty. It *means* something. With that single word I have declared that this little beast is *mine,* and that I have a responsibility to protect her.

The sound of my voice does not frighten the animal. Instead, she takes a step forward, then two. I watch, still as carved marble, while the lithe creature approaches, each step elegant and deliberate. When she is a mere eight feet away, I kneel to the snow and slowly extend my bare hand, palm up, in welcome. Only then does the fox startle and bolt into the woods.

SEWELL CHANDLERY

A man barges into the birthing room. He throws the door back, then flings off his coat in a single, smooth movement. I see this only out of the corner of my eye, however, because my patient—young Grace Sewell—is wailing and thrashing on the bed. This is her first labor, and she fights against every pang, then sobs through every respite. We have been at it all night and are both exhausted.

"Out! All of you," the man orders, and, because I recognize his voice, I ignore him.

I have not taken instructions in a birthing room since being apprenticed to an old, rusted battle-axe of a midwife in Oxford. Her name was Elspeth Horne, and everything I know about midwifery I learned from her. Thirty years have passed since then, and it will take more than the likes of one presumptuous man to make me shrink back from a patient.

"Did you hear me?" he asks.

"Yes," I say, not turning. For the first time in three hours, Grace is silent. She is only startled, and it won't last long, but for the moment her mouth is shut. Miracles never cease.

"Then why are you still here?" he demands.

"I do not leave my patients. And I do not answer to you."

"This woman is no longer your patient. She is mine. I have been called in to replace you."

I stand then, taking in every inch of Dr. Benjamin Page's pompous six feet.

"And this *patient* of yours, do you even know her name?" I ask.

"Mrs. David Sewell."

"Her Christian name, Doctor. The one that actually belongs to *her*. Do you know it?"

He sniffs. "Her name is irrelevant."

"Like it was irrelevant with Joshua Burgess?" I point at Grace. "You might not think a name matters in a room like this, but I assure you, it is vital."

I arrived at the Sewalls' the night before, having crossed the frozen river on foot, just before dusk. I was accompanied by the shop boy who works for David Sewell and had expected him to lead me to a private home across the street, but instead he took me right into the chandlery, where David was pacing back and forth behind the counter, looking very much like his older cousin, Henry, the town clerk.

"Where is Grace?" I asked, looking around the dim store at the piles of coiled rope and barrels of oil, the shelves filled with nails and bolts and boxes of soap.

He pointed to the ceiling.

"It is called an *appartement*," he'd said, exaggerating the French pronunciation, as he led me up the stairs at the back of the shop. "In England they call them 'flats,' but I prefer the European term. They're everywhere in Boston. A very convenient way to live and work."

He opened the door, then, and led me into the second-floor home that sat above his place of business. It consists of two small bedrooms and one larger room combining the kitchen, dining, and living area. His young wife was there, rocking slowly in a chair, lips pursed, and brow knotted. Her sour-faced mother sat beside her and held her hand.

"It hurts," Grace had told me. "I didn't think it would hurt."

"What did you think, then?" I asked, kneeling beside her.

"I don't know that I thought much about it all. This part was never explained to me."

I glanced at the girl's mother—the very proper looking Mrs. Hendricks.

"There was no need to alarm my daughter before she was ready."

"I tend to think of it as preparing them, not alarming them," I told her.

"I have prepared her to be a *lady*," Mrs. Hendricks sniffed. "Not that you can tell by this backwater village that her husband has chosen."

In reality, Grace had only been in the early stages of labor. So early, in fact, that had she been properly educated by her mother about the realities of childbirth, no one would have bothered to call for me until dawn. But I had sat up with the girl, regardless, timing her contractions all night. They came every thirty to forty-five minutes and lasted twenty seconds. Hardly birth pangs at all. And all the while I listened to Mrs. Hendricks complain about the long, hard journey from Boston, her difficulties on the bad rural roads, and her opinions of them as well.

The girl was inexperienced, and scared, and—when I performed an internal examination—barely dilated. Yet as the night hours dragged on, both Grace and her mother became more intimidated by the process. Impatient with the results and doubtful of my ability.

At some point, when I slipped out to use the privy, Mrs. Hendricks must have convinced David to send the shop boy for Dr. Page. And now he is here, trying to order me from the room.

"Let me see her," Page demands, attempting to edge me away from the bed.

"You will not manhandle me." I swat at his arm. "Cross to the other side of the bed if you wish to examine her. But I will not leave my position."

"Very well. I shall have to educate you, then." He turns to Grace. "It is unfortunate how many country women confuse false labor for the real thing."

"I beg your pardon—" I interrupt.

"Because it is obvious—"

"Her pains are now regular and promising."

"That this is a false labor," he says.

"Oh, for the love of God, Grace, do not listen to this man. I have been with you all night. Your labor is early but real."

The girl is of the stiff and straight variety. Well-bred and nicely mannered. If not pregnant, she would be slender and shapeless. Excellent posture. Tiny waist. Nose straight enough to be a ruler. Hair like a pane of glass. Grace Sewell has been bred to look nice in a gown and do as she is told. The problem is that she has always taken her orders from those with a pedigree and a formal education. So it makes sense that when she looks to Dr. Page and his fine coat, she finds comfort and familiarity. Whereas all she has gotten from me during these long hours of the night is an assurance that she must be patient, that the baby will come when it is ready, and that there is nothing to be done in the meantime but wait and walk and sleep if she can.

Mrs. Hendricks rises from her chair and joins him at the side of the bed. "What is your opinion, Doctor?"

"I believe," he says, setting his medical bag on the bed beside Grace and unzipping it, "that your daughter is suffering in the way that all women of higher birth suffer."

She waits for him to continue, her eyes round and her mouth curved into a moue of attentiveness, hanging on every word.

"It has been known for centuries that wealthy and beautiful women—those who lead delicate lives and are of an upper *strata*, such as your daughter—suffer a great deal more during childbirth than"—he looks at me—"*common* women."

"That is absurd," I tell him. "If you knew anything about women, much less birth, you would know the female body works the same regardless of class."

"And how many well-bred women have you delivered, Mistress Ballard? How many ladies? Or governors' daughters? How many wealthy women have you sat beside?" Dr. Page does not wait for me to finish drawing the breath that will school him on how many *hundreds* of women I have delivered, from all walks of life, before he plunges ahead, "As I thought. Now get out of the way and let me assist this woman so that I may relieve her of these false pains."

"Thank you, Doctor," Mrs. Hendricks says, voice breathy and submissive. "What can you do for her?"

"Administer laudanum. She will sleep and her pains will cease."

"Grace," I make my appeal directly to the girl now, "medical text-books do suggest laudanum for a false labor. Your labor is still early, but quite real, and this medicine will do you great harm."

Dr. Page clenches his jaw. "I am confident in my diagnosis."

"A diagnosis determined by what?" I demand. "You have not once checked her. Internally or externally."

"By observation. And medical skill. Remember which of us," he turns to Grace as he finishes, "has the medical degree in this room."

Grace looks at her mother, confused and terrified. "What should I do?"

"Listen to the doctor, darling. He went to school for this."

It is decided then, and I watch in horror as Dr. Page pulls out a bottle filled with reddish-brown liquid. "Fifty drops ought to do it," he says.

"That will knock her unconscious!"

"How else do you expect her to sleep? You've kept her up the entire night, chattering and performing needless examinations."

Dr. Page pulls out a dropper from a small velvet bag and begins to measure the drops into a tiny goblet. "Here," he says after a few moments, handing the cup to Grace, "drink."

"Please do *not* take that medicine," I all but yell.

But Grace Sewell tips the cup backward and drains the contents into her mouth. Shivers at the bitter taste. Swallows with a delicate gulp. Wipes her mouth with the back of her hand. Within moments her eyes are heavy and she's breathing slowly.

Dr. Page puts his things away and buckles his bag. "Have her husband call for me when the real pains begin. Though I do not expect that to be for some days yet."

I watch him go but say nothing as I do not want to discourage his departure. The sooner that fool leaves, the sooner I can care for Grace.

Mrs. Hendricks glares at me. "Aren't you leaving as well?"

"*Absolutely* not. Your daughter," I say, pointing to where the girl lies, sprawled on her back, "will soon be deep in the throes of labor. But she has been rendered unconscious by that idiot. It will be a miracle if he hasn't killed her and the child both."

"You don't really think that—"

"Of course I damn well do!" I shout, and am gratified by the look of horror on Mrs. Hendricks's face as she shrinks backward. "Why do you think I argued with him? I will stay exactly where I am until I know that your daughter and grandchild are well. But if they aren't, you will have Dr. Page to thank for that. Remember that the next time you panic and call a man to do a woman's job."

*

Grace sleeps for nine hours. I sit beside her the entire time, fretting, my fingers on the girl's wrist, counting each heartbeat. They are too slow, the contractions too weak. Not nearly what is required to press a child into the world. But they do not stop, and that is its own kind of miracle.

Finally, Grace begins to sweat. Each contraction hardens her belly, and she moans deep in her throat. It is the kind of sound a soldier makes when he lies near the cusp of death on a battlefield. Of a wounded animal in the forest. It is the sound of a woman arriving at transition—that painful shift between labor and birth. At first it is a panting. Then a whistling, followed by a groan from deep inside her chest. If she were awake, I could prepare her for what comes next.

When Grace starts to gag, I have only seconds to sit her upright and lean her over before she vomits a foul brown plume onto the bed. Grace is covered. Her clothes are covered. The bedding is covered. But she is finally awake and instantly aware that her body is deep in the work of birthing her child.

The voice comes from behind me. "Mrs. Ballard, I . . ."

When I look to Mrs. Hendricks, I can see her throat working hard to swallow the apology.

She looks away. "Can Grace manage the rest of her labor?"

Stupid, prideful woman, I think.

"Yes. But thanks to you, she is no better equipped to handle the next birth. She will only remember the worst of this one," I say, then order her away to gather warm water and clean linens.

"What happened?" Grace asks as the last of the laudanum fades from her system.

"I believe that you have learned exactly what kind of doctor Benjamin Page truly is. Now"—I look her directly in the eye as I begin to help her out of the soiled gown—"will you allow me to assist you with the thing that I do best?"

She nods. Swallows. Begins to cry. "Yes."

"Good. Your mother is bringing us a wash basin. And then we are going to meet your baby."

*

When Dr. Page comes running up the chandlery steps two hours later, I meet him at the door to Grace's bedroom. The girl is sitting up in bed, holding her new son with a sense of wonder and pride.

When Page tries to push past me, I set a hand on his chest. "You are not needed here."

"That is my—"

"No. She's *my* patient."

"You would do well to learn your place, Mistress Ballard."

I laugh at him. "I have been in my *place* for many, many hours now. You, on the other hand, knocked a woman unconscious and abandoned her to the ill effects of a dangerous drug. As a result, you were not present when she began to vomit in her sleep. Had *I* not been in *my place,* she would have died. But I am curious about one thing, however," I say.

He looks in alarm to the bed. "What?"

"Did you even bother to learn her name while you were gone?"

Any humility that might have been rising to the surface after learning his error is wiped away by a sudden flash of pride. "There was no need."

"Then you have learned nothing. Her name is Grace. And if you were an educated man—as you claim—you would know that the name means 'unmerited favor.' Which is exactly what God has shown by allowing both her and the child to survive your ministrations."

I close the door in his face.

POLLARD'S TAVERN

SATURDAY, DECEMBER 12

There is blood in the snow.

A crowd has gathered outside the tavern, and two men scuffle at its heart, arms and legs flailing. Amos and Moses Pollard stand on either side of the shrinking circle, arms out to block anyone from interfering. Abigail has wisely situated herself on the front steps, mug of steaming cider in hand, a safe distance from the fray. She looks on with disdain.

I have just come from delivering Grace Sewell and am ready to be home, but my curiosity wins out, and I cross the street to see what all the fuss is about.

"Men are a right bunch of fools," Abigail mutters when I reach her side.

"Yes. But which ones specifically?"

"The one that's bleeding is James Wall." Before I can ask a question or jump to any conclusions, she adds, "And the other is an officer of the court from Vassalboro. Came here to bring James in on charges, he did."

"Charges for what?"

She shrugs. "Dunno. But James doesna want to be brought. So they're deciding it amongst themselves. Like I said, fools. James shouldna resist, and the officer shouldna let him."

"Let?"

"Ye'll see."

And I do, soon enough, when the officer grows tired of the deba-
cle. He's an average-size man, under six foot, and not so much thin
as sinewy. It is clear he's been trained to box, however, and is quick
on his feet. A left hook makes contact with James's jaw, sending him
sprawling to the frozen mud. The officer is on him in a moment, tying
his hands behind his back with a length of rope.

"As I said," the officer pants. "You are to report to Fort Western
immediately to face charges for failure to pay your debts."

James spits a glob of blood onto the ground. "I already told you!
We got stuck in the river and couldn't make our delivery. So I didn't
get paid. And therefore I couldn't make my payment last month."

The young officer does appear sympathetic at this. But he straightens his back and stands over James. "The why of it is none of my business. That's for the court to decide."

The crowd watches as he pulls James to his feet and leads him to
a wagon parked beside the tavern. They step aside as James is hoisted
onto the seat and has his bindings tied to an iron loop attached to the
wagon's sideboard. It's a sailor's knot, meant for rigging, and there's no
chance it will come loose on the journey. Once satisfied that James is
secure, the officer unties the reins and climbs to his seat.

He tips his hat to the crowd, then flicks the leather straps and
shouts, "Ha!"

The horse turns onto Water Street and toward the north as the
residents of the Hook stare silently after them.

"He lodged here last night," Abigail says, pre-empting my question again. "Said his name was Barnabas Lambard, but we didna
know he was an officer of the court or why he'd come."

"He looks to be quite young."

"Aye. About twenty, I'd say. And that probably worked in his favor."

"How's that?"

"Moses told me he was asking around about James. Where he lives
and what he looks like. Everyone thought they must be old acquain-
tances. But it was the horse he was most interested in." Abigail takes a
sip of her cider and turns to me.

"Why?"

"A man's a man. But every horse is unique. That's what he told

Moses, at any rate. And 'tis well known that James rides a Narrangan-sett Pacer. He boasts of it often enough—says it comes from Wash-ington's own herd. Lies, probably. I couldna pick one out of a herd, mind you, but that officer could. Charged right out of the tavern the moment he saw James tie up at the post."

I look to where the horse stands beside the hitching post—confused and jittery thanks to all the excitement. It's of middling height with narrow hindquarters and, like so many other horses, is a warm chestnut brown. Black mane. Black tail. Black socks. The head and tail are held high, though, and I think that maybe a good horse-man would know a Pacer from a Hackney.

"What will you do with it?" I ask, nodding to the horse.

"Board him, I guess. James can settle the bill later."

The wagon is gone now but I look in the direction it left. "I thought debtors' prison was a thing of the past. How much does James owe?"

Abigail shrugs. "There wasna much opportunity for asking ques-tions once the punches started flying, was there? But I have heard James intends to start a distillery." She turns those moss-green Scot-tish eyes on me. Gives me a look filled with import. "And that he went to Judge North for the loan."

"Why him?"

"A wealthy man is North. Likes to have a finger in every pot. Or so I'm told."

I turn my head to the side. Take in the hulking form of the tavern behind us. "Has Amos . . . ?"

"He would *never*."

The crowd starts to disperse, and I see John Cowan—the young blacksmith's apprentice—saunter over to say a few words to the Pollards' oldest daughter, Catherine. We observe the pair in silence. Bowed heads. Low voices. At one point John leans closer and lightly touches Catherine's elbow when she says something. They both laugh. Blush. Then he says goodbye and walks away.

"And what do ye make of that?" Abigail asks. Once again, she sips her cider, then passes the mug to me.

It's good and rich. Tart and strong. I swirl it around my mouth, carefully choosing my words. "John is kind and hardworking. Charles Clark depends on him greatly. He's strong. Responsible."

"But?"

"I didn't say 'but.'"

"Not out loud ye didna."

I flash Abigail a quick smile. "He's a good man. I believe that. But not the brightest I've ever known."

"Your standards might be too high, Mistress Ballard. Not every man can be Ephraim." She looks at me with a smile of her own. "Or Amos."

"Sadly, no."

"Ye ken my meaning. If he was to come knocking on your door would ye let him court Hannah?"

Abigail and I have never discussed Moses's interest in my daughter, but it can't have escaped her notice. "It isn't John Cowan who plans to come knocking. Or at least if he did, your own Moses would knock him down."

We assess John's retreating form. It wouldn't be a fair fight, but neither of us say it aloud. We both like Moses too much.

"Aye, he would try," Abigail says with a rueful twist of her mouth.

"Regardless, Hannah appears to be spoken for, and Dolly is still a bit young for courting, but if the circumstances were different on either count, yes, I would open the door for John Cowan. And I believe Ephraim would as well."

"That's about how I reckon things, but I wanted to make sure," Abigail says. Then, as I turn to go, she reaches for her mug. "Martha?"

"Yes?" I hand it back.

"Dinna be surprised if Moses comes knocking a bit sooner than ye expect."

*

I set my quill on the desk and stretch my hand. It aches. From cold and age and the strain of small muscles put to work guiding a child into this world.

Friday, December 11. — Birth. David Sewell's son. Cloudy. At Mr. Sewell's. I was called to attend Grace Sewell yesterday evening. Her travail was mild. But she and her mother were intimidated and called Dr. Page who gave my patient fifty drops of laudanum which put her into such a stupor that her pains (which were regular and promising) became scant until she puked. Her pains returned and she was delivered at the seventh hour of a son, her first born. I received twelve shillings as a reward. Left her cleverly at ten and walked across the river.

Cyrus and Young Ephraim have long since crawled into their beds on the second floor, and I can hear their snores rattling down the stairwell. The girls have also retreated to their room and whatever dreams the night might bring. Jonathan, as usual, is sleeping elsewhere.

My brows pinch together in frustration at the thought of him, but I continue writing:

Saturday, December 12.—Clear and cold. James Wall was carried to Fort Western by an officer today. I hear a charge was given against him for failure to pay debts.

I stretch my back, listening to the wind in the pines and the creak of the house as it settles around me. I can hear a coyote yipping in the pasture and an owl hooting near the barn. The fact of the matter is that I am lonely.

And then I laugh. If anyone had told me two decades ago, when I was buried in small children and endless chores, that one day I would sit at my desk in a warm, quiet house while the snow fell outside and complain of *loneliness,* I would have slapped them. That future seemed as far away as Constantinople.

I blow a long, cool breath over the new entry to set the ink, then put aside my quill. I would very much like to join the rest of the house in slumber, but I can already feel the creeping wakefulness that often assails me at night. This is a new affliction, something that began once I rounded the corner of forty-five. I never understood what a gift sleep was until it vanished. Whereas, in all the decades before, I slept deep and heavy, soaking up every morsel of rest that was offered, I now skim the surface, fitful, easily woken, and unable to drift off again. On nights like this, no amount of physical exhaustion can induce my mind to shutter, so I read by candlelight instead. It is the only time I allow myself this indulgence. The joy of falling into another life, another world, is the one thing that mitigates the frustration of a sleepless night.

I change into my nightgown, brush my hair, slip under the covers, and reach for the candle on the bedside table. I scoot it closer, then open *Emmeline* by Charlotte Turner Smith. Ephraim purchased the novel on his last trip to Boston. The cover is tattered—I am not the first owner—but the print is clear, and there are no missing pages, which is more than I can say for most of the novels I'm able to get my hands on. Within seconds, I am immersed in a make-believe world of English aristocracy. But it does not escape my attention that, had my own ancestors enjoyed such comfort, I would be living across the sea, and not here in the vast wilds of the new world.

BALLARD'S MILL

The house smells of dead animal. Like hide and fat and wild game. The acrid scent will last for several days, but there's no help for that. The deer tallow is pungent, but once it has been made into candles and cured, the stench will fade. I have added dried, crushed lavender and rosemary—along with their oils—to each of the four rendering pots that sit on my worktable. In a week, the candles will simply smell like the forest. And the house will smell of home once more.

"There," Dolly says, tying the last of the linen threads to the end of a slender, foot-long branch. "Two hundred and forty."

I inspect her work, then nod in approval. Dolly tied the wicks while I readied the hardening racks along the edge of the room. Each branch will hold two candles, and each rack will hold forty-eight. Altogether, we should have enough candles to get through the winter, with extra for bartering.

We spent all morning rendering the deer fat given to us by Amos Pollard, then straining it until the tallow was smooth and pale. Dolly and I both wear aprons to keep the oily splatters off our clothes, and scarves around our hair to keep it from falling in our eyes. Candle making is hard, sweaty work, and not a task meant to make a woman look pretty. It is, however, one of the necessary parts of running a household.

We take our spots at the table and lower the first branches so that the wicks on either end drop into separate pots. The thick linen strings soak up the wax for a moment before we lift them out again. It takes a few seconds for the rendered fat to harden and then we plunge them in again. We repeat the process, watching each candle grow in width with every immersion. Once they are an inch wide, we set the branches across a drying rack so that the candles dangle as they harden. The task will take several hours to complete, but neither of us minds. Rarely do we get an entire day together.

It is one of those winter afternoons that is so bright the sun reflects off the snow and hurts my eyes if I look at it directly. I cannot help but worry about Ephraim working his way through the frozen marsh up north. His people are Welsh but have lived in the colonies for two generations and have grown acclimated to these northeastern winters. He insists that he no longer feels the cold. I know that he's lying, but he says it anyway. It's the game we play—a dance of concern and denial.

Hannah has been with Lucy, our oldest, married daughter, and her family on the other side of the river, near Fort Western, all week. Lucy had her seventh child—Hannah's namesake—earlier in the year and was eager for both her help and her company. There are eleven years between them, but they have always had a special bond. And now that Hannah is nearing the age of marriage herself, I suspect there are questions she would rather ask her sister. This reality makes me a bit uneasy, however, given Lucy's casual attitude toward things of a carnal nature. Her first child was born a mere five months after her wedding.

There are rules and rituals, of course, for young people and how they court. Usually, it begins at one of the seasonal Frolics. Just last month, May Kimble's family hosted one, and there will be another in January here at the mill. But still, young people always find ways to be together, away from watchful eyes, and anytime my children are out of sight, I wonder what they might be up to.

As for the boys, Young Ephraim has joined his older brothers in cutting trees in the forest today, and none of them will be home until dinner. Only Dolly and I are here, and it is both restful and strange. It seems as though only yesterday I had a baby on each hip and two more wrapped around my ankles.

I plunge the candles into the tallow, then pull them out again, watching the excess drip off and back into the pot. The rendered fat has cooled slightly and isn't as runny, making the process go faster, and I like the way the dried herbs speckle the tallow. But I keep an eye on the consistency because if it gets much thicker the pots will need to go back over the fire.

We work in companionable silence until Dolly says, "I took stew and bread to Mistress Foster yesterday while you were out."

"And is she well?" I ask.

"No better," Dolly says. "No worse."

Ever since Sally Pierce made her accusations, the Fosters' world has grown increasingly small. Many of those inclined to defend them now whisper behind their backs. They wonder. They gossip. Some neighbors avoid them altogether. Few in the Hook cared that Joshua Burgess was dead until their pastor was incriminated in his murder. And those who dismissed Rebecca's claim of being raped look at her askance now that she is pregnant.

I am thinking about what I might do for Rebecca when Dolly points at something out the window.

"Who is that?" she asks. It's a simple question, but there is a curiosity—a certain kind of *light* in her eyes—that I note before turning to the window.

A man has driven his wagon up to the garden gate and dismounted. He is young and agile, of average height, and I recognize him immediately.

"That is Barnabas Lambard."

"I've never heard the name."

"He's an officer of the court from Vassalboro."

Dolly finishes dipping her candles, sets the branch on the hardening rack, then moves to the window for a better look. She fists her hands on her hips and gives the man a curious stare, head cocked to the side, lips pursed. "Why would an officer of the court come here?"

"An excellent question," I say. "You keep working on the candles. I'll find out."

"My tallow has gone thick," she says, and I know she wants to come along. By the faint smile tugging at the edge of her mouth, I suspect that Dolly might find the young man attractive.

"Then melt it again. I'll be back shortly."

I keep my apron on and the scarf around my head when I go to greet Mr. Lambard. I pull the front door open before he has made it through the garden gate.

He tips his hat. "Good morning, Mistress . . . ?"

"Ballard."

"Good morning, Mistress Ballard, I'm—"

"I know who you are, Mr. Lambard."

He stops on the path, chin tilted to the side, an expression on his face that suggests he's trying to remember if we have met. "You do?"

"I saw you apprehend James Wall in the Hook yesterday."

He takes off the wide-brimmed felt cap and whacks it against his leg twice even though it isn't dusty. "Ah. Then you won't be surprised to hear that I've come to arrest someone else."

I like James and still think it unfair that a measly debt could land him in jail, so I can't keep the snide tone out of my voice when I reply, "Someone forget to pay their taxes? Or perhaps you're after a gossip?"

There, I've almost made him smile, but it doesn't quite reach the surface.

"A bit more serious than that, I'm afraid. I'm here to arrest a man accused of rape."

"You've come for Joseph North?"

He shakes his head, and a single curl flops onto his forehead and falls across his eye. It makes him look younger somehow, less serious. He shoves it away with the back of his hand. "No. I'm here for Joshua Burgess."

He doesn't know. How is that possible?

"Well, Joshua Burgess doesn't live *here*," I hedge.

"So I gathered. But now I'm known in town, after what happened yesterday. And it's always best to have the element of surprise when coming to arrest a man. I halfway expect him to have fled anyway. I thought I'd stop and ask the neighbors first."

"And you just happened upon us?"

"You are the first drive off the main road into town." He hooks one thumb over his shoulder and points north. "At least coming from Vassalboro."

"Well," I say, taking comfort in the coincidence, "I know for a fact that Burgess hasn't fled."

"But are you willing to tell me where he is?"

I pull the corner of my bottom lip into my mouth, thinking. "If you'll tell me something in exchange."

"And what would that be?"

"Why you haven't come for Joseph North?"

"Ah, I see." Barnabas scratches the back of his neck. "Direct orders from the court. I'm to let North come in on his own for the hearing."

"And why does he get different treatment?"

"Because he's a judge. And a colonel."

"James Wall was a captain, and you arrested him in front of twenty people."

He nods once but doesn't break eye contact. "There's a wide gap between captain and colonel, isn't there?"

"And a wide gap in favor too, I'd say. You think that is fair?"

"What I think has nothing to do with it. I'm only an officer of the court; no one asks my opinion."

"I just did."

He flashes a quick, bright smile. "I *think* that I've a single job, Mistress, to apprehend the men I'm ordered to. And I'm the sort of man who does my job."

Yesterday, when he was scuffling with James, I hadn't gotten a good look at him. But I take Barnabas in now, curious about this man who has stepped into the scandal enfolding our town. He has sandy-colored hair and eyes that might be hazel. Or perhaps brown. I can't tell from this distance. But there's something about his face and the way he moves that makes him appear unremarkable. It occurs to me that perhaps he does this on purpose, to seem nonthreatening. He's young to be an officer of the court, and looking nondescript—especially to strangers—would be an advantage.

"Your turn," he says. "I've answered your questions."

"You can find Joshua Burgess at Pollard's Tavern."

He flicks a glance to the house behind me, then back, another smile quirking the corner of his mouth. "Seems to be a popular place amongst the criminal element in your town."

"James isn't a criminal," I say. "He's a friend, in fact. And there isn't a man in this town who wasn't shocked to hear that he's failed to pay a debt."

Abashed, Barnabas nods once. It's not an apology—he doesn't

owe me one—but rather an acknowledgment that he's misjudged the man.

"Go to the tavern. Ask for Amos Pollard. Tell him I sent you. He'll take you to Burgess."

"I thank you for the help," he says, replacing his hat. He tips it, adds, "Mistress," then looks over my shoulder. Again, he offers that charming smile and tips his hat a second time. "Miss."

I turn to find Dolly leaning in the doorway, hand on her hip, scarf conspicuously missing from her hair. She watches Barnabas with an expression that I can only describe as proprietary.

Well, that's new.

"Good day to you, Mr. Lambard," I say, walking to the garden gate to see him off. He unties the reins and climbs onto the wagon seat.

Another tip of his hat. Another glance over my shoulder. A smile that twitches at the corner of his mouth. And then he is gone, unaware of the gruesome discovery awaiting him at the tavern.

Dolly comes down the walkway to my side. "Why didn't you tell him?"

"About Burgess?"

"Yes."

"Because he'd have gone back to Vassalboro."

"That's a bad thing?"

"If he goes home now, he'll never see the body. And if he never sees that body, he won't ask any questions about how Joshua Burgess came to be hanged, then thrown in the river." I look Dolly full in the face and see the vivid flash of understanding in her eyes. "I want as many people asking questions as possible."

"I think he will," Dolly says with a firm nod. She turns her gaze down the drive to where Barnabas and his wagon have already disappeared into the trees. "He seems clever."

It's a woman that does the choosing. I remember Ephraim's statement from a few days ago. *Anyone who thinks differently is a fool.*

Tuesday, December 15—Clear and cold. I have been at home. Made twenty dozen candles. An officer went by here looking for Captain Burgess with a warrant for his arrest.

DR. COLEMAN'S STORE

I am not the only woman who has come to Coleman's in hope of finding something today. There are two women at the counter waiting to be served and three more at the back when I step in, wicker basket tucked in the crook of one arm. I pause just inside the doorway to shrug out of my riding cloak and shake the snow from my hair.

The stack of pelts beside the counter hasn't grown any taller, but I don't like the bright, bushy red tail sticking out from the center. I am scowling when I turn and come face-to-face with Sarah White. The young woman takes one look at my expression, bursts into tears, and tries to push her way past.

"Wait," I say, dropping my basket with a thump. I grab Sarah's arm. "What's wrong?"

"I should have known better. Come early or late, Mother said, but not while the *Ladies* are out."

Ladies. A pejorative if I've ever heard one.

I lead her to the side. "Tell me what happened."

"Them," Sarah says, nodding to where three women huddle in the far corner, backs to the room. "Made it clear I wasn't welcome here."

"It isn't their store."

She sniffs and wipes two fat tears off each cheek with the cuff of her sleeve. "They sure act like it is."

If Sarah White had been born in another town, to different parents, she would have married early and well. Her face alone would have assured that. But her figure would have likely caused a duel. As it stands, she lives in the Hook, and her parents were ill equipped to protect such a lovely girl. A dalliance with a member of the Boston militia last year has left her with a bastard daughter and a ruined reputation.

"Did you find what you need?" I ask.

She shakes her head.

"Well, you'd best do it then. It isn't often you get out without the baby, and your mother won't like to see you come home empty-handed."

"But—"

"Let them answer to me," I say, nudging Sarah back into the shop.

I grab my basket and move to the back where Coleman keeps the sewing supplies. The three women sift through bolts of fabric spread along a table. They whisper amongst themselves, laughing, and I listen as one of them speaks in a tone bubbling with glee.

"Can you believe how *brazen* Sarah is? Flouncing around without that baby."

I look through the slats in the shelf to find Clarissa Stone running her hand along a bolt of soft blue cotton. Her face is angled toward the companion on her right, mouth twisted into a vicious smile.

"It's indecent," Rachel Blossom agrees.

Peggy Bridge chimes in then, unable to resist a bit of gossip, and a disapproving *tsk*. "There are hours for her to shop. Her mother should have taught her."

"*Oh,* her mother clearly didn't teach her *anything,*" Clarissa says, and I am opening my mouth to excoriate them all when she adds, "Did you hear about Sam Dawin?"

I step back to make sure they don't see me.

"What about him?"

"He and May were *married* in Henry Sewall's living room on Sunday. They went to housekeeping *immediately.* Her mother is furious."

Clarissa receives exactly the response she intended. *Hmms* and *tsks* and heads that shake in judgment.

"Doesn't it seem *odd*?" she asks. "They only posted their notice of intent six weeks ago."

Peggy, not one to be left out, adds, "I heard they made quite a public show of affection. My husband saw Sam kiss May right on the *street*!"

This last word is said with such an air of scandal that she may as well have implied they ran naked through town after church.

Clarissa nods, pronouncing her verdict with certainty. "May is *pregnant.*" The others gasp, but it's only for show, and she looks gratified when she adds, "Why else would they marry so quickly?"

It is an appalling display of hypocrisy, and I will not tolerate it a moment longer. I step out from behind the shelf, startling them. They spin around, horrified to find that their ugly conversation has been overheard. And by me no less. Varying expressions of shame, anger, and suspicion dart across their faces.

Both Clarissa and Peggy are heavily pregnant. Clarissa to such a degree that it looks as though she might already be past due. I let my gaze linger over their swollen bellies, let them grow uncomfortable beneath my gaze.

"Perhaps they married quickly because they are in love? Or because Sam nearly died a couple of weeks ago and that certainly makes a man think there is no time to waste." I move closer. Lower my voice. "There is nothing wrong with a man wanting to share a bed with his wife right from the start. What *is* wrong, however, is gossiping about your neighbors in such a cruel way. And not just Sam Dawin—a good man by anyone's standards—but Sarah White? That is *rich*. Even for the likes of you three.

"As I recall," I add, twisting the knife, "you delivered your first child four months after your wedding, Peggy. It was six months for you, Rachel." I look to Clarissa Stone and shake my head. "But you're the one who should be most ashamed of your pious outrage. It took a year and a bitter paternity suit before Paul would make an honest woman out of you."

I don't have to remind them how I know this, how I attended each of them in childbirth and that—in Clarissa's case—I received testimony as to the paternity of her child, which I later gave in court when she sued for maintenance.

"Not one of you has the right to speak," I say. "And if you had a lick of integrity, you would go apologize to Sarah this instant."

Only Rachel Blossom has the decency to blush. The others shift and glare before turning their noses to the ceiling and brushing past me.

"I am sorry," Rachel whispers as she turns her face to the floor and follows after them, but, like her friends, she does not say a word to Sarah on her way out.

I watch them go, imagining how they must be cursing me under their breath as they hustle back to their homes. They have left the bolts of fabric in disarray, so I fold and straighten them into neat rows on the table. A bolt of pale green silk catches my attention, and I pluck it from the pile. Run my thumb along the nubby weave. Check the price tag. Put it back. Pick it up again. Back and forth, five times, until I make up my mind and tuck it under one arm. I *do* need a new dress, after all.

I look up to find Sarah White standing in front of me.

"Thank you," she says. "You didn't have to defend me. I made my choices. But I'm glad you did nonetheless."

"It was the truth. And they needed to hear it." Sarah looks so sad as she's turning away that I reach for her hand. I want to ease her embarrassment, to reassure her that not everyone in the Hook considers her an outcast. "Their opinion of you doesn't matter, Sarah."

"It isn't just them, Martha. It's everyone. It's hard to stare down an entire town," she says, then goes to pay for the items in her basket.

I watch as Sarah leaves, her chin tucked against the collar of her dress to avoid the cold blast of wind. It pains me to think of her so alone and ostracized in this community. It will be harder for her to find a husband now that she's already borne a child, but she is not without hope, and I resolve to help find her a man who will love her as she is.

I turn back to the sewing supplies and ask, "Where are the needles?"

"Behind you, and to the left. Second shelf from the bottom. Green jar," Coleman calls out from the front of the store.

"You heard that?"

"I'm mostly blind, Mistress Ballard, but me ears work fine."

Sure enough, the needles are right where he said, and I take a packet from the jar, then sort through another beside it for buttons, before bringing everything to the front.

I set the basket at my feet and lean against the counter.

"I'm afraid to ask just how well your ears were working a few moments ago."

"Ye weren't taking great pains to keep yer voice down. And they deserved it regardless."

"Perhaps, but it wasn't very kind of me."

"And what they were accusing Sam Dawin of? That was kind?" he asks.

"Hardly. Although it is human nature, I suppose."

"Hypocrisy?"

"Well, yes. They feel better about themselves whenever anyone else is caught doing the same."

"But neither Sam nor May have been caught in anything."

"Which is why I didn't hold my tongue."

"And I like ye all the better for it," he says. Coleman turns back to his chessboard. "Now how can I help ye this morning?"

I slide the packet of needles across the counter, along with a small pile of buttons, and the silk.

"Will that be all?"

There are a dozen things that I would like to have: a new cast iron kettle for the kitchen, a set of blue glass bottles for my work room. But, as I do each time I step through these doors, I remind myself of what I *need*.

"Nothing. Unless you've heard where they took James Wall?"

"I hear he's been confined to the jail yard at Fort Western until his debt has been paid."

"So he posted bond then?"

Coleman nods. "Yesterday."

Being confined to the "jail yard" and being in jail are two entirely different things. The latter is as it sounds. Arrest and confinement for a set period of time. The former, however, is a loose arrangement in which those waiting trial, or those who have been arrested for unpaid debts, are able to post bail, and then go about their work during the day—within a set area—but must return to the jail house by dark. Sunrise to sunset. The bounds of their freedom include a distance of one mile on either side of the river, from Mill Brook to the bend in Water Street. In the rare instance when a home or business falls outside of that boundary, it is included as well.

Coleman studies me for a moment and I get the feeling he's

deciding whether or not to tell me something else. There's a bit of food stuck between his teeth, and he picks at it with his tongue for a moment, then says. "That new doctor of yours has created quite a stir."

"He's not *mine*," I protest.

"Most folks seem to be glad he's here. Having another *real* doctor is a boon to this town, they say. And he's got money." At this he offers a crooked grin. "So I don't hate him."

"Money?"

"Oh, aye. His young wife arrived on Friday. Bought up half the store so she can set up house." He gives me a knowing look. "She is *very* pregnant. Only a few months left, I'd say."

"They're renting rooms?"

"No." He shakes his head. "A house. Across the river. They've leased the old McMaster place right near the Chandlery."

"Well that explains a lot," I mutter.

"Be careful with him, Martha. He's made it plain that he doesn't care for you. Thinks you're a meddler."

"The feeling is mutual."

"Perhaps. But he's recruiting to his side. And that will hurt you in the end. What with the Burgess fiasco. And Grace Sewell's delivery."

"You know about that?"

"He's made sure that *everyone* knows. Says that *you* insisted he give that girl a near-lethal dose of laudanum. Adamantly opposed, he was. But he deferred given that you know the girl. Wanted to make nice with the local midwife after the dustup in court. Him being a genial fellow and all."

"That foul little bastard! I did no such—"

Coleman sets his hand on mine. "I know. But that's what you're dealing with, and you ought to be aware."

I groan and rest my elbows on the counter. Drop my head to my hands. "Damn that Burgess. If he wasn't already dead I'd kill him myself for all the trouble he's caused."

"As I hear it, he's still causing trouble."

When I look up, he's trying to wrestle a grin into submission. "Barnabas Lambard?"

"Got quite a fright, 'e did, when Amos pulled back that tarp. Demanded to know what happened. So Amos told him everything.

And then that officer marched right to Henry Sewell's office and looked at the court records. From what I hear, he seems to agree with your assessment."

"I am beginning to like that boy."

"Well, 'e don't like you over much right now."

"He doesn't have to like me as long as he keeps asking the right questions."

"You might regret saying that one day." Coleman laughs. "That boy don't seem the sort to stop."

I place everything into my basket and hoist it over my arm.

"Thank you. For the goods and gossip."

"Always," he says, and once more reaches out his old, weathered hand and grabs mine. "Be careful, Martha. Sentiment has turned against Rebecca Foster. It's turning against you as well."

Thursday, December 17.—Birth. Mr. Stone's daughter. Clarissa Stone was delivered of a dead daughter at the twelfth hour yesterday. The operation performed by Dr. Benjamin Page. The infant's limbs were much dislocated, as I am informed. The man knows not how to deliver a breech presentation.

Hannah brought the news this afternoon. One day after scolding Clarissa Stone at Coleman's Store, she went into labor. And instead of calling for me, as she should have, she called for Dr. Page. This is my fault. I'm certain of it. I know I was hard on her for shunning Sarah and gossiping about Sam. But this? It is too high a price to pay. For her. And for me.

I set my pen down.

Close my eyes.

Weep.

BALLARD'S MILL

Ephraim is dead.

That is the nagging fear that has plagued me over the last twelve days, and I have to drive it from my mind so it does not take root and fester. I feel his absence as though it were a missing limb, some vital part of me gone, and often find myself looking to the lane, watching for his return.

I must leave for Vassalboro on Tuesday, with or without him. I would prefer *with,* of course, but am growing less certain by the hour that he will make it home in time.

If he makes it home at all.

"No," I say aloud, taking that thought captive as well.

In his absence, I keep myself busy. Cooking. Cleaning. Spinning flax and weaving linen. I tend to the neighbors and my patients when they call, making tinctures and syrups in my workroom. I manage our small farm and assign work for my children. Cyrus runs the mill. Hannah and Dolly milk the cows. Jonathan tends the livestock. Young Ephraim oversees the chickens and tends to the horses. He has a soft voice and gentle hands, and I have never seen a horse startle or rear in his presence. Still, he's a bit young for the job, and I check on Brutus and Bucket once a day just to make sure all is well.

I slide between the heavy barn doors, a bucket of slops in each hand. It is time to feed the pigs, but Jonathan is nowhere to be found, which means he's slipped off again without telling anyone.

The barn was built as a large square with a peaked roof and four separate quadrants on the inside, one each for the horses, cattle, goats, and pigs, with a cross-shaped walkway between the pens. It smells of old straw and fresh manure, of alfalfa, hay, and barley stacked in the upper loft. It smells of warm animals and wet sawdust. The horses whicker as I make my way between the stalls. Both dairy cows are pregnant, and they shift and low at the sound of my voice, while the bull stomps and snorts in his pen. He is restless, eager for another chance at the cows, but he's done his job for the year and will have to wait until breeding season in June. The calves—one male and one female—are bored and they nap, oblivious, as the goats bustle in their pen, bleating out their request for dinner.

"Hush," I say. "It's not your turn. Jonathan will see to you later."

I lift one bucket and then the other over the pig pen rail and dump the contents into the trough, wincing at the wet, vomitous sound. I don't stay to watch the fat pink animals root and snort their way through dinner. I have never been fond of messy eaters.

I am almost at the barn door when I hear the thing I've spent weeks listening for: the heavy clop of horse hooves on frozen ground.

"Ephraim," I whisper and run out the door, an empty bucket swinging from each hand. They bounce against my calves as I hurry down the path, careful not to slip on the hard packed snow.

My smile evaporates the moment I round the bend and reach the front yard. Joseph North has dismounted his bay mare and is tying his reins to the gate post. His mongrel dog sits at his feet, looking at me as though I were a meal. He bares his teeth but doesn't growl.

I drop the wooden buckets with a clatter and set my hands on my hips. "What do you want?"

"I've come to see the results of Ephraim's survey. I stopped by the mill, but he wasn't in."

He may as well have said that he's stopped by for tea. Or to bring payment on a late bill. But his eyes are pinched at the corners, calculating, and I know that he came to see if Ephraim has returned.

"That's because he isn't at the mill."

"Where is he, then?"

"Out."

"*Where?*"

"I have never met a man who enjoys giving his wife an account of his every movement, Colonel. Ephraim goes where he pleases and returns when he will. As to the where and when, you'll have to ask him yourself because I certainly don't know."

North takes in my disheveled appearance: the tatty work clothes, dirty hands, and the scarf tied around my hair.

"I see that I have caught you in the middle of your *work*," he says. Perhaps it is my imagination, my dislike for the man, but I feel he emphasizes the word in a way that suggests only an unrefined woman would deign to perform physical labor. "Do tell Ephraim that I'm looking for him."

I hope he might leave then, but his departure is interrupted by Cyrus. My son rounds the bend in the path, coming from the barn, with a fishing rod over one shoulder and a string of blueback trout in his hand. As always, he is grinning, nearly bursting with good cheer. Yet, if I had a knife in my hand at this very moment, I would joyfully drive it through North's throat for the look of disgust that flashes across his face as he watches my son approach.

Cyrus Ballard is thirty-three years old, and he will never marry or have children of his own. He will never work away from the mill or go to sea—though it is his greatest desire. He will never explore the vast wilds of this untamed continent. Cyrus is thirty-three years old, and he is mute. He was robbed of speech at the age of twelve, and the loss has marked his life in irreparable ways.

There is no flaw in his intellect, or physical ability. He is tall and strong and handsome. He can read and write, and can communicate with his hands when necessary. It is a form of speech we have adopted, motions instead of words. But outside of our family, he is often pitied. Thought dimwitted. An illiterate population cares little for a man with beautiful handwriting, and—without speech, he cannot make them understand.

"Hello, Cyrus," North says. He glances back and forth between us, then grins. "Has your father returned from his surveying trip?"

Cyrus crosses his arms over his chest and glowers. He doesn't like North any more than the rest of us. After a moment he moves to stand beside me, protective.

"Why don't you take the fish inside," I tell him. "They'll want cleaning."

He nods toward the string, where a cut runs down the belly of each fish, to prove he's done it already.

"There is some talk about you in the village," North says.

Cyrus's hazel eyes pinch in suspicion. He is unable to take the bait, to ask what this talk might be.

"Apparently you got into a fight with Joshua Burgess the night he died. That is fascinating timing, don't you think?"

"What are you implying?" I ask.

"Only that your son thrashes a man in front of fifty people and several hours later that man turns up dead. I find it curious. Perhaps that officer from the court will, too. I hear he's been sniffing around."

"Should that happen, you will, no doubt, refer him to your own judgment of accidental drowning."

"A judgment made without benefit of all the facts." Joseph North smiles. "I cannot help but wonder if you knew of the fight when you testified before me, Mistress Ballard."

I owe this man nothing. Not answers. Not explanations. Not respect. And I give him none of it as I stand there, waiting for him to leave.

But he isn't done. "I want to know what Rebecca Foster told you. If I am to defend myself, I must understand the charges."

"The charges seem simple enough to me."

A small muscle twitches along his jaw. "The details are vital to my defense."

"Your defense is not my concern, Colonel. I am going to Vassalboro to testify on Rebecca's behalf, not yours."

"I am judge of this county. By law you cannot keep that information from me."

"It is my duty before the *law* to give my testimony to the *court*. As you well know. You will hear it, along with everyone else, next week, before the judge in Vassalboro."

"Perhaps."

He might as well have said, *If. If* your husband is present. *If* your husband is still alive. *If.* But perception means a great deal to Joseph

North, and he cannot break character in his role as the wrongfully accused. *Perhaps.* A more civilized, urbane, less threatening word. Still, there are oceans of meaning in those two syllables.

"No need to be concerned, Colonel. I am confident the hearing will proceed as planned."

He strides back to his mare. Gathers the reins. I watch him swing onto his horse, then turn her in a small circle. "You might consider all the ways your confidence is misplaced," he says.

As if on cue, Cicero growls.

"If I were you, I'd feed that thing before he bites someone."

"No point feeding a dog when it can take its own dinner by the throat," he says, then drives his boots into the mare's side. Joseph North canters down the drive, mongrel dog at his heels.

*

Friday, December 18——Cloudy and some snow. Colonel North was here. He examined me regarding what conversation Mrs. Foster had with me concerning his conduct toward her last August. I have been at home.

*

Saturday, December 19——Clear part of the day. Today is 35 years since my marriage. Mr. Ballard has not returned from his surveying. I have been at home.

SUNDAY, DECEMBER 20

Killing chickens is a bloody, awful mess. The task usually falls to Ephraim or Jonathan, but both are gone. So today Cyrus and I have undertaken the job of butchering and we usher three ornery cocks to the yard.

These are the last of our extra roosters from the spring. Mean things that torment us with beak and spur every time we go to collect the eggs. They are small and spindly, and I'm tired of them. It's no great sadness to see them put in the oven to roast.

"I hate the axe," I tell Cyrus. "We should use Revenge."

He gives me a questioning glance.

"Your father's blade. Down at the mill. That awful, hooked thing. Revenge. That's what we call it. Fetch it if you would."

It takes him only a few moments to go there and back. But the blade is in his hand when he returns. We silently debate which of us will do the job. He points at me. Holds his fist as though he's grasping something, and I agree because there is no good way out of this work. I'll face spurs or blade one way or the other. Better to be in control of the thing that cuts.

Cyrus grabs the first bird. He holds it upside down for several moments, letting the blood rush to its head. When its eyes close and its wings stop flapping, I know the cock has fallen asleep. Cyrus holds its head in his other hand and secures his grip on the feet. I *hate* killing things. But I hate these roosters more. And this is the most humane way to dispatch them. So I cut the fowl's throat with a quick, C-shaped motion and it's done. Cyrus hangs the bird by its feet at the fence so that the blood will drain. It goes quickly enough after that. One after the other. Once we're done, he goes to clean the blade and put it back at the mill.

I will have Hannah and Dolly dress and cook the birds once they're plucked. There's no clean way to finish the job, but it's better done outside than in the kitchen where the feathers and blood will get everywhere. I scald the birds in hot water to loosen the feathers, and then I set up my stool and carving stump in the yard and get to work. Soon, there is a pile of black and white feathers in the bucket at my feet. I have gutted the last rooster when once more the sound of horse hooves echoes down the lane. But there are two sets this time, and I do not even bother to get my hopes up.

When I lift my head, I see that North is back. And he's brought his wife with him. Halfway down the drive he holds out his hand and motions to Lidia.

"Wait here," he tells her, then kicks his mare into a trot.

Lidia North does as she is told and pulls her small gray horse to a stop. She's covered in a green riding cloak, and all I can see is her pale face peeking out beneath the hood. She looks unwell, and her hands are tucked into a muff to stay warm.

Dammit, I think, but go to meet North at the gate, hands sticky with blood.

"Colonel."

He's dressed in riding clothes and packed for a journey. Headed to Vassalboro early, no doubt. The cur is at his heels, eyeing me in that ravenous, predatory way.

"Ephraim?" he asks, not bothering to dismount or offer a greeting.

"On his way."

He snorts, unconvinced. "I would give you one piece of advice. When you stand before the judges," North says, voice just low enough that his wife cannot hear, his arm sweeping wide to indicate the house, the barn, the mill, "remember who I am. After all, your family depends a great deal upon my generosity."

"Are you threatening me?"

"I am *reminding* you," he says, "that, as an agent of the Kennebec Proprietors, it is *my* duty to confirm that you have met all the conditions required to obtain the deed on this property."

"Don't worry. I *remember* exactly who you are," I say. "Rebecca Foster told me."

I have been so consumed with the chickens that I didn't realize how miserably cold it is out here. The sun has passed its zenith and is sliding toward the horizon, dragging the last of the day's meager heat with it, and a breeze has come in from the east, whipping shards of ice into the air. It stings my cheeks and makes my eyes water.

Joseph North's voice is every bit as cold as the air when he replies, "Clearly there is more than one idiot living in this house."

I gasp at the insult. I could scream with fury. But I'm not the one who makes the sudden screeching sound. It comes so quick and so loud that I jump. Spin around. See nothing. But then there is a rush of air and the flapping of wings as an enormous bird dives toward us. It does a lazy circle around the house, swoops between me and North, then glides to the garden gate, gripping the wooden board so tightly that its talons gash open the weathered cedar.

Cicero yips and growls, but he too sees those lethal talons and keeps his distance. North pulls his horse backward in alarm, but I feel only a wild rush of relief.

"Percy," I whisper.

There are only three falconers in the territory of Maine, and only one in Hallowell. Ephraim is the only one who practices mounted falconry. So, when I say the bird's name, Joseph North loses all bluster and turns his horse away.

"I thought you wanted to speak with my husband?" I call after him. "As you can see, he is home now."

"It's getting late," North says, gravel in his throat. "I've no time left to dither."

On horseback, at a brisk walk, it will take four hours to reach Vassalboro. There is no chance he and Lidia can make it before nightfall. Which means they must find shelter along the way, or ride after dark.

"Pity," I say, loud enough that Lidia can hear. "I am certain my husband would love to speak with you about your visits this week."

"Cicero, come!" North snaps. He neither looks at me nor bids me farewell. The mongrel trots after him, skinny rump wagging with each step. North has met up with his wife, halfway to the tree line, when I see another horse and rider emerge. My heart soars for one brief second until I realize that it is not my husband.

Moses Pollard is riding his father's favorite stud and wearing his Sunday best. He has a bouquet of bright red sumac berries in one hand and a silly grin on his face.

"Oh good grief," I whisper.

Percy tightens his grip on the garden gate, and I hear the scratch of talon against wood. The jesses dangle from his feet, all twelve inches swaying back and forth as he watches the young man approach.

Moses has noticed the bird as well, and he pulls up ten feet from the gate. His horse prances uneasily.

"Did you pass Ephraim on the drive?" I ask.

"No."

Moses dismounts, holding the bouquet awkwardly in one hand as he gathers the reins in the other. He clears his throat, uncertain how to proceed now that he knows Hannah's father is not at home. It is obvious he has not prepared for this possibility.

Percy, however, is growing impatient and squawks loudly, bobbing his head.

"He's hungry," I explain.

For a moment Moses's eyes grow round with alarm, and I realize he's taken it to mean I might set the bird on him.

"Hannah!" I call, then tighten my lips to stop from laughing when Moses pales. Oh, how faint grows the heart of man when he plucks it—still beating—from his chest and lays it at the foot of a woman. When my daughter appears in the doorway I say, "You have company. And please send Cyrus out with one of those roosters. Percy is hungry."

Hannah's cheeks bloom with happy color when she sees Moses. She smiles at him, he returns the gesture, and I know that all is lost. There will be a wedding within the year.

"Is Father home?" she asks, looking at the bird.

"I don't know. But I have to get Percy to his mews."

Hannah ducks inside and returns a moment later with Cyrus, who is holding a plucked bird by the neck.

He smiles and dangles it above the ground. There is a teasing glint in those hazel eyes that suggests he might lob the bird right at Moses just to see what happens. Hannah is his little sister after all. He can't make it easy for her suitor.

Under different circumstances I might let him toy with Moses. "Toss it in front of the gate," I tell Cyrus. "Before he comes at you."

The chicken lands with a wet flop exactly where Cyrus intends. I back away when Percy launches off the gate and starts to savage his lunch right there on the path.

"Moses, why don't you go inside with Cyrus and Hannah and have some tea? I'll get Percy put away in the mill and will join you shortly."

"Of course, Mistress Ballard," he says, tying the reins and easing through the gate. He keeps a wide berth, careful not to watch the carnage, then follows the others into the house. He *would* come calling on an afternoon in which it is impossible to keep any sense of decorum. At least they will have a story to tell their children one day. Carefully, I ease to the side and wash the blood from my hands.

I am not ashamed to admit that I wait too long to collect Percy. I am hoping Ephraim will come down the drive at any moment and relieve me of the duty. But he does not come, and there is no sound of hooves anywhere in the woods. It grows quieter and colder by the moment.

"I am going to speak with your master about this," I say, pulling the shawl off my shoulders. It isn't enough protection, I know that, but it's better than nothing, and I wrap it around my left forearm. Percy could crush my arm with one ferocious squeeze of those talons. He could rip through flesh and bone. But surely Ephraim's training isn't for naught? This is what I tell myself as I hold my breath, close my eyes, turn my face away, and extend my left forearm at a right angle from my side. No sooner does it come to a halt than a wall of air and beating wings hits my face.

*

I ease the door to Percy's mews open with my foot. He did not, in fact, wound me. Most likely because I did exactly as I have seen Ephraim do a thousand times. Once Percy was stable on my arm, I looped the fingers of my right hand between his legs—just above his talons—then lifted him off my arm. After that it was only a matter of securing the jesses and walking, arm extended, down to the mill.

Still no sign of Ephraim. Every minute that passes makes the stone in the pit of my stomach grow heavier. All the terrible fears I have kept at bay for the last two weeks crash against one another, growing louder and louder. But I cannot entertain any of them now. I must prepare for my trip to Vassalboro on Tuesday. And I must play hostess to the young man who has come to court my daughter.

In hindsight, I tell myself, that is why I missed the obvious. There was too much happening at once. But I see it, finally, when I lean forward to put the bird in his mews.

Ephraim has tied a message around Percy's leg:

I'll meet you at the courthouse. Bring the book.

VASSALBORO

I unfold the note, then refold it as I sit on the bed in my rented attic room at the Silver Street Tavern in Vassalboro. I run my thumbnail along the crease, wearing it thin. Ephraim's handwriting is neat and concise, perfectly spaced letters drawn with a steady hand. I marvel at their beauty, at the exactness of each elegant line and curve. My husband is numbered among those who believe that a man's handwriting is a testament to his character.

The hearing starts in less than an hour, but Ephraim still isn't here. I made the trip alone yesterday, choosing not to travel with the Fosters, so I could have time and space to think, and arrived at sunset, expecting to find my husband waiting for me. He wasn't, so I skipped dinner and went to bed early, eager for a good night's sleep.

My stomach rumbles but the thought of eating makes me nauseous. I put up my hair, pull on my best dress, lace my boots, and tuck the journal into a leather satchel before leaving the room. I descend all three flights of stairs carefully, minding where I set my feet in the dim stairwell. Instead of eating breakfast, I grab a soft, wrinkled apple from a bowl on one of the tables as I pass through the main hall, then take it to the stables behind the tavern where Brutus is housed. It isn't much lighter in there than in the stairwell, and I am forced to dodge piles of manure on my way to his stall. A quick glance in all directions reveals that there is no sign of Sterling.

"Where are you?" I mutter under my breath.

Brutus whickers when I appear in front of him, and sticks his head over the stall door. I hold out the apple on my palm and he picks it off with his teeth.

"Don't bite anyone while I'm gone," I say, then rub his nose fondly.

I stand there, eyes closed, for a moment longer. The smell of hay and horse and manure grounds me. It is a fortifying scent that reminds me of home.

"Yes. I'm dawdling," I tell Brutus. "Sometimes a woman has to do a thing she fears."

He stares at me, brown eyes unblinking. Unsympathetic. Then he snorts, sending a puff of warm air into my face.

"Fine, then. Be an ass."

Unlike Hallowell, all court proceedings in Vassalboro take place at the Meeting House—a long rectangular one-story building that serves as church, courthouse, and community center. It sits directly across the street from the tavern, and once I step outside, I see that there is already a line of people waiting to get in. As in the Hook, court days always draw a crowd. Not wanting to lose an advantageous seat, I hustle across the muddy road and up the steps onto the boardwalk that connects all the shops and buildings on that side of the street. I slide in behind a group of whispering women and follow them into the Meeting House.

Half the benches are already filled, and I maneuver as close to the front as I can. Once I've chosen my spot, I tuck the satchel between my feet and wait. Because one of the defendants in the Foster case also happens to be a circuit court judge, this hearing has garnered a great deal of attention. That does not mean that it will be first on the docket, or that it will even be heard today. The Court of General Sessions has been known to run for up to three days. Though I suspect that won't be the case this session, given that Christmas is looming.

I can see Joseph North sitting to the left of a long table at the front of the room where an older man in silk robes and a powdered white wig studies the docket. Because it is the winter meeting, his robe is red. Black is reserved for summer.

North does not look pleased to be seated with the other defendants, and they do not speak to one another or anyone else. He sits ramrod straight, cleanly shaved, and wearing his best coat.

The room continues to fill, and there is still no sign of Ephraim. But at precisely nine o'clock, the judge bangs his gavel on the table and the room falls silent. I crane my neck to look for Rebecca Foster and find her in the back corner, sitting beside her husband. Her eyes are closed, and her face is turned toward the window, as though drawing strength from the meager light that filters through. She looks beautiful and broken.

Across the aisle and five rows forward is Lidia North. She is wan and deflated. Thin as a rail. Pale as a ghost. Cheekbones sharper, clavicles jutting out above the lace collar of her blue dress. I think her headaches must be worse of late. Yet she is not deterred from supporting her husband.

"The Court of General Sessions is now open," the clerk announces. "The honorable Obadiah Wood presiding."

Honorable is a term used loosely in that Wood—a physician—is, like North himself, an untrained justice of the peace, recognized by the state of Massachusetts and the District of Maine but not a lawyer by trade. He fills a specific gap in the legal system and has a rudimentary understanding of the law at best. Most of these judges rule by common sense, but some by partiality.

Because this is only a hearing, there are no lawyers present, there is no jury, and no verdict will be handed down. The court meets simply to ascertain the validity of the accusation and to set formal charges for a future trial, should one be required.

Obadiah Wood looks at the docket before him and says, "The court will hear evidence in the case of the Commonwealth versus Henry Jackson. Mr. Jackson, a barber, is accused of malicious injury while shaving Jacob Retton two months past."

Two men approach the long table and take turns arguing their case as the judge asks each of them a series of questions. The entire debate takes less than ten minutes, and Wood declares that Henry Jackson cut his client with a straight razor by accident, and no charges are filed, despite the fact that Jacob Retton will have a scar along his jaw for the rest of his life. Henry Jackson is ordered to pay a fine of twelve shillings in recompense.

And so it goes. He hears three cases of petty theft, two of slander, one divorce petition, one estate settlement, a breach of contract (said contract being a handshake), and five requests for the collection of debt. He orders a total of six fines, all of which are recorded by the clerk. It takes nearly two hours to clear these cases, and I am starting to feel stiff and numb from sitting so long. I regret not eating breakfast. I am wondering whether there will be an opportunity to slip out and find a privy to relieve myself.

"Next on the docket is the Commonwealth versus Joseph North and Joshua Burgess."

I tense as North stands. But then Barnabas Lambard slips from his spot at the edge of the room and approaches the table. He'd been so still that I hadn't seen him. He whispers something to Obadiah Wood then walks back to his seat. Barnabas does see me, however, and I cannot tell whether his expression is one of irritation or curiosity. I doubt he expected to find me here. If there is time afterward, I will apologize for not warning him about the body.

Obadiah Wood turns to the clerk and says, "Please strike Joshua Burgess from the court records. We have been notified that he is deceased. Also note that there may be a future inquiry as to cause of death."

"I beg your pardon, Your Honor." North takes a step forward and clears his throat. "I believe there has been a mistake. Benjamin Page, a physician in Hallowell, declared Joshua Burgess's death an accidental drowning."

I look to North, curious what he's up to. Not five days ago he threatened Cyrus, insinuated that he'd been the one to kill Burgess. And now he's pushing Dr. Page's assessment again? It doesn't make sense.

As though sensing my scrutiny, North's eyes flick to mine—tighten—then return to the judge.

Oh. It's a threat, I think. *To me. He knows I don't want Cyrus's name brought up in court regarding a murder investigation. He's reminding me that he has a card to play.*

"Mr. Lambard?" Wood asks.

Barnabas steps forward once more but removes his hat this time and lays it against his thigh. "Yes, Your Honor?"

"You went to apprehend Mr. Burgess?"

"I did. On the orders of this court."

"And what did you find?"

"That he is dead. I saw the body myself as it's being stored until the ground thaws enough for burial."

"And did it appear to you that the man had drowned?"

Barnabas shakes his head and two ringlets fall across his brow. "No, Your Honor, he—"

North clears his throat. "Again, Your Honor, if I may clarify?"

"If I want your clarification, I will ask for it. As you were saying, Mr. Lambard?"

I have been curious about Barnabas from the moment I saw him scuffling outside Pollard's Tavern with James Wall, and he continues to surprise me now.

"When I found the body of Mr. Burgess, I saw that he had count-less injuries. So I asked to see the court records regarding his death. I was obliged by one Henry Sewell of Hallowell." Here he glances at me and offers a nod so faint I barely catch it. "It is true that the official cause of death recorded is that of drowning."

The crowd murmurs quietly and Barnabas lets them.

"But," he says, after a moment, "the record also shows that there was a second, conflicting opinion as to cause of death—also recorded by a medical professional—that of murder. Specifically hanging. In my capacity, as an officer of the court, it is my opinion, given that Mr. Burgess is one of two men accused of a serious crime, this seems a matter worth looking into. In no small part because"—and here he does look apologetic—"during that same hearing, a man was accused of killing Mr. Burgess."

"What man?" Wood asks.

"Reverend Isaac Foster, sir."

Stupid boy, I think, and when Barnabas glances at me, he can safely judge my thoughts by my expression alone. His eyebrows pinch together in concern before he turns back to Wood.

"Mr. North," Wood asks, "was any proof of this offered to your court?"

He stands, and I can see that he is choosing his words carefully. "A young woman who used to work for the Fosters claims that she overheard Mrs. Foster say that her husband killed the man. But that point was also argued in my courtroom, so I had my clerk record the accusation but took no further action as it seemed to be a concern best left to another court." North offers a pinched smile. "Given the circumstances."

"Well, at least we can agree on that." Wood snorts, then whacks the table with his gavel. "The clerk will note that the question of Joshua Burgess's cause of death remains undecided and will be held over until the next session. As will any consideration of involvement by Reverend Foster or anyone else. We will move forward to the issue at hand. The case against Joseph North as it relates to the accusation of injury to Mistress Foster's person. All parties please come forward."

Rebecca moves to the front of the room, fingers knotted together at her waist, head held high. Isaac follows, a hand set protectively in the small of her back. She looks at Isaac, alarmed, when he pulls away from her side and approaches the table.

"I have a request to make before we begin," he says.

Wood looks at Rebecca, then at Isaac. "I presume you are Mr. Foster?"

"I am."

"Have no fear, Mr. Foster, the court will not concern itself today with the accusation made against you."

"That is not what I would like to address. Although, given that neither my wife nor I were in Judge North's court last month, and we did not have the chance to defend ourselves, I would like the record to show that I formally deny the accusation. I had no part in that man's death."

"Very well then, the clerk will record your statement."

Isaac Foster is just past thirty and is drifting from plain to homely, yet he still has the voice of an orator and it resonates through the room. "On the same day those scurrilous accusations were made against me, Joseph North filed fornication charges against my wife. I would like them dropped."

"That is highly unusual," Wood says. "Why were charges filed?"

Isaac opens his mouth to answer, but North, clearly nervous, interrupts. "Mistress Foster's young housekeeper brought that charge, not me. She claims that Mistress Foster is pregnant by a man not her husband."

"And would this be the same young woman, no longer in her employ, who also accused her husband of murder?" Wood asks.

"Ah." He clears his throat. "Yes. It would."

There is ice in Obadiah Wood's tone as he asks, "And you thought it appropriate to file these charges in a case in which you are the defendant?"

The courtroom is hushed, all eyes turned to the front of the room where this latest twist is unfolding.

North lifts his chin. "I thought to do my job."

"In this case you overstep. I order that all fornication charges against Rebecca Foster be dropped immediately." He turns to the clerk. "Cite a conflict of interest as the explanation."

In the Court of General Sessions, the lone judge has great leeway in these matters. The Court of Common Pleas, however, requires a majority ruling, so I am grateful that it is one man, and not three, hearing this case today.

"May I continue? Or are there other breeches of conduct you would like to inform us of?" Obadiah Wood folds his hands on the table and looks squarely at North.

"By all means, let's get this over with," North tells him.

I brave a glance at Lidia who, eyes locked on her husband, seems to be flushed now. But she has the good sense to keep whatever she is feeling to herself, and refrains from making any outburst.

Wood once again scans the docket, then looks up at the gathered crowd. "The charge states that on the night of August tenth, Joseph North and Joshua Burgess broke into the home of Isaac Foster and injured the wife of said Mr. Foster." He looks to Rebecca. "Is that the charge you are bringing before this court?"

Rebecca stands before the table, and when she speaks her voice does not waver. "No. It is not."

I am not alone in drawing in a hard gasp. *Oh God, what is she doing?* I think.

Obadiah Wood looks at his docket and then back up at Rebecca. "My notes indicate a physical injury. If not that, what is your charge?"

"Physical injures did occur," she says, and there, on the last syllable, I can hear the first break in her voice. "But they were because of a rape. That is my charge, Your Honor. On the night of August tenth, those men broke into my house and"—she clears her throat, swallows hard—"they *raped* me."

Wood tightens his brow. "That is a very serious charge. Do you have any evidence?"

"They left evidence enough right here." Rebecca sets a trembling hand to her belly and pulls the fabric tight so that the small, round protrusion is evident.

"Are you also charging that you are with child as a result of this assault?"

"I am."

After a moment, Wood turns to North. "What have you to say to these charges?"

All of the bluster is gone from his voice. "I deny everything this woman has said. I was not at her home that evening, and I did not do the things she accuses me of."

Wood. "Then where were you?"

"I had dinner at my home with one Major Henry Warren of the Boston militia. His regiment is in Fort Halifax now, but he will happily attest to this fact if given the chance. After dinner he left, and my wife and I went to bed."

"Mistress North?" Wood asks.

She stands, and when she speaks her voice is small. "It is as he says. My husband was at home that evening."

North does not look at Rebecca, but he does soften his voice. "I do not question whether someone accosted Mistress Foster, but none of what she claims happened by *my* hand. I have been falsely accused."

"A grievous assault may have been perpetrated against your person, Mistress Foster"—Wood points a finger in warning at North, who is about to interrupt again—"but I do find myself in the difficult position of being unable to verify your claims. Without a witness to this assault, we cannot *prove* that it happened. And to charge a man with a capital crime without any evidence is a difficult thing."

Isaac Foster begins to tremble. It starts in his voice and moves to his outstretched arm, pointing at North. It is the least composed that I have ever seen him. He is angry. Sweating. His spectacles slide down his nose, and he shoves them back in place. "He. Witnessed. This. *He* did it!"

Wood looks pained as he reminds Isaac that North is a defendant, not a witness, and that he has denied the accusations regardless.

"Please." Rebecca steps closer to the judge. "I do have a witness. She is in this courtroom. She can testify that I speak the truth."

I feel my stomach twist with a sudden rush of adrenaline, and my heart takes flight within my chest, beating hard against my ribs.

"I protest this witness!" North says, stepping forward again. "She does not—"

Obadiah Wood's voice is loud, clipped on the syllables. He is losing patience. "It is not your turn to speak, Mr. North. You will have your chance. Step back."

North does as he's told, but I can see the growing bubble of frustration in his chest, the way it puffs in and out with each breath. He is accustomed to having total control of a courtroom.

"Who is this witness?" Wood asks.

"Me," I say, standing. The entire room swings their heads in my direction. "I can verify everything that Rebecca Foster has just told the court."

"Please step forward, Mistress . . . ?"

"Ballard."

Judge Wood waves his arm, indicating that I should approach the table.

"I object," Joseph North says, abandoning all sense of propriety. "The law of coverture prevents any woman—even one as esteemed as Mistress Ballard—from testifying in court without the presence of her father or husband."

"And what concern is this of yours, Colonel?"

"*Great* concern! Every word of it. The law remains firm on the parameters of what testimony she can give."

I weave my way through the crowd, satchel in hand, ignoring North, and speak directly to Wood. "I am a midwife, and the laws of Massachusetts and the District of Maine allow me to give testimony in court apart from any covering, whether it be husband or father. I do so in Joseph North's courtroom several times a year, and he has never once objected."

North shakes his head, lifts a hand, finger pointed for emphasis, and comes to stand before the table himself. "The laws of Massachusetts state that a midwife may give testimony in matters of paternity. It gives her no such allowance in legal hearings such as this."

"One could argue that this *is* a matter of paternity," I say.

"That is an accusation that can *never* be proved!"

For the first time today, Obadiah Wood appears uncertain. He looks at North. Then back to me. But he does not speak or offer comment on North's objection. The longer the silence continues, the straighter North stands.

I tighten my grip on the satchel. "Please, Your Honor, my father died many years ago and my husband—"

"Is here!" Ephraim shouts from the back of the courtroom, right by the door. "I am here!"

It takes Ephraim a moment to reach the front. The Meeting House is so full—there is standing room only at this point—that he must squeeze between dozens of spectators to reach my side. When he does, he smells of horse, sweat, and wind, and I know that he has ridden hard to be here in time. He gives my hand one comforting squeeze.

"I'm so sorry," he whispers in my ear. "I will explain later."

Ephraim turns to the judge and smiles. He knows Obadiah Wood, but he announces himself for the benefit of those watching. "I am Ephraim Ballard, Martha's husband, and I apologize for the delay." He levels an unforgiving glare at North. "I was unavoidably detained."

"Thank you for coming, Mr. Ballard," Wood says, then motions to me. "Please, tell the court what you know of the events that happened on August tenth."

"I called on Mistress Foster on the nineteenth of August and found her badly injured. I am a midwife. I have been attending women for over thirty years. I know the damage done by rape, and Rebecca's injuries were some of the worst I have ever seen."

"She is lying," North growls.

"Is that your only defense?" Wood snaps at him. "That any woman who contradicts you is a liar? Continue, Mistress Ballard."

"The injuries from her assault were witnessed with my own eyes. She had multiple bruises and cuts. A split lip. I dressed her wounds and helped her bathe and listened to the details of what happened to her. She hasn't changed a word from that day to this."

Obadiah Wood scratches at his jaw. "How can the court be certain that you and Mistress Foster have not conspired to wrongly accuse Colonel North?"

I swallow a sigh. I will never understand why men think that women work so hard to destroy them. In my experience it is usually the opposite.

"I can prove it," I tell him. "If you will allow me?"

"By all means."

I pull the diary from my satchel, take it to the table, then set it before the judge and turn back to the entry on August nineteenth. I scoot the book closer for him to read.

"There," I say. "I recorded Rebecca's accusation in my daybook on the night she told me. You will note that I've made many months' worth of entries since and that I could not have gone backward to fill it in. What Rebecca claims is true. In every word and detail."

Obadiah Wood dismisses us so he can read the diary entries and deliberate. Based on how many people trickle out of the Meeting House, it feels as though the entire town of Vassalboro is present.

As Ephraim and I make our way to the door, I see Lidia North out of the corner of my eye. She is waving, trying to get my attention as she angles through the crowd.

Once she gets within a few feet of us, Lidia calls out, "Martha! Can we speak? I am out of tonic."

But by then we have reached the crush of people surging out the door, and Lidia is shifted away, her voice lost in the buzzing crowd. I don't look to Ephraim to see if he noticed her. For right now, it is easier to pretend I didn't hear. Once outside, I walk with Ephraim as he leads Sterling to the stables to be fed and groomed.

"You got my message?" he asks, searching for an empty stall.

"I nearly lost an arm in the process, but yes."

"Percy wouldn't hurt you."

"I'm glad you're certain of that. I had to feed him a plucked chicken just to make sure."

Once Ephraim has handed the reins to the gap-toothed stable boy and given him a shilling to tend the horse, I throw my arms around him.

"I was so worried you wouldn't make it."

"I almost didn't." He pulls me closer. Breathes in the scent of my skin. "The bog is wretched this time of year. We were nearly swallowed twice. If North assigns that lease, I'll call him a murderer. No one could survive there."

"Well, he certainly wanted to murder you just now," I say.

"Let him try."

"I would rather that he not, if you don't mind. I've lived without you long enough these last weeks."

Ephraim leads me back to the tavern, and we eat an uneasy lunch at a small corner table. The stew is flavorless and the bread dry. I long for our town and our tavern and the cooking of Abigail Pollard. We pick at our food until a man comes to stand beside me and clears his throat. I look up into an apologetic face.

"Mistress Ballard," he says, then nods to Ephraim. "Mr. Ballard."

"This is Barnabas Lambard," I explain to my husband. "Officer of the court. Much has happened while you were away."

Ephraim watches the boy but says nothing

Barnabas takes off his hat. "I did not know the Fosters were your friends," he tells me.

"You couldn't have."

"I certainly didn't intend to make their situation worse. I can see that I have, though. And that troubles me. I only reported what I found in Hallowell." He clears his throat, and the accusation is gentle. "What *you* sent me to find."

I do not look at my husband, though I can feel his curious gaze on my profile. "The fault is mine. I should have told you that Burgess was dead, but I was afraid you would leave without investigating. I stand by my assessment that he was murdered. But it was not by Isaac Foster."

"You know this for certain?"

I hesitate, but only for a moment. "Though I am old enough to be certain of little, I do know that Isaac is a bookish man, not a brutish one. And it was he who insisted that this case go through the courts. It makes no sense that he would take justice into his own hands before the process even got started."

"Well, I hope you are right." He returns the hat to his head. "I'd best be getting back."

Ephraim watches him go, and I can see all the questions building in his eyes. Once Barnabas has pushed through the door, he turns to me. "What was all that about?"

"I think young Mr. Lambard is trying to remain on my good side."

"And why exactly would he be concerned with that?"

"Probably because he's smitten with your daughter."

"I doubt Moses will be pleased to hear that."

"I doubt Moses will care. Barnabas isn't after Hannah."

Ephraim does the math. Frowns. "No. She's too young."

"Explain that to Dolly."

"I'd rather you explain what's happened while I've been gone. And quickly."

I open my mouth to do just that when we hear the sound of shouting in the streets. The judge is ready.

The spectators make room for Ephraim and me as we enter the Meeting House again. We find better seats toward the front this time. Wood waits until those involved are present.

"The case brought before the court today is difficult," Obadiah Wood begins. "Mistress Foster gave compelling testimony, and Mistress Ballard gave proof that she was accosted in August as she says."

Oh God, no, I think.

I can feel it coming, the "but" that will serve as justification for denying justice. I can feel it coming the way I sense a storm or an argument. Like lightning in the air. It rises in my blood, and I squeeze Ephraim's hand so hard that he hisses in protest.

"The difficulty is," Wood continues, "that the Court of General Sessions was established to settle petty matters, and there is nothing petty about the charges we heard today. I am thus referring this case to the Court of Common Pleas for additional advice." The room erupts but Wood bangs his gavel seven times. "The court will reconvene in Hallowell with a full bench on January twenty-ninth."

*

"What a coward! What a guttersnipe! What a foul, stinking codpiece!" I slam the door to my room at the tavern after Ephraim steps inside. I throw my satchel to the floor. Pace. "He just absolved himself of responsibility."

Ephraim lowers himself to the bed with a tired groan and pulls off his boots. "He sits on the Court of Common Pleas for Kennebec County. That means he'll be hearing the case again."

"He could have brought charges *today*! He could have sent it straight to the Supreme Judicial Court!"

Ephraim's voice is warm and soft. "The man was being shrewd, Martha. He knows that any serious charges brought by a lower court would likely be tossed out unless they go through the Court of Common Pleas first. But a majority verdict from the Sessions will be heard. What seems like cowardice might in fact be the only hope Rebecca has."

I can feel the anger rolling toward me like a fog, and I begin to tremble. My eyes burn.

Ephraim Ballard has long made a study of me. He can feel my moods shift like the wind. He pulls me down to sit beside him so that I can lay my head on his shoulder.

"It isn't fair!"

"No. It isn't."

And then I cry. Mostly for Rebecca and the tiny, unwanted beating heart deep within her womb. But also for myself. And our daughters. And for every other woman who lives, suffers, and dies by the mercurial whims of men. Three minutes later, when I have wrung myself dry, I lean over and pull the journal out of my satchel.

"What are you doing?"

"The only thing I can."

I take up my pen and, with a trembling hand, mix my ink. My rage makes my handwriting almost illegible.

Wednesday, December 23—A cloudy day. I went to Vassalboro as evidence in the Cause between the Commonwealth and Joseph North, Esquire. The charge was that North, on the night of August tenth, broke into the house of Isaac Foster and ravished his wife. My testimony was that Mrs. Foster on the nineteenth of August, complained to me that she had received great abuses from North and was gravely injured. The judge determined the Cause is to be laid before the Sessions next January.

*

When I bring dinner to the room several hours later, Ephraim laughs at me.

"What?"

He nods toward the jug of cider on the wood tray and the two mugs beside it. "Didn't they have any ale? You know I don't drink that stuff."

I look at the jug, and it takes a moment to remember what he's talking about. "That was a long time ago. And besides. My father was upset."

"He tried to kill me."

"Maim. Possibly paralyze. But I don't think he wanted you *dead*. Or at least not permanently."

Ephraim rolls his eyes. "I don't think a temporary death is what he had in mind when he threw the jug at my *head*."

The laugh surprises me. It is good medicine after weeks of angst, after such a disappointing day. "Perhaps he did want to kill you. Just a little. But I think we can both agree you deserved it."

Thirty-Five Years Ago

OXFORD, MASSACHUSETTS

DECEMBER 19, 1754

Ephraim ducked. The jug missed him by a foot and shattered against the doorframe, filling the room with an overpowering scent of fermented apples.

"It is his right, Mr. Moore," Joseph North said, stepping between my father and my husband. That word. *Husband.* So new I couldn't yet speak it aloud, the mere thought was startling enough. "They are married now," he continued, lifting the certificate in one hand as though to offer proof. As town clerk, North had the legal right to marry us. A fact Ephraim had known and exploited.

"I care nothing of his rights. It's my daughter's reputation that concerns me."

"There's nothing left of it, Father. Billy Crane saw to that."

They were startled to hear me speak, and every head in the room turned. I had remained silent that evening, speaking only when my turn came to say the vows.

I have forsaken all others and will cleave only unto thee.

The words were still warm on my lips, and I pressed them together, hoping to keep the sensation intact. For those few moments I was not afraid. Was not ashamed.

My mother had been crying for over an hour. Father alternately in a rage and puffing with relief that his disgraced daughter had been redeemed. North came as promised, arriving shortly after we did, documents in order. Ephraim held my hand as we walked through the door and refused to let me leave his side even for a moment.

"Billy Crane is *dead*," North said.

Father nodded. Crossed his arms over his chest. "And I do thank you for that."

"And Martha comes with me," Ephraim said firmly, drawing the conversation back to the topic at hand. "We go to housekeeping tonight."

Most couples—my parents included—did not begin living together for many months after the wedding, choosing instead to consummate but live separately until a house could be put in proper order. Tradition held that this was a way to gather all the necessary goods needed to keep a home. It also gave the groom time to complete living arrangements for the new couple. But in fact, the practice was often used by parents to ensure that their daughter had not made a grievous mistake in her choice of husband. Though not common, it was not unheard of for an annulment to be requested in the weeks after a wedding.

"She has nothing!" my mother wailed.

"She has me. And I have plenty to get us started," Ephraim said. "Hasn't enough been taken from her? Do you mean to withhold tradition as well?"

He referred to the communal gathering and gifting of household goods, dishes and linens and quilts, that usually took place after a wedding and before newly married couples made a home together. He wanted to make sure that the women of our community would still make me a wedding quilt. He wanted to make sure the town would not shame me.

"If this is her choice, she can do without," my father said, and even though I could tell he regretted the words as soon as he spoke them, he lifted his chin in defiance.

"I am saddened to hear you say that, Mr. Moore. I had thought better of you." Ephraim released my hand and moved his arm to my waist. He pulled me tight against his side. "You can send her trunk in the morning. But she comes with me tonight."

*

The cabin was bigger than I expected. Two rooms, the larger with a stacked-stone fireplace. In one corner there was a kitchen with a cookstove, a table, and a window above a long stretch of rough-hewn wooden counter. A bedroom. I glanced at the door. Looked away. Glanced back. My hands began to shake.

Ephraim released me and stepped away. "Do you like it?"

I loved the home, and I loved the man, and I didn't have the proper words to tell him either of those things. I hadn't answered his question, though, so I turned to him, nodding. "I do."

He noted the pleasure in my eyes and ducked his head with a bashful smile. "Say that again. I like the sound of it."

Our vows. He had grinned his way through them, beaming as if we were the only two people in my parents' kitchen earlier that evening. As if the room weren't crackling with tension.

I didn't realize I was shivering until Ephraim bent to light a fire in the hearth. Once it was crackling merrily and the bitter chill had been chased from the room, he went into the bedroom to light another fire in the hearth there.

He returned. Clasped my hand in both of his. "Come. I have something for you."

I dared a glance at the bedroom door. My hope chest still sat at home, filled with lace and linen and needlework. Filled with the things that I had been making since I was a child. The things that women use to create a home. But that was not the gift that men expected from their wives on the day they wed.

Ephraim stooped a little so he could look me in the eye. "Not that. You don't have to be afraid of me, Martha. I won't hurt you." He tugged me to his chest and slid his hands into the hair at the base of my head, into the wild curls I could never tame. "I would never hurt you. Not ever."

I pulled back to look at his face. "What is it, then?"

"There." He pointed to the long table in the kitchen, and I saw the wooden box in its center for the first time.

It was made of pine, and there were no nails or dowels. He had pieced it together in tongue-and-groove fashion. Only Ephraim. I placed my palm on the lid.

I gestured toward the rest of the house, finished perfectly and sealed against the weather. "You had extra time on your hands, I suppose?"

He liked the teasing note in my voice. Responded to it physically. Ephraim eased closer to me and set one gentle hand on my shoulder. I felt the weight of it, heavy and strong.

"The house was finished months ago. Then the furniture a few weeks past. A man needs something to occupy him at night."

Indeed.

I cleared my throat.

"Open it," he said. "It's all for you."

He nudged me with his forearm, and I lifted the lid on his gift. Inside was a book bound in leather, filled with blank pages. Ink cakes. A feather quill. And a King James Bible. I pulled them from the box and set them on the table one by one.

"What is this?"

"The beginning of your education, Mrs. Ballard."

I laughed. "You know I can't read."

"That, love, is exactly the point."

"I don't understand."

His face was unreadable, and I was about to ask for an explanation when his mouth covered mine. His hands were gentle as feathers on my cheeks, thumbs stroking my jaw. His tongue brushed my lips, begged them to part, to soften. After a moment they did. He tasted of salt and bread and apple cider. His hands never wandered from my face, but I felt the restraint it took him to keep them there. I felt the passion and the frustration in his lips. I felt the longing in every inch of his body. Ephraim Ballard kissed me for long, endless moments. He was breathing hard when he finally pulled away.

"I will not take your body tonight, Martha. I will not do it until you ask me to. No," he said, shaking his head. "Not until you *beg* me to. I will take nothing from you that is not freely given. Do you understand?"

My answer was but a ghost of speech. "Yes."

"There is only one thing I will ask of you. As your husband." He brought his face so close that I was certain he would kiss me again. But Ephraim only rubbed his nose against mine, brushed it back and forth until I closed my eyes. "Let me kiss you. *Please.* Whenever I want. Just like that. Will you trust me with that one thing?"

I was incapable of words. But I nodded and tilted my chin upwards. He took the offer. His hands did not drift beneath my col-

larbone. But they explored the base of my skull and the thick curls of
my hair. He made himself acquainted with my earlobes. Cheekbone.
Jaw. The cowlick at my temple. And his tongue went to work as well,
tangling with mine and tracing the shape of my lips.

"You liked that," he said when he pulled away.

It wasn't a question. He knew I did. Ephraim could read my face
the way he read his ledgers and his books. I was open before him.
"Yes."

"Good then." He nodded toward the bench beside the table. "Sit."

He straightened the Bible on the table. Always the carpenter, he
squared it with his own body, then opened it. It was new. I could tell
that much. The leather binding was clean and hard, with no cracks or
scuffs. The first page was blank, and I, of course, could not read the
second.

This was no concern to Ephraim. He read it to me. "Family register." He pointed first to one line and then those below it. "Husband
and wife. Births. Deaths. Our life will be recorded here, on this page."

He pressed the book flat with his hand, and a smile spread broad
across his face. The feather quill had been sharpened to a fierce point.
He mixed the ink with water in a little dish and dipped the quill
into the black puddle. I relaxed next to him on the bench. The small
movement brought me close enough to Ephraim that our thighs and
shoulders touched.

Ephraim tapped the quill against the rim three times, knocking
the excess ink off the tip. He raised it above the page. "On this, the
nineteenth day of December, in the year of our Lord, one thousand,
seven hundred, and fifty-four, I, Ephraim Ballard, do take as wife
Martha Moore."

"This is my name," he said, scratching the quill against the paper.
"This is how it's written." The letters were all angles, lines, and curves,
and they made no sense to me. But it was wonderful to know that this
collection of ink scratches was the name I had taken as my own. "And
this," he added, dipping the quill once again into the ink, "is yours."

I watched him write my name with a delicate hand. He couldn't
have been more gentle or precise if he had been drawing my face with
that quill. My name looked beautiful beneath his hand.

"Have you ever seen your name written before?"

"No."

"Your father never wrote it for you?"

"I never asked."

"I will write it for you anytime you ask. I will engrave it upon my own heart if that is what you want." He lowered his lips to my temple, brushed them against my hairline. "And I will teach you to write mine."

He rubbed his nose against my ear, my jaw, my temple. I couldn't think straight. After a moment it was clear to him that I wasn't thinking anything at all. Ephraim laughed, deep and warm.

"Well then, Mrs. Ballard, let us begin your education." He pulled the stack of parchment closer. Arranged the ink and quill. Then he flipped the Bible open to a section near the middle. "Do you know what book this is?"

I shook my head. How could I?

"It's one you'll never hear preached in church. And I'd wager your father never read it at the table after dinner."

"What is it?"

"The Song of Solomon." He traced the title with his finger, and I tried to follow along, wondering which marks corresponded to each word. "Shall I read you a little?"

"Please."

He set his fingertip beneath each word and moved it slowly as he read. I followed it with my eyes. "The Song of Songs, which is Solomon's," he said. "Let him kiss me with the kisses of his mouth: for thy love is better than wine."

I tried to hide my smile. He noticed before I had the chance to smooth it from my face. Ephraim repeated the verse, but this time he spoke the words against my lips.

Let him kiss me with the kisses of his mouth? Yes, I thought, *I will let him.*

I couldn't help but wonder if the book said anything about his tongue, because Ephraim made full use of that as well.

"The Bible says that?" I asked when he came up for air.

"Indeed, and a great deal more."

I had not noticed before how tired he looked. Stubble along his jaw and dark circles under his eyes. Ephraim yawned. There was only one bed in this house, and it was just barely big enough to fit the two of us. But he had taken even this into account.

He pulled me to my feet. "Come with me." He led me to the bedroom. Opened the door. He took me to stand beside the bed. Held my hands in his. "I've promised not to touch you until you're ready. And I will keep that promise if it kills me. But you are my wife, Martha. And I would very much like to share your bed."

"My bed?"

"I built it for you."

I answered him with a quick kiss.

"Was that a yes?"

I nodded. "I prefer to be warm when I sleep."

"Then allow me the honor."

Ephraim turned down the bed and left me in privacy to undress. I climbed in, wearing my shift, and expected him to join me, but he wandered through the cabin, blowing out candles. The room filled with the smell of candle smoke, and the only light came from the glowing embers in the hearth. When I heard his clothing falling to the floor, my heart exploded beneath my ribs. There was a weight in the bed beside me. A shifting of air as he lifted the blanket. And then the full length of his body was right there next to mine.

"May I hold you?" he whispered.

"Yes."

"Come here, then. And let us sleep."

Ephraim pulled me to his chest and tucked his legs behind mine. If we were vertical, I would be sitting in his lap. But we were not vertical. We were lying in bed, *not* consummating our marriage. And yet it was the most intimate thing I had ever done.

*

It was later, as I lay in a stubborn wakefulness, curled against Ephraim's back for warmth, listening to the slow and even pace of his breathing, that I let my mind wander to all the things we could have done in the dark that evening. I thought about what it would have been like to feel his hands along my body. What places he might have explored with lips and tongue. I thought of a coupling that didn't involve pain or fear or violence. I thought of myself surrendering to the warm and gentle hands of the man I loved, and my skin grew warm. The desire to roll onto my back and pull him with me was so strong that I could think of nothing else. Instead, I lay there, eyes open, nose pressed against the smooth, warm skin of his back, and I let him take me in thought only.

I was deep in this fantasy when I heard the deep rumble of his voice. "Does it feel good, Martha? What I'm doing to you? In your thoughts?"

I startled and pulled away from him.

"No," he whispered, reaching back to grab my arm and drape it over his chest again. He placed my hand on his heart and set his own on top. "Don't stop. I'm certain that whatever it is you're imagining is something I'm enjoying immensely."

"I thought you were asleep."

"I could feel your eyelashes brushing against my back," he explained. "That's how I knew you were awake. You were getting warmer by the moment." Ephraim laughed. "And I cannot help but wonder what you were thinking about us doing in my bed."

"You said it was *my* bed."

"Ah, that it is, love. And when you are ready to have me do in deed what you just had me do in thought, we will find another use for your bed."

3

A BLIZZARD

JANUARY 1790

Some rise by sin, and some by virtue fall.

—WILLIAM SHAKESPEARE, *Measure for Measure*

FORT WESTERN

I spend the first hour of the first morning of this new decade burying a baby. He is dead born. And small. No more than five pounds, and his arrival into this cruel world came well over a month early.

"It seems wrong that he should go into the ground without a name," Ephraim says.

"She refused to name him. Just as she refused to declare the father."

He shifts the small, wrapped bundle in his left arm and sets his other hand upon it. "Nathan," he pronounces.

"Ephraim," I warn. "We have no right."

"And who will know?" He looks around. Peers into the dark, cloud-covered sky. The forest. Then those intense blue eyes turn back to me, and I see the lantern light flickering in their depths. Again, he says, "He should not go into the ground without a name."

I am too tired to argue. My hands are blistered and bloody from digging the hole, and my back aches. "Fine, then. Nathan."

The grave is deep enough now—over a foot deep and wide— but was a misery to dig, requiring both hatchet and pick. Though Ephraim offered to do it, I'd insisted he stay inside with the family. It is only by luck that he is with me now anyway. The weather turned poor last night, and he was headed to Fort Western as I left. So we'd crossed together, and he met me at the home of the laboring woman once he was done visiting with James Wall.

There was nothing I could do for mother or child. The wee boy was already gone when he whooshed from his mother's body, and she—terrified and unmarried—had declared nothing, keeping the name of the father secret. She had only cried. Then screamed. Then started to shake. The shaking is normal. Most mothers find themselves unable to stop the trembling after giving birth. But this was different. It came from her core and continued. It was feral and unhinged, and I left the room only when she finally surrendered the tiny body, and her mother took over the vigil. Within moments, the girl fell asleep from sheer exhaustion. She is only eighteen.

Part of my remit, a thing required of me by law to be licensed as a midwife, is to bury a child born dead. Or one that passes while I am present. The requirement is meant to spare the mother this agony, but instead places the hardship directly on the shoulders of the midwife. And in winter—*oh God,* why must there be such a cruel season?—to shovel away the snow, then hack into the frozen ground, to dig a grave deep enough that any passing wild animal will not interfere. Rocks piled atop are usually needed as well.

In this case, the only possible location was beneath the boughs of a large, sprawling pine. It is the one place where the ground is almost soft enough to dig a grave. Still, it was not easy.

It is now the middle of the night, and I turn to my husband, reaching for the bundle in his arms. He does not hand the baby over immediately. Instead, he looks at the tiny, wrapped, linen parcel, and I see the sorrow pool in his eyes.

"It's time."

Ephraim shakes his head, dislodging the ghosts that reside there, then gently sets the child into my arms. Together we place him in the hole. Cover him first with dirt, a heaping of snow, then pine needles, and finally a stone cairn that cannot be dislodged by any wild animal. Afterward, my husband kneels beside the grave, lips moving in silent prayer. This sight is so familiar to me that I am nearly blinded by grief. Some memories never fade.

He looks to my face and the tears that freeze against my cheeks. "Let's go home, love," he says.

*

In the morning, after I've indulged myself in a rare cup of hot black coffee, I retreat to my workroom and go over the list of deliveries I have performed in the last twelve months. The Year of Our Lord, 1789, brought fifty new souls to Hallowell. Of those, I attended thirty-nine. The rest either were delivered by someone else or happened before I could arrive.

As has been true every year since I began my inventory, the majority of babies I delivered were girls. Twenty-seven last year. I do not consider myself a superstitious woman, but I find comfort in these numbers. Every midwife I have ever known has cautioned that an abundance of male births for multiple years in a row means looming war. One of them—old, bitter, and widowed—had buried every child of her own and, in the calcification of her grief, would refer to such boys as "the cannon fodder of kings." I have never delivered a boy— either from my body or with my hands—and not thought of those words. Of my own nine children, six were girls, and I have always taken this as a good omen. It makes me hopeful that the wars of this country are behind us.

Four of the births in the Hook last year were stillborn, though I attended only three of them. Each is a bitter loss, and I take my time reading the entries.

Thursday, February 25. Birth. Mr. Jacob Chandler's daughter. Mrs. Chandler was delivered at the 9th hour of a girl, dead born. . . .

Thursday, September 10. Birth. Mr. Pinkham's daughter. Clear. I was called to see Captain Pinkham's wife. I left home at the twelfth hour. Walked. My patient was delivered of a daughter, at the ninth hour in the evening. It was dead born. I tarried all night.

Thursday, December 17. Birth. Mr. Stone's daughter. Clarissa Stone was delivered of a dead daughter at the twelfth hour yesterday. The operation performed by Dr. Benjamin Page. The infant's limbs were much dislocated, as I am informed. The man knows not how to deliver a breech presentation.

Six days after he gave Grace Sewell a near-lethal dose of laudanum, Clarissa Stone called for that idiot doctor to deliver her child. The results were disastrous. And yes, I understand why she did not want me in attendance after the tongue-lashing I gave her in Coleman's. But there was no reason to go to Dr. Page. I am but one of five midwives in this county.

He is twenty-four years old. Twenty-four! I have thirty years on the man and well over twice as much life experience. Yet the young mothers of this town are dazzled by the mere idea of a Harvard-educated man. So much so that they put the lives of their unborn children in his hands, and the results are deadly.

It is not that every birth I attend goes well, of course. Last night's delivery is proof of that. But she had lost the child before I ever arrived, and that is the difference between Page and me. With a heavy heart I lift pen to paper and record the life lost yesterday:

Thursday, December 31. Birth. Ruth Emery's son. Clear and very cold. I was called to see Ruth Emery. Delivered her of a son that was dead. It was her first born. She continues in grief. I left her at midnight. Mr. Ballard conducted me there and home again as the roads are near unpassable.

I consider them *my* babies. I am not their mother, of course, but they are *mine,* and I can still feel the weight of grief hanging heavy in those birthing rooms. The only thing harder than losing an infant would be losing a mother, and I thank the great gift of Providence that I have yet to experience this myself.

Sometimes, however, the most difficult part of a birth is simply getting myself there in time. The river, as always, is my greatest obstacle. Frozen or free, it must often be crossed, and whether by ferry or foot, there is no safe way to do so. The weather, too, acts as villain against me more often than I think is fair. Together, these two forces make as much trouble for me as the patients themselves.

Earlier this spring I faced such a circumstance, and I flip back in my journal to the entry.

Saturday, April 6, Birth. Eben Hewin's daughter. A severe storm of rain. I was called at the first hour by Eben Hewin. We crossed the river in his boat. It was a great sea a'going. We got safe over, then set out for Mr. Hewin's. I crossed the stream near his home on fleeting logs but made it safely. But as we passed by Mr. Haines's, a large tree blew up by the roots before me which caused my horse to spring back, which spared my life. I was assisted over the fallen tree by Mr. Haines. Went on, and soon came to another stream but the bridge was gone. Mr. Hewin took the reins, waded through, and led my horse to the other side. We arrived safe and unhurt. Mrs. Hewin safe delivered at ten that evening.

Last year, two of the children I delivered were illegitimate, but only one mother declared the father while in travail. She has since wed. But poor Sarah White remains unmarried and much maligned.

Sunday, June 21, Birth. Sarah White's daughter. Clear morn. Yesterday I was called at the rising of the sun to Sarah White, she being in travail and is yet unmarried. She remained ill through the day but was delivered safe of a daughter at the 9th hour this morning.

Today it is not just the births that I take time to note. I also go back in search of three entries, noted by an ink blot in the margin. Keeping with tradition, I do not move on in my survey of the previous year before paying tribute. This time, however, I mark an important—and grievous—anniversary:

Saturday, June 26 . . . My daughter Triphene died twenty years ago today. She was four years old. . . .

Sunday, July 4 . . . My daughter Dorothy died twenty years ago today. She was two years old. . . .

Thursday, July 7 . . . My daughter Martha died twenty years ago today. She was eight years old. . . .

Of everything that I have suffered in my fifty-four years, these three scars are etched deepest in my soul. It does not matter that I had two more daughters after burying those three. The loss is still as fresh and painful as though it happened yesterday. When they died, generations died with them.

I leave my desk for a moment and go to the wooden box on my worktable. I pull out the Bible that Ephraim gave me on our wedding night so many years ago. On the family register, beneath our names, is the list he promised we would make together. Our own legacy, recorded in black-and-white. I run my finger down the birthdates of our nine children.

Cyrus Ballard—September 11, 1756
Lucy Ballard—August 28, 1758
Martha Ballard—April 7, 1761—died, July 7, 1769
Jonathan Ballard—March 4, 1763
Triphene Ballard—March 26, 1765—died, June 26, 1769
Dorothy Ballard—May 17, 1767—died, July 4, 1769
Hannah Ballard—August 6, 1769
Dorothy "Dolly" Ballard—February 20, 1772
Ephraim Ballard, Jr.—March 30, 1778

For twenty-three years, my primary work was to grow a family. Work I considered both honor and duty. Joy and trial. The fact that I am only fifty-four and have buried one third of that family is a sorrow for which there are no words.

I was eight months pregnant with Hannah that awful summer and—in my darkest moments—was convinced that the ache of it would put me and the child I carried in the ground as well. Rarely does a day go by that I do not look at Hannah and think her a miracle.

It hurts. Every year it hurts when I do this, but to forget would be the greater injury. Now that it is done, however, I push my book away and breathe long and deep through my nose. I listen to my daughters rattling around the kitchen. Smell the hiss of bacon and the sizzle of potatoes. I put away my journal and my Bible and go to be with the children I still have left.

BALLARD'S MILL

My family stopped attending public worship in July when Isaac Foster was removed as preacher. It was our only available form of protest, and while I do not regret the decision, it does feel strange to sit at home on a Sunday morning. But it is not *unpleasant* to rest before the fire, a warm cup of tea in hand, and read the Book of Common Prayer.

"He has shown the strength of His arm," I whisper, the nail of my right index finger running along the last verse of today's liturgy. "He has cast down the mighty from their thrones and has lifted up the lowly."

I close my eyes, pray that it might be so, and close the book. No sooner have I set it back on the shelf than I hear a gentle knock at the door. Hannah sticks her head outside, then looks back at me and says, "Mistress Parker is here."

"Is her husband with her?" I haven't seen Seth since the morning he and the others cut Joshua Burgess from the ice. He'd been one of the first to flee during my inspection of the body.

Hannah shakes her head. "She's alone."

"Didn't you invite her in?"

"She asked to speak with you at the gate."

"Is she ill?"

Hannah shrugs. "Not to look at."

Strange, I think, and pull my shawl off the peg, wondering at this need for privacy as I slip out the door. Mrs. Parker stands inside the garden gate, wringing her hands.

"Ellen." I look her over head to foot. "Are you unwell?"

"In a manner of speaking."

There is no wind, and the snow has a thin crust of ice on top where it has melted during the day and frozen again at night. My boots make an unpleasant crunching noise as I move across the yard.

"What's wrong?" I ask.

"I need to borrow a horse."

I know for a fact that her husband has two fine steeds tied up in their barn. "Why?"

Ellen Parker is a shy woman, the kind who drifts to the back of a crowded room, who blushes whenever too many people look at her at once. The cold has turned the tip of her nose red, but I think that the pink tinge on her cheeks is embarrassment.

"She's *back,*" Ellen whispers.

"Who?"

"*Her.*" Ellen's eyes widen, and she purses her lips as though this should be obvious. "The Negro woman. I need to see her."

"*Oh.*"

I heard her husband, Seth, mention this, at the tavern, when I inspected Joshua Burgess a month ago, but I'd forgotten in all the turmoil that followed. "Do you not want your husband to know?"

"Seth wouldn't approve. And if I take one of your horses, he'll not ask where I've gone."

"Where does he think you are now?"

"Here. With you. He saw me walk off. And he'll see me walk home. I'm not lying. Not much at least," she whispers.

Under different circumstances I might point out that a lie of omission is no different from any other kind, but I have no issue with lending her the horse.

"You can take Bucket. He's old and slow but he'll get you there."

"Thank you. I only need him for a few hours."

"Of course. But it's a hard ride through the woods. Are you sure there isn't something I can do for you here?"

"Yes," she says without explanation.

"I'll send Young Ephraim to the barn, then."

Ellen thanks me again, and I go to find my son and give him instructions for the horse. Ten minutes later I stand at the door and watch my neighbor ride away—not down the lane and toward the main road, but into the north pasture, toward the path that winds three miles through the woods to Burnt Hill.

Four times a year a Negro woman known only as Doctor comes to Hallowell. She arrives unannounced and might remain for a single week or months on end. No one ever knows. But her arrival is always whispered about, and the news spreads from house to house like a fine mist drifting beneath the door. Doctor is one of the only people I know whose medical expertise exceeds my own. Some have argued that she has the gift of healing. Others, of course—Seth Parker among them—call her a witch. It's an unimaginative accusation and one that I am frankly tired of hearing. *Witchcraft.* As though there is no other explanation for a woman who excels at her work.

Doctor speaks with a warm French accent and often describes herself as an *accoucheuse.* A midwife, same as me. Yet she is so much more. Doctor is a mystery to many in the Hook, and therefore they fear her. Yet I've never seen anyone who does not watch the woman with a kind of bewildered awe.

As of last week, there are one thousand, one hundred, ninety-nine residents in Hallowell. Families number one hundred eighty-four, and, of those, twelve are black. All free. There are no slaves in Hallowell, the Supreme Judicial Court having effectively abolished the practice in Massachusetts nine years ago by their ruling in the Mum Bett Case. The census counts everyone in the Hook except Doctor because she has asked those who live here to make sure the census takers don't know she moves among us. Doctor has sworn never to return should her presence be revealed, and we are more than happy to keep her secret given how many of us rely on her services.

When I can no longer hear Bucket snort and stomp through the woods, I return inside and go to my workroom. I mix the ink and dip my pen:

Sunday, January 3—Clear. I have been at home. Mrs. Parker borrowed our horse to go and see the Negro woman doctor. . . .

BURNT HILL

I approach the cabin slowly.

For much of the year the logger's base at the foot of Burnt Hill remains empty. In spring men come up from Winthrop and Pittston to camp and harvest timber that they later send down a heavily swollen Bracket Brook toward Hallowell, where it's bundled at the Kennebec and ferried south in rafts. But in winter, the brook fades to a trickle, and the remote camp is abandoned.

The tallest point in three counties, Burnt Hill—so named for a decades-old fire—is windswept and bitterly cold, barren at its rounded peak, except for brush and rocks. Its slopes are thick with a canopy of aging paper birch and sugar maple. As they're cut from the hillside, one by one, trembling aspen, balsam, and spruce rise to take their place. It is the aspen that I like best, however, not just for their pale, speckled bark, and astonishing show of gold each fall, but because every aspen in this great expanse of forest is connected by a single root system. They give life, one to another, and work to replace what the loggers take. There is much that men could learn from nature if we would only listen.

Beautiful though Burnt Hill might be, the only reason anyone would make the trek out to this place in the dead of winter is to see Doctor. Knowledge of her arrival is passed up and down the Kennebec in muted whispers, but she is only visited by those who strive to keep their secrets close.

As I ride into the clearing, a young Wabanaki family slips out the cabin door. A man, and a woman holding an infant swaddled in rabbit pelts. Both parents are draped in heavy wool blankets dyed a deep and startling red, and they wear the traditional leggings, tunics, and deerskin moccasins. The woman cradles her child close to her body and keeps her eyes on the ground, careful of each treacherous step through the snowdrifts. But the father looks to me and nods cautiously before taking the child, then helping his wife onto the horse. Once she is situated, he lifts the bundle to her again, then leads them from the clearing without a backward glance. Theirs are the only tracks in the two inches of fresh snow that blankets the clearing.

Fascinated, I wait until that flash of crimson is no longer visible between the pine boughs before I approach the cabin. In total, it is no bigger than my workroom and sits like a lopsided rectangle at the base of a small, stone outcropping. Smoke curls from the chimney, and I can hear humming within—a melodic rise and fall of voice that sounds both familiar and foreign.

I dismount Brutus and tie him to the side of a large covered wagon that sits beside the cabin. Behind it, and to the side, is a lean-to stable, built by loggers, and made from hewn, lashed timber. It rests against the rockface and is wide enough for only a single steed. Inside is the largest horse I have ever seen. Eighteen hands if he's an inch and so ruddy he gleams like fire in the shadows. Brutus snorts at him, and he returns the gesture while I shake my head.

"It's always a pissing contest with you men," I say, then turn to the other horse. "And who are you?"

If I have a weakness for anything in this world it is a big, beautiful stallion.

"He is Goliath," a voice calls out from inside the cabin. "And you, Martha Ballard, should come inside. *C'est froid.*"

It *is* cold, and I am grateful for the welcome, but I remember, at the last second, that I have brought a gift, and I go to retrieve the bottle from my saddlebag first. It is a bottle of syrup of currants and brandy, wrapped in a soft linen cloth and tied with a ribbon. I do not need Doctor's services today—not in the usual sense, at least—but I have not forgotten to bring payment.

"Good to see you again, Doctor," I say, as I step inside and shrug out of my riding cloak. I hang it on a peg and brush the snow from my hair, then close the door to shut out the cold that has drifted in after me like a fog. "How did you know it was me?"

Doctor offers a knowing smile, full lips curving around small, straight teeth.

"Oh," I say, as the answer occurs to me. "You recognized my voice."

"You would recognize mine, *non*?"

"Indeed."

There is a rocking chair on either side of the fireplace and a flat, round stump between them with a lantern on top that emanates a soft, golden light. Roughly a decade younger than me, Doctor has high cheekbones and a long, slender neck. She wears a green muslin dress, and her hair is kept up and away beneath a matching headwrap. There is a mortar in her lap and a pestle in her hand. Beside her is a woven basket, lid fitted tightly on top. No doubt a gift from the Wabanaki for services rendered.

Doctor sees me looking at the basket and says, "The woman you saw outside has gone dry. She has nothing left to feed *le bébé*."

I take this as my invitation to come in and sit down. As I arrange my skirts, she continues.

"It happens. No one knows why. But *le bébé* has not weaned. So they came to me for help."

"Are there none in her tribe who can nurse the child for her?"

"None with milk to spare." She looks at me as though I ought to know this. "It is winter. And many are hungry."

"What did you tell her?"

Doctor flexes the hand that has been working the pestle. Her fingers are long and thin. Elegant. But I can see that the pinky on that hand was once broken and healed poorly. It does not fully straighten like the others. "There is nothing so good as mother's milk, but feeding the child boiled walnuts mixed with cornmeal and water will get him to the spring when he can eat other foods."

I did not know this, and I tell her so.

She looks me up and down, and says, "You are not ill."

"No."

"Tell me why you're here, then."

I place the bottle of syrup beside the lantern. "Ellen Parker borrowed my horse this week to come see you."

"And you are curious why?"

"No. I have enough secrets to carry. I've little interest in adding hers to the pile."

"And yet you didn't come to visit." Doctor turns her gaze back to the mortar and pestle. She cups the rounded knob in her palm and rolls it in a counterclockwise motion against the mortar, crushing the fine, dry leaves into powder. It smells of black pepper and sage.

"Why shouldn't I?"

"No one does. There is always a reason."

"What about Hitty?"

Doctor looks up at me sharply, dark eyes still and steady as a lake at midnight. "Not even her," she says. "Not since she took up with *cet homme*."

"I thought they were married."

"Only . . . *aah* . . . what is the word . . . ?" She laces her fingers together and holds them up.

"Handfast?"

"Yes. Not that it matters. No law recognizes a marriage—handfast or otherwise—between your kind and mine." Doctor licks the end of her broken pinky and sets it to the fine powder in her bowl. She tastes it, thinking for a moment with eyes closed, then nods once, deciding it's the way she wants it, and sets the bowl on the floor beside her. "But again, you didn't come to talk about my daughter."

"No."

"Tell me then."

There are so many things about Doctor that I don't understand. Where she comes from and where she goes when she isn't in Hallowell? How she learned the craft of medicine and from whom? When she learned to speak English and how she became acquainted with the Wabanaki? How she travels so freely on her own as a woman in the wild? But if I could ask Doctor any question—and be guaranteed an answer—I would ask her name. What is it? Yet that is forbidden knowledge, a question that will have me immediately dismissed. So I ask what I came here to learn.

"What do you know about the herbs tansy and savine?"

Doctor answers without hesitation. "They are used to stop a child from growing in the womb. One brings *les régles*"—she sets a hand, fingers spread, on her lower abdomen, then clenches it into a fist—"and the other cramping. But you already knew that, *non?*"

"I tended a woman recently, Rebecca Foster, who took them together. A great deal from what I can gather. But she didn't lose the child."

"The baby wasn't welcome?"

"It was forced upon her."

It isn't so much that Doctor winces, but a shadow flickers through her dark, velvet eyes. Briefly. Just the ghost of an emotion, gone as quickly as it came. "So she wants to try *les herbes* again?"

"No. Or at least she hasn't said so. And I wouldn't recommend it anyway. I didn't give them to her in the first place."

"*Bon.* Savine is wicked. Kills a woman as often as it helps."

"But will it cause harm to the child afterward—since it failed to unroot? That is what I need to know." The idea of Rebecca Foster being left, not just with an unwanted baby, but with an invalid has made me lose more than one night's sleep.

"No more than the mother. Is she *bien?*"

"I fear she'll never be well." I tap my chest with one finger. "In here." Then I move that finger to my temple and tap again. "Or here."

"You are worried she will hurt *le bébé* when it comes? Or herself?"

"I am worried about ten thousand things."

Doctor laughs, a deep and rich timbre that fills the cabin. "Then you haven't learned much about being a healer." She sees the look of hurt cross my face but doesn't chase it with an apology. "Have you done all you can to help this woman?"

"Yes."

"Worry only about the care you give when called upon. The rest is not yours to fret about. Ah," Doctor says, holding up one finger. "Someone is coming."

"Who?"

"My next patient."

I turn to the door and listen. At first, I hear nothing but pine boughs creaking in the wind and the siskins who live deep within their branches calling to one another. But then, after a few long seconds, I detect the steady clomp of hooves making their way across the clearing.

"Who gave Madame Foster *les herbes* if it was not you?"

I glance at the woven basket beside her. "I believe it was the Wabanaki, though I cannot be sure. They have long been friends."

"Ah. That is why she did not die. As to why the child stayed rooted? You must ask them. I have yet to see the Wabanaki make a mistake with *les herbes.*"

Doctor remains in her chair, hands folded in her lap. She nods once. I have been dismissed.

"Thank you," I say, rising.

Doctor smiles. "For what?"

"Reminding me that I am not God."

Again, that laugh, like water over rocks. "Had you forgotten?"

"No. Only that there are some hurts I will never be skilled enough to heal."

Inscrutable as always, Doctor only stares as I go to the door. I slide into my riding cloak and pull on my gloves. We are not friends. Not in the traditional sense. I would like it to be so, but I can sense the wall between us. A barrier impervious to my admiration. Perhaps one day I will win her over.

A knock sounds on the door.

Doctor looks at me but speaks to this new arrival. "*Entrez,*" she says.

I feel the cold air on my neck, feel the sudden gaze of a startled stranger. And when I turn, I find May Dawin standing at the door.

"I'm sorry, I—"

"Don't worry. I'm just leaving," I tell her, and then, because I do not want the girl to feel awkward for bypassing me in favor of Doctor, I add, "How is Sam?"

It is no surprise whatsoever that Sam Dawin fell headfirst in love with the girl. Apart from the fact that large men often have a penchant for tiny women—a longstanding irritation of mine—she is lovely, like a doe, all soft browns—hair, freckles, eyes—and smooth skin. Her voice, too, has a gentle, soothing cadence.

"He is well, Mistress Ballard," she says. "Thank you for mending him. I don't know what I would have"—her voice thickens with emotion—"what I would do without him."

I set my hand on May's shoulder and give her a pat. "He loves you too. Never doubt that."

"I couldn't. Not if I tried."

"Good day, both of you," I say, and step out the door. As it closes behind me, I hear May introduce herself and then comes the usual response.

"You may call me Doctor."

May Dawin is inside, whispering with Doctor, but Sam stands beside the wagon, running his big hand up and down the bridge of Brutus's long, soft nose. He has never looked less pleased to see me.

BALLARD'S MILL

I lean against the edge of a worktable down at the mill watching my husband eat breakfast. Ephraim sits beside the woodstove, tin plate on his lap, and takes large but precise mouthfuls of scrambled egg and fried potato. The bacon is long gone. He ate that first.

"Thank you," he says. "I was about to start gnawing on my ankle."

"Not much meat there. Next time consider your arse."

"Can't reach it," he says, bending to the side and chomping the air with his teeth.

I laugh. It is good to be married to a man with a gift for levity. "I am glad you haven't dried up and gone to seed," I tell him. "So many men your age do."

"Not many of them have a wife that looks like you. I have incentive."

I slide off the table and cross the old, weathered floorboards, then take the plate from his hands and set it on the stove before straddling his lap and wrapping my arms around his neck.

"There is no need to lie, husband. We both know that I am not pretty. I never have been."

He says nothing for a moment, just studies me as though seeing my face for the first time. Then he makes one of those indistinguishable male noises. Half grunt, half sigh. He runs a finger down the bridge of my nose, over my lips, up one cheekbone, and down my chin. He brushes a few loose strands of hair away from my eyes and says, "When you were young, your eyes were dark. Chestnut like your hair. And do you know what the Bard says about chestnut eyes?"

"Nothing, I'm sure."

"An excellent color: your chestnut was ever the only color."

"I do believe you just made that up."

"In fact, I did not. It's from *As You Like It*. But that's not the point I'm trying to make. Your eyes used to be dark, but now they have lightened. Golden, like acorns."

I snort. "And I suppose the Bard would have something to say about acorns as well? No doubt from *The Taming of the Shrew*."

"He had much to say about acorns—he was a man well acquainted with nature, was Shakespeare. But my favorite line is also from *As You Like It*, though, unlike Celia, I did not find you 'under a tree, dropped like an acorn.' It was a field, the first time I saw you, and from what I remember, there wasn't an oak in sight. But my point is that something about you had to mellow with age, given that your temperament wouldn't budge an inch. It was left to your eyes to soften, and they are lovelier now than ever. So no, Mrs. Ballard, you might not be pretty, but I'll be damned if you are not the most *beautiful* woman I have ever seen."

"You are biased."

"I am *proud*."

It has been a few years since we made love in the mill, but given his honeyed words, I think this might be a good time to resurrect the habit. I scoot closer, hips rising, just as we hear a sound at the door.

A man almost laughs but saves himself at the last second by clearing his throat, followed by an *"Ahem."*

Barnabas Lambard—shaved and dressed in his Sunday best—leans against the doorframe with the kind of precocious grin best suited to a twelve-year-old boy. "Sorry to interrupt," he says.

"That makes two of us," Ephraim mutters, as he gently lifts me from his lap so that he can stand.

"That is Barnabas Lambard," I remind him.

Ephraim squints. "You are the officer of the court from Vassalboro."

"Yes."

I am pleased to see him and not afraid to show it, so I grace him with a smile. Ephraim notes this act of rare approval, takes the man in curiously.

"My wife says you're the one who told Obadiah Wood that Burgess was murdered."

Barnabas looks at me with an expression that falls somewhere between intrigue and annoyance. "I am. Though she could have warned me up front that the man was dead. Came as a shock. As she intended, I'm sure."

"Is that why you're here?" I ask.

"There are two reasons, actually, and that's one of them." He crosses the floor and extends his hand to Ephraim, introducing himself formally. "Barnabas Lambard. I am pleased to officially meet you, sir."

Oh.

I look him over again. There's a fresh shaving nick on his jaw, and his shirt collar has been pressed. The look that passes between Ephraim and me is so quick Barnabas shouldn't catch it, but he does, then his eyes narrow as his own gaze shifts between us.

Clever boy.

"Why would a dead man bring you back to Hallowell?" Ephraim asks.

"Because an inquiry has been opened into his cause of death. Judge Wood has questions regarding the circumstances and the manner of his demise and has instructed the Sessions to take up the matter on the twenty-ninth when they convene here in the Hook." He turns back to me. "I thought you might want to know that there is growing interest among the other two judges about the accusation made against Mr. Foster."

"The kind of questions that would behoove him to secure a lawyer?"

"Perhaps."

"Thank you for the warning."

"Now that the two of you have made amends . . ." Ephraim's voice is dry as toast. He looks young Barnabas over with renewed interest. "You must have ridden half the night to arrive so early?"

"I came in yesterday. Stayed at the tavern." His next words are chosen carefully, and he isn't afraid to meet Ephraim's eyes when he says them. "I didn't want to arrive smelling like the road."

"And why is that?"

They stand a foot apart, eyes locked on each other. Ephraim has him beat in height, but I think the boy might be a near match in terms of nerve. Without looking away, he takes off his hat and holds it in front of him. He grins, big and wide. Not the least embarrassed.

"That would bring me to the second reason. I thought I might say hello to your daughter."

Ephraim has guessed this purpose, of course. I did tell him about Barnabas's first visit and the interest Dolly took in him. But no man is ever really prepared when a boy comes knocking, and Ephraim—good father though he is—cannot keep the growl out of his voice when he answers.

"Hello? That's all you want to say?"

"I've heard it's a good place to start on a first meeting."

There's a bit of triumph in Ephraim's eyes. "*First* meeting? And do you even know her name, given that you've never spoken to her?"

"Dolly. Short for Dorothy, or so I've been told. A family name, I'd guess?" He looks to me in question.

"After my mother," I tell him.

"She is too young for courting," Ephraim says.

In fact, Dolly will be eighteen next month. A mere two months younger than I was when Ephraim first came to court me. He knows I'm thinking this, of course, so he stubbornly refuses to meet my gaze.

Again, Barnabas flashes that impish smile, a hint of confidence without hubris. If I am not careful, I will end up being quite fond of this boy. It is a rare man who can handle my husband.

"Well, I'm young too, which is good. But I never said a word about courting. I only said I'd like to say hello."

"And yet you've still not explained why."

He shrugs. "I like the way she looks. At *me,* I mean. Twice I caught her eye, and she didn't blush or giggle. There doesn't seem to be a silly thing about your daughter. From what little I have seen, she reminds me of Mistress Ballard. Clever, both of them. Same as my own mother."

It's a good speech, but Ephraim won't give in quickly. He lets Barnabas stand there a moment—long enough for a twinge of uncertainty to creep into the boy's muddy eyes—before he finally lifts his hand and holds it out. "Ephraim Ballard."

"Now that we've gotten that out of the way," I say, wiping my hands on my apron. "Would you like some breakfast? I believe Dolly is cleaning up the last of it now."

"I would like that very much."

I wait until Ephraim and Barnabas have gone up the path toward the house and then I pull the mill door closed. Outside, in his mews, Percy squawks his displeasure at our departure, but I pay him no mind. He's had his breakfast already, and soon Ephraim will let him out to fly.

I follow the men up the path, watching as they make their way between the snowbanks, noting how they walk. Ephraim like a bull— sure and strong—and Barnabas like a stag—young and ready. There is much, I think, that you can tell about a man by the way he walks. Nothing timid on the path before me, though, so I catch up and try to prepare myself for what will come next.

Dolly is waiting at the door. She leans against the frame just as she did the last time Barnabas Lambard came through the garden gate, one hand on her hip and her face flushed with curiosity. She must have seen him ride up, must have been hoping that we would come back to the house.

I poke Ephraim in the ribs and whisper, "Understand my father a bit better now, perhaps?"

He answers with an irritated grunt.

Dolly's cheeks are bright, and her hair is brushed, falling down her back in rivers of loose brown curls, but the prettiest thing about her are those eyes. Same as her father's. It may as well be midsummer for all the blue beneath her heavy lashes. And when she smiles at Barnabas, I can hear Ephraim's teeth grind together. I tug at his hand and pull him back a half step.

"Remember, *love*," I laugh, "it's a woman who does the choosing. You said so yourself."

"And I'm a fool for ever mentioning it to you."

Dolly lets Barnabas into the house, and we follow, neither of us quite ready to see our youngest daughter so easily felled by Cupid's arrow.

DR. COLEMAN'S STORE

"Aren't you coming in?" I ask.

Ephraim shakes his head. "Not today. I need to go across the river and inquire about a lumber order."

There are only two ways to cross the Kennebec: by ferry in warmer months, or by foot once it's frozen. It is nearly half a mile wide at points and deep enough that no one has ever touched the bottom. The current likely has something to do with that, however. The Kennebec is not the kind of river that you swim. Everything on the west side is considered Hallowell, and everything on the east, Fort Western, even though they are, in practicality, one village, split in half, spanning two miles in length. But each side has its homes and shops, its own community. Though it is treacherous, I almost prefer crossing the river on foot. The ferry takes too long.

"Be safe," I tell him.

"Not to worry, the ice is thick enough. And I'll only be gone an hour. Meet me at the tavern for a pint when you're done here."

Ephraim kisses my forehead, then steps off the boardwalk toward the well-trod path that leads down the bank and across the frozen river. I watch him begin the crossing—sure-footed as always—then I turn back to the store.

Coleman is doing steady business today, so I wait for a group of loggers to finish buying their tools before I approach the counter.

"What might you be needing today, Mistress Ballard?" he asks.

"Nothing. Unless you've come across something new to read?"

I hoist my basket onto the counter and pull back my cloak. My copy of *Emmeline* sits on top of two dozen neatly stacked candles. Their bottoms have been cut flat and their wicks trimmed.

"You've brought a new batch, I see." Coleman reaches out his right hand and plucks a candle from the basket. He sniffs the dried wax, then picks at a fleck of lavender with his thumbnail. "These are fancy."

"Just because something is useful doesn't mean it can't be pretty."

Most families in the Hook make their own candles, but there is always a traveler or housewife or shopkeeper who finds themselves in a pinch, and Coleman's is the first place they turn. He likes meeting the need, and I like the chance to barter. I come here at least twice a month in the hopes that he has gotten a new shipment of coffee, sugar, and chocolate from Boston, though the odds of those items having arrived since the river closed are slim. Most important, however, I am hoping to find something new to read. Having finished *Emmeline,* I am eager for another story.

Soon he turns his attention from the candles to the book.

"Any good?" Coleman asks, screwing up his eye to focus on the title.

"I liked it better than most. And the author is English. You'll approve of that," I say with a wink. "It's about a woman on the fringes of high society who refuses the traditional roles assigned to her, finding her own way, a love of her own choosing, and therefore ends up both wealthy and happy in the end."

"So it is a fantasy then?"

"Absolutely not. It is a *possibility.* Although, I must say, it felt rather . . . what's the right word . . . *gothic,* perhaps. Filled with wild, remote locations and mysterious happenings. I think you would enjoy it."

"Then I will trade ye book for book, Mistress Ballard," he says, reaching under the counter and pulling out a novel that is rather worse for wear and missing half the cover. "Although, to be honest, my damned eye is fading on me, and it won't be long a'fore I canna read at all. I'll have to hire a shop boy to keep the ledgers."

I take his book and turn to the title page. "*The Castles of Athlin and Dunbayne* by Ann Radcliffe," I say. "You have read it?"

"What was the word ye just used? *Gothic*? If that's what ye are looking for you will be satisfied. It's a full-blown medieval Scottish feud."

"Then it will suit my mood perfectly." I tuck the book under my arm and begin unpacking the candles.

"Anything else while you're here?"

"I'd love some coffee and sugar. But would settle for cornmeal and molasses."

"None of the former, I'm afraid. Not until the river opens. But I can give you a bag of cornmeal and a pint of molasses. More'n enough on yer account to cover it."

"How—"

"Mr. Sewell came in. Added money to your account and bought a pound of chocolate and half a pound of tea for ye as well. They're wrapped and set aside for ye."

Sometimes I am paid in coin before leaving a patient's house. Sometimes with food or livestock or bartering later in the year. But just as often, a grateful husband will add to my account at Coleman's or surprise me with a purchase left waiting for my arrival.

"Oh," I say, "that was good of him."

"To hear him talk, 'twas the other way around. He said his wife nearly died because of that laudanum and that you saved her."

I don't know what to say to this, so I don't say anything at all.

"I know you think that half the town has turned against ye, Martha, what with all the trouble you've had. But there are just as many who'll not hear an ill word against ye. Mr. Sewell counts himself in that number. And so do I."

*

Cyrus is at Pollard's Tavern when I arrive, and he waves me over to his table.

"What are you doing here?" I ask.

He slides a ledger across the table. Taps the line that shows a lumber order has been delivered and paid for.

"Chandler Robbins?" I read the name. "I take it he has another ship under construction?"

Cyrus nods. Shows the order details for seventy boards of white oak and two pine logs for the mast.

"His wife is expecting their first child soon," I tell him, as though it matters, as though he cares.

Although perhaps that isn't fair. Cyrus is far more interested in having a family than Jonathan. Which is the real tragedy of his circumstance. He is a good, strong, kind, intelligent man. But the simple fact of this world is that women look at him as though he's stupid. Simply because he cannot speak. They fear it is an illness. That it's catching. Some affliction that could be passed on to their children. So the girls of this town have always looked right through him. And he has built a wall around his heart in response.

"Every woman wants a man to whisper soft words in the darkness," Ephraim told me once, when I was lamenting Cyrus's lack of prospects. There was no malice in the statement, only heartbreak. And I have never forgotten it because it is true.

"Did you know that Chandler Robbins was one of the men who cut Joshua Burgess from the ice?" I ask.

If Cyrus heard me, he doesn't bother to acknowledge the question. His eyes are latched onto someone behind me, and he follows them through the room. He sits a little straighter, eyes curious, when a set of footsteps comes to a stop behind me. When I turn, Sarah White is standing there with a coin purse in her hand and a smile on her face.

"Hello, Martha," she says. "Cyrus."

My son gives her a broad, pleased grin in response, and I think that his cheeks have turned a bit pink.

"May I?" Sarah asks, indicating the bench.

"Of course." I scoot aside to make room.

She sits, arranges her skirt, then holds out a small cloth purse. "Here."

"What is this?"

"Six shillings for your fee. And another twelve for the court's fine. Exactly what I owe you. My Da' said he'd not pay a cent of it. That it was my responsibility. So I've been doing odd jobs around town for those who'd have me. I earned every bit of it myself."

The fining of unwed mothers is a cruel system, meant to humiliate women, and therefore dissuade them from carnal activity. But given that women do not conceive children on their own, and there is no law that fines men for their participation, it is the worst kind of hypocrisy as well. The minimum and maximum fines are set by law, but the amounts in between are up to the whim of each individual judge and can range from inconvenient on one end to crippling on the other. The law—grossly titled An Act for the Punishment of Fornication, and for the Maintenance of Bastard Children—states that any woman who commits fornication shall be fined no less than six shillings for the first offense and no more than three pounds. Every offense after that ranges between twelve shillings and six pounds. If a woman is unable to pay the fine, she is committed to the jail yard for a minimum of forty-eight hours, but the court can extend it to thirty days. Joseph North decides the cases in this county and is not typically known for his leniency. But for Sarah, he'd handed down the minimum fine—no doubt because I had offered to pay it myself, that day, as Sarah had not a shilling to her name. It has taken her six months to earn the money.

"Sarah . . ."

"I insist. It's my debt. And I want to pay it." She drops the purse into my hand and closes my fingers around it.

There is something in her eyes—a kind of light—that I cannot argue with. Sarah is proud of herself for accomplishing this, and I'll not take that from her. Cyrus senses it too, is leaning across the table on his forearms. I know that he wants to tell her something, that the words would come tumbling out if only he had the ability. Instead, he holds up one finger, then opens the ledger and rips out a page from the back. He grabs ink and quill from his case, and we both watch as he scribbles a short note, then slides it across the table.

You are a good woman, Sarah White.

She takes the paper and smiles at it with a frustrated expression. "I'm sorry, Cyrus. I canna read."

His gaze drops from hers. Falls to the table. He nods once, resigned. Embarrassed.

"He says you're a good woman."

And this makes her laugh. "He might be the only one in the Hook who does."

"Not the only one," I say. "Not by a long shot." And that's when the idea occurs to me. "What are you doing on Saturday?"

"Nothing as far as I know."

"You should come to the Frolic. It's at the mill this time. We would love to have you."

I look to Cyrus for confirmation, and he offers an eager nod.

"I don't know. . . ."

"It's just one evening."

"What about the baby?"

"Bring her. There won't be any shortage of arms willing to rock her while you dance." I can see her hesitate, look to the door for a way out. "Think about it? Please?"

Sarah gives me a half-hearted nod. "I will."

"Promise?"

She smiles again, but sadly this time. "For you, Martha, yes."

She says goodbye, but my gaze is on Cyrus as she leaves. He tracks her across the room and doesn't meet my eyes until she's out the door.

Oh. How have I missed this?

"How long?" I ask.

He flips his hands up as though asking, *What?*

"How long have you been in love with her?"

Cyrus clenches his jaw. Shudders. Then he grabs the note, wads it in his fist, and walks to the great, crackling hearth. He throws his missive into the flames and leaves Pollard's without another glance in my direction.

I blow out a long breath between pursed lips. "That long, I suppose."

*

The air outside the tavern is clear, but the breeze coming off the river is cold enough to burn. I untie Brutus from the hitching post and lead him the short distance to where Sterling drinks from a trough. The ice has been broken, but sharp little chunks float on the surface.

"You'll freeze your lips off," I tell the horse, scratching his great barrel chest beneath the leather saddle strap.

"It's a wonder he doesn't bite you." Ephraim lays a calming hand on my shoulder, knowing I will jump at his voice.

"How do you *do* that?" In all the years we have been married, I have yet to hear the man sneak up behind me.

He shrugs, taking Brutus's reins from my hands and inspecting the saddle and harness as though they're in danger of immediate failure. It isn't that he doesn't trust my ability with a horse, but rather he isn't willing to let me on one unless he's judged it fit to ride—certainly not one as willful as Brutus.

"You're late. You said you'd be an hour. It's been two."

"I picked up three more lumber orders at the fort. Then I had a bit of a chat with James Wall."

I lift an eyebrow.

"Did you know he's building a distillery?"

"I'd heard."

"He's leased a stretch of land along Farwell Brook. It's not big enough to use for mill trading. But it's cold and spring fed and just right if you're the kind of man intent on making whiskey. He pays the lease with what he earns from us."

"Us?"

"What Jonathan and Cyrus and I pay him to help us get the boards downriver."

"Ah. That explains a lot."

It's Ephraim's turn to give me the questioning glance.

"They never made their last delivery, did they? Got stuck in the river instead. And James had nothing with which to pay when the note came due."

"That's not entirely true," Ephraim says, then studies my face. "He was only ten dollars short. But that's because North required payment in full. For the entire loan."

"What's James going to do about it?"

"I offered to cover the difference. Part of me feels responsible. But he refused. Says he won't go into debt again. He plans on selling his horse to pay the note."

"The Pacer?"

"Aye. Says he can cover what he owes North, then buy a nag to replace it."

I've never understood James's obsession with that particular breed, but I'm sad to think of him losing the horse. And all because he went to the wrong man for a loan.

"Anyway," Ephraim shrugs. "That's what took me so long."

"Well, you missed something interesting as a result."

"And what would that be?"

I pull the coin purse out of my pocket and hand it to him.

"What's this?"

"My fee for delivering Sarah White. And the court fine. Eighteen shillings, paid in full. She brought it to me herself."

"That must have taken her—"

"Months. It isn't fair, Ephraim. There has to be a better way."

"And?"

"And what?"

He laughs. "I know you well enough to know when there's an *and*."

Ephraim sets a hand on either side of my waist and helps me into the saddle. Then he swings a leg over Sterling's back and settles into his own. We turn for home just as the sky begins to darken.

"I do have an idea," I say, trying to sort out my thoughts so they'll make sense. "Or two."

"I'm listening."

"Sarah can't afford another turn before the court. It will be jail time if she has another child out of wedlock."

"Are you saying she's not going to change her ways?"

"I am *saying* that the father of her child gladly took advantage of her body but left town long before the results of his lust brought her before the court. There is no justice in that."

"Sarah brought him to bed willingly enough. Or at least she's never said different. She's hardly innocent in the matter."

"Innocent? No. But she also has no legal recourse. The man is gone, and she cannot collect maintenance for her child."

"Her parents haven't turned her out."

"But they aren't supporting her either. She needs a real way to make a living. Not odd jobs that pay a shilling here and there."

"So what do you intend to do for her?"

"Exactly what you did for me."

It takes him a moment to figure out what I mean. "You'll teach her to read?"

"If she's to have any real chance in this world, that's where she has to start."

After a quarter mile we turn aside from the wide Kennebec, where Mill Brook meets the river. Farther on, Water Street narrows and becomes little more than a glorified cattle trail that passes through Vassalboro and follows the Kennebec up its banks, eventually disappearing one hundred fifty miles north, as does the river itself, into its source, Moosehead Lake.

"And this second idea of yours?"

"If she can't find a job, then perhaps I can help her find a husband."

"I suppose you have a man in mind?"

"I do."

"And you think it ought to be Jonathan?"

I open my mouth, stunned, ready to argue, but Ephraim mistakes my meaning and interrupts.

"I know it bothers you that he's taken no interest in courtship."

"He's twenty-six. He ought to be courting *someone*."

"That's the standard you have for him? Just someone? And Sarah would be your choice?"

"Sarah would be a great catch for any man, Jonathan or otherwise. But no, I hadn't thought of pairing them together."

"Who then?"

"Cyrus."

This does surprise him. "And what made you think of that?"

"You'd have thought the same if you saw the way he looked at her just now. I suspect he's been carrying a torch for that girl for some time."

I tell him about the note. How he threw it in the fire and stormed off.

Ephraim rides in silence for a while. "He won't appreciate you meddling, Martha."

"I'm not going to meddle."

He snorts.

"I am simply going to create an *opportunity*."

"For whom? Yourself?"

"For Cyrus."

"He can't speak, and Sarah can't read."

I smile at my husband. "Yet."

DAWIN'S WHARF

Sam Dawin is not happy to see me. I can tell by the set of his mouth and the way he rounds his shoulders as he throws a bale of hay over the fence. A giant red-and-white bull with long, hooked horns begins to tear at it, then he's muzzle deep, gorging himself. Within seconds, the hay is scattered, and Sam is stomping through the snow toward me.

"I know what you're here to ask," he says, "and it's none of your business."

The man has never been rude before, not in all the years I have known him, and this, more than anything, stuns me into silence. He can see his misstep though and has the good grace to stop.

"I haven't come to ask you anything."

"You haven't?"

"No. I've come to congratulate you on your marriage and to bring a wedding gift. Though I am a month late and I do apologize for that."

Abashed, color floods his cheeks. "I'm sorry. I assumed. . . ."

"What?"

"I thought you came to ask why May went to see Doctor."

"That's no more my business than it is yours to know why *I* was there."

"I'm truly sorry. I . . . that was very rude of me." Sam looks at the ground. "You have been kind to us, and I had no right to assume anything."

"You are right to be protective of your bride. No matter the supposed offense."

Sam darts a quick glance at my face, then returns the steady gaze to his feet. "I've already heard the rumors. They're spreading fast, you know."

"Rumors do that. And you did go to housekeeping quickly." I can see Sam stiffen again, can see the defensiveness creep in around the corners of his mouth. "I brought a quilt for May. I make an extra one every winter." It's a risk, but I take a step forward and set my hand on his arm. "No woman should go to housekeeping without a proper quilt."

I don't add that rushed marriages are nothing new in Hallowell, nor are the assumptions that go along with them. Tied to my saddlebag is the large, wrapped parcel. I undo the binding and hand it to Sam. He lifts it from my arms carefully, as though picking up a child.

"Your marriage is your own business, Sam. Don't let anyone tell you different."

"Thank you. May's mother wouldn't make her a quilt. She's too angry. Will probably never forgive me."

"Of course she will."

"You don't know her mother."

"I do, as a matter of fact. But regardless, my own mother forgave me, and Ephraim as well, after we went to housekeeping early."

He looks up at me. "You didn't wait?"

"No," I say. "Ephraim took me home that evening."

A different sort of young man might blush at those words. He might stammer or shift his feet. But Sam Dawin is staid and steady, practical, and he makes no show of being ashamed at the desire to bed his own wife.

"I am glad you understand," he says. "Not many do."

"You would be astonished at the things I understand, Sam."

I can see the decision running through his eyes, first the question, then the answer, one chasing the other. Finally, he asks, "Do you want to come in? I am certain May would like to see you."

"I would like that very much," I tell him, then go back to my saddlebag. Brutus is tied up at the post, drinking from a trough and grazing on the bale of hay beside it. I lift a bottle from my bag. "And I have another gift. But this one is just for May."

The house is small but neat, designed well so that Sam can add on as their family grows. It is set back from Water Street by a good fifty yards, but it has views of their wharf and the river beyond. Sam Dawin was fortunate to lease one of the last lots with river frontage and is therefore able to take advantage of both the mill traffic and his eighty acres of farmland. If he manages it well, he'll provide a solid living for his young family.

The front room is warm, clean, and smells of new wood and freshly baked bread. May sits in a rocking chair beside the hearth, a pile of knitting in her lap and a cup of tea on the small table to her left.

At first, she looks startled to see me, but then she smiles, and two perfect, round dimples appear at the corners of her pretty mouth. "Mistress Ballard," she says, "please come in."

Sam holds up the parcel. "Martha has brought us a wedding gift."

"How kind of you. Our very first," May says, trying to stand, but she isn't even fully upright when she plops back into her chair again, dizzy.

That's when I notice the bucket at her feet, and within seconds, May has grabbed it and leaned over, retching.

"I'm so sorry." She gags. Retches again. "Forgive me. I—"

Her words are lost in the gurgling, wet slop.

I am at her side immediately, kneeling, pushing the hair away from May's clammy forehead. A palm set against her forehead proves that she has no fever, so I put the bottle I've brought on the little table, and, operating on instinct, begin to give orders.

"Sam, go get a cold, wet cloth."

He's back in less than thirty seconds, and I press the fabric to May's forehead. "Lean back. Rest your head on the chair. Breathe through your nose."

The girl obeys without question as I pat her brow and cheeks with the cool cloth. "Are you ill?" I ask.

"In a manner of speaking."

One look at Sam proves my suspicions correct. He closes his eyes slowly. Sighs. Nods. May is pregnant.

This angers me. Not because the child was clearly conceived out of wedlock—that happens more often than not in Hallowell—but because it gives the gossipers room to gloat. I had hoped to suffocate that rumor.

"How far along?" I ask.

"I have missed two cycles."

And they've only been married one month.

Tears trickle down her cheeks, and I wipe them away. Then, when I'm sure the girl won't flinch, I cup May's face in my hands.

"No baby is conceived apart from the will of God, May. If you are pregnant, it means that you have been touched by Providence, and you will never hear me say an ill word about the child you carry. Nor will I let anyone do so in my presence. Do you understand?"

May nods. Continues crying. I cannot tell if she is afraid or ashamed or simply ill.

The act of mothering is not limited to the bearing of children. This is another thing that I have learned in all my long years of midwifery. Labor may render every woman a novice, but pregnancy renders every woman a child. Scared. Vulnerable. Ill. Exhausted. Frail. A pregnant woman is, in most ways, a helpless woman. Her emotions are erratic. Her body betrays her. Since May Dawin is presently without a mother of her own, I stroke her hair, encourage her to breathe, promise that her stomach will settle. And it does. The wave subsides, and then we are left in the vulnerable aftermath of confession.

I do not make eye contact with May. I do not look at Sam. Instead, I settle my gaze on the crackling fire and I offer them something that I rarely part with: the secrets of our neighbors.

"Every year I deliver children born out of wedlock in this town. You know those names. Most everyone in Hallowell does. They come to court just to hear me say them. Last year there were two. The year before, five. What you do not know is how many of the children I deliver are *conceived* out of wedlock. Four in ten. An *early* birth they call it. *Pre*mature. And not a one of them underweight. Our Puritan fathers would have us believe that lovemaking rarely happens outside the marriage bed. But I know better than most that it rarely happens—for the first time, at least—*within* that bed."

I am astonished to find that Sam is also crying now. He looks as though he wants to pluck May right out of my arms and run away with her. Words can be a gift, but so can silence. And that is the next thing I give to this new family. I rest my cheek against May's soft brown hair and let the silence settle around us like autumn leaves. I do not stand again until the need for it has dissipated.

"I brought you something," I tell May. I pick up the bottle. Hand it to her. "It is a syrup of bearberry leaf, cranberry, green tea, and mint. It helps calm infections of the urinary tract. These are common in newlywed women, . . . a result of . . . *er* . . . over*exertion*." I had wondered what it would take to make Sam Dawin blush, and now I know. His cheeks are flaming. "One spoonful morning and night, taken with a glass of water."

May runs a fingernail over the cork. "Thank you."

"Now, open your other gift."

Sam hands the parcel to May and she tears off the paper. The quilt is large, big enough to cover them both, and is made of scraps of fabric that I have gathered and kept over the years for this purpose. Every year I make an extra quilt, sewn in bits and pieces at night before the fire when my other work is done. And every year I choose this same pattern. It is called Wedding Rings, soft loops intertwined and set against a pale background with a solid border. I do this because every year there is a wedding. Sometimes rushed. Sometimes performed according to the standards of our town. Yet each young bride finds herself in a new home and does not know how to make it *her* home. This, a simple piece of bedding, is the answer. Everyone must sleep, and to do so beneath a warm quilt, tenderly made, is the first thing that helps a house become a home.

Again, there are tears, but happy ones this time.

"I don't know how to thank you." May presses the heels of her hands into her eyes.

"You don't have to."

I don't want to overwhelm the young couple any more than I already have, so I say my farewell, then add, "May is lucky to have you, Sam. Do not be overly hard on yourself."

He and May exchange a look that I cannot decipher, and the reciprocated smile dies on his lips.

BALLARD'S MILL

SATURDAY, JANUARY 23

Barnabas Lambard plays the fiddle. I cannot explain why this astonishes me, but it does. He'd seemed a more serious type, I suppose. One does not typically equate a law enforcement officer with being a musician. But those same hands that sent James Wall sprawling to the ground are every bit as nimble with bow and string. He stands on a large stump, in the corner of the mill, sawing his way through a lively rendition of "Soldier's Joy."

"I've always liked this song," Ephraim says, bumping his hip against mine. He's been playing host for the last hour, wandering around the mill, greeting everyone who arrives. "It's an old Scottish ballad that the pipers and fiddlers would play while soldiers chugged whiskey in preparation for battle."

"Let's hope a battle doesn't break out tonight," I say as my eyes drift to where Cyrus is spinning Dolly around the dance floor. I have not forgotten what happened at the last Frolic.

Ephraim shrugs. "You know how these things go. It isn't uncommon for fists to fly toward the end of an evening. After that nasty cider has been passed around for hours."

"That only happens when one boy thinks another has had more than his fair share of turns around the dance floor with a pretty girl.

Were that to happen, I'd put my money on Barnabas. I've seen his fists in action."

"So far Dolly has only danced with her brothers. There's no reason for him to get jealous just yet."

There is a cloud of fine, powdered sawdust in the air, kicked up by the swirling, dancing feet of sixty young people as they match the beat of the song. It's a wonderful kind of chaos, and the mill smells of dust and woodsmoke, joy and sweat, whiskey and apple cider. It also smells of mating. Not *sex* per se, that is entirely different—though none of the parents here tonight are fool enough to think it couldn't happen—but *mating,* that ritual common to all species. The flirting. Posturing. Choosing. Dancing. The occasional kiss, stolen in the dark, hidden from watchful eyes. It all has an ancient smell. Like dark soil and ripe fruit. Like humanity at the most basic, elemental level.

"The world must be peopled!" Benedick so helpfully observed in *Much Ado About Nothing.* It remains my favorite Shakespeare play for that line alone, though the rest of his monologue about Beatrice's virtues doesn't hurt. So it's no wonder there are fifteen chaperones at the mill tonight, parents gathered along the edges of the room, or sitting in the loft sipping from their own jugs of cider and ale and whiskey, keeping a weather eye on their children below.

When Barnabas grows tired after the fifth song, the dancers take a break. They fill their cups and wander over to the table for a bit of food. John Cowan—the young blacksmith's apprentice—weaves through the crowd and holds out his hand for the fiddle. He arrived with Catherine Pollard this evening and has been dancing with her since the first song. I look to where Abigail watches him with interest. More refined in her drinking tastes than most, she nurses a mug of mulled wine. It isn't only John Cowan she's keeping an eye on tonight, but Moses as well. He didn't arrive with Hannah given that we're hosting the dance, but he has stayed close to her side all evening.

"It isn't easy, is it?" I ask, after making my way to the loft where Abigail leans against the rail.

"What?"

"Keeping your eyes on two at once."

"That is why the good Lord gave me two eyes in the first place," she says with a grin. "It's you I pity."

"How so?"

"You've got four children of age down there, and only half the eyes needed to keep track of them."

"Ephraim is here."

She laughs. "But as usual, he only has eyes for you."

Abigail isn't wrong. I can feel the heat of my husband's gaze as he moves through the mill, and when I look to him, he greets me with a ready smile.

On the other side of the room, Barnabas whispers something to John Cowan. He no more looks like a musician than I a pirate, yet he climbs onto the stump, sets bow to strings with an exquisite gentleness, and begins to play. The tune that rises is every bit as lovely as the one Barnabas finished a few moments ago, though slower.

I recognize "Whiskey for Breakfast" after the first few notes. My father once told me that the song was an ode to those who stayed up so late that they, quite literally, had their whiskey before their breakfast. And based on the determined look in Barnabas's eyes, I see that he requested it on purpose. He flexes his fingers as he moves around the edge of the room toward Dolly. Her eyes light up at the sight of him.

And there it is, the ask.

Barnabas bows and holds out his hand in question.

Dolly curtsies and receives it.

And then they melt into the crowd of dancers, her arm around his neck and his hand at her waist.

Clever boy, I think.

After watching them dance for a moment, I leave Abigail and return to the main floor and go to stand beside the wide double doors, hoping for a draft to cool me down. When Ephraim sneaks up behind me and kisses me below my ear, I startle, then lean against him when he laughs.

"How long has it been?" I ask.

"Since what?"

"Since we last hosted one of these."

"Hmm." He presses his chin against my temple. "Must have been when Lucy was being courted by that Town boy."

That Town boy, I think. Aaron Town is his name, but my husband has never forgiven "that Town boy" for getting his daughter pregnant out of wedlock. He'd married her well in time for the birth, of course. They were in love, after all. But Ephraim remains inflexibly old-fashioned about such matters. "Do not take what doesn't belong to you," he has lectured our sons on endless occasions. I don't have the heart to tell him that—in one case, at least—I suspect the lectures have been in vain.

"Would have been sooner if your sons could be bothered to court someone."

"They're mine now, are they?"

"Only seems fair we trade off taking the blame."

It's hard to find anyone in the swirling crowd, but eventually I see Jonathan's bobbing head and then the flash of Sally Pierce's auburn hair. She has worn it down tonight, and it gleams in the lamplight. As usual, she looks at him with those ridiculous mooning eyes.

"Sally's convinced him to give her one dance, at least."

Her cheeks are round and her smile bright. Sally *is* a lovely girl. Tall but not towering. Buxom. And I notice that her gown has been cut to enhance these assets instead of her waistline.

"It's not the first dance," Ephraim tells me. "That's the third. You haven't been paying attention."

"It's not Sally I've been looking for."

"Who then?"

"Sarah White."

Ephraim puts his hands on my hips and turns me around to face him. "I thought you weren't going to meddle?"

"I'm providing options. That's all."

He smiles at me, broad and teasing to show he's not displeased. "I never said it was a bad idea."

"It would solve two problems at once. She'd be safe and provided for. And Cyrus could finally settle down with a family of his own."

"Does love not factor in?" Ephraim asks.

"I suspect he's there already. And yes, she might take a bit longer. But love can grow between two people. I've seen it happen more than once. Besides, we were lucky," I add. "For us it exploded."

"As it did for Lucy," he tells me, and I can see how the admission pains him. "As it is for Hannah now. And for Dolly too. They're nearly blinded by love out there on the dance floor. It's coming off them in waves, like steam from a pan. You'd want something *less* for Sarah?"

"It's a better future than raising a child on her own. I only want her to be open to the idea."

"And forcing it on her will do that?"

"I would never force anything. I just . . .'"

"What?"

"I want to see what would happen between them if the idea was given a chance to grow."

"It will never work if it's your idea. It would have to be hers."

I nod, understanding. "Because it's a woman who does the choosing."

"And you need to consider that perhaps she has already chosen."

"A man who got her pregnant and left her with a child? Clearly she chose *wrong*."

"Wrong or right doesn't matter. Sarah isn't here tonight. She's made that choice at the very least." Ephraim kisses me on the nose, then pats me on the bottom and goes off to join the other fathers in the loft.

Well, I think, *maybe she just needs another opportunity.*

The song ends and the dancers catch their breath, but then John Cowan begins his third song, "St. Anne's Reel," and a wave of laughter rises above the music. Cyrus and Young Ephraim are shadow dancing in the middle of the circle, each with an invisible partner. By the end of the first verse they're both clapping and stomping their feet, and by the end of the second, they've acquired real partners from the crowd.

I head over to the food table to see what I can do about my growling stomach. Abigail Pollard has brought an entire side of roasted beef for the occasion, and the other families have contributed as well, each bringing their specialties. There is chicken cooked in beer, venison loin stuffed with apples, and pork ribs to round out the meats. Any number of roasted vegetables including carrots, potatoes, turnips, and chard. A wheel of cheese—now deformed, with chunks pulled out of it by greedy fingers. Breads. Jams. Biscuits. Cakes. Pies—of both the fruit and meat variety. Roasted nuts and dried fruit and, of course, dozens of jugs of cider, ale, mead, and whiskey.

I'm debating among the assortment of sweets when Sam Dawin joins me at the table.

"What's a married man such as yourself doing here tonight?" I ask.

He shrugs, studying a plate of apple tarts, deciding which looks best. Plucks one from the pile. Takes a large bite. "May likes the music," he says, trying not to spit crumbs.

I saw them come in earlier. May has been in the loft most of the evening with a handful of other married women, watching the dance below. She looks tired—and a little green—but also happy. It doesn't seem that anyone else is aware of her pregnancy.

"Is she feeling better?" I ask.

"Depends on the day."

I nod at the table. "Bread will help. As will the cheese. Try the dried fruit as well. But I'd stay away from anything with lots of spice or salt. Give her mild foods over the next few weeks, and I'd wager she will feel better in a month."

"Thank ye, Mistress Ballard. I will."

I choose a rhubarb tart. These were made by Abigail as well, and the crust is made with butter, so flaky it crumbles onto my chin when I take the first bite. I expect Sam to load a plate for May, but instead he takes his own tart over to where Jonathan rests against the wall, taking a break from this new dance. Both men lean against a pile of stacked boards, a single foot propped up beneath them. Arms crossed. Heads bent. Talking. Both of their faces are clouded by some trouble that seems out of place this evening. Jonathan leans his head toward Sam's ear. Mutters something. Sam spits. Jonathan balls his fist. They are clearly angry, but not with each other.

Jonathan says something with an expression of finality.

Then Sam nods.

As though they've come to an agreement.

After a moment, their attention turns back to the dance, surveying the crowd.

Jonathan takes turns watching Moses and Hannah, then Barnabas and Dolly. He's not said a word to me about these new suitors, but clearly, they haven't escaped his attention. The gesture is protective and tender, and I am stunned to find that tears prick my eyes. For years I have vacillated between pride and worry when it comes to this boy of mine. I desperately want him to be a good man like his father. I am also painfully aware that you cannot make a child be anything he is not. But this—the watchful vigilance over his sisters—makes me feel as though all is not lost.

I turn away just as John Cowan launches into another thumping song. Someone taps my shoulder. And there is Cyrus. His dark, curly hair is mussed. Hazel eyes shining. He smiles, broad and handsome.

Then he bows.

And extends his hand.

You think it will break your heart to have a child who suffers in this way. One who is seen as damaged. You think, perhaps, that it is your fault somehow. That if only you'd done something different, taken better care of him, this would have never happened. And then he asks you to dance on a cold January evening, and you realize that perhaps you are a fool. And whatever his life may be now—different than you'd imagined all those years ago when he grew in your womb and curled into the hand you set upon your stomach—he is perfect.

I return the smile.

Curtsy.

Give him my hand.

Let my boy lead me onto the dance floor.

"I am sorry," I tell him.

Cyrus lifts an eyebrow in question.

"That she didn't come."

He shrugs, as though to say it isn't a big deal, as though he never thought she would. But there is a cloud of disappointment in his eyes. And just before we step into the song, I look up to find Ephraim standing at the rail of the loft. I can see it there, written on his face, plain as day: heartbreak. He wants for Cyrus exactly what he found for himself. Then the song swells, the beat rises through the floorboards, and I am swept away.

MILL CREEK BRIDGE

I don't see the lovers until I am right upon them, and even then, hidden as they are, it would have been easy to pass them by altogether. A man and a woman in a passionate embrace. Heads bent. Breathing hard. Hands roving.

It takes a moment to recognize the auburn hair of Sally Pierce.

It takes a few more after that to recognize Jonathan. The wagon is off the road, pulled beneath the shelter of three towering pine trees, and they are pressed against it, oblivious to my presence. Jonathan has one hand up Sally's skirt and another in her hair.

I stare in disbelief. It isn't so much *what* they are doing that has struck me dumb—I was young myself once, after all—but *where.* Anyone crossing the bridge could see them if they cared to look. Then again, perhaps that is why they chose the spot after all. They are two miles from the Hook. Secluded. Private. Out in the woods by themselves.

Except they aren't. And now I must announce my presence or move on, pretending I didn't see them. The latter is the better choice. The wiser. Both Jonathan and Sally are of age, after all. But I have not forgotten the accusations she brought against the Fosters, nor the shame and trouble it has caused my friends. So this seems the worst kind of hypocrisy, and I decide that I owe the girl no kindness today.

"Don't mind me," I say once I am certain that I can control the tone of my voice. And even then, it takes a few seconds for the words to register in their addled minds.

Jonathan and Sally jerk apart as if struck by lightning. The moment she recognizes me, her face floods, first with shock, then with fear. Those hazel eyes get wider and wider as her face crumples in dismay. She is about to cry. I only have to say a word to ensure it happens. Jonathan, sensing this, steps in front of Sally as she rearranges her clothing. He looks at me with an expression that can only be described as fury. Angry, not that he was caught, but by his *mother.*

This is how it has been between us for the last few years. I know why, but still, it hurts. The joy of having sons is that they *worship* their mothers. Until one day, suddenly, they don't. *I am not like you,* he realizes. *We are different.* Then, that boy—once small and sweet—begins the long, hard process of separation, until at last he rips the seam. But the holes where mother and son were once knit together remain.

"Sally has been at the house helping Hannah with a quilt." Jonathan clears his throat. "I was just escorting her home."

"Is that what you were doing?"

He doesn't bother explaining how they came to be parked beneath a tree, pressed up against the wagon. Silence stretches between us, long and awkward.

"Perhaps you'd best get her the rest of the way there." I meet Sally's eyes purposefully, then. "Lest you upset her *father.*"

Jonathan helps the girl into the wagon, then goes around to his side, flashing me a look of blatant hostility.

"Sally," I say, and nod farewell.

The girl cannot meet my eyes, cheeks and hair battling over which is brighter. Her voice is a barely a croak when she responds, "Mistress Ballard."

Jonathan climbs into the seat beside her and takes the reins.

"Jonathan?"

He looks up then, and I see the first glimpse of the boy he used to be. Sweet but clever, the way he was when caught with his hand in a jar of sweets. It's only a flash, but it comforts me. Reminds me that even though he is his own man, he is still my boy. Not even a ripped seam can alter that.

"We will speak about this later."

*

"Are you going to marry Sally Pierce?"

Jonathan startles. He had not expected to find me waiting for him in the barn. But I have long since learned that this particular son cannot be left to wiggle his way out of a confrontation. The only way to get his attention is to catch him by surprise.

"No," he says. "I ain't the type to leap over my sword. Not with her. Not with anyone. Marriage means children. And children mean responsibilities. I like my life exactly the way it is."

"Then you'd best leave her alone. You know well enough how children come to be."

"It was just a bit of fun," he says.

"I am not a fool, Jonathan Ballard."

"I never thought you one."

He leads Sterling to his stall then heaves the saddle onto its rack. He doesn't look at me, and I think he's finally showing a bit of embarrassment.

"Nor I, you. Which is why I am surprised at you being so reckless with that girl. *Her!* Of all people? How could you?"

"It was just—"

"Don't you dare say it was just a bit of fun. Because I saw her face. And she believes that she's getting a great deal more from you than that."

POLLARD'S TAVERN

FRIDAY, JANUARY 29

The Court of Common Pleas has come to Hallowell to determine whether charges will be brought against Joseph North. It is a special session, called by Judge Wood last month in Vassalboro, and marks the first time these men have held court in our town. Once again, we have gathered at Pollard's Tavern, but this time North wears neither robe nor wig.

Obadiah Wood is here, along with fellow Sessions judges James Parker and John Hubbard. As the officer assigned to their court, Barnabas Lambard has accompanied them as well. The tavern is packed, every seat taken, filled with friends and neighbors who've come to see one of their own face this serious charge. And that has made it worse for Rebecca, of course. The familiar faces. The whispers and judgment. It is one thing to give testimony in Vassalboro, before strangers, but something else entirely to do so before the people with whom you trade milk and eggs.

The way the air crackles with tension, the way I feel the glances of our neighbors, makes me think that they are hoping for another spectacle. Another outburst on my part. Half of them weren't here the first time, didn't see me held in contempt of court. It makes me angry, this voyeurism.

When we arrived at the tavern an hour ago, Ephraim had looked to the sky and frowned.

"A storm is moving in," he'd said.

I followed his gaze and saw the dark, angry clouds in the east, rolling in from the Atlantic. "Worse than usual?"

"Yes." He flexed the fingers of his left hand. "I feel it. In my bones."

"How long?"

"A couple of hours, if we're lucky."

In truth, the blizzard came in even quicker than Ephraim predicted, the winds picking up and the sky opening just as the judges arrived. Jagged bits of snow now whip through the air, scratching at the windows. A draft creeps under the door and swirls around our feet. I pull my skirt tighter around my ankles. Amos Pollard has built the fires to a roaring blaze, but they do little to beat back the creeping cold pushed forward by this storm. Ephraim drops his arm over my shoulder.

Jonathan and Cyrus chose seats at the back of the room, away from prying eyes. Whether they are here in support of us, or out of curiosity, I cannot say. But both insisted on coming.

North sits off to the side. But Henry Sewell is at the front as usual, performing his duties as clerk. He and Joseph North avoid eye contact.

Rebecca and I are at the front, flanked by our husbands, and when Obadiah Wood bangs his gavel, she nearly jumps out of her skin. *These court appearances are wearing on her,* I think. She had hoped that charges would be declared in Vassalboro, that the case would move to trial in Pownalboro. She had hoped that she would not have to repeat the details of her ordeal to the greedy ears of our neighbors. But Obadiah Wood had dashed those hopes, and collectively the judges chose to move this hearing to our community. Though I suspect that decision has as much to do with Joshua Burgess as it does Joseph North.

"This special session of the court has convened on two matters and will not take other issues into consideration," Obadiah Wood declares. "If you are awaiting judgment on a pending case, your last issued court date remains in effect."

Neither Judge Parker nor Judge Hubbard look pleased to be in the Hook, I think, and the latter keeps glancing at the windows and the storm clouds barreling closer. No doubt they will have to secure rooms at the tavern tonight. They cannot ride back to Vassalboro in this weather.

"The two issues before the court today are the accusation of rape against Colonel North, and an inquiry into the death of Joshua Burgess—also an accused in the first matter. As these issues are connected, we have chosen to deal with them together."

I can see Isaac Foster stiffen in my peripheral vision, and Ephraim squeezes my hand.

"I would like to request an extension," North says, stepping forward, "as I did not have time to secure an appropriate legal representative."

Judge James Parker, an older man with speckled brown hair and hooded eyes, leans across the table. "Denied. You have had a month. But no matter. This is only a hearing, not a trial. No guilt or innocence will be determined today. We are here on the advice of the lower court"—he glares at Judge Wood—"to determine whether charges will be filed."

John Hubbard clears his throat. Adjusts his collar. He looks like an owl in an ivy bush, wig frizzled and slightly off-center. "Now, to the first matter, that of Joshua Burgess," he says. "It came to our attention some weeks past that the body of the deceased is stored in this town as it is impossible to bury him until the thaw. We examined the body upon our arrival but would like to question those who first inspected the corpse, one Martha Ballard, midwife, and one Dr. Benjamin Page. Please come forward."

I do as asked, my chin lifted, hands folded at my waist, but I don't look at Dr. Page when he comes to stand beside me.

"Who examined the body first?" Hubbard asks.

I lift my hand. "I did, Your Honor."

He peers at his notes. "And you declared the cause of death to be murder by hanging?"

"I did."

"And how did you reach that conclusion?"

I am careful to present facts, not feelings. "All of the injuries to Captain Burgess's neck were consistent with hanging. A clean break and substantial rope burns. But the injuries to the rest of his body were those of a man who has been beaten. Numerous cuts and bruises and broken bones."

"And have you ever seen a hanging before?" he asks, and I dislike the tone of condescension I hear.

"Yes." A single word, no explanation, but I hope the certainty in that one syllable makes it clear that I do know of what I speak.

"I see. And did you find a rope on his person?"

"I did not."

"And did you not think it odd?"

"No. It only reinforced my belief that he had been murdered. If Burgess had hung himself, he would have been found dangling from a tree—rope intact—and not lodged in the river."

Hubbard scratches notes in his ledger. "Thank you, Mistress Ballard." He looks up. "Dr. Page?"

"Yes?"

"Please explain your original assessment."

"In my studies at Harvard Medical School I performed dissections on more than one man found dead in the harbor. Water can do tremendous damage to the human body. And given that there was no rope present on the deceased, it seemed likely that the injuries could have been made in a postmortem state."

"And were you able to determine how long the body had been dead before entering the river?"

"I postulated death by drowning, sir."

"Was there water in his lungs?"

"I did not perform a dissection on this man so—"

"It is possible that he was deceased when he entered the river?"

"I did not think so at the time."

Hubbard looks at me. "Mistress Ballard?"

"Yes?"

"How long do you think he was dead before entering the water?"

"I doubt more than a few moments," I say.

"Why?"

"The bruises. He had dozens of them, and they were fresh. Most were pink and swollen. Some were bright purple. But none the green and brown of a fading bruise," I tell the court, then add carefully, "In my three decades of tending patients, I have never seen a dead man bruise. Blood pools after death, Your Honor. It doesn't rush to the skin's surface."

He looks at Page. Lifts an eyebrow. "Is that correct, Doctor?"

"It is, but—"

"Have you ever seen a hanging, Doctor Page?"

"I have performed more than one dissection on such—"

"I did not ask you if you had ever seen a *hanged man,* but a *man hanged.* Have you?"

"No."

"Thank you. You may both be seated."

"If I may, Your Honor?" Page takes a step forward.

"Yes?"

"You asked me to explain my original assessment. But I would like the court to know that it has since changed."

"Pray tell why that might be?" Hubbard asks.

"Pertinent information was kept from me during my initial examination."

"Do explain."

"It has come to my attention that the victim was in a violent confrontation just hours before his body was found. Had I known that, it would have factored into my assessment."

I am sometimes astonished at how still I can be while my heart is racing. How *dare* Page?

James Parker takes over the questioning now. "Do you know whom Burgess fought that night?"

Page lifts his chin. Dares one sideways look at me. "Indeed, I do. He fought with Mistress Ballard's oldest son, Cyrus."

It is as though someone has taken a boot to a beehive, the way the room begins to buzz. These judges are not so quick to lose control of a courtroom as North was, however, and Wood brings it back to attention immediately with three hard whacks of his gavel.

Taking his cue, Dr. Page returns to his seat. I watch him wind through the room and deposit himself at a long table beside a pretty young woman. She's the kind of girl who will always look childlike no matter how old she grows. Small. Narrow. Fine boned. All of this even though she is—as Samuel Coleman told me not long ago—quite far along in a pregnancy. She rests her hand on her swollen belly and looks at her husband as though he has descended from Mount Olympus just for this occasion.

"Mistress Ballard?"

I lift my chin. Turn back to the judges.

"Did you know of this confrontation earlier?"

"Not when I inspected the body, Your Honor. I found out later that same day."

"From whom?"

I clear my throat. "Members of my household."

"And was this information delivered in the form of a confession?" he asks.

"No. *Absolutely* not. My daughters attended a Frolic the evening before with their brothers. Burgess was also there. And when he tried to force my eldest girl to dance, Cyrus stopped him. There are at least ten people in this room who saw the altercation and can attest to those facts. They all saw Burgess leave the dance in good health, and that Cyrus did not follow. But I do not think it has any bearing on this investigation."

"Is that your *professional* opinion? Or your personal one?" he asks.

"Both."

"And after the dance? Where did your son go?"

"He escorted his sisters home, then went to bed."

"Can anyone account for where he was in the middle of the night?"

What a poisonous bunch-backed toad, I think.

"He was in bed when I was called to a birth. At two o'clock that morning," I say, and it takes a great effort to keep the venom from my voice.

Obadiah Wood looks at his copy of Henry Sewell's court record. He asks, "When you first gave your testimony on cause of death did you include that information?"

"I did not."

"Why? Your son beat the man."

"There's no law against it," I say. "Not when he was protecting his sister from unwanted advances against a man who had already been accused of rape. And besides, Burgess walked away from that altercation. As witnessed by many people. Whereas the man I inspected in this tavern would not have been able to walk at all. Whatever happened to him occurred after he left the Frolic."

"Is your son in the courtroom today?"

I feel Cyrus's presence before I see him. He's come to stand behind me now.

"He is."

"State your full name for the court, please," Obadiah Wood says.

There is a long, painful stretch of time in which Cyrus says nothing.

"He has no speech, Your Honor," I explain.

The judges look at one another, mystified.

"He cannot speak at all?"

"Cyrus is mute."

I cannot bear the wave of embarrassment that washes over his face. The way he clenches his teeth then straightens his jaw.

"Is he deaf as well? Can he understand our questions?"

Acid laces each syllable of my reply. "He. Is. Not. Deaf. He can understand all your questions, and he can reply with the language of his body or in writing. Cyrus is fully literate."

Of all the men on the bench, Judge Parker seems most fascinated by this turn of events. He leans forward, resting his elbows on the table. "Did you get into a physical altercation with Joshua Burgess the night before he died?" he asks.

Cyrus nods.

"Did you kill the man?"

He shakes his head. Plainly denying the accusation.

"Is it true that you can read and write?"

He nods.

"We will require a written deposition in your own hand—preferably by the end of the day—stating your version of events as they relate to the altercation with Joshua Burgess. Are you willing to provide that?"

Again, the nod.

The judges huddle together at their table, heads bent, voices low, and fingers tapping their notes. After several moments, Hubbard straightens and says, "Mistress Ballard?"

I take a step closer to the table.

"You are hereby recused as witness in any capacity with regards to the investigation of the murder of Joshua Burgess. Please take your seat." Once I have situated myself on the bench beside Ephraim, Hubbard continues. "However, the court has determined that further investigation is needed. No official cause of death will be declared at this time. But we will address the accusation that has been made against Mr. Isaac Foster, husband of the defendant." He looks at his docket. "A Sally Pierce has previously stated before this court that she heard Mrs. Foster confess that her husband murdered Joshua Burgess. We will hear from her first."

I hadn't realized that Sally was present. She comes forward as asked, her father at her side, looking everywhere but at me. Sally still wears her riding cloak and has it pulled tight across her chest. It's as though she's consoling herself with its weight and warmth.

"Miss Pierce?"

"Yes."

Even though Sally looks at Hubbard, her eyes are unfocused.

"Please tell us what you heard Mrs. Foster say."

Sally clears her throat, but her voice shakes regardless. "She was in the middle of a conversation with Mistress Ballard who had come to tell her that Joshua Burgess was dead. And I heard her say, 'Isaac did kill him.' Plain as day she said it. And I never meant to get anyone in trouble, but I must tell the truth. That is what my father says." She looks at her feet then, and I can barely hear her next words. "He says I have to."

"Mistress Ballard?"

I stand again.

"Were you there that day? And is that what you heard?"

"I was there. And I did give Rebecca the news. I thought it should come from a friend. But because Sally was listening at the door, to a conversation that was none of her concern, she only heard half of what Rebecca told me."

"And what was the other half?"

"She said, 'I *hope* that Isaac did kill him.' And can you blame her?" I look to Ephraim, offer the ghost of a smile. "I would hope no less of my own husband in that situation."

"Miss Pierce?"

Her hands begin to shake. "Sir?"

"Is it possible that you heard only part of what Mrs. Foster said?"

William Pierce sets his hand on Sally's shoulders and, like he did the first time they came to court, I see his thumb and forefinger pinch the muscle between neck and shoulder.

"I have told the court exactly what I heard." A wince. "*Sir.*"

Sally can feel the weight of my gaze, and her eyes shift to the side when I speak again. "Though I'm certain Miss Pierce is a *paragon* of virtue, and that she would never *purposefully* deceive anyone, I remain firm in my certainty that she misheard the conversation."

I reach over and grab Rebecca's trembling hand, give it a reassuring squeeze.

The judges confer quietly for a moment, then Hubbard says, "We will move on to the next matter."

Isaac Foster jumps to his feet. Takes a big step toward the table where the judges are sitting. "Are you not going to ask my wife what she said? Or let me speak in my own defense?"

Obadiah Wood clears his throat. "The record already states that you denied the accusation. We did not feel it needed to be clarified as you were . . . ah . . . so adamant in Vassalboro."

Isaac's rage slackens, but only slightly. "Then I expect you will also give my wife the same chance to defend herself."

"Very well, Mrs. Foster," Wood said. "Please clarify for the court exactly what you said to Mistress Ballard that day."

Rebecca stands. "It is exactly as Martha said. I told her that I hoped my husband killed Joshua Burgess. That I wasn't sad to hear he'd died. And I do not regret a word of it"—and then she gives Sally a withering look—"because it is *true.*"

Judge James Parker leans forward, his great hawk nose jutting out. "Thank you, Mrs. Foster. Your testimony will be recorded by the clerk, and we will now move on to the other matter at hand. Will you please tell the court what occurred on the evening of August tenth?"

I can tell that Rebecca is frightened in a way that she had not been in Vassalboro. Her body seems to curl in on itself, making her look smaller than she really is. She steps into the open area before the table.

"My husband was in Boston, and I was at home, alone, with our two sons. It was close to midnight, but I was awake, reading, when someone began pounding on the door."

"And did you open it willingly?" Parker asks.

"No, I did not."

"Had you bothered to turn the lock before retiring for the evening?"

"Yes," she says, and I hear a note of acid in her voice. "Though most people in this village don't bother doing so. The Hook is known to be safe. Or so I am told. But I was not raised in these parts, and I have long been in the habit of locking my doors at night, even when my husband is home. I happened to be standing in front of it when they kicked it in."

"Did you sustain any injuries?"

"A bruised cheek and a split lip. The door hit me here." She lays a palm against her cheek where the ghastly bruises had marred her skin. It is a wonder the impact didn't shatter half the bones in her face. "That's how I ended up on the floor."

Obadiah Wood asks, "Are you saying that it was Joseph North who entered your house that evening?"

"Yes. And also Joshua Burgess. I have not forgotten him simply because he is dead."

He nods. "Continue, please."

The entire tavern listens, breathless, as she goes on with her account. The two of them had disagreed at that point about the noise and whether she was, in fact, to be harmed. In the end, Burgess helped her to her feet since she couldn't manage that herself. Black spots floated in front of her eyes, and she couldn't carry her own weight. They were happy to do the carrying. Straight to the bedroom.

Halfway blind, nauseous, dizzy from the impact, Rebecca hadn't made much sense of the questions they threw at her.

When will your husband be home?

Stop that noise. You don't want to wake the children, do you?

Where's the lantern?

Rebecca had explained to them, as well as she could, that Isaac wasn't home. Wouldn't be home for weeks most likely. They needed to go away. They needed to come back later. She didn't understand what was happening. She didn't understand why they were pulling her slippers off. Why they were pulling her stockings off. Of course she didn't want the children to wake. Why would she? It had taken nearly two hours to get them to sleep in the first place. The lantern? Did she own a lantern? She couldn't remember. Her head throbbed. Her vision spun.

It is gut-wrenching to listen to her. The way her voice catches in her throat. To see her wipe snot on the sleeve of her blouse. I hate every one of these judges for making her do this. But she doesn't back down. She withholds nothing as she continues her story.

Rebecca began to fight when they tossed her to the bed. Lying down made everything hurt worse. Only when they'd gotten her stripped to her shift did she begin to understand what was happening. And by that time, it was far, far too late.

Rebecca's voice grows calmer the closer she gets to the end of her horrible tale. "It was Joshua Burgess who went first," she says.

Burgess had been reserved up to that point. Keeping a few steps behind as North dragged her to the bedroom, quietly watching from the shadows as North stripped off her clothing. He was the one who'd forced her legs open. And North had pinned her there, spread-eagle and trembling while Burgess slowly, methodically peeled away his own clothing. Boots. Woolen socks. Then he ripped off the lace hem of her shift so that he could tie his hair back. What had happened to her shift after that she didn't remember, but it was gone when he climbed on top of her.

I have never seen a courtroom so quiet in my entire life. The testimony is horrifying. Rebecca spares no detail. She doesn't bother with modest speech or her own reputation. She has decided to shock and scandalize the neighbors who have insisted on being present to witness this public humiliation. She means to punish their curiosity. And I wonder if this isn't the first time that Isaac has fully heard her account, for he alternately seizes with rage and weeps openly beside her.

"It hurt." Rebecca's voice finally breaks.

I want to reach for Rebecca, to scoop her up and hold her the way I hold my own daughters when they are sick or hurt. I want to shield her from this awful exposure.

Rebecca's eyes find a safe spot on the wall behind Obadiah Wood, and she stares at it. Her voice slips into a monotone, devoid of all shock, all pain. She sounds like she is in another room, in another country, as she continues.

While Burgess made relatively quick work of his assault, grunting into the pillow beside her head, then rolling off her body, North meant to punish her. He was not content with resignation. After the blinding pain in her head subsided, after she stopped thrashing on the bed, after she stopped begging for them to leave, and grew quiet, he went to work. And he systematically dismantled her composure. Left her trying to escape the confines of her own skin.

Traitor. Whore. Indian lover. Jezebel. Temptress. Wanton. He accused her of being all these things and more.

Rebecca lifts a trembling hand and sets it over her left breast. "He flicked it," she says. "Over and over until Burgess had to hold me down with his knees so I'd lie still. After a while I couldn't feel anything else but that flicking. But it was the 'Indian lover' he kept repeating as he flicked. I couldn't scream," she gasped, the tears coming. "What if I'd woken the boys? What if they had come in crying? What would I have said to them? What would those men have done to my babies?"

North had taken her then, with Burgess holding her arms against the bed so she could not scratch or hit. It was well into the deepest hours of the night by the time he exhausted himself.

You'll not say a word of this to your husband. Or to anyone else. Do you understand? North said, pulling on his trousers with the drowsy movements of a man satisfied with his work. She had deserved it, he said, for bringing those Indians into their town after the militia had worked so hard to beat them back into the wilderness. They'd had no choice but to teach her this lesson. North told her this even as he wiped the beads of sweat from his brow.

They left her alone and naked and weeping in the soiled sheets. And she lay there, unable to move her limbs, listening to them tromp through the hallway toward the door, laughing, jesting about the way she'd begged them to stop. For one excruciating moment they paused at the bottom of the stairs and her heart pounded in her chest with the terror that they might go in search of her children. But they didn't.

The three judges sit there and stare at her for several long moments, unsure what to make of her accusations.

Finally, John Hubbard speaks. "And did you tell anyone? That day or the next?"

Rebecca's eyes are deep pools of grief when she finally opens them. "Who could I tell? Judge North was the one who would hear my complaint."

"And yet you have a witness?"

"Yes. Martha Ballard."

Hubbard calls me forward again. "It seems you are a busy woman, Mistress Ballard. How came you to be a witness in all of these matters?"

"They fall under the duties of my profession. I do not seek out such experiences, Your Honor."

"Go on then, tell us what you know of Mistress Foster's claims."

Once again, I tell the court exactly how I found Rebecca, the same as I had in Vassalboro last month. I tell them of her injuries. I show them my diary and the entries I've made, along with the interactions I've had with Judge North since.

"Thank you, Mistress Ballard, for your testimony," Parker says. "We will hear from the defendant now. Mr. North?"

He steps forward.

"How do you plead in this cause?"

"Not guilty. I have done nothing to this woman. She has no proof. No witnesses to the act she claims happened. Nothing but a friend who saw her much later. I ask that you dismiss these charges. They should have never been brought in the first place!"

"It is worth noting," Judge Parker says, "that there *was* a witness to the purported crime, but he is now dead. And that is a fact that this court finds both curious and rather convenient for you."

"Am I being accused of murder now?" North asks, hissing the words through his teeth.

"I am simply stating an observation, Mr. North. And reminding you that we will pursue all avenues of investigation as it relates to both Mr. Burgess and this case—seeing as how they are intertwined." Parker looks to Henry Sewell. "Please enter Mr. North's not guilty plea in the court records."

"My wife can testify that I was home, with her, on the night these events allegedly took place," North continues.

Lidia has gone from looking gaunt in Vassalboro to positively ill now. Pale. Lips thin and pressed together. Two fingers constantly massage her left temple. "He was home," she says.

"I would ask you to consider my own reputation in this town," North tells the judges, "versus that of Mistress Foster and her husband. These accusations are nothing more than a bit of petty revenge, a way of getting back at me for dismissing him as minister. He is *suing* the town for unpaid wages! Need you any more proof of their duplicity than that?"

I watch Lidia sink back into her seat and wonder how often she is awake these days past eight o'clock. How easy it would be for North to slip from bed with his wife unaware.

And so it goes, back and forth, becoming less about what happened to Rebecca and more about her husband versus the man accused of raping her. As if Isaac had any bearing whatsoever upon what happened to Rebecca in August. As if his insistence on being paid the full amount agreed to in his contract has any relevance on the situation.

"Have you anything else to add regarding the actual charges, Mr. North?" Wood finally interrupts.

"No."

"Then please take your seat. The court will now recess for a short time so that we might deliberate."

He bangs the gavel, then he, Parker, and Hubbard retreat to the storeroom to converse amongst themselves.

I sit with Rebecca. Hold her hand. We wait as the onlookers mill around the tavern and refill their mugs. Some go out to use the privy, sending a blast of cold air into the room every time they open the door. Others stretch their legs.

After some time—ten or fifteen minutes perhaps—the judges return to the tavern and lift their faces to Rebecca Foster. John Hubbard bangs his gavel.

"The Court of Common Pleas has decided that charges *will* be brought against Joseph North," he announces.

James Parker adds, "However, it remains the duty of the court to point out that there are no witnesses who actually saw Mrs. Foster being *accosted*. And without such a witness it would not be lawful to try this man in a capital case that could result in his death. It is therefore the decision of the court to declare charges of *attempted* rape."

The tavern erupts. People leap to their feet. Some clap their relief. Others shout their outrage. But I cannot bear to look at Rebecca, cannot bear to witness her heartbreak a second time. So I look to Ephraim instead and see everything I feel reflected in his eyes. Regardless of what might happen in the coming trial, Joseph North will not hang for what he did to Rebecca.

Obadiah Wood bangs his gavel to settle the outburst caused by this news. "We are not finished. It is our decision that this case go to trial before the Supreme Judicial Court three months hence. The defendant shall be remanded to the jail yard at Fort Western until that time. Colonel North, please step forward and acknowledge that you understand the charges, the parameters of your constraints at Fort Western, and that you will be present for trial."

Wood looks around the room. "Colonel?"

Lidia North remains in her seat, but her husband is not with her. He is not in the tavern at all.

*

I sit in my workroom, journal spread open on the desk, and write as the storm barrels in from the east, across the Atlantic, a monster building out in the ocean and pushing all that wind and snow across the coast and inland. Building, building until it is a wall of white that swallows everything in its path.

We are home now, and the household bustles around me. Hannah and Dolly make dinner while the men—Barnabas included—stomp in and out, with armloads of wood to prepare for what is coming. They close the shutters and build the fires, piling in warming stones that can be wrapped and taken to bed later. Ephraim insisted that Barnabas stay the night with us instead of riding the four hours back to Vassalboro. Apparently, I am not the only one who has grown fond of the boy.

Beside the hearth is a chessboard and—between chores—Cyrus and Barnabas take their turns. They've been at it for hours, quietly battling each other. I've never seen Cyrus lose the game, but something tells me that I should not discount Barnabas Lambard. Hannah and Dolly ignore them, of course. They've seen pissing contests before.

I finish the entry by stabbing my quill into the paper.

Colonel North fled from judgment and could not be found.

BALLARD'S MILL

I am wakened by a hand on my shoulder, shaking. Gently. A whisper. Warm breath on my ear. I hadn't slept well, too aware of the wind seeping through the chinks in the walls, of the plummeting cold, and the snow that was falling, not like a blanket, but like a burial shroud.

"Come look," Ephraim says, and I feel him reach for my hand.

He pulls me to my feet. Steps close as I wobble, his hands roving over my thin shift. Through my hair. Down my back. Across my bottom. A laugh, and then he leans over and pulls a blanket off the bed. Wraps it around my shoulders as I stand unsteadily beside the bed, still wondering why he's woken me.

Ephraim leads me through the dim house, our fingers intertwined. He's lit the candles and built the fire, but it can't yet be five in the morning and the household is still asleep, everyone in their beds, except for Barnabas who snores on a pallet by the fire. Or perhaps he only pretends to sleep. As I blink away the cobwebs in my eyes, I see his head shift toward us as we walk by, but his eyes remain closed.

A light sleeper, then, I think. *A cautious man.*

The chessboard lies beside him on the floor, unchanged from last night.

When we reach the door, Ephraim nudges me to the side, then pulls it open. Before me stands a wall of white nearly to the lintel.

Only six inches of pale, pewter clouds can be seen above the snow-drift. I've seen drifts pile up to three, maybe four feet. But only once before have I seen anything like this.

"It's still coming down," he says. "Not as heavy as earlier. But it doesn't show any signs of stopping."

I reach out a hand, palm flat, and press it into the snowbank. It is soft, but frigid, and my hand sinks in, leaving a print. I am awake now, aware of what my husband has been trying to say these last minutes.

"It's like it was in Oxford," I tell him.

He nods. Smiles. "So you remember, then?"

"Like that is a thing I will ever forget."

Ephraim Ballard takes my hand and leads me back to bed.

Thirty-Five Years Ago

OXFORD, MASSACHUSETTS

"What did you say?"

My cheek rested against Ephraim's bare chest, but still, even that close, I barely heard what he'd whispered. My hand lay on his heart, and he ran his fingers through my hair slowly, letting it slide through and fall back to pool around my bare shoulders. The sun wasn't up, but even if it had been, we wouldn't have known, for the storm still raged outside and the sky was as black as it had been for two days.

The cabin was warm, however, as were we.

The fire burned low and red in the hearth, casting a dreamy glow across the bed. Occasionally a draft of frigid air slipped beneath the door, and he pulled me closer, letting his skin warm mine. Nothing lay between us now. I'd taken off my shift with trembling hands the night before, and it remained on the floor, where it had fallen, when it slid over my shoulders and pooled at my feet.

"Hmm?" he asked, realizing only now that I'd asked a question.

I propped myself up on my elbow and looked into his cloudless eyes. "You said something. What was it?"

"Ah." I couldn't be sure, but I thought he blushed. "More Solomon."

"Oh."

Ephraim had been whispering the Song of Solomon into my ear

all night, calming me with ancient words that astonished me with the depth of their romantic understanding.

"You are altogether beautiful, my darling," he repeated and pulled me back against him.

As promised, Ephraim had not tried to seduce me in the first days and weeks of our marriage. He had waited patiently. Kissed me whenever he pleased, and held me through every long, cold night. He waited, first until I bled, and then longer, until we were both half-mad with desire. I had wondered at first if his determination was so that he would know whether any child conceived was his or not. Surely that mattered to a man. But soon it became apparent that it was an assurance he wanted *me* to have. To know, one way or another. To remove a question that might linger for a lifetime. And we knew, plain enough, a week after we were married. And that of course made our situation less complicated for a few days. Gave us a chance to learn how to live in the same space without constantly dancing around the tension of not yet having consummated our marriage. But soon my cycle ended, and January came and brought with it the kind of cold and weather I associate only with this month. It brought *winter* and forced us inside except for all but the briefest tasks. It forced us into prolonged closer proximity.

As promised, he let the decision be mine. And because I did not know how to surrender, I waited too long. Even then he did not complain. But last night, preparing for bed, I *knew*. We had been married a month, and, in that time, Ephraim Ballard had proved what kind of man he was. I had nothing left to fear. It was time for me to decide what kind of wife I would be.

So I did.

But first I procrastinated, brushing my hair as I sat on the small stool before the fire.

I let him strip naked—as he always did—and climb into bed. I let him sit there and watch me for several long moments. Let his eyes run over everything that he could see. Then I set down my brush and went to stand before him. The look on my face must have been clear because he froze. Didn't draw a breath. Our eyes remained locked as I tugged my shift off one shoulder.

"Are you sure?" he asked, voice husky.

I answered by baring my other shoulder so that the thin fabric could fall away. He said nothing as he gazed. Said nothing for long, uncountable seconds. But when Ephraim Ballard finally found his voice, I understood why he chose Song of Solomon as the text for my reading lessons. The words themselves were a primer, a perfect, exquisite example of how a man ought to take his wife to bed for the very first time. And, as Solomon had, Ephraim began at the top and worked his way down, illuminating the meaning of each line I'd so carefully transcribed into my book over the last month. Words that had seemed practical and agrarian but, when experienced as action, were nothing short of erotic.

How beautiful you are, my darling. . . .

Your eyes . . . your hair . . .

Your lips . . . your mouth . . .

Your neck . . .

Your breasts . . .

I will go my way to the mountain of myrrh and to the hill of frank-incense. . . .

You are altogether beautiful, my darling. . . .

You have made my heart beat faster with a single glance of your eyes. . . .

Your lips, my bride, drip honey. . . .

May my beloved come into his garden and eat its choice fruits. . . .

These were the words whispered in my ear as I surrendered to every gaze and touch last night while the storm fell upon us, roaring its approval. Never have I been so warm. Never have I felt so safe. And then, hours later, he pulled me tighter as though terrified I would slip from our bed and break the spell. He whispered the words again, intent on kindling this newly wakened desire, determined to stoke it into a blaze that consumed us both.

4

MIDWIFERY

FEBRUARY 1790

A sad tale's best for winter.

—WILLIAM SHAKESPEARE, *The Winter's Tale*

THE PARSONAGE

Monday, February 1. A snowstorm . . .
Thursday, February 4. It snowed . . .
Saturday, February 6. A very cold day . . .
Sunday, February 7. Clear and excessive cold . . .
Monday, February 8. Terrible, cold, and windy . . .

"God, I hate winter," I say, closing the journal and massaging my temples with the tips of my fingers. It is both a prayer and a curse, and I don't feel guilty for either. For nearly two weeks there has been little but cold and snow and a long, brooding oppression.

So, when the letter arrived this morning, summoning me to the Fosters', I was not annoyed. The fact that it came from a lawyer also piqued my interest.

Dear Mistress Ballard,
If it presents no challenge, would you be kind enough to meet me at the parsonage for tea this afternoon. 1:00 sharp.

Respectfully,
Seth Parker, Esquire

"Tell your father that Mr. Parker has summoned me to the Fosters'," I say, passing through the kitchen.

Hannah looks to the window where the snow is still piled high, then back to me as though I said I was going to jump off the barn roof. "It's horrid out there."

"Staying here won't make it any less so."

*

Rebecca Foster is six months pregnant and finally showing. With her first child it took longer, but with each subsequent child, her body has revealed the secret earlier. I marvel at how this varies woman to woman. Some blossom in the early months, and others wait until the final weeks.

Rebecca does not often leave her house now, and without Sally Pierce to help, the parsonage feels dusty and cluttered. It feels—perhaps not unjustifiably—as if its mistress has given up. Rebecca has made tea for those assembled, however, and there is fresh bread with butter and jam to go with it.

The two young Foster boys—blond like their mother—wander into the sitting room for a piece, then skip out with sticky fingers. I watch them go, wondering if they can sense the heaviness in the room or if they are oblivious to adult concerns.

"Thank you for coming, Mistress Ballard," Seth Parker tells me. "I hope it wasn't too difficult getting here."

"I managed well enough."

Esquire Parker is one of a handful of lawyers in Hallowell, but like most men in the area, he dabbles in both river trade and farming. There isn't much need for lawyering in this part of the world, so he isn't often called upon in that capacity. But now that the hearings are complete and charges—albeit minimal—have been filed, the Fosters need someone to represent them at trial.

"I have already taken Rebecca's deposition," he says, pointing to a small stack of papers on the little table in front of him. Beside it rests another blank stack, along with ink pot and quill. "If you will tell me everything you remember, I will write it down. You have only to make your mark at the end."

"I can write it myself," I say, voice clipped with irritation. "And sign my name as well."

"Ah. That's right. You keep a daybook."

"Yes. For many years now. I am quite comfortable with a pen."

"Very well then." He slides paper and quill across the table so they rest in front of me. "This will be submitted as evidence to the court in Pownalboro."

As I situate myself in front of the paper, Isaac Foster makes his way into the room.

"Mistress Ballard," he greets me, then kisses the top of his wife's head. He stands before the fire, warming his rump. It is winter after all, and none of us are ever truly warm unless butted up to an open flame.

Isaac pours a cup of tea as I begin my deposition. "Henry Sewall visited us yesterday," he tells Seth.

"Is that so?"

"He brought a letter."

I look up sharply, pen hovering over the paper. "Why?"

"A preacher by the name of Cobb has been offered my position. I am told he will start sometime in May. And he requires a permanent home as part of his salary. We have until the end of April to find new accommodations."

"But Rebecca is due to deliver at the end of April," I argue.

There is a note in Isaac's voice that I cannot identify. "A fact not taken into consideration."

"Where will you go?"

Seth Parker leans forward, his elbows resting on his knees. "Nowhere yet. I am filing an appeal citing conflict of interest given that Joseph North is the head of the church committee."

"And failing that?" I ask.

Rebecca pushes against her stomach, wincing. "To Fort Western most likely. To rented rooms."

"There has to be another option," I say.

"I can assure you that I am exploring every option on their behalf, Mistress Ballard. But if you truly want to help, the best thing you can do is finish your deposition."

Conversation predictably drifts to the weather as my gentle

scratchings continue. The storms. The snow. The ice that rises higher along the banks of the Kennebec. The terrible state of every road leading in and out of the Hook. *Why are men so obsessed with roads? I will never understand.* It is inane background noise to each deliberate word that I etch onto the paper.

Several minutes later, I set the quill down and flex my hand. "And how is your wife, Mr. Parker? Is she well?"

"Ellen? Aye. Right as rain I'd say. Why do you ask?"

"No reason. Do pass along my greetings." Whatever ailment caused Ellen to seek out Doctor has either resolved itself or remained hidden from her husband's knowledge.

I hand the paper to Mr. Parker and watch as he considers my neat, concise handwriting. After a moment he gives me an approving nod. "Thank you again for coming, Mistress Ballard."

"Of course. But since I'm here, I'd like to examine Rebecca. Make sure all is well with her and the child."

Child.

That's the point when Rebecca flinches, her mouth tightening at the corners. She turns away from her husband and heaves out of the chair, passing him on the way to their bedroom without a word.

*

Rebecca lies on her bed, in a cotton shift, as I move my fingers over her swollen belly, prodding here and there.

"I am sorry about the letter," I tell her.

"As am I."

"But the trial—"

"Will do no good." Rebecca looks at me, those brown eyes certain. "You saw what happened at the last hearing. Even if they find him guilty it will be for *attempting* a crime, not *committing* one. There is nothing left for us in the Hook. Isaac is the one fighting to stay. I'd rather start over. Somewhere new. Where no one knows what happened to me."

I open my mouth to argue, but she interrupts.

"You know I'm right. You just like me too much to admit it."

Oh, the *burning* that tears induce. Sometimes worse than fire. "You are right," I whisper. "I *hate* that you are right."

One of the greatest skills that I have as a midwife is to sit in silence. I cannot count the number of times that I have wordlessly held a hand as grief explodes in a room. The only antidote to this kind of despair is to create a bulwark of immovable calm. To sit and be. To pray and offer comfort. To watch the shadows cut tracks along the wall as the sun slowly moves across the sky. To say nothing when there are no words that can console. And it is in this laden silence that I feel the child in Rebecca's womb move. A thumping, strong and steady. I remain where I am, fingers spread wide across her belly, concentrating on the rhythmic taps that rise from her body—that shifting, squirming proof of life.

I wait a full six heartbeats before whispering, "How long since it quickened?"

"Not long. A month or so."

"You didn't tell me."

"I hoped it would stop." Rebecca turns away. Looks at the wall. "I still do."

*

A few moments later, I stand outside the parsonage, breathing cold air through my nose to calm my mind and still the rage. *It isn't fair.* This is what runs through my mind over and over like a dog chasing its tail. It isn't *fair.*

Vengeance might be the Lord's, but hasn't He appointed men to be the arbiters of justice? Where is it for a woman like Rebecca? And who can bring a judge to justice? As I trot up the narrow channel of packed snow on Water Street astride Brutus, a thought occurs to me—so quickly that I do not have time to reject it: if Joseph North cannot be hanged for raping Rebecca Foster, perhaps he can be hanged for killing Joshua Burgess?

*

Saturday, February 13—Clear and cold. The ice builds at Fort Western. I was summoned to appear this day at the house of Isaac Foster to give evidence to what I know concerning the cause there to be tried. Came home in the early evening. Mrs. Densmore here to cut me a gown of green silk. She tells me that the wife of James Bridge was delivered at the first hour this morning of a dead born son who is to be interred this evening. Doctor Page was the operator.

I am not angry that Clarissa Stone didn't call for me. There are other midwives, and she could have sent for any of them. But Peggy? After what Page did to Clarissa's child? There is no excuse for her pride. She had all the information she needed.

I can count on one hand the number of men I have ever truly hated in my entire life. But Benjamin Page is near the top of that list. Billy Crane takes first place. Followed closely by Joseph North. But since Page's arrival in Hallowell, he has been nothing but a pestilence. God, I'd strangle him with my bare hands if I could.

BALLARD'S MILL

"Why is he here?" Ephraim asks.

I've come down to the mill with lunch for Ephraim. He's been working on the waterwheel since dawn and somehow looks both sweaty and freezing. The wheel is still locked in the frozen creek, and my husband has determined that now is the best time to make much-needed repairs to several of the wooden paddles that have rotted or cracked.

"Barnabas?" I ask, looking over my shoulder. "I rather thought his reasons would be obvious."

I hand Ephraim his plate, but he sets it down on a stump. "He hasn't come courting," Ephraim says. "Look at him."

Barnabas is haggard. He's ridden hard and long with the wind at his face. His cheeks are red, his lips chapped.

"Perhaps he was in a hurry to see Dolly?"

Even as I say the words, I know that my husband is right. As always.

Ephraim pulls his mouth into a hard line. "That boy doesn't want to be here. He's scared."

Barnabas has brought the wagon. Lately he's been coming on horseback, but those were social calls. I've only ever seen him on that wagon—the one with the iron loop affixed to the sideboard—twice.

Ephraim takes a menacing step forward as Barnabas jumps down from his seat. He looks like he's swallowed a gallon of vinegar. He takes off his hat. Whacks his thigh. Looks to the clouds. Squints. Shakes his head as though arguing with the Almighty.

"Why are you here?" Ephraim demands.

It is the first time I have ever seen Barnabas Lambard out of sorts. He nearly chokes on the words. "I'm here to arrest your son for the murder of Joshua Burgess."

Ephraim's voice is low and deep. Dangerous. "Which. Son?"

The word must be painful for Barnabas, like cut glass on his tongue, and he struggles to spit it out.

After a moment, he looks to me as though pleading for help. It's a mercy he won't get. Not today.

"Cyrus."

*

The only thing our oldest child has ever wanted, in all his life, is to go to sea. Though I know he'd deny it, I suspect Cyrus wants to be a pirate. To climb rigging and perch in a crow's nest and see exotic locations. He wants—more than anything—a life of adventure. A life filled with salt air and blue water and a fist shaken in defiance at the stormy horizon. He's been robbed of this future, however, and makes do with sailing the Kennebec and navigating his father's logs to ports downriver. In winter, however, he is landlocked. And his only solace is Mill Pond, where he goes to fish almost every day.

So we trudge up the path—the four of us—in search of him. Ephraim. Barnabas—who looks as though he'd rather eat a pile of steaming entrails. Me. And Dolly. She'd seen him arrive. Of course she had. That girl looks for him like a first-century believer waiting for the return of Christ. So no sooner had we passed the garden gate than she came rushing out the front door, drying her hands on a kitchen towel.

But the girl is perceptive—more so than any seventeen-year-old I've ever met—and she knows something is wrong. No one will answer her questions, however, and now she's angry as well.

"Where are we going?" she demands. "Why is he here? Why won't anyone answer me?"

I give her a warning look that makes her swallow the next question, and I can see her anger turn to fear in the span of a single blink. She finally understands.

"He wouldn't dare," Dolly whispers. She grabs my forearm and squeezes hard. "He *wouldn't*."

"It takes decades to really know a man, Dolly. And you've barely had weeks with that one. I'd suggest you not assume anything about what he will or will not do."

It's a hard lesson, but it's best she learn it now.

Dolly falls silent, then falls into step behind me on the narrow path. Ephraim leads the pack. Twice Barnabas looks back at me and—judging by the look on his face—believes he's being led into the woods as a ritual sacrifice. I can't say the thought hasn't crossed my husband's mind, but mostly I suspect he wants to see if Barnabas has the courage to follow through with his mission.

Mill Pond is a half mile north of the house and sits in the middle of a sprawling meadow. The pond isn't all that big—only two acres across—but is quite deep in the middle and is the happy home to many hundreds of blueback trout. Cyrus discovered it within a day of our moving to this property eleven years ago, and promptly claimed it as his own. He stands in the center of the pond now, atop two feet of ice, holding a fishing line in each hand. He's kept the hole open all winter, and its sides are jagged from constant chipping with the hatchet.

Cyrus sees his father first and offers a broad smile. But Barnabas steps into the clearing next. Then me. Followed by Dolly. And the smile melts off his lips. When his eyes sharpen and his fists tighten over the fishing poles, I know he's understood the reason for this interruption.

Cyrus twists his lips in displeasure.

Mouths some profanity that will never reach the air.

Nods.

Then he pulls both poles from the water and trudges back across the ice. We watch as he collects his fishing paraphernalia—bucket, poles, string, hooks—and strides toward us.

He drops everything at Ephraim's feet, and then his hands move in a flurry: thumb pointing at himself, flat hand slicing through the air as though to say *didn't*, and then fist to the side of his neck in imitation of holding a noose.

"I know," Ephraim says. "But Barnabas here believes that you did."

"No. I do not. But arresting you is the job I've been given. Dr. Page's testimony was *damning*." He looks to the side and glares at me, as though I should have shared what I knew about the beating long ago. "And the court has ordered that I bring you in."

Cyrus studies him quietly, then turns to Ephraim and flaps his hand, indicating he's free to interrogate the boy.

"And where will you take him?" Ephraim asks.

"Vassalboro. He'll have to appear before Judge Wood. But once he posts bail, he'll be remanded to the jail yard at Fort Western."

"And what proof do they have?" Ephraim asks.

"Proof? None so far as I know. Only the testimony of Dr. Page, which was confirmed by at least five other people. So the court will look into the matter."

His voice is calmer now that he's had the chance to explain everything, but Barnabas still seems unsettled. He likes Cyrus. I know this for a fact. And he's not looked Dolly in the eye once.

She, however, hasn't stopped glaring at him since we arrived at the pond. "You cannot do this!" It's almost a shout, but not quite. Dolly isn't the type to descend into hysterics. But she does have a temper, and she's letting Barnabas see it for the first time.

He winces.

Then takes a deep breath.

Barnabas takes a step toward Cyrus. "I don't want to do this. Please believe that. But if you fight me, I'll have to fight you back."

I think of how handily he subdued James Wall. Barnabas, however, has never seen Cyrus throw a punch.

"When will he stand before Obadiah Wood?" Ephraim asks.

"Tomorrow."

"And the hearing?"

"At the end of next month. Friday, March twenty-sixth."

Dolly's head swivels back and forth as she takes in this conversation between her father and her suitor. And with every second that passes, her brows draw closer together and her cheeks burn hotter.

"No!" she says. "I will not have it. You will not arrest my brother. You said yourself he's done nothing wrong."

"I said that I don't *believe* that he has." Barnabas's voice is nothing but a whisper, and his eyes remain focused on Cyrus. He's waiting, watching to see if Cyrus will bolt. He is no longer the charming young man who has dined with us several times but rather the efficient, ruthless officer of the court.

"Dolly," Ephraim warns.

"Stop." She turns on her father, and he blinks in surprise. This may be the first time she has ever directly defied him. "You cannot let this happen."

"*This*," he warns, "has nothing to do with you."

"It has everything to do with me," she hisses.

Dolly leaves my side and trudges through the snow to stand in front of Barnabas. She isn't quite as tall as I am, but she raises herself to her full height nonetheless.

"Do not do this," she tells him.

"I have to." Still his gaze is pinned on Cyrus.

"*Please.*"

"You don't understand. I have—"

"I understand *perfectly.*"

I'd wondered perhaps if her feelings for Barnabas were rooted in infatuation. He is the first man who's ever paid her serious attention after all. And that tends to addle a girl's mind. But no. I hear it there in her trembling voice. She cares for him. But she loves her brother.

"If you arrest him, I will never speak to you again. Not one time. *Ever.*"

It's the wrong thing to say. And she knows it the moment the words have slipped into the cold, brittle air. But she is stubborn, like me, and won't back down now that she's taken a stand.

His eyes shutter and his spine stiffens. My husband was right. This has nothing to do with Dolly. And the fact that she's inserted herself into a matter of the court has disappointed Barnabas Lambard.

His voice is as cold as river ice when he answers, "I am sorry to hear that."

Barnabas doesn't see the slap coming. I'd guess he hears it before he feels it. But by then she's turned away and is marching down the path toward the house.

He is dumbfounded.

But Cyrus is grinning.

And Ephraim can't decide whether to laugh or charge after his daughter.

So I'm the one to speak.

"Cyrus didn't kill anyone," I say.

"I know that." Barnabas's voice is strangled. And he spares one, longing glance at Dolly's retreating form. "I do. And it will bear out in court soon enough. You'll see. There's nothing. Not a single witness who saw him near Burgess after the Frolic."

"Then why is the court doing this?"

"To prove that they've followed through on the matter. That they were thorough. In case questions are asked."

"*Are* questions being asked?"

"Yes. But not about Cyrus. The concern is to do with North. He got away, and they don't want their authority being called into question. More has happened in this county during the last four months than in the last four years. Every single judge on that court is under a lot of scrutiny."

"From whom?"

"The Supreme Judicial Court."

"So my son has fallen prey to politics?"

"I wish I could say it isn't true."

Ephraim narrows his eyes. "And you're willing to be part of this?"

"I'm the sort of man who does my job, Mr. Ballard," Barnabas says, directing his gaze briefly to my husband. "If nothing else, I hope you can respect that."

After that one quick glance he turns his focus back to Cyrus. It's like he's preparing for the fight. Wagering if it will be man to man, or two against one. I can see he's not pleased about either option. But he is ready for them.

"Are you going to fight me?" he asks Cyrus.

It would be one hell of a fight. And were they other men—*any* other men, actually—I might pay to see it.

The woods are quiet. So quiet I can hear the breath of everyone present. There is no wind. No birdsong. No chatter of squirrels or the sliding of snow from pine boughs.

My oldest child takes a step forward.

He balls his fists.

He grins, mischievous, and damn it all if I don't realize he's enjoying this.

Then Cyrus holds his hands out, wrists pressed together, and waits for Barnabas Lambard to bind them with a rope.

WHITE SADDLERY

The saddle shop is all but hidden from the road. It sits a block off Winthrop Street in the middle of the Hook, accessible only by a path through the snowdrifts. It is attached to a small, timber home with wooden shingles, and I can hear the *tap-tap-tap* of a leather punch, then the clean *whoosh* of a strap cutter as I lead Brutus through the narrow channel of dirty snow. The entire place smells of leather. Not like a tanner's shop, all rank and fetid with tallow and carcass, but rich and burnished. Like belts and bags and boots. Jeremiah White crafts other things as well: reins and gloves, mostly. But he makes his real living on saddles. I still use the one I bought from him a decade ago, and I slide out of it as I dismount Brutus before the hitching post.

After unbuckling my satchel, I go left to the front door since my business is not with Jeremiah today. But the door swings open before I can knock.

I haven't seen Rachel Blossom since I found her, Clarissa Stone, and Peggy Bridge gossiping that day at Coleman's Store. She pulls up short when she finds me on the step. Then, glancing behind her, she closes the door.

"I want to apologize to you as well," she says, lifting her small, pointed chin in defiance, as though I think her incapable of such a thing.

"As well?" I ask.

"I've just apologized to Sarah for what we did that day. You were right. It was disgraceful, and I'm sorry."

She offers no defense for her actions, doesn't chase the admission with a *but,* and I respect her all the more for it.

"Clarissa and Peggy are your friends. It can be hard to speak up."

"It shouldn't be." She looks away. Blinks back tears.

When Rachel meets my gaze again, she sets a hand to her stomach and pulls her dress tight to reveal the small mound. I would have never noticed otherwise. She's maybe five months along.

"Will you still deliver this one? I won't call for Dr. Page. They shouldn't have either."

I pull Rachel close and wrap my arms around her. "Of course. It would be my honor. And I am sorry for Clarissa and Peggy. If they'd called for me, I would have come."

"I know." Rachel pulls away and clears her throat. "I like Sarah. I hope she'll let me visit again."

"I like her too. And I think she'd be a good friend to you."

Rachel bids me goodbye, and I watch her disappear around the corner of Winthrop Street.

I turn back to the door and knock but don't have to wait long before it is thrown back by a small woman with graying hair pulled into a tight bun.

"Martha!"

"Mistress White." I nod in greeting.

"Do come in." She wipes her hands on her apron and ushers me inside. "It has been too long since I've seen you. To what do I owe the pleasure of this visit?"

"I've actually come for Sarah. If you don't mind."

Alice White is startled to hear this but doesn't say so. "Of course. Busy day for her. She's in her room with the baby now. I'll get her. Please, have a seat."

I take one of the two polished wooden chairs before the window and tuck my satchel underneath. There is whispering in the other room. Urgent. Possibly frustrated. But I can't make out the words. After a moment Alice slips back out.

"She'll just be a moment," she says. "Don't mind me."

There is nowhere for the older woman to retreat, so she picks up her knitting, goes to the kitchen table, and makes a show of spreading out her yarn and needles.

Sarah White lives with her parents, still sleeps in the same bedroom she occupied as a child. Only now there is a cradle against the wall and a general aura of sadness permeating the house. After a few minutes she comes out, baby tucked into the crook of her left arm, as she tries to button her blouse with her other hand.

She joins me at the window while Mrs. White knits a pair of socks and pretends not to listen.

"It is good to see you," Sarah says.

"And you." I lift the plump little girl from Sarah's arms and fold back the blanket from her face. "You both look well."

"Forgive me for taking so long. I was nursing."

"I thought you might be."

"She eats so much. All the time! But it doesn't seem to matter. I am still making more milk than one baby can consume. It's"—she waves a hand in the air—"relentless."

"Consider yourself blessed. I've known more than one woman to go dry long before a baby is nine months. Nurse her for as long as you can. It will do the both of you a world of good."

Typically, I give this advice for the baby's health and also to help a young woman regain her figure. However, it does not appear that Sarah is struggling in that regard. Her dress reveals the same hourglass figure she sported before, if not a bit heavier on top.

Sarah looks at me, large eyes curious. "I heard about Cyrus. It's outrageous, what happened. Is he all right?"

Though I hate that news of his arrest has spread, I am encouraged by her interest.

"He's as well as can be expected. The jail yard is difficult in winter. So few hours between sunup and sundown. Hard to put in a full day's work. But I'm certain the charges will be dismissed. Cyrus had nothing to do with Burgess's murder."

She lowers her voice to a near whisper so her mother cannot hear. "You are certain it was murder?"

"I am."

"Good," she says, then smiles fondly at her daughter. "Good riddance to him."

"Sarah." I shift the baby in my arms and lean closer. "Did you ever have trouble with Joshua Burgess?"

"No more than anyone else. He could never keep his eyes to himself. But there was one time that he . . ." She blushes and turns to the window but looks more angry than embarrassed.

"He what?"

"Offered to pay me. So I'd go to bed with him."

My stomach twists into a knot. "Oh God. The fee you paid me last month . . . ?"

"No. I refused him of course. But he was steaming mad. Said I was a whore now and couldn't afford to be picky."

"Having a child out of wedlock doesn't make you a whore."

"I know that. And told him as much."

"Did he threaten you?"

"No. But if I was in town, he had a habit of being there. Always watching. It scared me. So I wasn't sad when I heard that he'd been killed. Less sad when I heard that you'd called it murder."

"You aren't alone in that."

"I think about it though, what he said, that I can't afford to be picky. He was wrong. I *have* to be picky." She nods toward the baby. "Because I have her now."

The child in my arms is astonishingly pretty. Round cheeks. Round eyes of the same blue gray as her mother's. Chestnut hair that is already flipping outward in small ringlets. Chubby, dimpled knuckles. And such an easy smile! She flashes her gums at me, delighted to be so readily admired.

"What have you named her?" I ask, my voice now at a normal level.

"Charlotte. After her grandmother." Sarah looks to the table, catches the flinch on her mother's face, and adds, "On her father's side."

"Ah." There is little more that I can say, for every word is a pitfall.

"Henry *will* come back." Sarah looks at me with the steely kind of defiance that only a jilted woman can summon. "That's what I'm waiting for. He *promised* to come back. Henry *is* going to marry me."

If wishes were horses, then beggars would ride, I think. It's what my own mother used to say when my fancies outgrew reality. I keep the saying to myself. It will do Sarah no good and would hurt her besides.

Charlotte is eight months old, and this is the first time I have heard Sarah speak the father's name, as she had refused to do so in the birthing room. I am curious, though. There are several Henrys in the Hook, and it's possible Sarah made up her story about the father being in the militia to protect a married man right here in Hallowell. Such a thing is not unheard of.

"Henry?" I prod.

Sarah knows what I'm doing. Knows that I am fishing for more. She lifts her chin. "Henry Warren."

I am immensely relieved. I know of no man in the Hook by this name.

"Major Henry Warren," she adds, "of the Boston militia."

That name takes a moment to settle in my mind. Like a rock dropped to the bottom of a pond. Then there it is, the realization of what she's just admitted.

Oh.

Major Henry Warren is the name of the man that Judge North gave the court as an alibi for the night that Rebecca was raped. That is the man who abandoned Sarah, with child, in ill repute. She sees the expression of dismay on my face but does not know the cause.

"He *will* come back," she insists.

I cup my hand at the back of Charlotte's head. Smile at her. She returns the grin in earnest, so happy she nearly jumps out of my lap.

"Is that why you didn't come to the Frolic?"

Sarah nods. "He wouldn't want me acting as though I am free."

Alice White watches me—I can see her in my peripheral vision— daring me to shut down this dangerous line of thinking that continues to seduce her daughter, but I keep my eyes on Sarah. That's who I came to see, after all. And it's none of my business what goes on between mother and daughter. I won't get in the middle.

"Well," I say. "I have an idea that might help you pass the time."

And I am afraid it will be a very long time, I think.

"What do you mean?"

"Something occurred to me when I saw you at the tavern last month—"

"I earned every shilling honestly—"

"I don't doubt that for a moment," I say, pulling the baby up and laying her against my shoulder. I pat until a raucous burp erupts and then—much to my astonishment—a tiny giggle.

"What then?"

"It has to do with Dr. Coleman."

Sarah waits, unsure where this is leading.

I clear my throat. "He is getting older. And his eyesight is starting to fade. That doesn't matter so much with the shop inventory. He has a system and knows where everything is. But it's becoming a problem with the ledgers."

"I don't understand what you mean."

"I think you might be of some help to him in that regard. He mentioned that he wants to hire a shop boy. Perhaps he would consider you."

"I am not a boy."

"I know."

Sarah looks down at her hands. Flexes her fingers wide, then curls them into a ball. "You know I canna read."

"Yes. Is that all?"

"All? You may as well be asking if I speak Latin."

"Well, that would do you no good whatsoever. Coleman is deeply prejudiced against all the Romance languages. He prefers English, it being of Germanic origins. And those letters are easy enough to learn."

"How?" There is suspicion but also interest in Sarah's voice and she leans forward slightly.

"I could teach you."

The next obstacle presents itself in the form of Alice White. "That is preposterous!" she says. "What an idea. Sarah has no need of sums or letters."

"Why shouldn't she learn?" I ask, turning to her pinched, angry face.

"There's simply no point."

"What ought she to do instead?"

Alice clamps her hand around the knitting needle. "Take care of her child."

"Of which she is doing a fine job. It's obvious just looking at Charlotte. And besides, reading won't interfere with that at all. But it might"—and I am careful here, as though performing a tight rope walk on the edge of a razor blade—"provide her *opportunities*. A source of income and a viable way to provide for her daughter on her own."

It is my turn to stare at Alice now. My eyes are wide, my lips pursed, daring her to contradict me.

It might keep her out of trouble, I want to scream. *It might distract her from this fool's hope of ever seeing that baby's father again.* I only admit the real reason to myself, however. *And Cyrus cannot court her if she cannot read.*

Alice is clever enough to understand my stern look. "How would you even go about it?" she grumbles.

I hand Charlotte back to her mother and bend down to pull a small book out of my medicine bag. "The same way I learned," I tell her. "And the same way I taught each of my children."

I hold the book out for them to see. The cover reads, *The New England Primer: or An easy and pleasant guide to the art of reading.*

There is a hungry look in Sarah's eyes but uncertainty in her voice when she asks, "Don't you think I'm a little old to learn?"

"Not at all. I was about your age when I did."

Sarah wrinkles her brow. "Who taught you?"

"My husband," I say. "After we were married."

BALLARD'S MILL

Lidia North is in terrible pain. The headaches have increased in frequency, and she has long since run out of tonic. That's why she's come all the way out to Ballard's Mill without her husband's knowledge or consent. His escape from Hallowell last month made that part easier, no doubt. But God only knows what she's done to assuage the unrelenting pain in the meantime. Often, when the aches descend upon her, Lidia shuts herself in a dark room and goes to bed. Sometimes for days on end. I have seen her only three times since September when she purchased her last bottle: once when she and North passed by on their way to Vassalboro, and twice in court.

The sky is dark and gloomy, fat, lazy snowflakes drift to the ground like autumn leaves, but Lidia shades her eyes with one hand as though the sun is shining. She stands on the threshold, uncertain. From my seat before the fire I can see that her eyes are watering from the pain, that Lidia is dizzy and nauseous from her illness. Her hands shake. Her face is pale. But still, I cannot bring myself to welcome Judge North's wife into our home. Twice now the woman has lied on his behalf.

It is Ephraim who remembers his manners. "Please, Mistress North," he says, "come in."

"Thank you."

Lidia removes her cloak and her gloves. Hands them to Ephraim. Then, with a cautious bob of her head, makes her way to where I sit before the fire and gingerly lowers herself into the opposite chair.

"Martha."

"Lidia."

Oh, this miserable dance. Pleasantries and politics. I want no part of it. So I am blunt, crueler than I intend, in my approach.

"You have run out of tonic?" I ask.

"Yes. Months ago. I can barely think most days. My head throbs as though someone is pounding on it with a hammer. I cannot sleep. I can barely eat. *Please*"—Lidia sets a leather purse on the small table between us, and I can hear the metallic clink of coins—"I will pay you anything."

Though we have been neighbors for many years, Lidia and I have never been close. Certainly not *friends*. We have always been cordial, however, each respecting the other's station. What bothers me most about the woman—apart from her unyielding loyalty to a man I despise—is that Lidia North is a weak woman. Timid. Milquetoast. She has no metal in her spine, no opinions of her own. I need my friends to be *interesting*. To have vim and vigor.

I try to keep the judgment out of my voice. "May I ask you a question?"

"Of course."

"It has to do with your husband."

Lidia narrows her eyes but says, "All right."

"Major Henry Warren?"

"What of him?"

"Did he dine with you on August tenth?"

Her eyes narrow. "Yes."

"You remember it? That night specifically?"

"I do not keep a guestbook if that is what you're asking."

She has no recollection of that night, I think. *She's only saying what North told her to say.*

"Were you awake, Lidia? You told the court that Joseph was home with you the entire time. But were you actually awake to see him there?"

"Of course he was home."

"That is not what I asked."

Lidia pulls her bottom lip into her mouth and chews on it with the edges of her teeth. "My husband does not cavort about. And I do not need to stay awake an entire night to know that for the truth."

"So you lied?"

"Of course not!" Her voice cracks. "He cannot have done the thing he is accused of."

I lean forward, press with my words. "Were you awake?"

It takes several long seconds for her to admit the truth. Lidia shakes her head.

"And will you admit to that at trial?"

She shakes her head harder this time. "I will *not*. And no one can force me to do so. I am a judge's wife, after all, and I know the law. I cannot be compelled to implicate my husband."

"Then I do not want your coin," I say, as I push the small leather purse back toward her, "because I will not make your tonic."

The woman is stricken. "How can you say that? How can you be so cruel?"

"If I am cruel, then I am only matching the example you set for me. You won't tell the truth about that night, nor would you tell the officer of the court where your husband has fled."

"I have already told them! A dozen times at least," she cries. "Joseph has gone to Boston on business."

"A very convenient fiction."

"The only fiction is the one being told by that Foster woman. She lies. Joseph would never lay a hand on anyone in the manner she claims. But do his friends and neighbors believe him? No! They've taken the word of a heretic's wife. A woman who hasn't lived in this village for five years. And now the very court my husband serves is after him? You tell me where the justice is in that, Martha Ballard. *Tell me*."

"I will tell you the same thing that I told the court. The same thing I saw with my own eyes. Rebecca isn't lying. The real cruelty is happening to her. And you would realize that if only you bothered to learn where your husband goes at night."

"I know Joseph! And I know the law," she says, half weeping and half spitting with anger, "and I don't have to tell anyone where he's gone. Not you. And certainly not that whippet of an officer from the court. Not if it means acting against my husband."

"Then come back when you are ready to tell the truth."

I hear the wind pick up outside and the snowflakes spin and hiss through the air, getting tossed against the windowpanes where they stick, then melt. In the distance I hear thunder.

Lidia North rises to her feet, unsteady, the tears openly running down her face. "You think you're *so* clever. That you understand everything. But you never ask the right questions, Martha. Certainly not of your little pet Rebecca. Do you even remember what it was like in the District of Maine before the war against the French and Indians? Do you? Because Joseph does. And he fought to clear the Kennebec of that vermin. Samuel Coleman was there. He fought with Joseph. *He* could tell you. But no, you only listen to Rebecca. And she brings them back into this town?" Lidia shakes her head. "That woman deserved whatever she got. But my husband had nothing to do with it. Tell her, Ephraim! Tell your wife that she is wrong. About everything. Tell her to make the tonic."

"My wife knows her mind, Mistress North," Ephraim says. Then he looks up and directly at me. "And I'll only tell her to follow her conscience."

Throughout the entire conversation, Ephraim has been sitting at the kitchen table, bent over his ledger, as he balances the accounts. But when Lidia walks across the room and lifts her cloak from the hook he goes to hold it for her. The physical effort to ride out to the mill must have cost every bit of energy she had in reserve.

"I thought better of you, Martha," she says, pulling on her gloves and stepping out the door.

Once it is shut, Ephraim turns to me. Leans against the frame. "So did I."

So rarely have I been scolded by my husband in these last thirty-five years that I can feel the heat seeping into my cheeks. "You would have me make her a tonic? When she has lied to the court? When those lies may well mean the difference in whether North faces some kind of justice or none at all?"

Ephraim goes back to the table and gathers his ledger, tucking it under his arm, and there is sadness in his voice when he says, "I did not take you for the kind of woman who would punish the innocent for the sins of the guilty."

CLARK FORGE

My conscience stings, and I've just changed into my riding skirt and cloak to go after Lidia—she can't have gotten far—when there is a pounding at the door. Huge fists pummel the wooden timbers. I can see them shake from ten feet away.

When I pull it open, John Cowan stands at the threshold stomping his boots on the flagstone to knock off the snow. He takes in my attire, nodding once in approval.

"Good," he says, "you're ready."

"For what?"

"To ride."

It takes a moment. My mind is elsewhere, and I wasn't expecting the young blacksmith's apprentice. So it's a full five seconds before I realize one of the Clarks needs my help.

"Which one of them is ill?" I ask over my shoulder as I go to get my medical bag.

"Mary," he says, then adds, "the baby. She's been having fits."

John Cowan has not bothered with the wagon this time, having instead ridden Charles Clark's draft horse, Sampson. Better suited for the plow, he looks ridiculous with a tiny saddle on his broad back, as though someone has tacked a square of leather to a Highland steer. He stamps at the gate, impatient.

"Let me get Brutus and we can leave."

"No need. Your husband's already gone for him."

"How—"

"I passed the mill on my way in. Told him you'd been summoned."

And sure enough, he has. For no sooner do I reach the garden gate than Ephraim comes down the path from the barn, leading Brutus. If he is sorry for his harsh words, he doesn't show it. He simply helps me into the saddle and wishes us well as we head for the lane. I look back once, hoping to meet his eyes, but he's already turned back to the mill.

I can handle being out of sorts with half the town, but this— Ephraim's disappointment—pains me. Sorting that out will have to wait, however.

At a full gallop, it takes less than ten minutes to reach the forge, and then John leads the horses to the barn for water and hay while I make my way to the house. I can hear Betsy Clark crying from the other side of the door. But still I knock, to be polite. Sometimes people would rather keep their tears to themselves. It's a choice I always try to give when possible.

Charles opens the door with one hand, and I see that he is holding the baby snug in the crook of his other arm. They both exhale in relief when they see me. "Come in," he says. "Please."

I shed my riding cloak. Set my bag on the floor. "What's wrong?"

"It started last night," Betsy says. "At first I thought it was just a shudder. You know how they do sometimes when they pass water? But then she did it again. Later. And again, in the middle of the night, and both those times her hippen was dry."

"It got worse this morning," Charles adds.

I take a seat beside the fire and reach for the bundle in his arms. He hands the baby to me, and I set her in my lap—head at my knees, feet against my belly—so I can unwrap the blanket. Mary Clark is still scrawny, but she's gotten longer and fills my entire lap now. "When was her last fit?" I ask.

Betsy sniffles. Wipes her wet cheeks with the back of her hand. "An hour ago. Right before we sent John."

The cabin is warm, and the baby doesn't protest when her swaddle is fully removed. There are no signs of injury. No lumps. No bruises. She looks at me with large, round eyes as I run my hands across her body. I feel her legs and back. Arms. I prod her torso gently and move my fingers up the side of her neck, around her ears. "Has she fallen? Perhaps off the bed?"

The baby is too young to roll over, but falling happens sometimes accidentally.

"No."

I press my fingers lightly against the base of her little skull. Temples. Crown. There doesn't seem to be any swelling. "Has she been dropped? Perhaps by one of the girls?"

Betsy shakes her head.

"Have they carried her to you? Maybe once when she was crying? Or just around the bedroom and you didn't know?"

She hesitates. Looks at Charles.

"I'll go ask," he says, and slips into the bedroom where their other two daughters are playing quietly out of the way, as they've been instructed.

"They would never," Betsy whispers.

"It wouldn't have been on purpose."

Charles comes out a moment later. "Neither of them dropped her. They swear on it."

"And you're certain they're telling the truth?"

"Yes. Both of them are terrible liars." He almost smiles. "They get it from their mother. None of them have a talent for it."

I am finished with my examination when it happens again. Little Mary Clark goes stiff and still in my lap, then there is a sudden jerking of muscles. Her eyes roll back until I can see the whites. Betsy wails. Charles curses. And I hold the child's head in one hand and reach into her mouth to make sure she hasn't swallowed her tongue and blocked her airway. She hasn't, so I pull her tight against my chest. I can feel all nine pounds of her quivering against my ribs.

Forty-five seconds. That's how long the seizure lasts. And when it is over, Mary doesn't cry. Her face is placid, and her eyes look to the ceiling, unfocused.

"I don't think this was caused by any injury," I say.

"What then?" Charles asks. It is strange to hear the voice of a big man crack in fear.

I think I know, but I cannot be sure. And I don't want to share my opinion yet. If I am correct, this is a disease I've never treated. A disease that might not even be treatable.

"Go fetch John for me," I tell Charles.

He hesitates, curious, but does as he's told and is soon back with his apprentice in tow. He's been at the anvil and wears a heavy leather apron. Sweat beads his brow.

"Mistress Ballard?" he asks.

"Is Sampson still saddled?" I ask.

"No."

"Then you can take Brutus. But be careful," I say, noting his startled expression. "He bites. And he's thrown every rider that's ever sat him. If you value your life, do not pull too hard at the reins."

John Cowan swallows once. "Where am I taking him?"

"To Burnt Hill. I need you to bring Doctor back with you."

"I did not think she made house calls." John looks at the baby. Back at me. "I was told you have to go to her, and I do not think that Mary . . ."

He doesn't want to say it aloud, and I do not blame him.

"Then let us see if she will make an exception. Tell her that Martha Ballard begs that she come with you."

*

It takes almost two hours before we hear pounding horse hooves. John escorts Doctor through the door with the kind of dazed expression I'd expect of a man who's just been strapped to the top of a carriage and driven off a cliff. I felt much the same way the first time I rode Brutus at full tilt.

"Please, come in," Charles says, motioning Doctor forward. "I'll help John with the horses."

It's been too much for Charles. He paced while his wife nursed the baby. He paced while I changed her hippen. He paced the entire time we waited. At one point, he tried to give me the fee for the child's birth—now overdue—but I'd refused, curling his fingers back over the coins and telling him to pay Doctor instead. He'd paced then, too, afraid of what that meant. So this task, the managing of beasts, is a relief to him. It is a thing he can *do*, and, like all men, that is where his instinct goes.

Just do something! And fix it if you damn well can, the mind of a man screams. By and large they are useless at a time like this. And it is a relief to all of us when both Charles and John are gone. Betsy relaxes, as does Doctor. Her riding cloak goes on the hook beside mine, and she takes a seat with us.

"Her name is Mary," I say, handing over the tiny bundle. "The fits started yesterday."

Doctor lays the baby on her lap, exactly as I had, but is far more cautious. She turns to Betsy and asks, "May I look at her?"

I am aware that this is a permission I never thought to ask.

"Of course," Betsy says.

Only once she's been granted approval does Doctor strip the child naked and begin her examination. It is a fascinating thing to watch. She looks for injuries, as I had, pokes and prods in all the same places. But then she turns the baby onto her forearm and runs the pad of her index finger all the way up her spine and back down again, checking for deformities in every vertebra. And all the while Doctor whispers to herself.

Several minutes into this, Betsy leans toward me. "What is she saying?"

I shrug. "I don't speak French."

Doctor's voice is deep and calming, and soon the whispers turn into song. A lullaby of some sort, hummed as she bends her ear to the baby's chest. Listens to her breath. I can see Doctor count each heartbeat with a tap of her finger.

The next seizure is not so violent as the last, but still, Betsy jerks in her chair as though she has been stung by a wasp. It may be a thing that she never grows comfortable with. Doctor, however, remains calm as Mary twitches in her lap. She holds the baby's arms down and I hear her counting in French, though I don't know the numbers past three.

"*Trois. Quatre. Cinq. Six. Sept. Huit. Neuf. Dix . . .*" She keeps going, until the seizure stops. "*Vingt-trois.*"

When the fit is over, Doctor dresses and swaddles Mary, then hands her back to Betsy. "Give her the breast if she will take it. It is the best thing for her right now. But pull away if she has another episode."

As directed, Betsy unbuttons her blouse and puts the baby to her nipple. Mary latches on, though not as forcefully as I would like.

Doctor looks at me, motions with her head. "Let us talk outside."

*

The snow has turned to rain, and we stand outside the cabin, unprotected from the downpour. Doctor slides back into her cloak. She pulls on her gloves. After a moment she nods to my riding skirt. "That is very practical."

"It was easy," I tell her. "I can show you how to make one."

"Next time, perhaps."

Charles stomps his way back from the barn. He glances at me, then hands Doctor a small leather pouch filled with coins. "Your fee," he says, then slips inside to tend his wife and child.

Doctor looks to the door where he has just disappeared. "He is a gentle man."

"He is learning," I say, but do not bother her with our history. "I've heard of children, adults as well, with that condition. But I don't know what it's called. I only know it as 'the fits.'"

"I believe she has the falling sickness," Doctor tells me, then adds, "Epilepsia. Sometimes they grow out of it. Sometimes they do not. Time will tell."

"You've seen it before?"

"A handful of times. In France. Mostly in children. Often the seizures come in clusters. Lots in a day. Or for several days in a row. Then nothing. Weeks can go by. Months before another one. If you are very lucky, they never come back after childhood."

"Are they deadly?"

"They can be."

"Is there no treatment? Nothing I can give her?"

"*Oui.* Valerian. Skullcap. Horseradish. In various preparations. There are other things too, but none of them grow here. And I wouldn't give them to a child regardless. *Les herbes* might do more damage than good. She is too young."

"When? How old must she be?

Doctor is unwilling to give an exact answer. "Beyond childhood . . . if she lives that long."

"Will it cause damage?" I tap my left temple with a finger. "Here?"

She gives me a weak smile. "I cannot say."

When I look up, Betsy Clark is at the window, Mary's little head against her shoulder, watching us. "I suppose we should go tell them."

"*Non.* You will tell her. They are your friends. Your patients. They called for *you.*"

"And I called for you."

"Which is why I came. Otherwise I would not have interfered."

"Thank you. I do appreciate it."

"I am glad to help," Doctor says. "The people in this town revere you. That is why they come to me, sometimes, you know."

"No. They go to you because you are more skilled."

She shrugs as though the point is up for debate. "They come to me when they want to preserve your good opinion."

"Not all secrets are bad," I argue.

"Just because a secret isn't bad doesn't mean it's harmless. Speaking of which, how is your other patient? The Foster woman?"

"As poorly as you would expect. And growing ripe with child."

Doctor sets one hand on my shoulder. Smiles. "*Bon courage.*"

Bon courage. Be of good courage. Courage is good, I think, wishing that I had more than a grain to spare.

As Doctor walks to the barn to collect Goliath, the rain turns hard and cold. Like stones tossed by an angry boy.

Hail.

Hell, why not make a bad day worse?

Epilepsia.

Epilepsy.

It makes so much more sense now. I have read of this disease in three different Shakespeare plays but didn't know what it meant. Brutus described Julius Caesar as having "the falling sickness." Othello raged and foamed as if he had "fallen into an epilepsy." And Kent told Cornwall in *King Lear* that he wished "a plague upon your epileptic visage." Leave it to the Bard to name a thing that has hitherto gone unnamed. This realization is no victory, however.

I turn back to the cabin to give Betsy and Charles the news.

*

Wednesday, February 24——Snowed and rained and hailed. I was called to see Charles Clark's daughter who is destitute by reason of the fits epilepsia.

THE ROBIN'S NEST

"I told Dr. Page that his services would not be required today." Mrs. Ney, the prim, gray-haired housekeeper, shuts the bedroom door behind me, adding, "He was none too pleased."

"I don't care what pleases him," Eliza Robbins says, breathing through her teeth, air hissing in and out as the contraction seizes her. She stands at the window, hands upon her belly. Even in travail I can hear the sophisticated lilt of a well-bred Englishwoman. "I won't let him anywhere near me."

"Your husband wasn't pleased either. He called for Dr. Page, after all," Mrs. Ney chides.

She rolls her eyes. "He has no say in the matter. Not unless he wants to push this child out."

Clever girl, I think. Despite the slow encroachment of modern obstetrics into the realm of childbirth, it is still—thankfully—a woman's prerogative to decide who will deliver her child. Although I worry this, too, will change.

Mrs. Ney appears unperturbed. "Dr. Page did not leave. He's keeping Mr. Robbins company downstairs."

Eliza snorts. "With lit pipes no doubt."

"They are attempting smoke rings. The sitting room will have to be aired out tomorrow."

"Harvard men." Eliza shakes her head. "Always trying to act like Oxford men."

She groans then, deep and guttural, and I spring from my chair to go stand behind the young woman to make sure she doesn't fall.

"I'm fine," she says, voice thick with pain. "It's just that this one . . . ggggrrrr."

I'm not sure why the girl is still standing. Most women—those in labor for the first time at least—refuse to walk the room after a certain point in labor. Eliza isn't in transition yet, but she is close—her water finally having broken an hour ago—and she paces before the window, hands on her lower back, wet footprints trailing behind her.

She wears only a shift, and her fine, brown hair is loose, curling against her damp forehead. With the warm glow from the hearth and the candles scattered about the room, she looks like something out of a Renaissance painting. Pink cheeks and round body. Every so often, I tend a patient who makes the act of birth a thing of beauty. They make it look like what it really is, at its most elemental—right and natural—and I cannot help but marvel.

Eliza Robbins has no family in attendance—or at least none that are blood related. Mrs. Ney—once her governess, now her housekeeper—has been friend and family since the girl was born in Manchester. When Eliza married Chandler and moved first to Boston, then to Hallowell, the wiry sprite of a woman came as well, and is at ease in the delivery room as before the cookstove. It is not duty that brought Mrs. Ney here, but devotion. The woman, widowed young, has no children of her own. So it is Eliza she lives for, and soon, the child she carries will inherit that devotion.

Upon my arrival, Mrs. Ney assessed me, head to foot, and pronounced that I would do nicely. Eliza Robbins has not questioned my instructions once as a result.

"May I ask *why* you sent Dr. Page away?" I ask.

Eliza answers with another grunt, rounding her spine and grabbing onto the window sash for support. After thirty seconds the contraction subsides, and she takes a long breath through her nose.

"Because Grace Sewell told me he is an idiot. She said he nearly killed her with all that laudanum. Said you were right about everything, but no one would listen—not even her." Eliza finally makes her way to the bed, and we help her scoot back against the pillows. She sighs in relief. "This might be my first child, Mistress Ballard, but I am the oldest of five myself, and I've seen several come into the world. Haven't I, Ney?"

"More'n enough."

"Chandler and I tried for two years for this baby, and I don't want some clod of a doctor killing me before I can see it."

Chandler Robbins hails from Boston—as so many of the newer residents in Hallowell do—and, like his friend David Sewell, is a Harvard graduate. But whereas Sewell set his sights on starting a business across the river, Robbins has, for the last several years, been methodically building a boatyard on the peninsular outcropping of Bumberhook Point, a mile and half south of the Hook. Like any good entrepreneur, he knows that profitable industry relies on raw materials, easy transportation, and ready energy. The Kennebec provides him all three. Hallowell and its booming lumber trade provide the rest. He owns the point and everything on it, but his home is in the Hook, on Water Street, overlooking the river. It sits on a rise and has been dubbed the Robin's Nest, no doubt a nod to both its elevated position and the crow's nest atop every ship that Chandler builds.

For all his wealth and prominence, he chose a wife who—at first glance—seems below his station. Eliza is not pretty. She looks rather owlish with her big, brown eyes and feathery hair, but what she lacks in appearance she more than makes up for in heart and intellect. Having met her, it isn't hard to understand that Chandler—resourceful, practical, affluent—has chosen a partner and not just a wife.

"Eliza," I warn, "I will have to touch you now. To see how far along you are."

"Do what you must. But don't think less of me if I curse. My mother was French."

And that is all it takes for me to like the young woman. Sometimes it is easy to bond with a patient. Sometimes it is impossible. Usually, I don't bother myself either way because I have only one job in a birthing room. But the instant camaraderie does make that job easier, and I help Eliza scoot her shift up under her breasts. I can tell by the shape of her belly that the baby has dropped into the birth canal.

"Ready?" I ask.

"No." Eliza laughs, then gasps as her stomach turns to a vice.

My inspection will hurt less during a contraction, so I slide my hand into Eliza's body once the grinding pain reaches its peak. Inches. That's all it takes before I find what I'm looking for. "The head is down. Your baby is in position. Are you ready to push?"

Those wide owl eyes fill with tears, but not of pain. Fear. It is the most natural emotion, and I grab her hand.

"I am here. So is Mrs. Ney. You can do this. And we will help you. But on the next contraction you must begin to push."

And she does. Not hard or well. Eliza is tired and inexperienced and afraid. But for the next hour she bears down over and over and over. Crying. Panting. Grunting. And swearing—but only once, and in French, an astonished *merde!*—when the head, covered in thick black hair, pops from her body. One and a half more pushes for the shoulders and then I pull a slimy, wiggling baby boy from Eliza's body.

"Hello little one." I greet him as I do every child, but this time I laugh.

He is enormous. Easily nine pounds. I roll him over, counting fingers. Toes. I rub him down with a soft cloth. Check his palate. His eyes. And, when the afterbirth is delivered, I snip and tie the cord with a smooth, practiced movement.

I set the boy gently on Eliza's chest so they can meet each other. He is bawling, loud little lungs shrieking his displeasure at all the light and noise. He does not like the air on his skin. He does not like being removed from his safe, warm home. But when Eliza says, "Thomas, hush now," he stops crying, and, much to everyone's astonishment, lifts his head right off her chest and looks directly at his mother. And in that short silence, as we are speechless at the strength of this new little Robbins, we can hear his stomach growl. I choke out a boggled sort of laugh.

Mrs. Ney jumps into action then, plucking Thomas up with one arm and helping Eliza prepare to nurse with the other. "Let's get you a meal then, hungry boy." She looks at her young ward, beaming with pride, and says, "Your boy has arrived wanting meat and potatoes!"

The rest of my job is easy. There is no tearing. No excessive bleeding. Only the bathing and changing. The wrapping of linen cloths and the disposal of afterbirth. I help Eliza get Thomas latched onto her breast, then Mrs. Ney and I sit by the new mother and praise all her good work. We commend her on a beautiful baby. And, once they are situated, Mrs. Ney slips away to prepare a simple, cold meal for me and the famished new mother.

It is well after sunset when I tell Eliza, "I will be back shortly," and I leave the room with the bucket of waste.

"Will you ask Chandler to come up?" she calls after me.

"Of course."

I slip through the kitchen and out the back of the house to the privy. First I relieve myself, then empty the bucket.

"Leave that here," Mrs. Ney says, nodding toward the bucket, when I come back inside. "I'll wash it."

I watch the older woman cut cheese and bread and thick slices of smoked ham. She pours milk. Arranges shortbread. Makes tea. Clucks like a proud mother hen.

"Eliza is lucky to have you," I say.

There are tears in her eyes when she looks at me. "'Tis is the other way 'round. Her mother would be so proud of her."

"Is she . . . ?"

"Aye. Not long ago. Passed the year after Eliza married. A terrible shame. She was a good woman."

"I am sorry to hear that." I pat Mrs. Ney on the shoulder. "I'll go get Chandler."

Dr. Page is passed out, on his back, on the chaise in the drawing room, one arm thrown over his face, and a leg dangling off the side. There is an empty brandy snifter balanced on his chest and it wobbles with each breath.

He has no staying power, I think. Then I look at Chandler, also asleep, but sitting upright in his chair, head lolled to the side. The pipe still sits in his hand, curling gentle strands of smoke into the air. *The men never do.*

I gently shake Chandler's shoulder, and he snorts awake. "You have a beautiful, healthy son," I whisper.

He leaps up and is about to shout his joy, but I set a firm finger across his mouth, shake my head, and point to Dr. Page. I would rather not have to converse with the man again unless I have to, so I guide Chandler into the hall and close the drawing room door behind us.

"Eliza was magnificent. They're both resting upstairs."

"A son." He runs his hands through his hair. "What will we name him?"

"Thomas, apparently. But if you disagree, you'd best tell your wife soon. She's been calling him that from the moment she saw his face."

"Thomas." He smiles, wide as the ocean, and then, as if realizing for the first time that he's still holding his pipe, puts it to his lips. He draws in a mouthful of smoke, then forms his mouth to make a ring. No such luck. The smoke comes out in a white ball, then dissipates, but he is undeterred. "Thomas it is!"

Ever since being called to the Robbinses' this afternoon, I have wondered how I would broach this subject. There is no easy way, so I dive right in.

"May I ask you something? Quickly. Before you go up?"

"Of course."

"It's a strange question, so bear with me."

"All right."

"You helped the others cut Joshua Burgess from the ice that morning? In November? He was found right off Bumberhook Point, near your boatyard."

"Yes, he was. They came to me since the property's mine. There were seven of us who did the job. Eight maybe. I can't remember. It was dark and cold, and it was months ago now."

And you were drunk by the time I got to the tavern, I think but do not remind him.

"But you had lanterns that morning? You saw well enough to cut him out? To know who it was?"

"Yes."

I am careful, lowering my voice to a whisper in case Dr. Page has woken. "And what did you think?"

"Same as you, Mistress Ballard. That he'd been hung. Seemed obvious enough. All of us thought so."

"But there was no rope?"

"Only the one they pulled Sam Dawin out of the river with. But nothing near the body."

The sharp wail of a baby's cry interrupts us, and Chandler looks to the top of the stairs.

"Thank you," I say. "Now go see your son."

He turns away and is about to bound up the steps, but I grab his jacket just in time.

"Not with this," I tell him, and pluck the pipe from his hand. "No smoking near the baby. Bad for his new lungs."

Chandler runs up the steps two at a time, and when he's out of sight, I put the pipe to my own lips and draw. Chandler's tobacco smells of cherries and chocolate. It is cased with molasses and topped with vanilla but tastes—as all smoke does—like smoke. Only a nicer, classier kind of smoke. The kind you pay for. The kind that comes in little pouches and smells of gentlemen and scholars. *Tobacco.* There is no soot or ash, and I don't bother trying to blow a ring. I simply stand at the bottom of the stairs and let the cloud rise around my head as I ponder what Chandler has told me.

"Give me that," Mrs. Ney says from behind me. For one moment I think the housekeeper is going to scold me. But instead she adds, "You're doing it wrong."

Then the wiry old silver-haired woman puts the pipe to her lips, hollows her cheeks, pulls, puffs, and blows out a perfect smoke ring that grows and grows as it rises until—a foot wide—it dissipates altogether.

POLLARD'S TAVERN

As I pass the tavern on my way home, two drunken patrons stumble out, and I catch a full, warm whiff of Abigail's cooking. Mrs. Ney and I nibbled at dinner, but I'd had no appetite for the meal knowing that Dr. Page was in the next room and would likely wake at any moment. I'm not in the mood to handle his abuse. So I'd left the happy family and headed home for my own bed. But this? The smell of a hearty meal is all the motivation I need.

The fire is blazing inside, and the lanterns burn bright. The room is only half full of guests but overflowing with laughter, and I am met at the door by Moses. His cheeks are rosy and his smile wide.

"Are ye ill, Mistress Ballard?" he asks, taking one look at me.

"No. I've just come from a delivery. I was on my way home when I smelled your mother's cooking."

"Ah. Let's get ye some of it then. Fortify you for the ride."

I follow him to a table at the back and sink onto the bench with a groan. This is a new thing I've discovered about myself in recent years. The *noises*. Stand and groan. Sit and grunt. Some days it seems that I can hardly take a step without some part of my body creaking or cracking and this—even more than the gray hairs and the crow's-feet at my eyes—makes me feel as though I am racing down the final stretch of middle age.

Within moments, Moses sets a plate in front of me. "Cornish hen, roasted on the spit, along with carrots and onions and potatoes." There is also a slab of generously buttered bread, yet before I can even thank him, much less lift the fork to my mouth, he whispers, "Did ye hear about the Burgess homestead?"

"Hear what?"

Moses looks to either side to see if anyone is listening, then drops to the bench across from me. "I guess ye wouldna have, since ye've been at a birth all day."

He clearly wants to tell me the news, but I am famished, so I take a bite of potato while he backs into his story. *Oh God.* It is even tastier than I remember. I will never understand how Abigail Pollard can make the same meal that I do and yet it is always ten times better. I'm able to sneak in another bite before he continues.

"Someone burned Joshua Burgess's home to the ground earlier this month. But it was only discovered this morning."

It's a wonder I don't choke. "*Why?*"

"Dead men don't get many visitors, I suppose. But a pair of trappers mentioned it at breakfast. My Da' thinks that's where Judge North hid after the hearing. But only for a few days, just long enough to ride out the storm."

I sit a little straighter. "Why not longer?"

"It's been burned for several weeks."

"So how does he know it was North?"

"The barn didn't burn. And it was littered with dog prints. That's where Da' thinks he kept Cicero."

"He didn't take the dog with him?"

Moses shakes his head. "I saw it on the porch at North Manor this afternoon. Must have taken it home before he left town for good. But honestly, it was clever of North to hide there. Burgess is dead. No one would look there."

It's a good point and I tell him so.

"But why burn it?" I ask. "It makes no sense to destroy an empty house."

"Unless there was something in the house that he wanted gone." He shrugs, then stands to go back to work.

He may as well have slapped me with his bare hand. "Moses?" I ask, "What happened to Burgess's belongings?"

"He dinna have much to start with. One horse. Two cows. Some chickens. And the cabin was only just the one room, from what I've heard. There wasna much in it. The animals were given to the neighbors when he died."

I tear off a piece of bread, then pop it in my mouth. I chew slowly as a dozen little fires ignite in my mind.

"What of his saddle? His weapons? Were there any personal items?"

"Da' put them in the shed. With him." Moses shrugs. "Henry Sewell sent a letter to Boston looking for his relatives. Hasna heard back, far as I know."

"You'll let me know if you hear anything else?"

"Aye. I'll send word."

"Or you can bring it yourself. I'm sure Hannah would be pleased to see you again."

There are few things that I enjoy more than making a young man blush, and Moses obliges me in spectacular fashion. "Aye. I'll do that," he says. "Can I get ye anything else in the meantime?"

It's a risk. I know this. But I should have thought of it months ago.

"Yes," I tell Moses. "I'm going to need a lantern."

*

The Pollards call it a shed, but the structure behind the tavern is more like a small barn. Though only one story, it has double doors and could easily house several head of cattle comfortably. They use it to store extra supplies and feed, for barrels and crates. Also the body of Joshua Burgess. The path isn't as well-worn as others near the tavern—the stables in particular—but it's clear that someone makes the trip regularly, so my visit shouldn't be noticeable in the morning if Amos comes out to collect a side of beef or a slab of bacon.

The door latch creaks as I lift, then it flops over with a thump. I look back over my shoulder to see if anyone has heard. No lights go on in the upper windows of the tavern. No voices call out. So I pull the door open and slip inside.

The shed is well-ordered. Foodstuffs and supplies stacked in neat rows that are accessible on either side. Six large sides of beef and ten ham hocks hang from the ceiling. There are bags of wheat and wheels of cheese. I hold my breath for several seconds before realizing that the expected scents of death and decay are not noticeable. The shed smells only of hay and salt and sawdust. Of dried apples and smoked fish. But it is cold as river rocks inside, and everything is frozen. At first, I cannot find the body, am worried that it has been moved or stolen. But then, in the back corner, I see the pile of hay. It makes sense. Even if you know it's there, you don't want to stumble upon a corpse every time you come out for a tub of butter. They have hidden Burgess out of sight.

Satisfied, I close the door behind me. I can see footprints on the dusty floor and scattered hay where the judges from Vassalboro stood around and inspected the body a few weeks ago. It has since been heaped back over the body in a sloppy pile.

I set the lantern down and push through the hay with the toe of my boot until the oiled leather tarp that covers Burgess comes into view. I have no interest in examining him again—once was more than enough—so I move in the other direction, kneeling now, and scooting piles of the dry chaff aside with my hands.

There, the swell of a saddle. I push the straw back and find all the tack in place: blanket and bridle, bit and reins. I cover it again and keep searching. Beside it is a woolen blanket wrapped around a rifle and hatchet. Not what I'm looking for. I move on, sliding my arms in now, up to the shoulders as I feel my way farther into the pile.

"Finally."

My fingers slide over the leather strap of a saddlebag, and I pull it from the hay. It is dusty and cold and heavy. The night presses in around the circle of the lantern light, and my heart ticks faster. This is wrong. I know that, but I unbuckle the bag anyway. Inside are Burgess's pistols, along with a coin purse that sits heavy in my hand when I pull it out. An empty bottle that smells of whiskey. Three envelopes. And there, at the bottom of the bag, a strip of lace.

I stare at it aghast, remembering what Rebecca told the court, how Burgess ripped a piece of lace from the hem of her shift and tied his hair back before he went to work on her. He kept it, a souvenir, and my stomach turns at the sight.

I pull each of the envelopes from the bag, squinting curiously at the broken wax seals and the return addresses written above them.

The first reads: Colonel Joseph North, Hallowell, District of Maine.

The second reads: The Kennebec Proprietors, Boston, Massachusetts.

But it is the third that has me pinching my brows together in confusion.

"What in Satan's hell?" I mutter, running the pad of my thumb over the familiar, elegant handwriting.

It reads: Ephraim Ballard, Hallowell, District of Maine.

I am turning the flap to open this last letter when I hear the loud thud of a door being slammed, then a mumbled curse, and the heavy clomp of footsteps stomping toward the shed. I shove everything back in the saddlebag and blow out the lantern. If light can explode, then darkness can swallow, and I am consumed in an instant.

"Damn fool of a boy," growls the rough, guttural voice of Amos Pollard, followed by what I can only guess is a string of German profanity. "*Arschgeige! Arsch bit Ohren! Dünnbrettbohrer! Kotzbrocken!*"

And then there is the loud creak of the latch being lifted, followed by the thump of it dropping into place across the door. Before I can call out or warn him that I am inside, Amos Pollard has stomped away, still cursing under his breath.

I ease my way to the front of the shed and push against the door with my shoulder. It does not budge. I am locked inside.

"You are a fool, Martha Ballard," I say, and my voice sounds hollow in the darkness. "Of all the professions you could have chosen, you found the one—the only damned one—that would get you locked up with a dead man in the middle of the night."

Thirty Years Ago

OXFORD, MASSACHUSETTS

"I don't know a thing about delivering babies," I told the boy.

He couldn't have been ten years old, but still, he looked at me as though I was a simpleton. "You got one on your hip. And another inside the house. You must know somethin' 'bout it."

"That's different from delivering someone else's," I said. "And besides, are you sure she meant me?"

The boy groaned. Rolled his eyes. "You Mistress Ballard, ain't you?"

"Yes."

"Then you's who she meant. Said she wants *your* help and wants you to come quick." Impatient, he shifted from foot to foot. "Well? You coming?"

I looked to where my husband sat at the table, watching Cyrus eat a bowl of mush. He was three and a half and handy with a spoon, but, when left unattended, liked to finger-paint with his meals.

The look I sent to Ephraim plainly said, *Rescue me,* but he didn't.

"You should go," he said. "I will stay with the children."

"But—"

"Go."

"I could be gone a long time. They—"

"Will be fine, seeing as how I've been a parent as long as you have. Go help Elspeth."

The woman in question—one Elspeth Horne—was a terrifying old midwife. Wizened and angry but fiercely competent in the birthing room. That's why I'd sought her out when I had Cyrus, and then later, Lucy. But I could not fathom why she'd sent the boy for me.

Ephraim rose from the table and reached for Lucy. She dove into his arms with a wild giggle, and he plopped her on his shoulder like a sack of grain. "Go."

There was nothing left to argue. Lucy was weaned, after all, and I couldn't use that as an excuse. So I kissed Ephraim, grabbed my coat, slipped on my gloves, and followed the boy at a brisk walk down the path and onto the snow-packed road toward Oxford. The tavern where we were headed was only a mile away, and we made easy work of the distance, what with my long stride and his quick steps. All the boy would tell me was that the woman laboring had been staying at the tavern for a week, and that he'd been sent to fetch me. He didn't know her name or how long she'd been in labor.

When we arrived, he darted to the stairs, looked back, and waved for me to follow. Up, up we went, all the way to the attic room, and every step I mounted left me feeling more of an idiot for being there in the first place. By the time we reached the short, slanted door, I'd convinced myself to turn around and go home. But the boy threw it open without knocking, ran to the old woman seated by the bed, and kissed her on the cheek.

"Here she is, Gran."

"Thank you, Walter. Now go wait on the stairs in case I need you again."

I watched him go, then turned to Elspeth. With one old, gnarled hand she stroked the arm of a girl who lay on the bed, her huge, rounded stomach pointing to the ceiling. The girl looked every bit as alarmed at my presence as I felt.

"Mistress Ballard?" Elspeth asked, and I realized I'd not said a word since entering the room.

"Yes?"

She turned at the sound of my voice and suddenly I understood. I'd not seen Elspeth in eighteen months. And her eyes had been dark then, darker than mine. But they'd turned a total milky white since. Elspeth Horne was blind.

"Come in," she said. "And take off your coat. You'll need your arms free."

"I will?"

"Get on with it. You're letting in a draft."

I shut the door, shrugged out of my cloak, and peeled off my gloves. Then I took a deep breath and went to stand beside her. I told her the truth. "I don't understand why you called for me."

"You are going to help me deliver this child."

The girl was plenty young. She still had the full, round face of adolescence and the scared look of a child. She didn't wear a wedding ring, but that didn't mean much, as half the men I knew were too poor to give one to their wives.

"Has she no women?" I asked.

"She won't say, one way or another. But then she hasn't said much to begin with. No one knows where she came from or where she's going. Only that she showed up, Wednesday last, and has plenty of coin to pay for her room. The innkeeper called for me early this morning when he heard her crying. Rightly assumed her pains had begun. Walter got me here, but he's no use otherwise. So it's the two of us who will get the job done." She paused, nodded toward the light. "There should be another chair somewhere in the room. If not, send Walter to get one from downstairs."

There was one, beside the window. I grabbed it and joined her beside the bed.

"Why me?"

Elspeth pushed a long, silver ribbon of hair away from her forehead, but it flopped forward again, and, absentmindedly, I reached out and tucked it behind her ear. She felt the gesture. Tilted her head. Looked at me without seeing.

"Because you don't panic in a birthing room. You didn't with Cyrus—and that was as hard a birth as any I've ever seen—nor did you with Lucy. And if I'm going to teach what I know, then I want it to be someone not given to hysterics. Ain't nothing worse than a screamer or a crier or a silly girl in a room like this."

An hour ago, I was eating lunch with my little family, and now I'd just been told that—without my knowledge or approval—I'd become apprenticed to this woman.

The girl lay there, looking back and forth between Elspeth and me as though she wanted to stand up and run. But there'd be no running for her, not for a long while, because I could see the first hard wave of pain wash over her. The groan that followed was familiar, and I winced in sympathy. I was almost twenty-two when I had Cyrus, but this girl couldn't be seventeen.

I reached forward and set a hand on her belly, feeling it harden. "I am sorry that you don't have anyone with you for this," I told her. "But I've done it twice, and there is no better midwife in the state than Elspeth. We will help you."

"She's *blind*," the girl hissed.

"She has my eyes for seeing, and her hands work just fine. There's no need to worry."

Elspeth patted my knee, and I knew I'd said the right thing.

"What do you need me to do?" I asked.

"Ask her name." Elspeth must have sensed my confusion because she added, "The first thing, the most important thing in a birthing room, is to ask the woman's name. If you mean to put your hands on her body, she must trust you. And she will never do that if you don't even know what to call her, because you will be doing a great deal more than simply putting your hands *on* her by the end."

"My name is Martha Ballard," I said to the girl. I felt silly. Like a child standing before a cranky teacher, but I did it anyway. "What is yours?"

I could see her debate, as though saying it aloud would be a total surrender to our care. But another contraction hit her, this one worse than the last, and when it ebbed several seconds later, she said, "Triphene. My name is Triphene Hartwell."

Elspeth nodded. "Good. Now hand me my medical bag. It's at the foot of the bed. I will tell you what every item is for, and you will do with them exactly as I say. And Martha?"

"Yes?"

"By the end of this night, you will know whether midwifery is a thing to which you have been called." Those pale, watery eyes bored into me. "Or not."

5

THE GRIEF THAT DOES NOT SPEAK

MARCH 1790

If you have tears, prepare to shed them now.

—WILLIAM SHAKESPEARE, *Julius Caesar*

BALLARD'S MILL

I finish yesterday's journal entry while Ephraim reads the letters. There are three in total—one of them in his own handwriting—and I can hear the papers crinkle between his fingers as I record the details of Eliza Robbins's delivery in my journal.

Sunday, February 28. Birth. Chandler Robbins's son. Snowed in the afternoon. I was called to see Mrs. Robbins who is unwell. Mrs. Robbins lingered until four p.m. when her illness came on. Doctor Page was called but she did not wish to see him when he came. She was safe delivered of a son, her first born, at the tenth and one half hour last evening and is as well as can be expected. I tarried and watched. Mrs. Ney was there and she only.

I'd recognized Ephraim's writing on the envelope, of course. There is no mistaking the precise and lovely lines, how the stem of every *d* curls up and to the left, making a perfect half loop above the letter. The only mystery is how a survey that my husband completed almost twelve years ago had come to be in the saddlebag of a dead man.

Ephraim wanted the entire story, of course—where I'd been and what I'd been up to—not to mention how I got out of that shed. He wanted it the moment I got home, but, exhausted and stiff, I'd promised to give him every detail if he would wait until the morning.

Now, I tap my quill on the little pewter dish to knock off the remaining ink and push my journal aside. I turn to Ephraim. Wait.

"But"—Ephraim drops the letter to his lap and looks up at me, staggered—"this says—"

"I know what it says."

"They can't."

"They can, apparently. With that affidavit from North."

Ephraim folds each letter methodically and places it back in its envelope. Bits of wax seal break off and fall to the floor, but he doesn't notice. He taps the letters against his thigh. Then he's up and pacing.

"This is an eviction notice."

"Yes. I read it."

And I had. After dressing this morning, but before leaving our room, I sat on the edge of the bed and read each of the letters in Burgess's saddlebag: a survey drawn almost twelve years ago by Ephraim of our eighty acres, along with a detailed property description; a certified letter to the Kennebec Proprietors from Joseph North stating that the Ballard family had failed to meet the third condition for acquiring the deed to this property; and a response from said Proprietors noting that the Ballard lease is heretofore canceled and—as North suggested—reassigned to one Captain Joshua Burgess.

The fact that the saddlebag came home with me last night is another thing I will have to explain to my husband. He hasn't asked yet. Therefore, I haven't volunteered.

"But it's a lie. Everything he said in that letter is demonstrably false. We have met every condition."

"Not the third. Not technically."

"Only because next month will mark our twelfth year on this property. But we have most certainly maintained a permanent residence. There are hundreds of people who will testify to that!"

"Will that matter if North refuses to certify the claim? He is the Kennebec Proprietor, not you. And it would require a lengthy appeal regardless. And in the meantime, we would have been evicted. Turned into the street so Burgess could have all we've built."

"Except he's dead. And we are still here."

I shake my head. "That's the part I don't understand. Why would North go to all the trouble of transferring the mill to Burgess only to kill him?"

He looks at me with those steely blue eyes. "You believe it was North?"

"It's the only thing that makes sense. He's the only one to profit from Burgess's death."

Ephraim goes to stand before the window, the letters pinched between two fingers on his left hand. His back is straight and strong, as is his profile, and I watch him stare into the distance. After a moment he scratches at the scruff along his jawline.

A thought occurs to me, and I sit up straighter on the stool. "Oh."

"What?"

"When is North's letter dated?"

He pulls it from the envelope. Holds it at arm's length. Gives it a myopic squint. "October first. Why?"

The date is familiar. So I reach for my journal and flip back to October first, looking for a clue. And there it is, in black-and-white, written by my own hand.

Thursday, October 1—Clear except some showers. We had company this afternoon. Mr. Savage here, informs us that Mrs. Foster has sworn a rape on a number of men, among whom is Joseph North. Shocking indeed! I have been at home.

"That was the day that Rebecca Foster came forward with her accusation of rape."

"What are you saying?"

"I think North was buying Joshua Burgess's silence with this property."

"So why kill him?"

It's a valid question. One that I can't answer with any degree of certainty. "I don't know. Not yet at any rate."

"All your scheming hasn't produced a solution?"

"I do not *scheme*."

"If that were the case, you wouldn't have found yourself locked in the Pollard shed in the middle of the night. Or come home with a saddlebag that does not belong to you." Ephraim leans against the wall. Gives me a stern look. "Do not think I have not forgotten simply because of"—he holds up the letters—"these."

I take a deep breath. Puff it out. "I did think I was in trouble for a moment. It had gotten as cold as a well-digger's arse in there, and I couldn't decide whether or not to call for help."

"Intrigued by the idea of freezing to death, were you?"

I glare at him. "It hadn't gotten to that point. And besides, I had no way of explaining what I was doing there or why I had that damn saddlebag over my arm."

"Well, I'm guessing you didn't walk through the wall or dig your way out. So who rescued you?"

"Moses." I laugh. "Amos had gone back in and flayed him in German for leaving the shed door unlocked. Didn't take him long to figure out where I'd gone with that lantern. It did, however, take him a while to come for me. He had to wait until his father fell asleep."

Ephraim runs his fingers through the hair at his temples. Shakes his head. Growls. "You will be the death of me, woman."

"All's well that ends well."

He does not think it funny, this use of the Bard against him, and his eyes thin to slits of irritation.

"I would have got out. Eventually," I say.

"Maybe. Maybe not. But I see you have not solved our current predicament."

"Which is?"

"How in the name of seven hells we are going to explain how you came to be in possession of that saddlebag."

"No one is asking that particular question just yet."

"They will. The moment we go public with these letters. Which we'll have to do because, *technically*, we no longer have a legal right to live on this property."

I am about to tell him that, by the time anyone thinks to ask that question, we'll have figured out a way to answer. But that's when Jonathan throws back the door to my workroom without knocking.

"Yes?" Ephraim asks.

Jonathan looks at his father with pity and dread. "Something has killed Percy."

*

The wooden slats have been torn apart, and there is blood on the floor. A riot of feathers litter the mews. It is a grim scene, not much different from the block I use to butcher chickens.

I watch Ephraim. He stands still—too still—as he takes in the sight.

"What was it?" Jonathan asks.

Ephraim steps back and inspects the ground. There are paw prints in the snow. A mad tangle of them, crisscrossing and mashed together.

"A coyote," he says.

"Not a wolf? Those are big tracks."

"It was a big coyote." He kneels and draws one finger along the print. "See, the toes are oblong, and the pad is scalloped. A wolf has round toes, an angular pad."

"I'm sorry," Jonathan says. "It's a shame to lose that bird."

Ephraim grunts but doesn't answer immediately. Instead, he walks around the mews, hunched over, until he finds a set of prints leading into the forest. These are wider apart, like the animal was running, and there are small drops of blood splattered between them.

To me it looks as though the coyote ran off with Percy between his jaws, but Ephraim returns, shaking his head. "I don't think he's dead."

"Dad, are you . . . ?" Jonathan's voice trails off when I shake my head.

Let him be, my expression says.

"If it got him, it would have torn Percy apart right here." He points to the ground in front of the mews.

"There are a lot of feathers," I say.

"It got into the mews. Took a few swipes, no doubt. But I think Percy got his licks in, scared the thing, and flew away."

We all three look to the sky as though the falcon might be circling above us.

"Will he come back?" I ask.

Ephraim is less sure about this, and a frown clouds his expression. "I suppose we'll see how well I've trained him."

POLLARD'S TAVERN

FRIDAY, MARCH 5

James Wall gives Brutus a longing glance as I tie up at the post beside the nag he's bought to replace his Pacer. I recognize that look. It's a kind of longing mixed with jealousy. The sort of gaze an unhappy husband would settle on another man's wife.

He scratches the long bridge of Brutus's nose. "You're still riding this beast?"

"Why wouldn't I?"

"He's a lot of horse."

"And you think he's too much for me?"

James won't dare answer that question aloud, so he clears his throat. Looks at the ground. Grins.

"Well, you're not alone. My husband believes Brutus to be a villain as great as his namesake."

"Yet he allows you to ride him?" .

"*Allows?*" I laugh. "I am fifty-four years old. Ephraim doesn't *allow* me anything. I do as I please."

"Well, if you ever decide to sell him, I'd like the chance to make an offer."

I know, for a fact, that James cannot afford this horse, but his suggestion is the opening I need. It's the entire reason I crossed the street

when I saw him dismount in front of the tavern. So I follow him up
the steps, and he holds the door open for me.

"I thought you only rode Pacers?"

"I prefer them, no question, but I'm not as picky as people think."
He scowls over his shoulder at the nag. "As evidenced by that bag of
bones."

We shrug out of hats and coats. Stomp the snow off our feet. It's
midafternoon and the sun is shining, but it's dim inside the tavern,
and it takes a moment for our eyes to adjust.

"Are you drinking or visiting this afternoon?" I ask.

"Drinking. I'm not much in the way of company these days."

"Oh I doubt that. Let me buy you a pint. Consider it a consola-
tion prize for having to ride that old plug out there."

James laughs, and Moses is there, ready to take our orders, by
the time we've found our seats. Then he's off to get our ale and cider,
cheerful and efficient as always while we settle in.

"I am sorry that you had to sell your horse," I tell James.

He frowns. "I knew better than to go to Joseph North for a loan."

"Then why did you?"

"I ain't proud of it. But it happened before that business with
Mistress Foster. I would have never—"

Moses is back and he plunks two mugs onto the table. They're
both overfilled, and foam dribbles over the rim as the rich, amber
liquid spills onto the table. James drinks his down to a manageable
level as he waits for Moses to wander off again.

"Point is North had the cash and the willingness to invest. Went
on and on about how we need a distillery in the Hook. And the terms
seemed good. I had no trouble making the payments until the river
froze."

Most families make their own home brew, and while the qual-
ity of the beer varies, it isn't an arduous task. Same for cider. The
barrels used to ferment them are often harder to come by than the
ingredients. But liquor is another story. All the rum, gin, and whiskey
consumed in the Hook is shipped in from elsewhere. James is smart
to recognize that need and try to meet it. Even I can't fault him for
taking the financial risk. After all, last summer North was just another
businessman willing to invest in local commerce.

"You didn't have anything saved to cover the loan during the winter months?"

"Not enough to pay it in full. Which is what North demanded, even though that's not what he really wanted."

"What do you mean?"

"He gave me two options when I went to him and said my December payment would be short. Said I could pay the entire loan, plus interest, in full, right then, or sign over a portion of the distillery to him."

"But you've only just started construction."

He scowls into his ale. "North said it was his way of 'investing' in the business. But what he really wanted was thirty percent off the top." James can tell by my expression that I am outraged on his behalf. "I refused, of course. Ended up in the jail yard and had to sell my Pacer to get out from under his thumb."

"Thirty percent is *outrageous*."

"That's North. Don't you see what he's doing?"

I shake my head.

"He wants to own the entire town."

BALLARD'S MILL

"Well done!" I say.

Sarah White beams at me across the table. Between us is the *New England Primer* and three sheets of loose paper, along with my quill and ink.

Sarah's letters are clear and straight—not at all like a child's—and they only slant downward slightly as they go across the page. She has successfully written her name, along with those of her parents and her daughter. Sarah has taken great care with this last, C. H. A. R. L. O. T. T. E. spelled out in capital letters. She is proud of the name, and the child.

"I can tell you've been practicing."

This is our second lesson. The first having commenced last month when I extended my offer and left the primer in her possession. I am hoping to draw this one out long enough that she will stay and join us for lunch.

"Every night," Sarah tells me. "It's not as hard as I thought it would be. Not once I memorized the sounds. And the pictures help." Her face fills with color, and I think she is embarrassed. "I know that's silly."

I set my palm over the back of Sarah's hand. "Not at all. That's what the pictures are for."

At first Sarah balked at doing this lesson in front of Hannah and Dolly—it was a dose of humble pie she had not intended to consume before an audience—but my girls, having learned to read at my knee as well, are delighted to have Sarah at our table, and they take turns playing with Charlotte while she does the lesson.

Dolly comes to stand behind Sarah and peers over her shoulder at the primer. "The pictures were always my favorite part. I still want a nice illustration every now and again when I read." She pats Sarah's shoulder, then wanders off again to knead the bread that has finished rising.

"Hannah?" I ask.

She looks up.

"Will you go tell Cyrus and your father that lunch is almost ready?"

"I'll tell Father," she says. "But Cyrus is gone. He rode off not five minutes ago."

Dammit, I think.

"Where did he go?"

Hannah shrugs. "On some errand for father."

I stifle a sigh. This is the best chance I've had to get Sarah and Cyrus in a room together in over a month. His confinement to the jail yard complicates that, of course, given that he's home only during daylight hours. Having Sarah do her lesson here had seemed the perfect solution.

I turn back to Sarah and tap a small square on the left side of the page. Inside is a simply drawn hourglass with flowers in the corner. "Let's try one more page before lunch. Start here."

Sarah furrows her brow, and I see her lips working to sound out the letters before she speaks. "As . . . runs . . . the . . . glass . . . man's . . . life . . . doth . . . pass."

"Excellent! Now the next."

"My . . . book . . . and . . . hear—No!—heart. It says *heart*. My book and heart shall never part."

The pictures help, but so does the rhyming, and the farther we go down the page, the more comfortable Sarah feels reading the words aloud. It isn't just the writing she's been practicing every night, but the reading as well. And in the absence of shame, this new skill begins to bloom.

I sit back—pleased—as Sarah continues without my prompting.

"The lion bold, the lamb doth hold. The moon gives light in time of night. Night. In. Nightingales! Nightingales sing in time of spring."

On we go for the rest of the page, and when I look up, I see my daughters watching with expressions of pride. They are proud of Sarah. They like her, and the girl could do worse than marrying into a family in which she is liked. I only have to figure out a way to make it happen, a way to make Cyrus stay put long enough to try.

When lunch has been consumed and Sarah has bundled herself against the cold and tucked Charlotte into a sling beneath her coat, I see them both to the door, then watch as Jonathan bundles them onto the wagon. Once they're gone, I go back to the fire and sit beside my husband. He's nursing a glass of brandy and barely hiding a smile.

"Why the sour look, love? Have you been thwarted?" he asks.

"You warned Cyrus off, didn't you?"

"I sent him on an errand. We still have a business to run despite your schemes."

"Last I heard, you liked this scheme."

"I do. But it still has to be her idea."

"Well now she's gone off with Jonathan."

Ephraim shrugs. "He could do worse."

I swipe his glass and take a sip of the brandy. "No. Jonathan is the last thing Sarah needs. He's going to find himself in a great deal of trouble if he doesn't stop bedding girls before he marries one."

That shocks him at least, and I'm glad to have his full attention.

"You're certain he and Sally have . . . ?"

"More a suspicion than a certainty." I tip the last of his brandy into my mouth and swallow. "But it's going to end badly for that boy of yours. Mark my words."

"He's mine now, is he?"

"When they cause trouble, they're yours."

I stand and head toward my workroom, but Ephraim grabs my wrist.

"Look," he says.

He leads me to the window. A long, dark shadow flies out of the woods, fifty feet above the ground. It circles the mill once, then comes to rest on the weathervane.

Ephraim was right. Percy is alive.

McMASTER HOUSE

We sit outside the mill in a rare patch of winter sunshine, our feet propped up on a stump. Ephraim usually isn't one to smoke, but ever since Percy returned in good health, he has taken to having an afternoon smoke break. I join him when I can. As for the bird, Ephraim has no plans to rebuild the mews. For now, Percy has been left to flit around the mill and roost where he pleases. I watch my husband produce an old, ornate pipe from his pocket, along with a pouch of tobacco. He lights. Puffs. Rolls the smoke around his mouth and then out again in a smooth stream. He's not one for smoke rings given that he isn't a pretentious man, so he doesn't make a show of his good mood.

I am reaching for the pipe to practice the technique that Mrs. Ney showed me when I hear the heavy clomp of horse hooves coming down the lane. As I turn, the person I least expect emerges from the wood.

Grace Sewell's mother, Mrs. Hendricks.

She of the high ideals and sour expression.

I've never seen a person look more uneasy on horseback. Nor a horse less pleased to be ridden. Her spine is straight. Her arms stiff. And her eyes are filled with the kind of terror that any horse could smell. It's a wonder she's made it here alive. Brutus would have thrown her five seconds into the ride.

"Mrs. Hendricks." I greet her with a forced smile. "How can I help you today?"

Her teeth are clenched so tightly she has to stretch her jaw before she can speak. "My daughter Grace."

"Is she unwell?"

"It is the child. She sent me to collect you."

*

"You said your daughter called for me." I turn an accusing stare toward Mrs. Hendricks. "You lied."

Though today marks the Ides of March, it is still bitterly cold. Most years the river has opened by now and the ground is starting to thaw. But not this year. Winter still holds us in its bitter grip. Even though the sun is out, and shining, it gives no warmth. I look to it and frown. I am tired of winter. And I am angry at being tricked.

"If I had told you the truth, you wouldn't have come," she protests.

"Of course not! I want nothing to do with that man."

"Well, his wife is going to die if you don't go in. And I will be *thrilled* to tell the entire town that you left her to do so because of some petty grudge."

"Petty grudge? Two women in this town have buried children. And my son is in jail. All because of him!"

Mrs. Hendricks straightens her back. Lifts her chin. "He is no good at this birthing business. I'll give you that. And I will also concede that, had you not been there, my daughter and grandson would likely be dead. It's a debt I'll owe you for the rest of my life. But his incompetence doesn't mean that another woman and child should be buried. Not if *you* can help."

I take a step back and peer at her suspiciously. "What is any of this to you?"

"His wife and my daughter have become friends." Mrs. Hendricks huffs out a sigh. "I will be leaving in two months. If that girl dies, Grace will have nothing."

I would hardly count a husband, a child, a home, and a community as *nothing*. But I am in no mood to argue with Mrs. Hendricks.
Besides, we are standing in the street and could be overheard at any
moment. Yet before I can stop her, she pulls the rope beside the door
and bells chime inside the house. Within seconds I hear the heavy
tread of footsteps.

"Did Page call for me?"

"No," she admits. "And perhaps he will be angry. But I'm sure he
wants a dead wife less than he wants your help. That's why I walked
across the river and borrowed that demon of a horse from the tavern."

Said horse—Beulah—is nearly as old as I am, and whatever teeth
she has left are long and yellow. She's as placid a beast as God ever
made. Still, neither had seemed pleased with the other's company, and
when Mrs. Hendricks slid clumsily off her back, I didn't know who
would bite first. I was pleased to see Beulah do the honor.

I had believed Mrs. Hendricks at first. Had followed her into the
Hook, where we'd put our horses at the tavern. Then walked across the
river. Mrs. Hendricks remained quiet most of the way, and I thought
nothing of it. Worry does that to a mother. But it wasn't until she
walked right past the chandlery and down the street that I began to
suspect something was amiss. And when she stopped in front of the
old McMaster place, I knew I'd been duped.

Like Beulah, I might be getting a little long in the tooth. But I am
not so old that I forget basic facts. Like Samuel Coleman telling me
that Dr. Page has rented the McMaster home.

I am just about to turn and walk away when the door is thrown
back. This Benjamin Page looks nothing like the arrogant, well-kept
physician who has plagued me for months. He is a wreck. Hair sticking on end. Sweaty brow. Glassy eyes. Clothing rumpled. Still, he
musters enough animosity to insult me.

"What the hell is she doing here?" he demands.

If you had asked me in December if there would ever be a scenario in which I would thank the Almighty for Mrs. Hendricks, I
would have laughed. And yet, all those months ago I'd never seen her
in her true form. As a Boston matriarch. The sort of woman who can
intimidate a Harvard-educated man. That is the version of herself that
she presents to the petulant, frightened Dr. Page.

"Stand back, young man!" she orders. And her voice is so loud and so sure that he stumbles two steps backward into the dark hall. "I called for this woman, and you will do exactly as she says."

"But I—"

"Shut up. Take us to your wife."

He is flummoxed. So beside himself that, for once, the man doesn't argue. We follow him down the dark hall. Up the dark stairs. Into a bedroom so dark that I can barely see the hand in front of my face.

"Where is she?" Mrs. Hendricks demands.

"There. On the bed."

I see only a shadow surrounded by other shadows.

"Why is it so dark in here?" I ask.

Dr. Page snorts. "*Because,* science has proven that a dark room relaxes the patient. If you knew anything about medicine, you would know—"

A whimper from the bed silences him.

"How long since her pains began?"

"Yesterday. Early."

"And how long since she was last up and moving?"

"She hasn't been up. She must keep her strength!"

If he was closer, I'd slap him. "And since she last ate?"

I can see only the outline of his face in the darkness, but I hear the disdain in his voice clearly enough. "As I'm sure you well know, Mistress Ballard, a full stomach will cause indigestion in a laboring woman. She's eaten nothing since her first pain."

The man's an idiot, that much is clear. And I will not argue with him. "Do you want me here?" I ask.

"No."

"Does your wife want me here?"

"She has no say in the—"

Mrs. Hendricks has finally had enough. She grabs his ear and twists so hard he lets out a howl that would rival that of a dying dog. Dr. Page swats at her hand as she hauls him to his wife's bedside. When she releases him, he plops to the mattress like a marionette that's had its strings cut.

Mrs. Hendricks leans over the bed, and I must squint to see her put her palm to the young woman's cheek. "Hello, dear," she says. "We've come to help. Would you like that?"

There is a muffled answer that sounds affirmative.

"Very good. This woman here is a midwife. Her name is Martha Ballard. And she saved my daughter's life. If you would like, she will help you get this baby into the world."

Again, the affirmative.

"Excellent," Mrs. Hendricks says. Then she turns to Dr. Page and says, "Go find a chair and sit somewhere out of the way. Perhaps you will learn something."

I am still standing near the door, medical bag in hand, when she waves me forward. "Martha. If you don't mind."

I go to the window instead of the bed and throw the curtains open. Afternoon sunlight floods the room, and I can finally see the doctor's wife. She is curled into a ball in the middle of the bed. Pale as a ghost. Half asleep. Sweating.

"Mrs. Hendricks?" I ask.

"Yes."

"Can you stay?"

"I can."

"Good. The first thing I need you to do is go to the kitchen and get this woman something to eat."

"How will that help?"

"If she is to deliver a child today, she must wake up. And there are only two things in all of creation that wake a human. Sunlight and food."

Dr. Page snorts. "That is preposterous. Coffee—"

"Only increases heart rate," I tell him. "But if you have some, by all means go make it. She'll need that too."

When Mrs. Hendricks reaches for his ear again, he jumps off the bed and speeds from the room. She follows. Only then do I approach the girl.

"Hello, Mrs. Page," I say, sitting beside her.

"Hello."

She is young. Eighteen or nineteen perhaps. And small boned, like a girl. It does not surprise me that Page chose a diminutive wife. Someone he could intimidate. But that fact will not make my job any easier. If she is as small of hip as she is of shoulder, we might well be in trouble.

"I am here to help. I have delivered many hundreds of babies. Would you like my assistance in delivering yours?"

She nods. Then groans.

"Good. But before I can help you, I must ask one thing of you."

She looks at me, eyes wide. "What is that?"

"You must give me your trust."

"How do I do that?" she asks.

"You do everything I say. No matter if it doesn't make sense or if your husband argues with me."

"And what do you want me to do?"

"Only two things for now: eat what Mrs. Hendricks brings you, and then get up and walk the room. I will help you with every step."

"But I'm so tired."

"I know. Did your husband give you medicine? Laudanum perhaps?"

She nods. "Yesterday."

My guess is that it was a lower dose than he gave Grace. Otherwise, she'd be dead. But I don't dare hope the man has learned anything about messing with the natural order of a birth.

"It probably hasn't fully worn off. But there is one thing I can promise you. If you stay in this bed, if you eat nothing, you and your child *will* die. It will be slow and painful. Exhaustion will swallow you both. And there is nothing I will be able to do for you." I grab her hands. "But now? Now is not too late. So. Will you trust me?"

It is easy to assume that for a birth to go badly, something specific must go wrong. A breech presentation. A hemorrhage. An infection. I have faced all these difficulties, and more, but it is often the mortal threat of exhaustion that can cause a woman's life to ebb away. There is no condition on earth more draining than that of labor, and few ways to rouse a woman once she has succumbed to exhaustion.

Mrs. Page listens to me. I watch her think for a moment and then she nods. "I can do that."

I push her pale blonde hair back from her face. I press my palm to her forehead. She is warm but not feverish.

"I have to touch you now," I tell her. "To see how far along you are in this labor."

"Okay."

"But there is something very important I must know before I can
do that."

"What?"

"Your name."

"Mrs. Page."

"No," I tell her. "Page is your *husband's* name. And missus is the
thing you became on your wedding day. What is the one you were
given at birth?"

"Melody."

"It is very nice to meet you, Melody. My name is Martha. And I
will help you through this."

*

Melody Page has to walk the room for five grueling hours before
she hits transition. And it takes another full hour of pushing before
her tiny daughter makes an entrance into the world. Even then, it is
ten o'clock before the work is done. And eleven before I have finally
packed my things.

Mrs. Hendricks joins me at the bedroom door as I am leaving. "I
do not like you," she says, apropos of nothing.

It makes me laugh. "Nor I, you."

This earns the first real smile I have ever received from the woman.

"But I do respect you," she tells me. "And I am sorry for the trouble I gave you with Grace."

"That is more than enough for me," I say. Then I look behind her
to the bed where Melody is cradling her little bundle. "You will stay
with her?"

"Through the night."

"Thank you. Call for me if you have any concerns."

"I will," she says, then returns to Melody's side without another
word.

I am turning for the door when Dr. Page calls out. "Mistress Ballard?"

A sigh.

"Yes?"

"Let me walk you out."

I nod. We walk in silence down the hall, the stairs, and to the first floor. He opens the door and leans against the frame, blocking my exit.

"What is your fee?" he asks.

"I do not want payment."

"I cannot allow you to leave here without coin," he says. "I refuse to be in your debt."

"You have no say in the matter. I will accept nothing from you but an apology."

"You are a stubborn old bitch, aren't you?"

Suddenly I find myself missing Mrs. Hendricks. She'd likely rip his ear clean off at those words.

"Is that what you really think of me? After today?"

"I think you are full of yourself. A country woman bloated with the idea of your own skill."

I nod sadly. "And yet you still want to pay me?"

"It is the right thing to do."

"Let me ask you a question," I say.

He looks at me but doesn't respond.

I stick my finger in his face. "Have you ever successfully delivered a child?"

"In medical school I assisted any number of doctors in—"

"No. That is not what I mean. On your own?"

"I don't see how that—"

"So the answer is no. And the result is two of Hallowell's children dead born. Such things might not matter at Harvard. But here they matter immensely."

Page lifts his chin. "You do understand that they call it the *practice* of medicine for a reason, don't you? The consequences of such practice can be unfortunate. But no doctor expects less. Nor should the citizens of any town."

"And yet you are willing to practice on your own wife. Shame on you."

He says nothing.

"Here is what I require for payment. You stick to doctoring. I will do the delivering."

His eyes are blank. Uncomprehending.

"You will never attend another woman in childbirth. Not in this town. If you are too arrogant to call for me, then call someone else.

I care not. But I do not ever want you to set your hand to a laboring woman ever again. Do you understand?"

The young Dr. Benjamin Page grows still. Then pale. I see his jaw tremble with rage. But he steps aside to let me pass, and before he closes the door, he nods. Just once.

And that is enough.

DR. COLEMAN'S STORE

The ice is thickest in the shallows, near the riverbank. Toward the center of the Kennebec, however, it creaks beneath my feet. Like old floorboards. Like old bones. And even though I know it will bear my weight, I proceed carefully, medical bag in one hand and the other outstretched, each footstep purposeful, listening for popping sounds, feeling for shifting and sinking beneath my feet. Sam Dawin is not the only man to have fallen through the ice, though he is one of only a handful to survive. The river is at least four hundred feet wide in most places, deep in the middle, with a ruthless current and, at this time of year, lethal temperatures. If you go under, you are gone. And if they find you, it is usually bobbing in a Boston boatyard weeks later, your skin and clothing torn to shreds.

After attending to Melody Page, I am the kind of exhausted I used to think impossible. In my youth, when I first took to this profession, it was not uncommon for me to spend multiple days rushing from one birth to another. I could function on minimal sleep and sporadic meals. But something shifted once I turned fifty. My body started rebelling at the inconsistent schedule. And now my entire physical being protests the long night. The combative conversations with Dr. Page and Mrs. Hendricks have left me drained. My neck is stiff, and my eyes are dry. My bones feel loose at the joints, but my muscles tight. I am hungry.

"Home soon," I mutter as I traverse the midpoint of the river.

It takes an effort not to hasten my steps, but I continue the careful, methodical passage until my right foot lands on firm ground. It is a short hike up the bank, and then I stomp my feet on the boardwalk, knocking the snow from the soles of my boots.

The moon is bright, and the clouds are wispy and low, making the sky look like an oyster shell, striated with shades of gray. I will be home in an hour if I am lucky, and then it's a cold dinner and my own bed. But first I must collect Brutus from where I left him stabled at the tavern. Though the residents of the Hook are comfortable walking back and forth across the river, few of us are brave enough to ride a two-thousand-pound steed over the ice.

I am turning toward Pollard's when I see that the lanterns are lit in Coleman's Store. Odd. He usually closes shop by six o'clock. The front door is only a few steps away, so I go left instead of right and try the knob. It turns easily in my hand, and I step inside to the sound of bells tinkling merrily above my head.

Samuel Coleman looks up from his place at the counter. "Who's there?" He asks, milky eye squinting at me.

"It's only Martha."

"Ah," he says. "You're out late."

"I've been at a birth across the river."

"And who's the new parent?"

I laugh at the absurdity. "Dr. Page."

"He called for you?"

"He most certainly did not. And I can honestly say, his is the first child I have ever delivered against my will."

"But all is well?"

"It is. No thanks to him."

"All's well that ends well, I suppose. But that does not answer why you've brightened my doorstep this evening."

"I saw the lights were on."

"And you were worried about me?"

"Only curious what has you up so late."

Samuel Coleman lifts his ledger. "This. Going over it again. Making sure I've gotten my accounts right. It gets harder every day."

On my way to the counter, I make sure there is no silver fox pelt among those for sale. As I have every time I've entered for the last few months, I breathe a sigh of relief upon finding nothing but rabbit, stoat, and beaver. The occasional raccoon. And the one red fox.

"Are ye looking for a skin, Mistress Ballard?"

"No. I'm looking to make sure one isn't here." When Coleman tips his head to the side in curiosity, I add, "There's a silver fox that roams our land. I think she's made a den under the old live oak down by the creek. To be honest, I've grown fond of her."

"A pelt like that would fetch a pretty penny. Traders from Russia and China in particular value them. A single one is worth twenty dollars. Sometimes thirty if it's in good condition."

"But would you pay that?"

"I've never had the chance."

I lean closer. "But if one were offered? Let's say, by one of those trappers who come in on occasion. Would you buy it?"

He pulls at the corner of his mustache. "Would it matter? Since the wee beast would already be kilt?"

"It would matter to me."

"Then I reckon the answer is no. But I get the impression that ye dinna really want to talk about pelts."

"No. I had no reason other than curiosity for coming in. But now that I'm here, I thought I'd ask you about Sarah White."

"I barely know the girl."

"But do you dislike her?"

"Not at all."

"But would you dislike having her around?"

"I dinna want another wife, Mistress Ballard. And I am too old for her besides."

I laugh, long and loud. I cannot help myself. The thought hadn't even occurred to me. "Gracious, no! That is not at all what I mean."

"Then explain what ye do because I canna fathom what it might be."

"You told me that you were looking to hire a shop boy. Someone to work the counter and keep the books. I think Sarah would do well, and it would give your eye a break. Not to mention the rest of you."

"Yer saying I am old and feeble?"

"You basically said so not two minutes ago." I am glad to see the flash of humor in that eye, the bobble at the corner of his mouth that suggests a smile he's trying to hide. "You are nearing seventy. You have one eye and a grand total of six fingers spread between both hands. I am *saying* that having help in the shop a few days a week would be no great burden to you. I think you should consider Sarah."

"That is an interesting suggestion, Mistress Ballard," Coleman says. He leans across the counter and squints at me in such a way that his eye seems to disappear inside his face altogether. "And I do wish ye'd brought it to me sooner."

"Why is that?"

"Because just yesterday I accepted an offer on the store from a man in Boston."

"You've sold it?"

"I will have, next month, when he arrives with payment."

I am sorry to hear this—for more than one reason. I will miss Coleman, and I tell him so.

"There's nothing to miss. I'll be staying on to help the man until he's up and running. Ye'll see me often enough."

Coleman winks, and it is both endearing and macabre. It makes me curious again, how he lost the other eye. I have always feared that it would be an insult to ask, but I'm emboldened by my disappointment in losing this chance to help Sarah.

"What happened?" I ask. "To your eye? Your fingers? I have always wondered."

"You dinna take to the theory of piracy? That's the rumor I've heard whispered most around here," he says with a jolly rumble in his chest. "And do ye ken that no one has ever come out and asked me directly?"

"You do cut an intimidating figure," I say.

"Pfft. Nonsense. Being scarred and being scary are not the same thing."

I wait, not wanting to prod him any further in case it's an answer he does not want to give, but after a moment, he lifts his hand and turns it in the air. Waves those stubby fingers.

"It was during the Battle of Signal Hill. And wouldn't that be my luck? To get maimed in the last battle, after being at war and unharmed for seven years." He looks at me. Smiles. "I still consider myself lucky. I just lost bits and pieces. Some men lost their lives. And others? Well, Joseph North fought too, and he could tell you what it's like to lose a soul."

He says it so cavalierly. As though a soul is something you can lose as easily as a game of chess.

"What do you mean by that?"

There are great depths to that one milky eye, and I watch them settle over me as he ponders how to answer the question. When he finally speaks again, I worry he's lost the thread of our conversation.

"She had beautiful hair, you know," he says.

"Who?"

"My wife. It was bright. Shiny. Like a copper coin left in the sun. We'd been married three months when a Huron brave cut it from her head. I was told later that"—here he must clear his throat—"that it was sold to a Frenchman for thirty francs. They were going for head-count, see. Proof of a dead English enemy."

This is the part no one talks about anymore. Not in civilized company at least. When a war is over, you stop discussing the cost. The reality. The blood-soaked soil or the grave markers or the collateral damage. The ways we kill our enemies in order to claim victory. History is written by the men who live. Not the ones who die. But I've heard these stories myself. I know it isn't so easy as the French were bad and the English were good. *Ha!* The English? No. You'll never hear me defend their methods. My people came from those shores because they had no options left.

"The English weren't innocent of that either," I say.

"No. They weren't. Much to their shame. But to them, the taking and selling of a human scalp was *optional.* Yet that option made Joseph North a very wealthy man. By the time war was officially declared in 1756, an Indian male scalp was worth one hundred and thirty pounds to the English. A female, less. Always worth less, the women." I cannot tell whether that last bit is an apology or an observation. "They fetched fifty pounds. And how do you think Joseph North built that fancy house on the hill? How do you think he hands out loans like candy?" Coleman asks and looks me dead in the eye. "Like I said. Lost his soul."

POLLARD'S TAVERN

FRIDAY, MARCH 26

Cyrus stands before the table and faces all three judges. Once again the Court of Common Pleas has come to Hallowell with the honorable Obadiah Wood, James Parker, and John Hubbard presiding. As Judge North hasn't been seen by anyone in the Hook since the end of January, he was automatically removed from this hearing.

Seth Parker stands beside Cyrus ready to assist in this legal matter. He has assured us that the court has no legal grounds to keep our son imprisoned, but I have a bad feeling about these proceedings. Cyrus's case is the only one on the docket today. He has arrived freshly shaven and in his Sunday best. He looks more like his father than ever today. A man in his prime. But he's got a cheeky air about him that leaves me fidgeting in my seat. Cyrus looks like he's gunning for a fight.

"How do you plead?" Obadiah Wood asks Cyrus. "In the charge of murder against one Joshua Burgess in November of last year?"

There is a stack of papers on the table beside him, and he bends over the pile, quill in hand, to write his response.

Not guilty.

Once again, half the town is here. The tavern is packed. Beer and cider flow freely, but the room is silent. The accusation against him—

though invalid—is one that most of the people here would consider just. No one is whispering today.

Judge Parker leans across the table. "As you have heard, there are seven men here who testify to the fact that you got into a physical altercation with the deceased on the night of November twenty-fifth. Do you deny having done so?"

No.

Parker notes this in his ledger. "What was the cause for your altercation?"

Cyrus takes his time writing out his response. After a moment he shows the paper to Seth—who nods—but before he can hand it to the judge, Parker interrupts.

"In order to keep these proceedings expeditious, we will allow your attorney to read your answers, Mr. Ballard."

Cyrus hands the paper to Seth instead, who reads his answer aloud. "Joshua Burgess put his hands on my sister. I defended her honor."

This, too, was verified by the judges earlier in the hearing, when seven different witnesses came forward to describe the events of November's Frolic. But they want to hear from Hannah directly, so she goes to stand beside her brother.

"Please state your name for the court," Judge Parker says.

"Hannah Ballard."

"And what happened on the night in question?"

I can see Moses standing beside the fireplace next to Barnabas Lambard. His arms are crossed, and he scowls at the sight of her interrogation. He doesn't like her being put on display in this manner, and I can't say that I blame him. The boy is in love and protective, but Hannah insisted on defending her brother. As did Dolly who—for her part—sits with a stiff back and lifted chin doing all she can to ignore Barnabas.

"Joshua Burgess asked me to dance all evening, and I refused him," Hannah says. "It wasn't just me, though, he went around the room several times, but never found a partner. But I was the last one to tell him no. So he got angry. Grabbed my arm and dragged me onto the dance floor. He left bruises."

Moses was not aware of the bruises, I think, and he takes a step forward, fists balled. Calmly, casually, Barnabas sets a hand on his shoulder and pulls him back. Whispers something in his ear.

They've become friends, I think. And I am glad to see it.

"Is that when your brother came to your defense?" Judge Wood asks.

"Yes. It didn't take long. Five or ten seconds, maybe. And the fight didn't last much longer than that. Then Cyrus and a couple of other men tossed Burgess into the snow."

Wood taps the table with one finger. "Who were these other men?"

"Sam Dawin and my brother Jonathan."

"Are they in the courtroom today?"

They are. And they quickly confirm Hannah's testimony. Jonathan looks testy, and Sam uneasy, but the judges don't question them further. The Ballard family has taken up an entire table and two benches at the tavern. Seth and Sam have joined us as well, and I like to think that the sight is a bulwark for Cyrus.

"Cyrus had nothing to do with Burgess's death," Hannah says. "He stayed inside the remainder of the night, and then he took me and my sister home."

It's Judge Hubbard's turn to speak. "And what of your other brother?"

Again, Jonathan stands. "After the dance I left with Sam. We had an order of lumber to deliver. That was the night the river froze. We got locked in at Bumberhook Point."

"That's where the body of Joshua Burgess was discovered?"

"Yes sir, we were the ones who found him."

Hubbard looks to his colleagues, then directly at me. "Mistress Ballard?"

I stand. "Yes."

"You testified previously that your children returned home from the dance shortly before you were called to deliver a child?"

"Yes. Roughly an hour or so."

"And are you certain that Cyrus remained in bed after you left?"

This talking in circles is exhausting, and it takes more effort than I would like to keep the frustration out of my voice. "I have no reason to believe that he didn't."

"And when the rest of your household woke later that morning, was he among them?"

Young Ephraim. God bless his little lion's heart. The proceedings have been too much for him. He's scared for his older brother and smart enough to know that the judges are looking for something—anything, really—that will give them cause to proceed with a trial. He leaps to his feet and says, with a voice that cracks on the first word, "I can answer that!"

At first there is a titter of laughter behind us, and his cheeks blaze. But he stiffens his back and sticks out his chin.

"Young man? Your name?" Wood asks.

"Ephraim Ballard. The s-s-second," he stammers.

There's a smile at the corner of Wood's mouth. Just a flicker of kindness. "Continue please. Can you verify that Cyrus was home when the household awoke?"

"Yes! We share a room. And he was right there in bed when we were woken at five. Sam Dawin fell through the ice, and it caused a big ruckus when he was brought to us. At first we all thought he was dead."

This seems to be enough for Wood and Parker. Both of them lean back in their seats. Nod. Set down their quills. But Hubbard—it would seem—is feeling obstinate today and is not so easily charmed by my youngest son.

"And what of the three hours in between?" he asks. "Can you verify that your brother was home? Three hours is plenty of time to sneak out and finish the job he'd started with Burgess."

"I was asleep," Young Ephraim says, as though it is the most obvious answer in the world. "And so was *Cyrus*."

All this time Seth has watched the proceedings. He's taken notes of his own in some scrawl that I can't read, but now he folds the paper in half, stands, and approaches the judge's table. "If I may speak, Your Honors?"

It is his right as Cyrus's lawyer, and they allow it.

"I move to have these charges dropped immediately. Nothing has been accomplished during this hearing apart from dickering over the hours between two and five in the morning. It has been established that Cyrus Ballard did not go after Mr. Burgess that night. It has been established that he escorted his sisters home, went to sleep, and was there, in his own bed, when Sam Dawin was brought to the house. No witnesses have come forth saying otherwise. Nor has the court produced a single shred of evidence tying him to the murder. Every judge on this bench has argued at least once that charges in the Foster case could not be brought because there was no witness to the actual crime. Yet here, in the case of *murder,* that same standard is not upheld? No. This hearing is not only a gross misuse of the judiciary but a colossal waste of time. The court has no cause whatsoever to proceed beyond this point."

Somewhere, at the back of the tavern, there is scattered clapping, and the judges retreat to the storeroom to deliberate.

*

Friday, March 26.——Cloudy and cold. The Court of Common Pleas convened at the Hook to consider the charges brought against Cyrus in the matter of Captain Burgess. They agreed that Cyrus should be released from the jail yard but the charges remain pending.

POWNALBORO COURTHOUSE

"Let's go," Ephraim says. "I'm hungry."

Our rented room is in the corner of the second floor and benefits from having three windows. Two facing east and one north. There is a bed, desk, and washstand. It is spare but clean. The sun has made a rare appearance this morning, and I lean into the soft, warm light streaming through the windows. It likely won't last long, however. There are clouds on the horizon.

I follow Ephraim out the door and down the stairs into the tavern where the other guests have already collected.

Like many public buildings in the colonies, the Pownalboro tavern serves multiple purposes. It is a three-story white clapboard building with a long addition attached to one side. The first floor is a tavern, the second comprises six rooms for rent, and the third is living quarters for the family of Samuel Goodwin: Kennebec Proprietor, captain of the guard at Fort Shirley, and owner of this fine establishment. The addition, built thirty years ago, comprises a small jail and courthouse.

Four of the other rooms have been rented by the judges who sit on the Supreme Judicial Court. They have traveled from Boston for Joseph North's trial. But unlike North and his colleagues in Vassalboro, they are all lawyers by trade. They all have private practices in the city. They are men of wealth and distinction. But—to hear them mutter as they fill their plates at breakfast—none of them are pleased to be here.

The judges typically make the trip only twice per year: once in December and once in July. But the severity of the Foster case has forced a special session of the court. Adding to the complication, however, is the Kennebec itself. Usually, they sail from Boston to Bath, then upriver to Pownalboro, but they were only able to get as far as Bath yesterday, then had to rent a carriage for the remainder of the journey. The frozen river alters every facet of life for those who live along it, yet the judges take the inconvenience as a personal slight.

"That is Robert Treat Paine," Ephraim whispers to me as we choose a table in the dining area.

I am careful not to stare. The man is a legend in the colonies. One of fifty-six men to sign the Declaration of Independence, Paine is a lawyer, politician, judge, as well as a founding member of the Pennsylvania Abolition Society. He has worked most of his life to outlaw slavery in what are now these united states, and while many believe it is a fool's errand, I am hopeful the cause will prevail.

"Is he fair?" I ask. "Will he listen to the facts of the case?"

Ephraim nods. "I am told his moral compass points straight north."

"And the others?"

"The one with the dark hair, there to the left, is Nathan Cushing." Ephraim tips his chin slightly to indicate the judge. "He was appointed to the bench by John Hancock in January. His brother, William, is one of the five justices on the United States Supreme Court."

"He is no stranger to the law then?"

"Indeed. It's a family legacy. The one next to him is Increase Sumner. As solid a jurist as can be found. He's been on the court for eight years. Also appointed by Hancock."

"And the last?"

"Francis Dana. A delegate to the Continental Congress. Signed the Articles of Confederation. I don't know a man who doesn't respect him."

"All of them Harvard men?"

"Yes."

I sigh. "I must admit to being weary of Harvard men just now. They've caused me nothing but trouble of late."

"Well, I don't think Rebecca Foster could ask for a better set of jurists. They are nothing like the men who have heard the case thus far. If she has any chance of justice, it will be here."

I shift in my chair, then look at Ephraim with an expression of unmasked concern. "Have you seen the Fosters yet?"

"No." The look he gives me is equally wary. "They aren't staying here. Or at least they haven't arrived yet. I paid extra to reserve the last room for them. But there are a dozen places in Pownalboro they could be lodging."

I watch the judges at their table across the room. They look like mere mortals, just men of varying ages, at breakfast. In a few short hours, however, they will don their black silk robes and their powdered wigs and transform into symbols of power and authority. Those four men will determine whether justice is available to all, or only a select few.

*

Baths are a luxury. It has been several years since I enjoyed a long soak in a real copper tub, but I do now as we wait for the trial to begin. I'll pay extra for the privilege, since Captain Goodwin's children had to haul a dozen buckets of hot water upstairs to fill it. I don't care. It's worth every shilling to sit here and soak for an hour. I have soap, clean towels, and a quiet room where I can sort through my thoughts.

I sit in the water until my fingers prune, until the water goes from hot to warm, from warm to cool. I sit here, wet hair dripping over the curved rim of the tub, listening to the hustle and bustle of a household I do not have to manage today. The running of this tavern is a family affair—much like it is for the Pollards—and I listen to the footsteps and muted conversations. The slamming of doors and the constant sound of children running up and down the stairs. Their laughter and happy bickering. Below me, above me, the sounds of life, of a big family, are everywhere.

It is just the respite my nerves need. As the shadows shift and the water grows uncomfortably cold, I finally push myself out of the tub and step onto the mat. I towel myself off, then dress in the green silk gown that I paid Mrs. Densmore to make for me. It fits perfectly and has the shiny, stiff feel of a dress that's never been worn.

Ephraim is waiting for me in the room when I return, and I can tell that he, too, is fortifying himself for the afternoon. His face is to the window—watching clouds the color of steel roll in—and he doesn't turn when I walk through the door.

"They will hear four cases," Ephraim says. "I just got word from the clerk downstairs. North's will be the last."

"I thought his was the only one on the docket?"

"It was. Until last week. There are three other cases of a . . ." he pauses, considers his word choice, ". . . *carnal* nature that have been elevated from the lower courts. They thought it best to kill four birds with one stone—as it were—rather than wait until July. Perhaps they hope to get out of that trip altogether."

Ephraim finally turns around. Looks at me. Whistles long and low.

"What?"

"That is a new dress."

"It is."

He crosses the room. Runs one finger just beneath the collar. "You look lovely in green."

I study a spot on the wall behind him. "I thought that I should . . . that it matters. Today. That I don't look like some country woman trying to make myself important." I struggle to explain. "These are respected men. And they are deciding the fate of my friend. I wanted . . ."

Ephraim pulls me close, as he does every time that tears take me hostage. I am not a weepy woman. But today *does* matter. And we have come a long distance to finally put this case behind us.

"You look *lovely*," he says again, his voice a warm whisper curling into my ear. "Now let us go find the Fosters."

*

"The Supreme Judicial Court is hereby called to order," the court clerk announces to a full room. "Please stand for the honorable Justices Robert Treat Paine, Nathan Cushing, Increase Sumner, and Francis Dana."

Six dozen men and women stand when the four judges enter the courthouse. They look nothing like the men at breakfast this morning. Each wears his robe and his wig. Two have donned spectacles. All appear distinguished and severe. There are no smiles, no nods of acknowledgment between one neighbor and another. Only solemnity and a near-tangible sense of purpose. Despite all my years giving testimony, I have never been in a courtroom so serious as this.

Ephraim insisted that we sit at the front this time, as close to the bench as possible, even though North's case will be the last called. Ephraim did confirm that North is in Pownalboro, having made his first appearance since the disappearing act in Hallowell.

"Do you see the Fosters?" I ask. Thirty minutes of inquiring up and down the main street of Pownalboro did not yield our friends, and a hard knot of worry has begun to grow in the pit of my stomach.

Ephraim cranes his neck from one side to the other, looking for Isaac and Rebecca, then shakes his head. "Not yet. I don't blame them for not wanting to sit through other people's misery as well as their own."

"What about Seth?"

"At the back of the room. Keeping quiet and out of sight until the Fosters' case is called."

"Good," I say, then turn to look at him. "That's a good sign."

As usual, Seth appears nondescript in his wool breeches and coat, boring but not shabby. He's shaved and trimmed his hair for the occasion, and I can see that all the buttons on his waistcoat have been polished. I try to catch his gaze, but he's watching something out the window.

Judge Nathan Cushing stands. "As stated, and then later codified in the laws of this colony, on December 17, 1623, all criminal acts, and also matters of trespass and debts, will be tried by the verdict of twelve honest men, impaneled by the authority of this court, to form a jury upon their oath," he tells the room. "Look to your left to see the men gathered today for this purpose."

The men sit, stone-faced, in two rows of six. They range in age from twenty to eighty. Some bearded, some shaven. They are local men. Farmers. Merchants. Sailors. Blacksmiths and carpenters. To the best of the court's knowledge, they have no relationship with any of the defendants.

Cushing holds up his copy of the docket. "Our first cause is an appeal, that of Hannah Barker who was convicted by the Court of General Sessions of Lincoln County for slandering one Polly Noble, Miss Noble being a daughter of a justice of the peace on said court. All parties involved in these proceedings come forward, please."

Four women and one man approach the long table where the judges sit.

"How do you plead, Miss Barker?" Cushing asks.

Hannah Barker is so thin she wouldn't leave prints if she walked across a muddy road. Nor is she pretty, her face pocked and scarred from chin to hairline. But she stands straight and doesn't waver when she speaks. "Not guilty. I ain't said nothin' but the truth."

The truth, or at least Hannah's version of it, could have been stated a bit more politely, because when Cushing asks the two witnesses what Hannah told them about Polly, their answers are ruthless.

" *'God of Heaven!'* That's what she said, Hannah, I mean," the first woman tells Cushing. " 'What do you think has happened to Noble's family? Polly has gone up to Boston and had herself a Negro bastard.' She said it to me just like that, last summer coming out of church." This last word is whispered, as though the real sacrilege was the location and not the accusation.

"And do you have any children, Miss Noble? Illegitimate or otherwise?"

"No, sir."

"Have you ever been to Boston?"

"With my father. And he can testify that I never left his sight."

Cushing looks to the father, and he nods. Notes are made on the docket, and Cushing continues. "Next witness."

A second woman steps forward. She bears such a resemblance to the first that I assume they are sisters. "Hannah told me that 'Poll has been with several men and that her father had even catched her under the counter once.'"

These accusations are also denied, and the father swears his daughter was up to no such behavior. Polly, when her turn comes to address the court, weeps and says her reputation has been "ruin't." She begs the jury to uphold the conviction.

And they do. When Cushing hands the case over to the jury, they leave the room to deliberate alone in the tavern but are gone less than fifteen minutes.

Cushing reads the verdict aloud. "We the jury find Hannah Barker guilty of slander." Cushing makes his note on the docket, then adds, "This court sustains the previous conviction and fines Miss Barker the sum of seventy-five dollars."

More wailing, but from Hannah Barker this time. It is a fee large enough to financially destroy Miss Barker and her family. I look over my shoulder, searching for the Fosters. I fear Rebecca will take the judgment to mean that the justices will show partiality to North. For once, I am relieved not to see her.

Increase Sumner bangs his gavel on the table this time, calling the court back to order, then stands to announce the next cause to be presented.

"The court will hear the cause of Thomas Meloney, who is charged with living in sin with his own sister, Johanah, and murdering the infant born of her body. Please bring forth all witnesses," Judge Sumner says, then takes his seat once more.

Instead of Johanah, two men come forward. One from the back of the room and the other through a side door, from the jail. Father and son, if I have ever seen a pair. One old and bent, the other stiff and defiant. Neither of them has acquired a lawyer.

"Not guilty," Thomas Meloney says, when asked.

His father, however, tells a different tale. "They is brother and sister. And they has lived in one house together ever since Johanah had her first child. Three of 'em she has now, but I don't know who is the father of them children."

Neither the act of incest nor the murder of an infant can be confirmed by the court as there are no witnesses who saw either take place. All that can be confirmed is that brother and sister live under the same roof, and that Johanah has a habit of bringing illegitimate children into the world. This causes some consternation between the judges, because it is obvious the law has been violated and a child is dead. But without Johanah or her testimony, the case is sent to the jury on speculation alone.

Ten minutes later, Sumner reads the verdict. "We the jury vote to acquit Thomas Meloney on charges of incest and murder due to lack of evidence."

I stiffen in my seat, and Ephraim reaches for my hand. He squeezes it just hard enough to make me hiss.

"Careful," he whispers.

"What? I haven't said anything."

"You were about to."

"Only that a woman gossips," I mutter in his ear, "and is fined enough money to buy three horses, but a man breaks laws, both divine and human, and walks out of court with his hands in his pockets."

"Would you have them hang him from a tree without a stitch of evidence? Not a single witness came forward to support the accusation."

"And nary a single concern that Johanah's men stood in court without her?"

Ephraim squeezes my hand again, but harder this time. "How many worries would you have me carry today, love? Those of a stranger as well?"

It's a fair question, but I cannot help but feel unsettled that a young woman is out there in the world with no one to protect her from those closest to her. My only comfort is that Sumner looks equally disturbed as he makes notes on his copy of the docket.

The third case called before the judges is of great interest to me, and once again I search the courtroom for signs of the Fosters. Still nothing. They are cutting it awfully close.

Judge Francis Dana takes his turn to address the room. "The court will hear an appeal from Nathaniel Whitaker, convicted by the Court of Common Pleas of Lincoln County of the attempted rape of one Milly Lambard."

"No relation to Barnabas, I hope," Ephraim mutters.

The courtroom listens as Milly Lambard states that, four years earlier, Nathaniel Whitaker assaulted her in a field in Canaan. He denies this emphatically. Her family testifies that she told them about the assault on the morning that it happened. His family testifies that it couldn't have happened because he was with them, it being a Sunday afternoon, and they all sup together after services. Questions are asked. Accusations made. But in the end this case also goes to the jury without a preponderance of evidence. The earlier conviction is overturned, and Nathaniel Whitaker walks out triumphant.

*

"Where are you going?" Ephraim asks.

"Privy. We've been sitting here for hours."

"They're about to start."

"Better now than later and miss my chance to testify."

I weave my way through the crowd—most of the people standing to stretch or gossip about what they've heard—and step into the
bracing air. Fine little puffs of snow drift down from the steely clouds
that hover above Pownalboro, and I glare at the sky. I am tired of
winter. Of snow. Of ice. Of cold. I am tired of the world being held
in suspension between these mercurial seasons. But I do not control
the four winds, cannot command the sun to burn hot again. I can,
however, empty my bladder and make myself a bit more comfortable.

The line to the privy is long—at least twenty people deep—
and I shift from foot to foot. The human need for relief is impolite
and inconvenient, but really, the tavern should have more than one
accommodation for such needs.

Five minutes. Ten.

Fifteen.

I glance over my shoulder as the sound of a gavel banging the
table resonates through the chill air. Only two more people in front
of me.

By the time I close the outhouse door and throw up my skirts, my
relief is replaced by fear, and I do my business as quickly as possible.
By the time I make it back to the courthouse, half the room is standing. People crane their necks. Whisper. There is a buzz in the air, like
static. It makes me tense. Makes me feel as if an itch is snaking its way
across my body.

"What took you so long?" Ephraim asks when I squeeze back to
the front of the room.

"*Them.*" I indicate those around us. "The line was long."

"Well, they called North."

"I see him."

He stands off to the side, head bent, whispering with a man I have
never seen before.

Ephraim sets his hand to the small of my back. He means to calm me, but the gesture has the opposite effect. "They also called the Fosters. They aren't here."

"That can't be."

"Five minutes, Martha. They haven't come forward. I've even looked outside. They aren't here. And Seth hasn't seen them either."

"But—"

Judge Robert Treat Paine does his best to call the room to order. He bangs his gavel again. Slowly the room settles. People take their seats.

"This is the last call for Rebecca Foster," Paine says.

Seth makes his way to the front of the room.

"Are you Mr. Foster?"

He shakes his head. "No. My name is Seth Parker, the attorney representing the Fosters."

"Are your clients here today?"

He clears his throat uncomfortably. "I do not know. But I am prepared to argue their cause regardless. And they also have a witness present who has traveled from Hallowell to testify on their behalf." He points to me.

"It seems that you take these proceedings a great deal more seriously than your clients, Mr. Parker."

"Please excuse Rebecca, Your Honor. She is eight months pregnant as a result of the assault—"

"*Alleged* assault." The man standing beside North steps forward and introduces himself. He is tall and smug and wears a fine, dark coat. "Henry Knowland, esquire, attorney for the defense." He approaches the table and hands Paine a small square calling card. "I traveled here from Boston with my client."

"Well, at least Lidia didn't lie about where he went," I whisper to Ephraim.

Paine nods. "Thank you. As Mr. Parker was saying . . ."

He glares at Henry Knowland. "Regardless of how you *define* the assault, the fact remains that my client is eight months pregnant as a result. No doubt why she is not present today, Your Honor. Travel of any kind at this time would prove to be a burden. Yet this circumstance should not prevent this court from moving forward with the trial. I am prepared to argue on her behalf. I have brought depositions, and her witness has evidence as well."

"Bring the depositions forward," Paine says.

Seth hands both recorded testimonies to Judge Paine, then returns to his place at the front of the room. He reads both accounts aloud for the benefit of the courtroom. No one shifts or speaks until he's done.

"Mistress Ballard?" Paine asks, and I stand. "Do you confirm that this was written by your hand and that all of the details are true?"

"Yes, Your Honor."

"And have you brought this journal mentioned in your deposition?"

"I have."

"Please bring it forward."

I lay my book on the table in front of the judges and flip to the pages mentioned in my deposition.

"I would like the jury to note that everything is in accordance with her written account. Thank you, Mistress Ballard, you may be seated."

Ephraim takes my hand, rubs the base of my thumb with his. The *whisk-whisk* of his calloused finger on my skin is comforting. Grounding.

"We will move on to the cause between the Commonwealth and Joseph North," Judge Paine says. He reads the charges aloud for the benefit of the court. "It is stated that on the night of August tenth, Joseph North broke into the house of Isaac Foster and made an attempt to ravish his wife despite her many attempts to exert herself against him. She on oath affirmed this at two prior hearings in Kennebec County and has deposed the same. How do you plead, Colonel North?"

North looks distinguished this afternoon. Hair and beard have both been trimmed. His suit is new. Shoes polished. He comes to stand before the table with his attorney. "I plead not guilty, Your Honor."

"Then what have you to say regarding these accusations?"

Henry Knowland takes over for his client. It is a wise move given how North tends to argue and interrupt when not in command of a courtroom himself. "Depositions notwithstanding, *accusations* notwithstanding, there are no witnesses who can attest that these things did in fact happen as claimed. No one saw my client coming or going at the Fosters' that evening. No one *saw* any crimes perpetrated upon her person that evening. Her only witness is a midwife who tended to her nine days later, who herself is taking Mrs. Foster's word about these events. Was she hurt in some fashion? No doubt! Is there any proof, whatsoever, that *my* client is responsible? None. We have only the word of a woman who did not even bother to show up today to testify on her own behalf. How seriously can she truly take this fabrication? Gentlemen," he implores, turning to the jury and addressing them directly. "*Come. Be reasonable.* Will you ruin the life of a good man, a *respected* man, an upstanding member of a fine community, a man who has served this country honorably in not one, but two wars? A colonel! A judge! All on account of rumors and speculations? You are smarter than that. And you are far more honorable."

Knowland returns to his place and Judge Paine motions for Seth to take the floor. "Mr. Parker, do you have any additional words for the court?"

Seth looks around the courtroom, searching for the Fosters one last time, and I wince at the desperation in his eyes. Finally, he takes a deep breath and turns to the jury. "How is it *honorable* to ignore the undisputed facts that a woman was raped and is now pregnant as a result? No one denies that. They only question her word. *Her* account. They shout '*witness!*' as though crimes such as this are ever performed in broad daylight. In the middle of a street. Evil is always done in secret. You know that. Rebecca Foster *is* a witness! And her account should not be discounted simply because a late pregnancy—one that was *forced* upon her—has made it impossible for her to travel. She has asked this court to render justice. The real question is whether you will deny her that justice. There is no reason whatsoever to doubt her claims. The defense certainly has not provided any. The truth has been clearly presented, and you must act upon it—as the good men, the *honorable* men that you are."

Seth Parker returns to his seat, jaw clenched in fury, and does not make eye contact with anyone.

"The court gives this matter over to the jury for deliberation." Robert Treat Paine thumps the table once with his gavel, then leans back in his chair.

*

We do not leave the courtroom. Most of those gathered here do not feel the same sense of urgency, however, and they wander out to stretch their legs when the jury retreats to deliberate. The judges slip away as well to make the most of this break.

The first thirty minutes isn't bad, but when the time crawls toward an hour, I start to get tense. Sensing my mood, Ephraim grabs my hand and stops chattering about the weather and what we'll plant in the spring. Seth Parker remains as well, but across the room, deep in the throes of a good and angry sulk. There are only ten people left in the courtroom when the twelve men deciding Rebecca's case return. There is a mad scramble outside when word spreads and it takes another five minutes before everyone has taken their seats.

The jury foreman hands the slip of paper to Judge Francis Dana. He unfolds it. Reads the words carefully, not once, but twice. Then he hands it to Increase Sumner, on his left. I scrutinize their faces for any indication of how the jury has ruled. Nothing. There is not a single clue written on their faces.

Increase Sumner hands the paper to Nathan Cushing.

He reads and his eyes are inscrutable.

He passes the paper to Robert Treat Paine.

Once again, the man gives not even the barest glimpse of emotion as he takes in the jury's verdict. There is nary a scowl. A sigh. No lifted eyebrow or deep inhale.

Paine leans across the table and hands the slip of paper back to Sumner.

He pushes his spectacles onto the bridge of his nose. "We the jury," he reads, voice certain and clear, "declare the defendant, one Colonel Joseph North, acquitted on the charge of attempted rape as it concerns one Mistress Rebecca Foster."

Twenty Years Ago

OXFORD, MASSACHUSETTS

JULY 7, 1769

The plague fell upon our house during the hottest days of summer. Diphtheria. That old, wicked scourge. And even though it did not discriminate among the homes of Oxford, we felt as though it treated our family with particular malice. Ephraim and I waited, certain it would consume the two of us as well, but it did not. Maybe that was the miracle, but it was a bitter one, for we watched each of our children tumble into fever, one after the other, after the other. All six of them limp and coughing, their throats swollen and rashed so badly they could hardly swallow the broth we dripped into their mouths.

That wasn't the worst of it. The thick gray mucus that coated the backs of their mouths and throats was enough to drive us to our knees. They couldn't swallow. Couldn't speak. Could barely breathe.

"Is there nothing we can do?" Ephraim asked, holding Jonathan against his chest, both of their shirts soaked through with fever.

"Cold baths. Broth. Licorice and chamomile for their throats, but that will only soothe the pain, not treat the sores," I told him.

We did the best we could. We hauled buckets of cold water from the well every day. We soaked the children in the washtub one by one, but no sooner had we dried and clothed them than the fevers returned.

And they cried. Not the angry or frustrated cries that we had grown accustomed to in a house full of children, but whimpers. Soft and weak and helpless. Like mewling kittens.

I held them all as often as I could, but I had six children and only one lap. And even that was crowded by the seventh that grew heavy beneath my ribs. But holding them only seemed to make them worse. Hot. Sweaty. Restless. And yet they all reached for me with limp arms anyway, looked to me with glassy eyes, desperate to feel better.

Our prayers accomplished nothing.

"Why is this happening?" I asked Ephraim that third week in June, as we collapsed into bed, the windows thrown open to let in a meager breeze. We'd spread pallets across our bedroom floor to keep the children close. "What have we done wrong?"

He pulled me to his chest and cupped the back of my head with his big, calloused hand. "It rains upon the just and the unjust, love. And we no more deserve this than our friends or neighbors do."

We watched our children weaken. Watched their throats swell. Watched the gray caul spread across their windpipes. Watched their lips turn blue and their breath grow shallow. It was Cyrus we worried most about. For two days he hardly moved at all. Our boy, a mere twelve years old, hovered at the point of death for weeks.

But it was Triphene who went first. Triphene, the girl we had named after the first woman I attended in childbed. Five. She was only *five* years old. One night our daughter crawled into bed with us, tucked herself between our bodies, and when we woke, she was gone. Cold and still, her hair a pale blonde curtain thrown across my arm.

We sent for Elspeth. And even though she could neither see nor help, she stood with us while we took turns doing the impossible. Ephraim dug the hole, then I placed Triphene inside, then he filled it in again, and I set the stone on top. We could not leave the others alone inside lest one of them expire in our absence. We could not expose Elspeth to their illness. But neither could we do what had to be done without comfort or witness. Elspeth was both for us. It was a cruel thing to ask, but she never faltered.

And then she did it again eight days later.

At dusk this time. But Dorothy was only two. She was the child I had named after my mother. And I cradled her in my arms as I wept beside her grave. It lay beside that of her sister, the soil on top still fresh and dark from the week before. The sight of them was fire between my ribs. A void within my soul.

Three days after that we called for Elspeth a third time.

Martha was the one who should have lived.

Martha, our second daughter, the one that Ephraim insisted be named after me. She was eight years old and looked like her father. She seemed the least ill of them all. She never wheezed, never seemed to lose her breath. Her throat was never covered with the rancid gray sores. But her heart—*oh God,* her heart—grew slower and slower as her illness progressed. It slowed and then it stilled and then the next breath never came. And the weight of her in my arms, wrapped in linen, was the weight of a thousand heartaches.

I don't remember if I screamed. Or if I cried. In that whole, awful ordeal, it is the one detail I cannot summon from the depths of my memory. I've never asked Ephraim. I don't have the heart.

I was certain then that the sickness would take them all. It would take them and then it would take us and then it would all be over. It's possible that I even wished for that to happen as it would be the only way we could be together again. As a family. As God intended.

But Cyrus got better. The morning after we buried Martha, he sprang out of bed like a wobbly new calf, wanting water and toast. But when he came to me, asking to be fed, his voice was gone. I'd only heard that voice crack a single time with looming manhood. But now it was gone. Paralyzed by illness. And though we waited—days, months, years—it never returned. Never more than a gentle croak or groan that he soon became too embarrassed to use. His life was spared, but his voice was stolen. And with it, any chance of a normal future.

Jonathan recovered the day after Cyrus. Then Lucy the one after that. Their fevers broke and their coughs faded and their lungs cleared. Their voices never so much as wavered. And when they asked after their sisters, we had only tears for an answer. Though you never think it possible, you can celebrate and grieve in the same breath. It is a holy abomination.

"I want to leave this place," Ephraim told me as we stood beneath the oak tree where our daughters were laid to rest. "I want to move somewhere else where there is more land. Where we can have a real farm, not just a garden. Somewhere we can start over. Perhaps build a mill."

"What?" I looked at him as though he'd spoken some other language. I could not comprehend his words. He had carved Martha's name in the third stone that morning. We had only just set it upon her grave ten minutes earlier. The tears were still fresh on our cheeks, our hearts still an open wound. And he wanted to *abandon* them? "No," I told him. "We cannot leave our girls."

"Martha," he whispered, pulling me tight against him. "Our girls have left *us*."

Only once before had I been so angry that I'd slapped him. And, as he had on that hillside the day we married, he grabbed both wrists, startled by my fury.

I shook out of his grasp.

Ephraim pointed to the graves. "They are not here. Not anymore."

I turned and left him there, alone.

6

THE RUSHING RIVER

APRIL 1790

Is that a dagger which I see before me, the handle toward my hand?

—WILLIAM SHAKESPEARE, *Macbeth*

BALLARD'S MILL

I stand on the path, fifty feet from the mill, and watch Isaac Foster ride away. Ten days. That's how long it took him to finally return to the Hook and explain their absence at the trial. He came today without Rebecca, spoke only to Ephraim, and even then, he didn't stay for a total of fifteen minutes.

I walk the rest of the way down the path—tin plate with Ephraim's dinner balanced in my hand—as Isaac follows the drive into the trees, then disappears among the shadows. The days are longer now, and the sky brighter as winter loosens its ruthless grip. It hasn't snowed in a week, and the air no longer burns my lungs. The river is still frozen, however, but it has started to crack and pop occasionally, hinting that it won't be long until the thaw.

Inside the mill, Ephraim stands at his worktable, furiously stripping bark from a slender pole with his draw blade. It's a two-handled thing, straight as an arrow, and two feet long, with an edge sharp enough to cut bone. He knows what he's doing and is careful, but still, I wince at the sight of that glinting metal sweeping toward his torso. He wears a long leather apron over his shirt and britches, but one wrong move and he will need stitches. Or worse.

"Where have the Fosters been?" I ask, careful not to startle him.

"In Vassalboro. Isaac appealed his lawsuit to Obadiah Wood."

Ephraim looks up, then wipes a trickle of sweat from his brow. "They negotiated a settlement."

"Of?"

"One hundred dollars. It's only half of what Isaac is owed, half of what he was promised in his contract with Hallowell. But it will be paid at the end of the month and is enough to get them settled somewhere else."

"And did he say anything of North's acquittal?"

"Only that he truly believed they'd get a guilty verdict. He doesn't understand how a jury of 'twelve honest men' couldn't see the truth of what happened to his wife."

"They couldn't see her at all! Rebecca didn't bother showing up to trial." My voice is louder than I intend, and Percy rouses in the rafters of the loft. That bird has the nerve to squawk at me.

"Isaac said she refused to go. Said she didn't have the heart to stand before another group of men and give them details of her shame."

"It isn't *her* shame."

"I know. And so does Isaac. But what was he supposed to do? Drag her to Pownalboro and force her into the courtroom? Physically threaten her so she'd testify? He isn't a cruel man. Besides, Seth had her written testimony. You were there as a witness. Isaac thought it would be enough. And I can't blame Rebecca for not wanting to go through that again."

I set Ephraim's dinner on the worktable and lower myself to the stool. "She told me this would happen. That even if the court found North guilty, it would only be for *attempting* a crime, not *committing* one. And what's the worst punishment he would have gotten? A *fine*?"

There is only a small section of bark left on the pole, and I watch my husband strip it methodically away. The blade makes a whooshing sound as it reveals the pale wood beneath. I watch him for a moment, thinking.

"The jury acquitted every man tried of rape that day," I say after a moment. "But they fined a woman into poverty for spreading lies about a judge's daughter."

The pole is bare now, and Ephraim sets down his draw blade. Takes off the leather apron. "I believe it would have been different with Rebecca. She's pregnant. That's harder for a jury to ignore."

"If they'd had the chance to see her, *listen* to her," I say.

"I'm sure that's what North realized in January when she gave her testimony. He expected them to bring charges of rape against him that day. He knew that a jury would believe Rebecca, so he ran off to Boston and hired a fancy lawyer."

"And escaped doing his time in the jail yard," I add.

"But he didn't miss his chance for a bit of revenge when he had our son brought in on murder charges."

"You think North was behind his arrest?"

Ephraim nods. "I do. During the inquiry, Judge Parker pointed out that Burgess's death was very convenient for North. I think he sat in that courtroom believing he'd be charged with rape and suspecting that murder charges would follow. So he bolted. And then he found a way to have Cyrus charged instead. I aim to prove it too."

"How?"

"I'm going to have Paul ask around about this lawyer, Henry Knowland, while I'm in Boston."

Paul. He always says it so casually, as if the man he's speaking of isn't Paul *Revere.* Yes, an old friend, but also a national hero. The silver ink dish he gifted me is but a small part of the favor he owes my husband. If anyone can help Ephraim get to the bottom of what North was planning with his lawyer in Boston for those two months, it is Paul.

"Eat your dinner," I tell him. "It's getting cold."

Ephraim goes to the plate and nods in approval. He stabs a potato with his fork and pops it in his mouth.

"When do you leave?" I ask.

"First thing in the morning."

"And how long will you be gone?"

"Ten days. Perhaps a fortnight, depending on how difficult it is to get information about Knowland and make my case before the Kennebec Proprietors."

In the week since North's trial, Ephraim has been collecting written testimony from friends and neighbors who will swear to the fact that we have lived on this property since assuming the lease. He will take all of that—along with the letters I found in Burgess's saddlebag—to Boston. But it means he is leaving again, and though the matter needs to be settled—and quickly—I don't like the idea of him being gone.

Percy watches us from his perch in the loft, his noble head swiveling this way and that. If I didn't know better, I'd think that he talks to Ephraim sometimes. In his own way. Every so often, I can hear his squawk and screech from the house if the air is still. Sometimes I think I can hear Ephraim answer.

"The ice is moving in the river," I say, "and not a moment too soon. I am done with this winter."

He looks at me cautiously. "Perhaps it is not yet done with us."

"And what do you mean by that?"

"The waterwheel. It hasn't budged. You will know winter has gone for good when it turns again and brings its music back."

Percy flaps his wings as if in agreement.

I glare at the bird. "He took another chicken yesterday."

Ephraim crooks an eyebrow. "You're the one who gave him a taste for the things. What did you expect?"

"I expect him to be a gentleman about it and take only what's offered."

"Percy is no gentleman, Martha. He's a wild beast. Don't mistake him for anything else."

"A beast perhaps, but a tame one."

Ephraim studies his bird with a quiet thoughtfulness. "There is no such thing."

"Well, speaking of wild things"—I smooth out a wrinkle from my skirt—"Jonathan was supposed to put netting over the chicken run last week so Percy couldn't get in. He hasn't done it yet."

"There are lots of things that Jonathan is supposed to do and doesn't. And plenty that he does but shouldn't."

"Then you'd best deal with him as well when you get the chance. And eat the hen on your plate before your bird steals it too. I didn't bring it for him."

Ephraim tucks in to his dinner as I sort through the contents of his haversack and pack basket to make sure he has everything he needs for the trip to Boston. It all looks to be in order.

Once done with his dinner, Ephraim still has a hungry look in his eye, and, after putting his plate down, he eases me up against the wall. "What will you do without me?" he asks, sliding his hands around my waist.

"I have no lack of things to keep me busy."

"Oh?"

"There's much to do in my workroom. Syrups. Salves."

Those hands drop lower, exploring the small of my back. My hips. My arse.

"Flax to spin. Cotton to comb," I tell him.

Slowly, too slowly for my liking, in fact, Ephraim begins to ruck up my skirt. He kisses the side of my neck.

"Cooking . . . cleaning . . ."

"Sounds terribly boring." His fingers brush against the soft skin of my thighs.

"If you have thoughts on a better way to keep me occupied, I would love to hear them," I say.

"I think words are wasted at a time like this." Ephraim lifts me up and sets me on the table, drawing my skirt up around my knees. "I'd rather show you."

DAWIN'S WHARF

SUNDAY, APRIL 18

"Is it twins?" May asks, lying on her back, in a soft white shift.

I run my fingers across the wide expanse of her swollen belly. She is six months pregnant but looks eight.

"I feel only the one head." I press my fingers into May's side, just above her hip bones. "Right here. And here"—I slide my palm to the other side and cup another small mound—"its backside." Finally, I tap the base of May's ribs. "And little feet, right here, which I'm sure you can feel."

"Constantly." She laughs. "But I'm *so* big. There must be two?"

"No. Your *belly* is big. The rest of you is quite little."

May is small and narrow, and she carries every inch of her baby out front. I think this might suggest a boy—there is some truth to the old wives' tales—but I don't mention it aloud. I have long since learned not to raise a woman's hopes. If they want one thing, they'll almost certainly get the other.

"It's just the way you carry," I tell her. "Your ribs haven't spread, so you're going out straight instead of wide."

"Is that bad? My ribs?"

"No." I give her a reassuring smile and continue the examination, poking and prodding. "Does anything hurt?"

"Only my back. And only sometimes. Like when I walk. Or sit. Or stand." Another laugh, this one helpless, as if to say, *What can I do?*

"Roll to your side."

May heaves herself over with a grunt, and I work my fingers across the dip of her back. "Where?"

"Lower. Nearer my . . ."

"Ah." I pat the top of her bottom, the way I might with a baby, and May giggles.

"Yes. There."

"The baby is putting pressure on your back. You might ask Sam to rub it a bit at night. If he wouldn't mind."

I can see only her profile, but a dimple breaks that one cheek. "It's never taken much convincing for him to put his hands on my arse."

I'm delighted that May is comfortable enough with me now to joke. There is nothing more important in a birthing room than trust. "I'll make sure to tell him myself, as well, before I leave. Where is he?"

May pushes up on her elbow and blows a strand of hair out of her eyes. "The barn. Working on the yoke, I think. He wants to start training the new oxen at first thaw."

I look out the window to the dirty, gray landscape and the pines no longer frosted white. Hallowell shows every indication of going from ice directly to mud.

"He's optimistic," I say.

"He's a farmer. He has to be."

I help May off the bed and back into her dress. Together we go downstairs, and I leave her with a syrup of goldenrod and bearberry to help reduce the swelling in her ankles.

"Only one teaspoon per day. Any more than that and you'll be thirsty," I instruct. "Take it just before bed so it can work overnight. But don't be surprised if you're up several times to use the chamber pot."

May thanks me, then sees me to the door, and I am startled to realize the air is neither frigid nor unwelcoming. I drape my riding cloak over my arm instead of my shoulders.

Brutus is tied at the hitching post, fidgety and kicking at a dirty mound of old snow.

"Just give me a moment," I tell him, "then we'll go home."

I walk around the side of the house and toward the barn. I can hear Sam inside, banging on something and cursing rather artfully. "You piece of shite! You broken, filthy cock robin." Two loud thumps as though something heavy has been dropped, then kicked. "Dirty *bastard.*"

Uncertain what I might find inside, I tap the barn door with my knuckles before stepping through. I was right about the kicking. The oxen yoke lies on the barn floor, bent at a strange angle, and Sam gives it one more good whack with his boot. He's been at it for quite a while by the looks of him. Hair askew. Jacket off. Sleeves rolled up and shirt damp from sweat along his back.

"I've never known a thing to get fixed by being kicked," I say. "What's wrong with it?"

Sam looks up, startled. Then he points at the yoke. "The beam is twisted."

"And cursing it helps?"

"Aye. Helps me feel better about being stupid enough to leave it out all winter to get wet and warped under the snow."

Sam shrugs then and lifts the heavy piece of wood off the ground to hang it on a rack by the stall. His forearms are bare, veined and covered with the same coarse red hair that sits on his head.

"Let me pay you," he says, shoving his hand into his pocket. When he pulls it out there is a mishmash of things in his palm: an old button, a rusted nail, a chunk of salt, a strip of tattered lace, an arrowhead, a piece of twine, and a handful of coins. The flotsam and jetsam typical of any man who works with his hands throughout the day. He starts to count out the money.

"Save your fee until the child is born," I tell him. "These visits are included."

He looks at his palm and frowns, but he doesn't argue as he returns the collection of odds and ends to his pocket. His hands are filthy from work, and when he notices my careful observation, he drags them down the front of his shirt.

"How is May?" he asks.

"Very pregnant and uncomfortable," I say.

"She's well, though? Nothing is wrong?"

"She thinks that she's carrying twins."

The look on Sam's face is one of abject terror. "Is she?"

"Just the one, as far as I can tell. Though it does seem to be rather large. Like its father."

"Is that dangerous?"

"Not any more than two small ones." I smile. "But there is something she needs."

Sam lets out a long, relieved sigh. "What?"

"A back rub. As many times a day as you can manage. A lot of the weight is against her lower spine. And she's little to start with. There's nowhere for the baby to go. So the discomfort might begin to move down her legs soon."

"I can do that."

"Good. And call for me if she's in regular pain."

Sam walks me to the hitching post, and as we say goodbye, someone calls my name in a tone of voice that can only be described as abject fury.

"Martha Ballard!"

I flinch because I know that voice. So I close my eyes and gather my wits because he is one of the last people I want to speak with at this particular moment.

But he repeats my name, angrier this time, and when I look up at Sam Dawin, I see that a storm cloud has gathered in his eyes and his fists are clenched. Perhaps he has grown fond of me after all. Or at least protective.

William Pierce sits astride his horse, glaring at me.

"Mr. Pierce." I nod, as polite as I am able. "How can I help you today?"

"You can come with me."

"I am not in the habit of taking orders."

"Then let today be a first. Because Sally is dying. And it's your fault."

PIERCE FARM

"Sally isn't *dying*," I tell William Pierce. "She's in *labor*. Pray tell how that would be *my* fault?"

Instead of answering me, he looks to his wife, and what passes between them is a kind of marital shorthand known to every couple who has been wed for any length of time. They can read each other's expressions. The lift of an eyebrow. The flare of a nostril. Gritted teeth and lifted chin and eyes that gloss over with anger and fear. Volumes pass between them before William points his finger at her.

"You explain it," he orders, then he turns on his heel and leaves the bedroom, slamming the door on his way out.

"Please excuse my husband," Bonnie Pierce says. She is unperturbed by his outburst. "William is the sort of man built for having sons. Instead, he got five daughters. He's never quite got the hang of it."

"There's no one to blame but him. Sally is your youngest. He's had plenty of time."

"You can give a man all the time in the world, but he's never ready for his daughter to turn up pregnant. He wasn't with the others. And it's no different with Sally."

Well, isn't this a day of revelations.

"How long have you known?" I ask.

"Almost three months. I discovered her secret the day after North's second hearing, in January. I walked in on her while she was standing in the washtub. There was no hiding it then."

"And did you tell William?"

"Not right off." Bonnie levels me with an appraising glance. Looks me over head to toe. There is a frankness in it that I appreciate. "He would have only been angry with Sally. We kept it from him as long as we could. He's known for a month."

"It is hard to hide a pregnancy that long."

"My husband is many things, Mistress Ballard, but attentive is not one of them. And it is winter. And we all do what we can to stay warm. She's tall and stays bundled. It would have been harder in summer, no doubt."

"You do not seem much distressed by her condition."

Bonnie shrugs. It's more accepting than nonchalant, but still, I am surprised given William's pious outrage in court this year. "She didn't get into this situation by herself."

Sally's forehead is beaded with sweat, and her eyes are scrunched closed. She does not see the curious glance I throw in her direction.

"Are you saying this child was forced upon her?"

Bonnie laughs. "Not to hear her tell it. From what I can gather, my daughter was an enthusiastic participant."

A stone settles to the pit of my stomach.

Mentally, I turn back the clock. The last time I saw Sally was at the hearing at the end of January. Her father had forced her to testify—again—about all she'd overheard the day I was in Rebecca's sitting room. The blizzard was howling in from the east, and I thought nothing of the fact that she'd worn her riding cloak during the hearing. Half the people in Pollard's had done the same that day. Six months. She would have been roughly six months pregnant. Give or take.

How did I not know?

And at the Frolic a week earlier? I only remember thinking that she'd looked rather buxom, that her dress had been cut to accentuate that part of her figure. Had it been loosened elsewhere? There was nary a whisper in that room about her changing figure. Because no one had noticed.

Because no one has seen her since.

Because.

Because . . .

All five of the Pierce girls inherited their looks from their mother. The auburn hair and the hazel eyes and the full lips. The height they got from their father, however, and this, I think, more than anything else, has enabled Sally to keep her secret. A long body, coupled with a long torso and a generous bosom, can hide a multitude of sins. Especially early in a first pregnancy.

"Sally?" I ask.

She ceases writhing on the bed and looks at me, then shrinks back, her pretty eyes clouded with pain. She is afraid. Both of what is happening to her and of me as well. When I set a hand upon her bare foot, her flinch confirms this suspicion, and this saddens me nearly to the point of tears. I have never had a laboring woman respond to me this way. I have only ever seen relief in their eyes.

"There is something I must ask you."

"No." She shakes her head.

"The father," Bonnie whispers. "She thinks you're asking about the father. I've done the same, a hundred times at least, and she'd tell me nothing other than that she loves him and went to bed willingly. If you can get it out of her then you're more of a miracle worker than people say."

"I am not asking you about the father," I tell Sally.

Not yet, I think.

Sally visibly relaxes. "What then?" she pants.

This conversation would have been far easier three hours ago, before transition, and the otherworldly sense of agony it brings. The brain ceases to function. The body knows nothing but pain and the desperate need for survival. Lucy, my oldest daughter, has three times forgotten her own name in transition. Names and numbers cease to exist. Reality shrinks to a pinpoint of primal existence.

"I need to know if this child is early or late. I need to know when you last bled. The life of your baby may depend on it."

It is a miserable thing I am asking of Sally Pierce as she lies on her bed, head thrown back, sweat beading on her lip. I do not think of myself as an unkind person, but this is perhaps the cruelest thing I have ever done, asking a laboring woman to do math.

"Summer." The word is hissed out between clenched teeth, and I wipe a bit of spittle off my chin with a wrist. "Mid July, I think."

I count backward and am relieved to determine that we are well within the window for viability. She's at term.

Bonnie Pierce clears her throat. "I stopped keeping track of their cycles years ago."

"It wasn't your job to do so. I know nothing about motherhood other than children will do what they will do and there is not a damn thing *you* can do about it."

So far as I can remember, my mother never cursed in all her sixty-eight years. And I'm by no means a sailor, but I find that every year that passes, I grow more comfortable with the art. And if I never really liked Bonnie Pierce before now, I am sorry, because she laughs at that.

"Every one of my girls has found themselves in this position."

When I look at her in surprise, she laughs again. "Didn't know that, did you? None of them hid it nearly this long, but yes, all of them took a turn around a hayloft once or twice and ended up thick at the waist before their wedding. I just didn't . . ." She pauses to gather her thoughts. "With the others I *knew* what they were up to."

"My oldest daughter as well," I say, and if two women can become friends with one admission, we just have. "Time will tell with the others."

Bonnie Pierce shrugs. "I've always wondered if it was a trait I passed on to them. William married me quickly, of course, but I wasn't much of a maid when he did."

I am tempted to tell them both about the woman that Ephraim Ballard married—and the scandal that enfolded us—when Sally screams.

Here it is, then. She's ready.

It isn't fast and it isn't easy and it isn't enjoyable for a single one of us in that room. It takes Sally Pierce nearly two hours to heave her child into the world. The damage is no worse than what I often see in rooms like this. But she will require stitches, that much is sure.

"Hello, little one," I say, and if my hands are shaking as I lift the squalling newborn and inspect him, it is only because I know what is coming.

He is beautiful. Big. Healthy. Not a single deficiency that I can detect. I want to pull him to my chest. Cradle him. Kiss his face. Sniff the dark, chaotic hair. This instinct is so strong that I hesitate to hand him to his mother.

But there is Sally with her arms held out, waiting to receive him. This girl who has always managed to avoid directly meeting my gaze has no such trouble now. Those big, calculating hazel eyes challenge me to ask the question required by law. She has waited for this moment, defying all other attempts to coerce her into speaking the father's name.

I will not give in so easily, however. I take a different tack instead. After wrapping the baby in soft, clean linen, I hand him to her and watch as she puts him to her breast.

I watch her first awkward attempts.

I watch the grimace and hiss of pain when he finally latches on.

I watch Sally watch me, and though it is cruel, I let her squirm in silence. Then I pull needle and thread from my medicine bag.

"You shouldn't feel much," I tell her. "But if I don't do this, you will bleed for days."

The only sound is that of a newborn grunting and gulping as he tries to eat his first meal. Every few seconds Sally winces. Hisses. Yet I don't know if this is because of the vice that has attached to her left nipple or because of my needle. There is no bringing new life into this world without pain, however, and sometimes it assaults us at both ends.

"What did William mean?" I ask Bonnie. "When he told you to explain her situation?"

"He thinks I know who the father is."

"Do you?"

"Honestly? I haven't the slightest idea who it could be."

"I find that there are many mysteries in this world. But I do not consider the father of this child to be one of them."

Bonnie Pierce, God bless her, gives me this moment. She does not ask me to clarify, but rather allows me the pure, unadulterated pleasure of stealing every ounce of thunder from her daughter. There is no surprise here, and Sally takes no victory.

Once the stitches are done and the thread has been clipped, I sit back on my stool. Take in the full measure of this girl who has caused such trouble over these last few months.

"You have a beautiful boy," I tell her. "What will you call him?"

I know the answer already because I have seen the truth of it with my own eyes, yet it is a hammer to my heart when she speaks the words aloud.

"His name is Jonathan. After his father."

*

Sunday, April 18——Clear and pleasant. Birth. I was called from the Hook to attend Sally Pierce who I found to be in labor. She was safe delivered at 1:00 p.m. of a fine son. Her travail was severe, but she managed well, and I left her cleverly with her own mother. Sally declared that my son Jonathan was the father of her child.

I break the quill. That's how hard I press against the paper. It snaps in half, in my hand, and I sit back to watch the ink run down the pad of my thumb. I do not typically pour my feelings into this book of mine, but today there is so much more that I want to say. Yet I am out of ink. I've used the last of it just now, and I've no energy left to wander down, in the dark, to the mill, where Ephraim has left the other disk. So I wash my hands instead and go to bed. But I do not sleep. I lie awake, aware that my son never came home tonight, and I wonder if he is out cavorting around, or whether he has gone to meet his newborn son.

NORTH MANOR

MONDAY, APRIL 19

I need another quill and more ink. I meant to send one of the girls down to the mill this afternoon, but they are gone now—my entire brood of children—off to the Hook to shop and socialize for the evening, and there is no one to run the errand for me. So I gather my journal and make my way down the path.

Even now I am rehearsing how I will tell Ephraim that he has another grandson. I doubt he will be surprised at the news. Or even displeased—I have never known a man who enjoys being around children more than Ephraim Ballard—but the handling of Jonathan will not be pleasant. As far as I'm concerned, my husband cannot get home soon enough.

It is odd to be in Ephraim's space without him. He's been gone over a week, but it still smells of him. Yet without his voice and the constant fluttering of Percy's wings, the mill feels abandoned. No matter. There's the ink, on his worktable, along with a jar of new quills and the rest of his tools.

Ephraim's draw blade and Revenge sit in a neat row with the chisels and handsaws. Cleaned and oiled. Precise. Just like the man who keeps them. I do my best not to mess with his things while he's gone but I do pull a blueish gray quill from the jar and press the sharpened tip against the pad of my thumb.

My husband had been collecting feathers for a week before he left. Some from the loft where Percy now roosts, but others from the forest. One can't simply dip a feather into ink and write, however. Ephraim prepares each quill by hand.

I'd watched him strip the lowest, finest feathers, then place the shafts into the ashes of the wood stove to harden.

He'd looked at me. Winked. Laughed and said, "I wouldn't mind if you hardened *my* shaft tonight."

I had no intention of waiting until nightfall but didn't mention it then or the quills would be ruined. I'd simply returned his leer and watched as he took the feathers and laid them on his worktable. He flattened the shafts slightly, until they took on an oval shape, then rounded the tips with his fingers. It didn't take long for them to cool, only moments. Then he shaved off the points at an angle with his knife, followed by a slit at the top so that the ink will draw into the shaft.

Such simple things, paper, quill, and ink. But I cannot imagine more tangible symbols of my husband's love. I miss him and there is much I want to tell him, but no ability to do so yet.

I spread my journal open on the worktable, mix the ink, and dip my quill instead.

Monday, April 19—Clear morn. Cloudy afternoon, the wind very chilly. Mr. Ballard is still in Boston. My girls are at the Hook. My boys also.

I cannot say why it is so important that I make this daily record. Perhaps because I have been doing so for years on end? Or maybe—if I am being honest—it is because these markings of ink and paper will one day be the only proof that I have existed in this world. That I lived and breathed. That I loved a man and the many children he gave me. It is not that I want to be remembered, per se. I have done nothing remarkable. Not by the standards of history, at least. But I am here. And these words are the mark I will leave behind. So yes, it matters that I continue this ritual.

The ink is still wet on the page, and I leave it open on the table to dry. I'll collect everything later, when I get home. For now, my conscience burns, and I must go see Lidia North.

*

The tonic is in my medical bag. It weighs but a few ounces. Yet to me it may as well be an anchor, for it feels as though I am dragging the full weight of my conscience up the front steps to Joseph North's house.

Still, I knock.

Once.

Twice.

Three times I pound the knuckles of my right hand against the wooden door. Finally, after several minutes, it is answered by Lidia. I can see I've woken the woman. Her hair is mussed, her eyes watering, and there are pillow creases along her right cheek.

"Martha," she says, wary, "what are you doing here?"

"I have come to bring your tonic."

"But I thought—"

"I was wrong," I tell her. "And I am sorry for being cruel. Will you let me in?"

The house is dark, all the shades drawn, when Lidia leads me through the front door and into the parlor. It is not a manor home, far from it, but as one of the largest houses in the Hook, that is what it's called. North Manor. It sits against a large sweep of hill on the west side of Water Street, overlooking the river. Four full bedrooms upstairs. A kitchen, study, sitting room, and dining room downstairs. There are glass windows and velvet curtains and wood floors. But I can think only of the fact that Joseph North purchased this house with bounties paid on the heads of his enemies. I wonder if Lidia knows. Or if she cares.

"Do sit down," Lidia tells me. "I can build the fire."

"No need. I won't stay long." I lower myself onto the sofa beside her. "Where is Joseph this evening?"

Lidia shrugs. "Out for an evening walk."

It's best that way. I haven't seen him since the trial and certainly don't want to run into him now. "How have you been?"

"Worse. I wish it wasn't so, but . . ."

"The headaches?"

"Every day. Sometimes for hours at a time. Joseph is so patient with me, but I know they wear on him as well."

"I should have come sooner. I am sorry for that."

Lidia looks at her fingers. They are long and thin, like twigs. She flexes them several times before answering. "It hasn't been fair. For a lot of us."

The medical bag sits at my feet, and I lean down to sift through the contents. Each item is as familiar to me as the faces of those I love, and I let my fingers roam, looking for the right one.

There.

It is small, with a slender neck and a wooden cork. The bottle feels cool against my palm when I pluck it out of the bag and set it in Lidia's hand.

"You mustn't take too much," I tell her. "Only two teaspoons a day. Once in the morning. Once in the evening. Would you like me to get you the first one?"

"Please."

"Stay here. I'll get a spoon."

I leave her, head tilted back against the sofa. The kitchen is small and tidy, located at the back of the house, and I find what I'm looking for in a small basket on the counter. A set of pewter spoons. Neatly stacked. Everything in its place. The house feels sterile to me. Devoid of all the life and noise and chaos that I am accustomed to.

"Here," I say, once I am back in the sitting room, as I carefully pour a spoonful of the tonic and tip it into Lidia's mouth. "You should feel better soon."

She swallows the pale amber liquid. "Thank you."

I expect her to shudder. The tonic is bitter and the reflex normal. But on Lidia's thin frame, it looks like a seizure. I watch her carefully for a moment to make sure she is well.

"Let's get you to bed. Rest will help."

Lidia lifts an arm, flapping absentmindedly at the ceiling. "Upstairs."

She can get there under her own power, but I follow her up the stairs, just in case. The last thing I need is for Lidia to take a dizzy tumble. But once at the top, she guides me down the hallway and into the bedroom she shares with her husband.

I help Lidia into bed and draw up the blanket. The woman looks so small and frail, in so much pain. She mutters her thanks and is asleep within moments.

I have known only two other women who suffer from the dreaded mygreyn, but neither were this debilitated. When the headaches descend upon Lidia, she is all but crippled, requiring a cold, dark room and no interference. Watching her now, I regret my cruelty. The woman is suffering, and I had no right to deny her any form of relief. Regardless of what her husband has done.

"Let me know when you need more," I tell her.

I set the bottle and teaspoon on the small bedside table, then tiptoe from the room. Down the hall. Back to the parlor. I collect my medical bag and am almost at the entrance when I see that North has left the door to his study open.

*

I would have thought him a tidier man. But no, there are papers littered across his desk, books cracked open at the spine on every flat surface. The small, paneled room smells of pipe smoke, dust, old books, and candle wax. North has a straight-backed chair and a bookcase behind the desk. There is a wooden trunk beneath the window, and on the far wall, a side table with a decanter and two crystal glasses. The candles are all burned to an inch, and I reach out to touch the one on his desk. There are flakes of rosemary and lavender in the pooled wax.

They're mine, I think. *I made these.*

Of all the things to give me pause. Just a candle. A simple thing. But a reminder that I am a woman who makes and heals, not a woman who snoops and schemes.

But if not me, who? If not now, when?

I turn, intending to leave, but my gaze falls on his desk. It is an orderly sort of chaos. Letters, surveys, and maps are strewn across the polished wood surface. Many of them are in Ephraim's hand, and all of them relate to North's work with the Kennebec Proprietors. I recognize the map of Hallowell and the survey of our property.

There is a letter—only partially drafted—in North's handwriting. I lift it from the desk. Read it aloud. ". . . As per our discussion last month in Boston, please find the enclosed land surveys of three hundred acres between Mill Creek and Burnt Hill. I think you will find the lumber quantity and access to the river meets your growing needs to supply the shipyards in Boston. I am ready to assume the lease immediately. And, as agreed, I will take ownership of the aforementioned neglected Ballard lease—twelve years to be prorated to myself, and the deed finalized in April. Having a closer proximity to the property will better allow me to supervise the clearing of this forest. . . ."

I stand there, paralyzed, gripping the letter. He has intended to take our land all along. And not just ours. He wants half of Hallowell. The realization is sickening, but I am out of time because I hear the sound of boots on the porch and then the front door swings open.

"Lidia?" North's voice echoes through the first floor.

He is twelve, perhaps fifteen feet away when I make my decision. My last seconds are spent stuffing the letter into my medical bag. I am at the side table, decanter in hand, when he steps through the door to his study.

"What are you doing in here?" North demands, his voice laced with fury and contempt. Beside him, Cicero growls low in his throat.

When I turn, I lift one of his crystal glasses. A finger of amber liquid sloshes at the bottom. "Brandy. For your wife. It will help settle the tonic in her stomach."

The dog takes a menacing step toward me, and I see a freshly healed wound on his head, a long, jagged pink scar that runs diagonally across his snout. No doubt a run-in with a sharp set of talons.

Well done, Percy, I think.

I do not apologize for being in his study, nor ask his permission as I brush past him and go up the stairs, medical bag tucked in tight beneath my arm. He follows closely behind, furious glare burning into the back of my head as I wake Lidia and help her drink the brandy. Once more I give instruction for the tonic, and again Lidia thanks me for coming.

I neither look at North on my way out of the house, nor do I wish him farewell, for I do not trust myself to speak.

POLLARD'S TAVERN

My hands are trembling when I push through the door to Pollard's Tavern. I need a moment to gather myself before riding home. And I also need a whiskey. Or perhaps two.

"Mistress Ballard, is everything in the right?" Moses follows as I make my way through the crowd toward the only empty seat in the tavern.

I nod, but don't speak. I drop to the stool with a huff. All the tables are full, and the atmosphere is merry. Loud. There are more people here tonight than usual. I listen to the laughter and chatter as I settle into my solitary place in the corner. One of two rickety stools arranged beside an old wine barrel for a table. It's where Amos and Abigail usually perch, but they are bustling around the tavern, busy with their guests, and I know they won't mind me taking their place.

"I'll take whiskey if you have it," I tell Moses. "And whatever your mother has made for dinner."

"'Tis stew and bread," he says, eyeing me with concern. "But tonight she has cheese as well, along with roasted chestnuts."

I wag a hand at him in approval. "All of it, please."

I relax for a moment, face pressed into my hands, and when I finally look up, it is into the quizzical gaze of my daughter Hannah. Dolly sits beside her at one of the tables, and Cyrus and Young Ephraim are here as well. Their backs are to me, and each of them looks like Ephraim from behind. Broad shoulders and dark hair. They tuck in to Abigail Pollard's food. The table is full. Barnabas Lambard has come down from Vassalboro and sits by Cyrus. Dolly isn't so much ignoring Barnabas as Cyrus now. She keeps her back to her brother, resisting his attempts to reconcile her with the young officer of the court. My daughters do not forgive so easily as my sons. For his part, Barnabas seems content to bide his time. He may have lost the battle, but he knows he's won the war.

The youth of Hallowell are out this evening, enjoying this first glimmer of spring, a night with no bite in the air. Brothers accompanying sisters. Sisters dragging their little brothers along. Young men with their minds bent toward courtship, and young women making them wait for a stolen kiss.

Every so often I see Cyrus turn his head to the door. Waiting. Watching. Hoping for Sarah White, I'd guess, but she never arrives.

The other tables are equally packed, mostly with men I do not recognize, and I am grateful that my sons are here tonight—along with Moses and Barnabas—because more than a few interested glances are being cast toward Hannah and Dolly.

Once Moses has delivered my food and drink, I ask him who all these strangers are.

"The Boston militia," he says. "They just rode in from Fort Halifax this afternoon. Word is they'll be here for a week before heading south again."

It's been a year and a half since the militia last rode through Hallowell. A year and a half since Sarah White was seduced by their leader. This reminds me of something, however, and I grab Moses's shirtsleeve.

"Do you happen to know who's in charge? A Major Henry Warren by chance?"

I think the odds of Sarah's beau returning to the Hook are slim. Men of his sort usually turn to new hunting grounds.

"I can ask around," Moses says.

"Thank you."

Hannah slips from her seat and comes to give me a hug. "We didn't know when you'd be home. So we decided to have dinner here.

Honestly, none of us wanted to cook." She shrugs. "Dad was gone. You were gone. . . ."

"And Moses is here?" I ask.

Hannah smiles, broad and lovely, her brown eyes crinkling at the corners. "Aye. He is."

"You don't have to explain. I'd rather eat Abigail's cooking than my own any day. Go on, enjoy your evening. I'm heading home as soon as I eat."

"You don't want to stay?"

"I'm tired."

She studies me with those dark and steady eyes. "There's more to it."

"Aye. There is."

"But you won't tell me?"

I brush a bit of hair away from her eyes. "It's nothing you need to trouble yourself with tonight."

"Then I'll leave it be," she says. "For tonight."

Hannah wanders back to the table, and I watch the delicate mating dance between her and Moses. He brings her a mug of cider, and she touches his wrist. She smiles, he blushes. He makes a joke, and she laughs. It is all so simple and innocent, and I am struck by the realization that the dance of new love is many miles behind me.

I could warn Moses and Barnabas that I expect them to get my daughters home safely tonight, that I don't want them near any of these militiamen, but there's no need. I doubt either man intends to let my girls out of his sight. Dolly might be making a show of her anger toward Barnabas, but I can see her lean in his direction when he tells a joke. I can see her try to hide her smile. And he sees it as well. The boy has a great deal of work ahead to win her back, but she has chosen him, and that is obvious to anyone who cares to look.

Moses is back again. "I asked some of the lads about Warren, but they say he isn't here."

"I figured as much."

"That's a problem?"

"No," I tell him. "More like a relief."

Young Ephraim shoves his plate aside and goes to play dice with the youngest Pollard child. Matthew, he's called. The stable boy. They both have the rangy look of boys who are no longer little but who

won't be men for some time yet. All teeth and elbows and knees, they
need haircuts and baths. They are in that grubby, delightful no-man's-
land between those who play and those who work, and I am glad that
Young Ephraim's brothers and sisters brought him tonight. It is hard
to be the youngest.

Jonathan pushes through the tavern doors as I tuck in to my dinner. He sees his siblings at their table. Grins. He joins them, giving
both Hannah and Dolly a kiss on the cheek. Ruffles his little brother's
hair. Gives Cyrus a jolly slap on the back. It is a rare bit of camaraderie
that I never get to see. He's a bit sterner with Barnabas and Moses,
offering only a handshake, but it's friendly at least. Once he's found a
spot, he looks up to find me watching. It's been many years since I've
seen him blush, but his face floods with color at the sight of me. He
has been with Sally, apparently. All last night and today if the dark
circles beneath his eyes tell the story right.

He nods at me once then turns away.

I finish my dinner and sip my whiskey, marveling as I watch my
children. This is a new, bittersweet milestone of motherhood. They
have gotten bigger, as have their problems. But they have also grown
wiser, and that is a miracle because wisdom is not a thing you can
acquire for your children. As I rise from the table, it occurs to me
that part of what I feel, watching them, is a sense of betrayal. I carried
these children into the world, paid their entrance fee with dues rendered upon my own body, and now they no longer need me.

I bid them all good evening with a kiss to the brow—even Jonathan, and I am glad when he doesn't turn his face away.

"We need to talk," I whisper in his ear, then I walk alone into the
night.

BALLARD'S MILL

I am almost to Mill Creek Bridge when it clicks. The thought. Loud and clear as though someone has just snapped their fingers beside my ear.

Lace.

Twice Rebecca mentioned Joshua Burgess ripping that strip of lace from her hem. He used it to tie his hair back before he raped her. And I found a piece—just as Rebecca described—at the bottom of Burgess's saddlebag. It is hers, no doubt. He kept it as some macabre souvenir.

So why does Sam Dawin have a piece of lace in his pocket?

I saw it yesterday, with my own eyes.

Was it only yesterday?

Time has started to play tricks on me. All or nothing. Minutes or years.

I have been at home.

This is the phrase I write most often in my journal. And that is true. Untold hours I've spent in my workroom, puttering about with the normal business of domestic life. But I have also lost days at a time with births and deaths and burials. I am in the business of mortality. Its beginning and its end.

Yes, *of course,* I am tired. That is nothing new. I have spent the better part of the last thirty years tired. Elspeth told me to expect that.

"We are midwives," she told me once. "We will sleep when we're dead."

That was the first thing I thought when she passed. When we buried her in Oxford.

Sleep well, my friend.

None of this has anything to do with Sam, of course. Or the lace. But that is how the mind works late at night, after a good meal and a good cry.

Yes, I cried leaving the tavern. So much has happened in such a short amount of time.

Questions skitter across my mind like shooting stars, all of them possibilities that flare, then burn out quickly for lack of sense. I cannot find any scenario in which Sam fits into the Foster case. But the connection was right there, in his palm. Tied with a knot.

If I only knew what I was seeing.

I let my mind wander, hands loose on the reins. Brutus senses my mood, slows his pace from a trot to a walk, and drifts off the muddy center of the road and onto the edge, where the heavy clop of his hooves is muffled by tufts of old grass peeking through the fading snow. He knows the way home, and for once, I am content to let him lead.

Lace.

It is important, though I cannot fathom why.

We continue like this for another quarter of a mile—Brutus meandering very much like my thoughts—until the bridge comes into sight.

I press against his side with my left knee.

Tug gently on the reins with my left hand.

Home.

Sleep.

That's all I want.

But, as so often has been true in the last three decades, I cannot have it.

*

I wait up for Jonathan. Long after his brothers and sisters get home and go to bed. I wait up so long that my eyes are heavy, and the fire is low. A clever move on Jonathan's part. See if he can wait me out, sneak in once I've finally given up and gone to bed. No doubt he'd be up early and off to work before dawn to avoid me again. But I've been thinking about what I want to ask him all day, and I won't miss this opportunity. Not even if it means that I must sit here until dawn.

It is after midnight when I hear the squeak and rattle of the wagon coming down the drive, and another fifteen minutes before he's done putting up the horse and makes his way to the house. I count his footsteps—seventeen—slow and wary, as they approach the door.

Then the latch.

The hinges.

A breath of cool air at the back of my neck.

And, finally, a heavy sigh.

"Hello, Mother."

"Jonathan," I say, then sniff. "Are you *drunk?*"

"I've had a few pints. You'd be in your cups too if you'd a mother waiting at home to scold you."

"I am not going to scold you, Jonathan."

He looks up through eyes that are heavy with drink, uncertain whether to believe me.

"That'd be a first."

It would be easy to arm myself in return, fire off a wounding shot. But I am too tired for that, and besides, it would do no good. What's done is done. Instead, I pour two fingers of brandy into a glass and hand it to my son. A peace offering. He takes it warily. Downs half in one greedy, desperate swallow.

"Did you know?" I ask.

"No," he says. "It was as much a shock to me as everyone else."

It is the first time he makes full eye contact, and I see that he's not entirely drunk after all, wrapped up in warm flannel, perhaps, but there's no cloud drifting across the blue sky of those eyes. They are every bit as bright and clear as an October afternoon.

"But when I found you two in the woods in January, she had to have been near six months. Maybe you couldn't see it under all those clothes, but certainly you could have felt it."

Jonathan has the good grace to blush. "It wasn't her belly that I was touching at the time. Not that you need the details."

"I'm not asking for details, Jonathan. I'm asking how something that important could have escaped your notice. She got pregnant in *July.*"

"And every stolen moment since has been rushed. Hasty. She gave plenty, and I took what I could get, and that time in the woods was about as much privacy as we ever found. Now you know. Are you happy?"

"Happy? I'm the farthest thing from it."

"You and me both."

"Self-pity is not a thing you get to feel right now, son. You can't take a girl like Sally Pierce to bed and not think there will be consequences."

"I didn't take her to *bed,* Mother. I took her to the *barn.* In July, as we've established, after the summer Frolic."

He isn't fully sober. I know that. Which is the only reason I don't hold this admission against him.

"Have you not seen her since January?"

"Only once. At the hearing."

He drains his glass, swishing the last mouthful of brandy around his mouth before swallowing. He sets it down on the table, and I add another finger to the glass.

The look he gives me is quizzical. *This is new,* it says.

I smile. It's a sad one. I can feel it there in the tremble at the corner of my mouth.

"What are you going to do? Sally has declared you the father."

"I won't abandon them if that's what you think."

"But will you marry her?"

"I don't have a choice, do I?"

"There's always a choice, Jonathan. You had one in the beginning. And you have one now."

"You'd have me pay maintenance but leave him a bastard?"

I am strangely encouraged by how appalled he is at the idea. "I would have had you marry a girl before getting her pregnant. But we're long past that. I just want to know what you will do now."

"I'm not so bad a man as you might think, Mother. I posted our intent to marry outside the tavern tonight."

This news is both a relief and a sadness. It is past time for him to settle down, but I would have hoped that love would factor in.

"He looks like me," Jonathan says, and I detect a note of wonder in his voice.

"Yes. He does."

"I didn't expect to feel anything when she handed him to me." His eyes are glassy, whether from drink or tears I can't really say. "But I did."

That feeling he doesn't yet recognize is love. And if he loves his son, I have hope that he might yet grow to love Sally as well.

Jonathan watches the fire pop and fizzle. He does not apologize for anything, but neither is he antagonistic with me any longer. This is the decision I made while sitting here all evening: sacrifice one thing to gain another. Sally Pierce, puzzling though she might be, is not a piece of the puzzle I need to solve right now. Rather, my mind is bent on untangling the question that has been nagging at me the last few hours.

I reach out. Pat Jonathan's hand. "Can I ask you something?"

Again, that wary look. He draws away as though I might bite him. "Yes," he says. "I'm certain Sally got pregnant on purpose."

"I suspected as much myself. But this has nothing to do with Sally."

Jonathan nods, still cautious. "What then?"

"That night, last November, when Sam fell through the ice?"

"Yes?"

"You've never really told me what happened."

"There isn't much to tell." Jonathan settles back in his chair, takes another sip. I note that his eyes go to the fire and stay there. He does not look at me again. "We set off from Sam's wharf well after midnight."

"That's a late start."

"We'd originally planned on leaving the next morning. But the river was closing, so we decided to leave after the Frolic. But we were late getting out. And a good thing too. If we'd left earlier, we'd have been two hours farther downriver when he fell through. No way I could have gotten him here in time. He'd be dead."

"Instead, you found a dead man."

He works his jaw back and forth, like a cow chewing its cud.

"None of us were happy about that. Particularly Sam. But it makes sense if you think about it."

"How?"

"Everything gets caught at Bumberhook Point. The peninsula reaches out into the water. Ice or no ice, that's where logjams happen."

"How long do you think Burgess had been there?"

"Couple hours. Probably. It was his hair—all frozen in the ice—that stopped him from sinking into the current."

I am careful, so careful with my next question. "You said Sam was upset to find him?"

"I reckon anyone would be. But Sam cursed more 'n I ever heard 'im."

There. *Finally.* Jonathan's enunciation slips. Just a bit, but it's enough to convince me that I can press harder.

"Did they know each other?"

He shrugs, a sloppy lift and fall of the shoulders. "They wasn't friendly."

"What do you mean?"

"Sam's never liked the man. But after what he did at the Frolic . . ." Jonathan's voice fades off and is replaced by a scowl that he directs at the hearth.

"What happened after you got Sam out of the water?"

"The shock hit him. All that cold, all at once." Jonathan runs the glass along his lower lip—back and forth—before tilting the liquor into his mouth again. He empties it with a single swallow. "Sam's lucky he had that rope. 'E would've been swept away otherwise."

Click. There it is. Another piece of the puzzle snaps into place.

"You told me before that the rope was looped at Sam's waist?"

"Yes." Jonathan leans his head back against the chair, eyes closed, fingers loose around his glass.

My final question is asked with the voice I used when reading him to sleep as a child. Soft and deep. Comforting. It's not a benign question, but I do everything in my power to make it seem so.

"Was it bloody?" I ask.

It takes him so long to answer that I think he's fallen asleep. The glass tumbles from his hand, and I reach out to catch it as a single word slips out in the form of a whisper.

"Yes."

*

I reach out to shake Jonathan's shoulder, to wake him up, when I am startled by a soft knocking at the door, followed by a voice calling my name.

"Martha." The voice is female and heavily accented in French. Doctor.

I'm up and at the door. When I pull it back, I see that she hasn't even bothered to dismount Goliath, but has ridden him through the garden gate and right up to the door. She sits on his back, regal. Impatient.

"You must hurry," she says. "Rebecca Foster is in labor."

THE PARSONAGE

We ride, hell-for-leather. The wind tears at my face and whips my hair into a frenzy. There was no time to pull it back before leaving. I'd had to saddle Brutus as well. Not to mention pack my medical bag and change into my riding dress. I met Doctor at the trees, and we were off.

Now we gallop, heads down; Brutus and Goliath sense the urgency and propel us forward as mud kicks up at our heels.

"Rebecca Foster did not send for you," Doctor shouts, and the wind nearly rips her voice away.

"What do you mean?"

"Her husband called for me at the cabin. He was very specific that I *not* alert you."

"Then why did you?" I shout.

"Because Rebecca is *your* patient. I know you care for her." Doctor points one long finger at me. "And I have long since learned that people only come to me when they are keeping secrets. You will forgive me for being wary of such motives."

It stings, this knowledge that Rebecca would hide her labor from me. That she wouldn't want me there. I delivered both of her sons.

"How long has it been? Since you saw Isaac?"

"Less than an hour," Doctor says.

"When did her pains begin?"

"I do not know."

It is nearing one o'clock in the morning now, and I urge Brutus faster. At a full-blown gallop, it will be a ten-minute ride to the Hook. Without knowing her condition, it could be ten minutes too long.

The sky is clear and dark as ink, with only a slice of waning crescent moon to guide us. If not for that and the scattered stars, we would have no light at all. As we cross over Mill Creek Bridge, I see a shadow dart out of our way. Black and silver with eyes of amber.

Tempest watches us speed away.

*

We can hear screaming from the yard.

Doctor slides off Goliath's back and tosses the reins to me. "I will meet you inside," she says.

I dismount, then lead both horses to the hitching post to tie them off. They've run hard and bend their heads to the trough for a long, cold drink.

I gather my medical bag, uncertain what's waiting for us inside. Isaac is nowhere to be seen, but I know my way around and go directly to the bedroom.

Rebecca is arched back against a stack of pillows, shift rucked up to her ribs. Legs open. Knees bent. Eyes closed. A fine trickle of sweat drips down her temple. Her hands fist the quilt beneath her, and her jaw is clenched.

Doctor looks at me in that calm, unnerving way of hers and shakes her head slightly.

"Is she ready?"

"*Non,*" she says, indicating the hard ball of Rebecca's stomach. It is still high, under her ribs instead of flat and wide at her hips the way it needs to be for her to push. Doctor waves me over. "Come."

I slide out of my riding cloak and set my bag at the foot of the bed. A single glance tells me that the baby's head has not yet dropped, that despite the pain, this labor is far from over.

Once the contraction subsides, Rebecca's eyes flutter open. If she is surprised to see me, she doesn't show it. Or perhaps she doesn't care.

"I asked for Doctor," she says.

"I know. But I am here regardless. I will not leave you alone in this. Where is Isaac?"

Rebecca lifts her arm and points to the ceiling. "Upstairs," she pants. "With the boys. They're scared."

She has no women to attend this birth. No family. No friends. It is only Doctor and I. And I fear we will not be enough.

"Make it stop. Please," Rebecca begs when another contraction begins its relentless march through her body.

I look to Doctor, not because I don't know what to do, but because she is Rebecca's choice and I don't want to press my help where it isn't wanted.

"The baby will not turn down. I have already tried," Doctor says.

"You have tried from the inside as well?"

She shakes her head. "*Pas encore.* That requires *deux. Une* for turning. And *une* for holding the mother down."

Rebecca is wilting, exhausted from the long effort of trying to expel this child from the confines of her body.

I plunge my hands into the wash bucket, scrub them with lye soap, then join Doctor at the foot of the bed. It has been stripped, all the blankets piled in a corner, and an old quilt is folded beneath Rebecca to catch the blood and water. There is—mercifully—not an alarming amount of either. But the scent of birth permeates the room.

The human body has a smell. Not just perspiration. Or defecation. Flatulence. Blood. But the deep parts of a person. Damp and earthy, tinged with the metallic bite of iron. All the moving, beating things that comprise our inmost being. They smell like the natural world, humid and verdant, like soil after the rain. But those are scents that a person rarely notices until a moment like this. Births. Accidents. Injuries. The various ways in which we are turned inside out.

"When did your pains start?" I ask.

"After . . ." She grinds her teeth together. "Noon. In the afternoon."

"Why didn't you send for help earlier?"

There, the desperation in her eyes speaks the truth. "Because I do not want this baby to come."

Rebecca has been laboring for nine hours with a breech presentation and is fast approaching the limits of what her body and soul can bear. Her movements are weak and rubbery, exhausted.

"It has to come, or you will die," I tell her.

Slowly, the realization of what I am saying hits her. "My boys . . ."

"They still need you. Isaac still needs you. So we must get this baby out. In order to do that, we have to turn it."

"All right."

"But we cannot do that from the outside." A pause and then I say, "It is going to hurt. Do you understand what I'm saying?"

Rebecca bobs her head, but I can't tell whether it is a nod or a shake. And whether it hurts or not, the work must be done if Rebecca is to survive this night.

Doctor presses her palms together as though praying, then brings them to her face, thumbs brushing her nose. She whispers something in French, and the only word I recognize is *Dieu*.

God.

When Doctor opens her eyes again, her only focus is the entrance to Rebecca's womb and the child trapped beyond.

"We must wait until the pains ease," she says. "It cannot be done before."

This contraction is long and crushing, deep in Rebecca's back, and she arches against it, wailing so loudly that the air catches in her throat, making her cough, then gag.

"Breathe," I say. "In through your nose. Out through your mouth."

The sound of her agony is the most difficult part, but it must be set aside, even knowing that with her boys, Rebecca birthed them in steely, resolved silence. Nary a moan the entire time. So this difference—the shrieking terror—unnerves me, and I cannot help but wonder how much goes beyond the physical pain of the child's arrival and lies with that of its conception.

"Go up. Beside her. When I tell you, press on the top of her belly." Doctor taps the heel of her hand. "With this."

I do as I'm told, and as we wait for the last waves of the contraction to fade, I brush the wet hair away from Rebecca's brow and the tears from her eyes.

"I'm sorry," Rebecca whispers, "for not calling for you. I didn't . . ."

"Hush. You have nothing to be sorry for."

"I didn't want you to be here because . . ."

Doctor nods to me and I set the heel of my hand on the top of Rebecca's stomach.

The moment her belly slackens, Doctor leans forward, whispers, "*Je suis désolé,*" and slides first one, then the other hand into Rebecca's body.

She pushes and turns, and I can see the small muscles in her forearms begin to tremble with the effort. For her part, Rebecca splits the air with the kind of scream that is rarely heard off a battlefield. We are all sweating from the exertion within seconds, but when Rebecca's belly ripples from one end to the other, I think that perhaps the wrestling match is won. A gush of water floods the bed, soaking the quilt.

"*Bien,*" Doctor pants. "The head is down, but backward."

Oh God, I think, *that will double her pain.*

"She doesn't have the strength for that."

"She does not have to. But we must work quickly. Turn her over. Hands and knees. I can do the rest."

It takes both of us to roll Rebecca onto her side, then get her up on all fours. She hisses and spits through her teeth, like a wounded cat. Rebecca's arms shake, and I fear she will fall face-first into the pillows. Her strength is gone. But this position seems to help immediately, gravity pulling the baby's head away from her tailbone and into the birth canal.

The groan comes, deep and ragged, and I know that another contraction ravages her body. At its peak, Doctor slides two fingers inside Rebecca's body.

"I am lifting the head," she says. "In a moment I will guide it out. But you must lift Rebecca's shoulders up. Her body will do the rest."

I climb onto the bed and pull Rebecca up so that her arms are draped over my shoulders and her head is pressed into my breastbone.

"Now," Doctor says, sliding her other hand inside. It is immediate. Rebecca's stomach deflates as the head drops farther into the birth canal. "*Push.*"

She has no choice in the matter. Her body recognizes that this journey is almost over. It seizes as though being compressed by some external force, and as she bears down, the baby's head emerges halfway.

"Again," Doctor demands.

Rebecca obeys with the last of her energy, and the baby slides, slick and angry, into Doctor's hands. Even from where I kneel at the other end of the bed, I can tell that the cord is far too short. Twelve inches where it should be twenty. No wonder the child hadn't turned.

Doctor slices through the cord with a small pocketknife and I ease Rebecca down onto the bed once more, then roll her onto her back. Below us Doctor hums as she inspects the child for injuries or defect. Finding none, she lifts the baby.

"*Vous avez une fille.*"

I move to the bottom of the bed to clean the child as Doctor tends to Rebecca. As I'm wrapping her in a soft linen cloth, I notice that she has a strawberry birthmark behind her left knee. It is identical to the one on Joshua Burgess's temple. It is proof of Rebecca's claim. It is heartbreaking.

"Hello, little one," I tell the red-faced, squinty little thing. Then I look up at Rebecca. "You have a daughter."

I bring the bundle to Rebecca and hold her out. But she does not reach for the child. Instead, she looks to the tiny, squalling girl once, then turns her face into the pillow, and says, "Throw it in the river."

THE KENNEBEC RIVER

I pull Brutus to a stop in the middle of the boardwalk outside Coleman's General. The snow is all but melted in town, there are muddy tracks cut down the center of Water Street, and the snowdrifts are shrinking on either side. The Kennebec groans on my left as the ice splits and forms small glaciers that crash against one another in the building current. It is an astonishing thing to behold, though not altogether safe. The river often floods when it opens, and the banks have been known to shear away as those blocks of ice roll and tumble downstream.

The squirming infant in my arms cries out again. The child is hungry and cold and fussed all the way here as I held her against my chest, snuggled in tight beneath my riding cloak. She needs a mother but has none. And I have been asked to do the unspeakable.

We begged. Cajoled. Both Doctor and I did all we could to urge Rebecca to put the girl to her breast, but she refused. Would neither look at nor hold the baby. An hour, then two. Surely, we thought, Rebecca would relent. But she hadn't.

"We cannot hide this much longer," Doctor whispered, placing the writhing bundle in my medical bag. "You must go. *Now.*"

We stood in the hallway outside Rebecca's room, listening for Isaac.

"I cannot . . . I have *never* . . ."

"The child is not safe here. You told me as much when you came to my cabin in January. She does not want this baby. Nor can we blame her."

"It is wrong." I shook my head. "I cannot—"

"If you love her, you must do this," Doctor said. "Leave Rebecca to me. Take care of the child."

I left, carrying my medical bag. Doctor will tell Isaac that the child was dead born, that we have done our duty and buried the remains. She will lie so that Rebecca can heal. Perhaps. One day.

Once astride Brutus and away from the tavern, I pulled the baby from my bag and tucked her tight to my chest, praying that my angry, tired steed would not throw us both to the ground. I walked Brutus through the Hook, keeping a finger beneath the infant's nose to make sure she was breathing. Every outraged, hungry cry was a reassurance that she was not stifled beneath my cloak. All the while my heart raced, and my thoughts did their best to keep up.

But now I must make a decision, and there are no good ones before me. I look to the river, listen as the blocks of ice scrape and grind together. I could do as Rebecca asked. No one would ever know. No one will ever come looking for this child.

But that is unthinkable.

Hungry and confused, she cries out in my arms once more, and I pull her close.

"Sshh."

Dawn is still hours away, and the sky above is spread wide, midnight blue and littered with stars. The shadows mingle, dark and darker, all around us. Brutus twitches beneath me, impatient, and I settle him with my voice. A pat of my hand.

The baby shifts in my arms. Whimpers again.

"I know, I know, little one. It is cold. And I am sorry."

But I have made my decision now and will not turn back.

I peel back the blanket until I can see the wide eyes and the tip of that tiny nose. I think of the daughters I buried so long ago, of their graves, two hundred and twenty miles away in Oxford, three in a row, beneath an oak tree. They are lost and gone, and I would give most anything to hold them again. I would give my own life if it meant they could have theirs back.

"What your mother does not yet understand," I tell the baby, my voice choked with emotion, "is that there are some losses in this life that we do not live long enough to fully grieve. And I'll not give her another one."

I tuck the baby girl under my riding cloak once more—safe from the cool night air—and turn Brutus onto Winthrop Street.

WHITE SADDLERY

Sarah White answers the door. I did not expect her to be awake, much less dressed, but there she is, as though expecting me, as though I've been invited. And here I thought I'd have to get through her mother first.

"May I come in?" I ask.

"Of course," she says, and pulls back the door to let me in.

I don't realize at first why she throws a questioning glance over her shoulder. But once I've knocked the mud off my boots and stepped inside, I see a man sitting beside the fire. He is young and handsome, and there is a bundle in his arms.

When the bundle squirms, then snores, I realize that he is holding Charlotte.

Sarah opens her mouth to explain, but there is no time.

"I need your help. Please."

"Come in," she says. "Tell me. I will help in any way that I can."

I do hope she truly means that, because when I get to the fire and pull back my riding cloak to reveal the newborn squirming baby, she gasps. The man does as well, although he adds a colorful invective to go along with his stare. Abashed, he sets his palm over Charlotte's ear. Says it again. But whispers this time.

"She was born almost three hours ago and has not eaten. Are you still making enough milk for two?"

God bless Sarah White, and may He curse anyone who speaks a harsh word against her ever again, for she immediately drops into the other chair and begins to unbutton her blouse.

I look to the man. Back to Sarah. "Mmm. Perhaps he ought—"

She laughs. "Don't fret about my modesty, Mistress Ballard. He's seen it all before." Sarah reaches for the baby, smiling as though she's just been offered a prize and not a burden. "This is Charlotte's father, Henry Warren. I told you he would come back for us."

Well.

I need to sit down.

I lower myself to a chair beside the hearth. Gape at him while Sarah lifts the baby to her breast. The little girl clamps onto her nipple with a ferocity that amazes me. She sucks and gurgles, slipping off the breast. Screaming. Starving. Angrily swatting the air with her tiny fists. She grabs hold again, little mouth working in desperation while Sarah expertly adjusts both child and breast for a better fit. She rocks the baby. Shushes her. Strokes her ear and temple with a long, soft finger. And all the while Henry watches in wonder, as though Sarah is nursing his child and not a stranger's.

"Does she have a name?" Sarah asks.

I shake my head.

She looks at me through long, dark lashes, and I can see her mind work. "Does she have a *mother*?"

Again, I shake my head.

"I see. Am I to keep her, then?"

"Only as long as you're willing. I must confess that my only thought was to get her fed, not what happens next. But I will think of something. I promise."

"I am happy to help you, Mistress Ballard. It's the least I can do. Considering all you've done for me."

"Thank you." I sigh and lean back, then close my eyes for a moment and let the heat from the fire seep into my body. When I open them again, I see that the young man is staring at me now. "I'm sorry. I've failed to introduce myself. I am Martha Ballard. A midwife. And a friend of Sarah's."

I extend my hand, and he accepts it. "I'd gathered as much. I'm Major Henry Warren, Sarah's fiancé."

I look to Sarah, stunned.

"He asked me this evening. Walked right in the door and asked me. We plan to post notice tomorrow and be married within the month." The smile Sarah gives me is almost pitying. "I know you didn't believe me. No one did. Everyone thought I was a fool. But they don't know Henry. He promised and I believed him."

It is as though someone has tossed my mind beneath the stampeding hooves of a charging herd of horses. There is so much to make sense of all at once. But before I can reckon with the fact that Sarah's lover has returned for her, there is one thing that I have to know.

I turn to Henry. "Do you know a man named Joseph North?"

"Isn't he the judge in this town?"

"Yes."

"I know him by name only. I have never met the man."

"Well, he claims differently."

I do not know this Henry Warren any more than I know Latin. Or Chinese. But I do like the way his eyes pinch in alarm and how he pulls Charlotte tighter against his chest.

"What do you mean?"

"Judge Joseph North has sworn to the court that he was with you on the night of August tenth last year, when he is accused of raping a woman in this town."

"On August tenth, I was three hundred miles west of here. Same as I've been for the better part of a year. Until December, when we got orders for Fort Halifax. And there are two dozen men at the tavern who will testify to that."

I ponder this. Nod. "I had to ask," I tell him.

Henry doesn't seem the least bit offended. "I wouldn't expect less of anyone who cares about Sarah. But I don't like that he's used me as an alibi. I'm happy to write to the court and certify otherwise."

"The trial has come and gone, and North has been acquitted."

"I don't care. I don't want my name associated with his. Tell me who I must speak with about this. I want it official."

"His name is Seth Parker, and we will deal with that later. But thank you." Now that that is out of the way, I have another question for him. "Did you know about Charlotte?"

"No. But I . . . ah . . . knew there was a *possibility* of a child. I had to finish my enlistment with the militia. That's what took me so long. I've made arrangements for us. Here. In Hallowell."

Sarah beams. "He's bought Coleman's Store!"

"You're the man from Boston?"

"I am. And I thought that's where we'd have to live. But my grandfather died last year. Left me a bit of an inheritance. And that gave me the option of moving here instead."

When I told Samuel Coleman about the story of *Emmeline* by Charlotte Turner Smith, he had laughed. Said it sounded like a fantasy. And yet here is a woman who did the very same thing as that character. Sarah has lived on the fringes of society. Yet she's chosen the course of her life. She's found love on her own terms. And I'll be damned if she likely won't end up wealthy and happy as a result. Just wait until I tell Coleman how very real the premise of that novel is after all.

I am overwhelmed, with both joy and exhaustion, and the sensation feels very much as though I am a candle, wilting over an open flame, with my wick burning at both ends. I have so little energy left, and I can feel my mind getting fuzzy. It is time to go home.

"Martha?"

"Yes?"

Sarah tilts her chin toward the baby. She is milk drunk and has fallen off the breast. Asleep. Her mouth open, milk dribbling from one corner.

"What should I call her?"

I smile. "I think Emmeline would be a fine name."

MILL CREEK BRIDGE

It is nearing five o'clock in the morning when I urge Brutus into a lope. I am too exhausted to ride this hard, but I want nothing more, at this point, than my own bed, my own pillow, and the soft, worn quilt on top. Now, with home only moments away, and my nerves still raw, I cross the bridge and turn west, up the lane. Once again, I nudge Brutus to go faster, but we've not made it a quarter mile when a living shadow melts out of the woods. Tempest darts into the road in front of us. Her eyes are an amber flame blazing in the dark. The fox barks out a ferocious warning, and Brutus rears back, forelegs pawing the air in alarm. The movement catches me off guard, but not so much that I'm unseated.

Tempest looks directly at me, warning and fear and something else reflected in the light of the moon. She sniffs the air, searching for my scent, and takes another step forward. Brutus flicks his tail. Snorts. He sees only sharp teeth and wicked claws. He knows nothing of my fondness for this creature.

I am unprepared for the buck.

Off balance. Arms akimbo, and then, before I can adjust or pull in a full breath, I am tumbling through the air over his head. The horizon—now pale and silver—spins, and the earth rushes toward me. I have gone forward, arse over teakettle, and though I try to land on my feet, I cannot tell up from down. And there is no time to judge my position in the air.

I hit the ground, hard, on my back—breath rushing from my lungs in a guttural *oof*—before I can protect myself from the fall. I feel the impact everywhere. My ribs throb, my head aches, my hips feel battered, and even though it is dark, bright little lights spin in front of my eyes, dancing to some nauseating rhythm. I taste blood and know that I have bitten my tongue. The thing that scares me most, however, is that my mouth opens and closes but my lungs refuse to pull in air. I gasp and flail like one of Cyrus's fish when pulled from the pond.

I cannot breathe.

I roll onto my side, trying not to panic. It takes another long, frightened moment, but I am finally able to pull a thin stream of air into my burning lungs in a ragged, wheezing whistle. It feels like water and fire, life and death, and I lie there drinking in both, my lungs aflame. Drowning. Burning. The sound I make, trying to breathe, would have me on my knees, begging God for help, if this were a birthing room and I heard a woman in this state. But it is only me, beneath the stars winded and wounded.

Think, breathe, think, breathe, I tell myself. *You cannot die here alone in the middle of the road.*

Brutus is fifty feet away, stamping the ground, impatient for me to get up. I'd kill him if I could, that's how much I hate that stupid, ruthless brute of a horse right now. Worst decision I ever made. Worst money I ever spent.

Wheeze.

Gasp.

A breath, deeper now, but still the burning.

I am *furious.*

My own horse has tried to kill me.

I glare at the damned, stubborn stallion. I should have castrated him when I had the chance. Ephraim was right. That's the only way to tame a wild beast.

The cold and wet seep into my clothing, my bones, and I know that I should get up. That I cannot lie here forever. I am certain— mostly, I think—that nothing is broken, but my body is slow to rise.

There is a soft padding near my head, the tiny crackle of little feet moving through leaf and mud. And then there she is. My fox. All dark and silver in the moonlight, her startling eyes locked on me.

Tempest.

I say nothing.

Don't budge an inch.

I barely allow myself the air that my lungs are screaming for.

Because the fox is sliding forward, one delicate paw after the other, and now she is only a whisker's breadth away, staring at me as though *I* am the most curious creature on earth. I would never have believed such a thing could happen, have never heard of such a thing in my life.

Tempest—my own little fox—eases her slender head forward and sticks out her pink tongue. Once. Just once she licks the tip of my nose. It's a greeting. A peace offering. Some acknowledgment that we are one and the same. But it is fleeting. Gone as quickly as it came, just like her, because in one bound, she springs over my head, nose pointed toward the house, tail toward Water Street, and begins to bark.

There is nothing comely or tender about the sound this time. They are vicious little snarls that rip the air and snap my senses into order once again. I struggle to my feet and back away. Not because I am afraid of Tempest. Certainly not. But because I realize that these are warning barks.

We are not alone in the woods.

But in the distance, I hear an answering call. Another fox. Her mate, perhaps, somewhere closer to the house.

I turn to Brutus just in time to see him spin around and bolt in the opposite direction. That traitor has run off and left me.

"Et tu, Brute?"

*

I limp toward the mill. My ankle is sprained, and a cut runs the length of my right forearm, dripping blood into the cuff of my sleeve. My breath comes easier now, but still, there is a whistle at the end—a dispute, lodged by my body for its recent treatment. Brutus is gone—run off toward the Hook—and has taken my medical bag with him, so I do not even have my bandages.

I am still cursing the beast when I step out of the woods and see a lantern burning in the mill window.

"Ephraim," I wheeze, and shuffle faster.

A horse is hitched to the post, snorting deep in the shadows, and a long rectangle of pale light slips out from the door and falls onto the muddy yard.

I turn sideways and slide through the narrow wedge of open door. "That damned horse threw me again," I say. "Mark my words, I'm selling him for glue."

At the sound of my voice a low, angry growl fills the room. Cicero. He lies on the floor beneath Ephraim's workbench. He lifts his head from his paws and rounds his spine slightly, all the bristly hair standing on end. Teeth bared. Eyes flashing. No wonder the foxes are barking tonight.

His master stands a few feet away, flipping pages in a book that I immediately recognize as my journal. He looks up at me, dispassionate.

"I would like to know," Joseph North says, ripping a page from the spine, "what you were really doing in my house yesterday?"

*

"Get out," I say, grabbing onto one of the large central posts for support.

"No."

"Ephraim will be home any moment."

"That excuse didn't work the first time," North says, tearing another sheet of paper from the book. It falls to the floor and settles at his feet. "And I'm rather weary of hearing it. Your husband is in Boston. Petitioning his claim to this property."

"My children—"

"Are all in bed. Asleep. You are alone, Martha. The question is whether you are *afraid.*"

Rrrriiiipp. The sound echoes through the mill. This time he wads the page with his fist and throws it to the corner.

"No. I am not afraid of you."

"Rebecca was afraid when we went to her that night. You should have seen the way her legs trembled on that bed." He says it so casually. As though he doesn't care that he's confessing to a crime. "Don't worry," he adds. "I'm not incriminating myself. I've been *acquitted,* remember? I can't be tried again."

"*Get out,*" I tell him, the air hissing through my teeth, ribs creaking in protest. I wonder if I broke something after all.

Cicero leans forward at the note of anger in my voice. Bares his teeth.

"No. You and I are going to have a little talk. And we're going to start with why you were in my house."

"Medicine. For your wife."

His eyes narrow. "You're hurt."

I wince but do not answer him.

"Well, that will make this easier." He turns another page in my journal. Reads a benign entry aloud. Pats his mouth as though yawning. "Where is my letter, Martha?"

"I don't know what you're talking about."

"You are a terrible liar."

"I wish I could say the same about you."

He laughs. "No doubt I've had more practice."

I summon every bit of nerve that I have. Stand as straight as I'm able. "Get away from my journal. And get off my property."

"It's my property now. But I think we might come to an understanding." North holds up the journal by its spine, then yanks out a fistful of pages. If one could rip my soul in half, that would be the sound. He shakes them in front of me. "I underestimated you. I never knew you kept this book. Until the first hearing."

I need to run. Everything about North—his demeanor, his words, everything—feels dangerous. Unhinged. But I wouldn't make it to the path before he caught me. I could scream. There's a chance one of the children would hear me. But which one? Hannah? Dolly? Young Ephraim? I would pray for Jonathan, but he was passed out drunk, not five hours ago. Cyrus is the best option, but there's no certainty he'll be the one to come running.

"If not for this, Rebecca's claims would have never made it past the first hearing." North yanks at the book again, and my eyes sting as I watch a week's worth of careful documentation being torn in half.

I ease back toward the door, but Cicero is on his feet now, growl-

ing deeper, edging closer, and I stop. I lift my hands, palms out to ease
him back. He sits back on his haunches in the middle of the floor.

North snorts. Tears out another page.

"Why did you rape Rebecca?" I ask. Stalling is the best option I
have now. Keep him talking. Give Cyrus time to get up and get to
work.

"I taught her a well-deserved lesson."

"You broke her body and destroyed her life. You forced a child
upon her. What did she *ever* do to you?"

North looks at me, lips twitching in fury. "She brought those
damn Indians into this town! Not once. But two dozen times. Do
you know how long it took us to root the Wabanaki out of this place?
Seven years. Seven years of war with the French and their barbaric
allies. And she waltzes into the Hook with her high ideals and that
idiot husband and invites them into her *home*. It could not be tolerated."

"Who she associates with is none of your business."

"*Everything* to do with this town is my business! I was here before
any of you, and I'll not have this place polluted by our enemies."

I shake my head. He truly believes what he's saying. "You raped
her because of the *Wabanaki*? Because of a grudge held over from
some old war? You are a judge. You had no right to violate your oath
of office."

"I had every right!" He thumps his chest. "*I* am the judge. *I* decide
what is just."

"You are a disgrace."

He laughs, but there is no mirth in the sound. "Rebecca Foster is
just a cunt. Same as you. Same as every woman. Just a nice wet hole
to dump a bit of seed. Nothing more."

Samuel Coleman is right. This man has lost his soul. It is the only
way to justify such a belief. He was born of a woman after all. He has
a wife *and grown daughters*. He moves through a world that is equally
filled with women.

"What happened to you?" I ask. "During the war?"

"Nothing *happened* to me. I learned the greatest lesson of my life."

He sounds more like a judge again, and less like a zealot. His voice
has slipped into oratory, the kind he uses from the bench. There is no

courtroom to lecture, however, only me, and I use this bit of space to test the strength of my wounded ankle. The jolt of pain that shoots up my shin is reminder enough that I cannot run.

"If you see something," North says. "If you *want* it, then you must *take* it. That is how you survive not just a war, but a life. The French and Indians taught me that."

"So you are a thief as well as a rapist?" I lift my arm and indicate the mill around us. "You take land. Women. Scalps." He flinches at this. "And then call yourself a *victim* when challenged?"

It is risky, but I need more time. So I press harder. Fold my arms across my chest.

"No," I shake my head. "You're no hero. No *founding father.* You are a coward who runs in the face of justice. *You* are the kind of man who hides in a dead man's house instead of facing the jail yard."

North looks at me, eyes wide, as though astonished I could have figured this out.

"Let me guess," I say. "You couldn't find the eviction papers. So you threw a tantrum and torched Burgess's homestead?"

"*You,*" he hisses. "You have them."

"No. Not anymore. They are currently in the possession of your employers. And I would imagine the Kennebec Proprietors will find this little scheme of yours quite illegal. See it, want it, take it only works when there is no one around you to stop you, Joseph."

He is not a man given to silence. Swollen by self-importance, impressed by the sound of his own voice, Joseph North always fills a void with vain and stupid words. But, for the first time in our long acquaintance, he closes his mouth.

Ten seconds.

Twenty.

For thirty long seconds he shakes with rage.

"There is no one to stop me now, is there, Martha?"

I should have known where this was headed. He'd made it clear up front with his nonchalant confession. But it isn't until he tilts his head and the look in his eye changes from pious to prurient that I understand the point he has come to make. Joseph North intends to take a pound of flesh.

"You have caused me a great deal of trouble. And there is a price to pay for that."

"You wouldn't *dare* touch me," I say, shifting as best I can toward the worktable. I need something, anything, to support my weight.

"I admit that I have not fantasized about you the way I did with Rebecca. At least not in many years. You were quite lovely when you were young, though. Billy Crane thought so at least, didn't he?" He licks the corner of his mouth as he makes a roving assessment of my body. "Your breasts were smaller then, but your legs just as long."

Billy Crane.

I haven't heard that name spoken aloud in at least a decade. Maybe more. And the fact that North says it now, with his own threat hanging in the air, makes my heart trip harder.

"Oh, don't look so surprised. You think I don't remember? We hung him from a pine tree. No trial. And I learned a good lesson in the process. Don't get caught."

He takes a step toward me.

"Touch me and you will regret it for the rest of your life." I edge back, looking for something with which to protect myself. "You will not find me such an easy victim. And you do not have help tonight."

"I can admit that Burgess was a mistake. He enjoyed it too much. Wanted another go at her when he was done. But I didn't need him then, and I don't need him now."

I take another step toward the worktable. Force the fear out of my voice. "So why take him? It was such a stupid risk."

"It was *brilliant*. People might have believed her if she said one man raped her that night. But two? It's ludicrous. A story cooked up by a vengeful woman who's just seen her husband fired. I took Burgess with me so that no one *would* believe her. You saw how well that worked for me in court. Charges of *attempted* rape. And then an acquittal."

"An acquittal only because she wasn't there to testify."

"And whose fault was that?"

"*You* are the only one at fault here. Don't you dare try to blame anything on her."

I have to keep him talking. That's the thing. He's just so damn *impressed* with himself. Always has been. And the more he talks, the lighter it grows outside. Men aren't so brave in the daylight as they are in the dark. My children might be asleep, but not for long. This is a farm, after all. And besides, the thing that I want is here, three feet away. But if I lunge for it, he will block me.

"Come now, Martha, we have business to attend." North untucks his shirt. Pulls at the laces of his trousers.

"Don't you dare." I edge another step closer toward the table.

"Go on, try to run. But I don't think you'll get far. Not with that ankle."

Cicero swishes his tail across the floor, kicking up a fine cloud of sawdust. He bares his teeth and the dark gums above them.

When North tugs his trousers down, and then the drawers beneath, I do not deign to look at the thing he strokes in his hand. Instead, I watch his eyes, wait for him to charge, knowing that I will have only one chance. If he reaches me, or knocks me down, the fight will move to the floor, and any leverage I have will be lost, along with any hope of defending myself.

"It must vex you to know that you can't scheme your way out of this," he says.

I am sweating. At my temples. Under my arms. My upper lip. I haven't sweated in six months. Maybe seven. Not since the last time I worked in my garden. Winter has stripped this experience away entirely. But here it is again. Assaulting me. Unwelcome. The air feels thick and heavy inside the mill. I can smell North's breath. His sweat. His crotch. I can smell the anger seeping from his body.

Thump. Thump-thump. Thump-thump-thump. Thump-thump-thump-thump. Faster and faster and faster my heart beats.

Smell and memory are linked together. Nothing conjures the latter like the former. And now, my entire being is seized with a memory from thirty-five years ago. Billy Crane. The shed. Four horrendous minutes with my face shoved into the dirt.

"I *knew* you were scared," North says.

And I cannot deny it. The proof is there in the rapid rise and fall of my chest. The breath that I cannot force into submission. I can hear the blood rushing through my ears, like a river that has broken loose from winter's grip. Raging. Violent. I know what is coming. My body is aware. It *remembers*. And it will not be calmed.

I lurch toward Ephraim's worktable when North takes that first step in my direction. He is faster than I am with a sprained ankle, and he catches me by the hair. Yanks me backward, hard.

I scream.

The pain is so startling that the sound has escaped my lips before I realize I've drawn the breath to cry out. Cicero jumps to his feet again. Growls. Inches forward. I sound wounded, like an animal. I sound like prey, and he salivates at the noise.

North winds his fingers through my hair. Pulls me closer. Whispers.

"What a pretty penny this would have earned."

"Let go of me!" I scratch at his hands.

"Oh no. You are going to be *quiet* about this. While I'm doing it, and afterward. You'll not say a word, because no one will believe you. They'll think it's some bit of petty revenge, just your way of getting back at me after losing in court."

No one will believe you.

It's the line spoken by every man who has ever used a woman in this way. The trouble is that so often they are right. But I am *angry* now, and I do not want to be used in any way by Joseph North. There is only a foot between us, and we are near the same height, so I do the only thing that I am able. I tilt forward as though trying to move, and when he grips my hair tighter, I smash my head backward into his face.

It is North's turn to scream. Then he grunts. Curses. He drops my hair and clutches at his bleeding nose.

When he lets go, I dive for the worktable, scrambling for Ephraim's wicked, curved blade. Revenge. Hilt in hand, I turn. The knife feels heavy in my palm. Unwieldy.

"You aren't going to kill me," he says, laughing.

And it's that arrogance—the certainty—that enrages me.

"I have no intention of killing you."

Even though I could.

"Then put down your toy and take what's coming to you."

I grip the knife tighter, lift the blade, and slash the air. Just once. Just close enough that he flinches and raises his arm to block me. Revenge cuts a clean swath through his sleeve. A three-inch slit that exposes the skin of his wrist.

North looks at it, stupefied.

"You stupid, little c—"

"Don't touch me."

I swipe again, and he stumbles backward this time. Two steps. He nearly trips over his pants, and it's enough that I can maneuver into a better position. Press my hips against the worktable. Support my weight.

Anger. Fear. Both mingle to make my voice unreliable. I do not want to sound weak, so I clear my throat. Even so, it is better to reply one word at a time. "You. Will. Not. Touch. Me."

"I don't take orders from women," he says. And then he lunges, hands out as though he would take me by the throat and throttle me.

I drop down.

Ignore the blinding pain that cascades through my knees when they hit the floor.

Lean forward at a slight tilt.

And bring my arm down in a quick, purposeful slash, just as his hands grab hold of thin air.

I do not swing blindly.

I do not miss.

And I am not sorry.

The blade catches him right between the legs. It is a clean cut, the kind that takes a moment to feel.

But when he does, his scream rises high in the early morning air, for Revenge has done its job. Joseph North will never rape another woman as long as he lives.

*

North falls on top of me, and now we are a tangle of arms and legs, and Ephraim's blade toggling between us. I try to scramble away but have no leverage, so I must use my arms to create some distance. I feel him shift on the ground beside me, and I swing wide, again, but connect with nothing but air.

North isn't coming for me, however. He is bent over himself, hands cupped at his crotch, blood flowing between his fingers. Cicero goes insane, unsure whether to defend his master or attack, the smell of blood making him frantic.

"What did you do? What did you do!" he gasps, then begins to cry and curse and swing his arms in my direction, and I feel each drop of blood hit my face. It smells of copper and rust and salt. It smells of fear.

I can hear the words that he hurls at me, but they do not make sense together. Random insults, violent but utterly impotent. He screams. Gags. Curses.

"I told you not to touch me," I say. "I told you to *leave*."

I scoot away from him and use the worktable to pull myself up. Wipe the blood on my skirt. I grip the blade as Cicero takes careful, measured steps around his master. He has made his decision and identified me as the threat, the cause of all this pain and screaming. One large paw glides through the slick red puddle, and when he sets it down again, the print is perfect, as though stamped in wax.

Revenge is ruthless but might not do much good against those teeth if Cicero gets them around my arm. Or throat. My hand is shaking now anyway, and the hilt is slippery in my palm. The dog senses this, edges closer.

I had thought that the rising sun might bring one of my sons to the mill for work, but it brings the sound of hoofs thundering down the drive instead.

It brings an unholy screeching as well. It rings in my ears. It makes my teeth hurt.

Blood.

It spreads on the floor beneath North. I feel no pity for him, but neither do I want him to die here, in my husband's mill, in such a way that I will bear the blame. My intent was to maim, not kill. To teach him a permanent lesson. To ensure that he had one less weapon with which to wound the women of this world. I shrug out of my shawl and throw it to him.

"Use that," I order. "Staunch the bleeding."

He screams at me. Curses through a slobbering haze of fury.

"Calm down and do as I say. Or you will die."

I expect Cyrus or Jonathan but instead it is Ephraim who steps through the door. I stare at him, stupefied.

"What the bloody *hell*?" Ephraim asks when he sees North sprawled out, blood pooling between his legs, as he tries to press my shawl to his groin.

Cicero is backing away now, alternating between growls and

whines, when Percy swoops through the door and dives for him. The dog yelps, as though he's just been branded, and runs for the door. Percy takes a sharp turn and is after him, talons extended.

My journal is on the floor, torn to shreds.

And I am crying at the sight of my husband. I drop Revenge. The blood feels oily on my hand, and I wipe it against my skirt.

"He was waiting for me when I got home." I look directly at Ephraim and try to communicate everything in two sentences. "I told him not to touch me. He wouldn't listen."

My husband goes still. Quiet. His pupils dilate, and he takes me in, looking for injury, then he turns to the gory sight of North twitching on the floor. He understands what I am trying to say.

"Are you hurt?"

The question is both gentle and ferocious.

"Only because Brutus threw me."

"I thought as much," Ephraim says. "I caught him on Water Street."

I test my weight on the sprained ankle, limp toward Ephraim anyway. "North needs a doctor."

Ephraim studies him on the floor. "There isn't time," he says.

"But—"

"It will take too long to get him to the Hook. Without help he'll bleed to death. If he's to be saved it will have to be by your hand."

Saving Joseph North is the last thing I want to do, but we cannot let him die here. Not after all that's happened.

Ephraim moves toward him, and North growls, "Do not touch me!"

"You would give me orders? In my own home? After what you have done?" Ephraim goes to stand over him. "If you aim to die, it will not be on my property."

Still, North howls and spits and curses at me, and through clenched teeth he heaves every possible insult he's ever heard for the female species.

A moment ago, he thought me weak. Vulnerable. And perhaps I was, but I am not helpless.

"It is a pity you hate women so much," I tell him. "Because you are going to spend the rest of your life pissing like one."

There are a thousand things I want to know about how Ephraim came to be here in this moment, but, given the look on his face as he surveys the gravity of North's wounds, my questions will have to wait. He has only just realized what his blade has done.

"Martha . . ." he says, and I hear the note of uncertainty in his voice.

"I will need my medical bag. And a great deal of ice."

*

I am a midwife.
  I am a healer.
  I do not take life.
  I shepherd life into this world.

This is what I tell myself as we staunch the bleeding. Ephraim applies the pressure as North slips in and out of consciousness, his eyes growing wide in alarm, then rolling back until only the whites are showing. Every time he comes to, his body twitches, but then the pain takes him away again and he flops back to the floor.

The bleeding is the main problem, but once we have it under control, I go to work with needle and thread. There isn't much left to sew. The cut was clean and effective, and time will have to do the rest. I rinse the wound with a tincture of witch hazel so that infection will not set in.

Once I've tied off the last stitch, I pile a mound of ice on top of the wound. This will both temporarily numb the pain and shrink the blood vessels. But North is restless, twitching. He won't stay asleep for much longer. What I wouldn't give for Dr. Page's bottle of laudanum.

When I look at Ephraim, there is an ocean of sadness in his eyes.

"I told him not to touch me," I say.

"Stop. You will not blame yourself for what happened here tonight, or for showing him mercy."

"I doubt North will ever call this mercy."

"If it hadn't been mercy, you would have gone for this throat."

"I cut exactly where I meant to, Ephraim. An eye for an eye."

"Then we'll call it *severe* mercy, love." He comes to sit beside me on the filthy, stained floor. "Will he live?"

"I don't see why not. Assuming there is no infection or fever. Which there shouldn't be if the wound is kept clean."

"And are you going to do that for him?"

"Absolutely not. He will get no further ministrations from me. He can find his own nursemaid."

"What should I do with him, then?"

"Take him to Dr. Page. As I recall, the good colonel here has a great deal of respect for that buffoon's *medical experience.* We'll see how satisfied he is with the care he receives."

"And what will I tell Dr. Page about these wounds?"

I look around the mill, at a loss for an answer, but then I settle on Ephraim's worktable and the row of clean, shining knives.

"It isn't uncommon for inexperienced woodworkers to have an accident with the draw blade. Particularly when they don't wear that leather apron."

"And if North argues that explanation?"

"Then he can explain that he broke into our home, attacked me, and was castrated in the process. But if I know anything about the man, that's not a story he'll want known."

Ephraim looks at the blood on my hands, on my dress. "And what about you?"

"I'm fine."

"No, you're not."

"I will be. Eventually."

"And until then? What will you do?"

"I have not slept in twenty-four hours. I am going to bed."

WEDNESDAY, APRIL 21

Tired and battered though I was, I couldn't sleep when I made it back to the house. I could only wash my face and hands and light the hearth fires.

By the time the children got up and about, I'd collected myself and they didn't know there was anything wrong. Nor did they think it strange when I asked them to draw and heat water for a bath. It was only when Ephraim came home and stomped right to our bedroom that they cast wary glances at one another. Not finding me there he'd come to the workroom, and we have been shut inside together ever since, whispering, the door locked.

He pulls a new journal and a box of ink from his satchel and lays them on my table.

"For you," he says.

And that is when I begin to cry. It is a heaving that begins deep within my chest, a current that bursts the dam of resolve that I keep so firmly in place. I weep. Long and loud enough that I know our children can hear it on the other side of the door. Ephraim pulls me against his chest and lets me wring out every tear.

After several long moments, he pulls away and takes in my appearance.

"You need a bath," he says.

"I know. The girls are heating water."

"Get undressed," he tells me. "I'll collect everything."

Soon I am standing in the washtub as Ephraim pours hot water over my body. It is only three feet wide, certainly not as luxurious as a copper tub, but it is better than nothing. And I am filthy. Covered with the muck of birth and mud from the road and blood from North. It has been less than eight hours since I delivered Rebecca Foster. Five since I left her daughter in the care of Sarah White. Three since Ephraim loaded North into the wagon and made for the Hook.

"I caught Brutus on Water Street. That's how I knew you were in trouble," he says. "I grabbed his reins and tore home as fast as I could. But when I heard you scream . . ." Ephraim takes a deep breath. Shakes his head. "Brutus had gone for help, and you'll not convince me otherwise. That horse loves you."

"I thought you hated him?"

"Not anymore."

"He tried to kill me. How many times does he have to throw me to prove that?"

"If he threw you, he had a reason."

"It was the fox. She darted out in front of him. I think . . ." I pause because I know it will sound ridiculous.

"What?"

"I think she was trying to warn me. She knew that North and Cicero were waiting for me."

"That makes sense."

"Oh! *That's* the thing that makes sense to you in all of this?"

He looks out the window, to the giant live oak that grows in the south pasture. "Foxes and coyotes are natural enemies, love."

Something about the way he says this makes me think that he is no longer speaking of Tempest and Cicero, but my mind is filled with all the things he doesn't yet know, and I must keep them in order, so I put this observation aside.

"Sit." Ephraim points at the tub. "I'll wash your hair."

"There's no room."

"There's room enough."

For my bottom only. My knees are bent and my feet rest on the floor, but the water comes up to my ribs, and sitting feels much better than standing on my lame ankle. He pours a pitcher of water over my head, and it runs down my neck, down my back. I tilt my head back. Look at his worried face. Smile sadly.

"Thank you."

"Tell me everything," he says.

I wrap my arms around my knees and start at the beginning, with Jonathan and Sally and our new grandson. He is neither surprised, nor entirely displeased in our son's choice of girl.

"He didn't choose her," I say. "She trapped him."

"You cannot have it both ways. Only recently you were complaining that he hadn't yet found a wife."

"He still hasn't. Not really. He's only found a girl willing to let her skirts be thrown up in the woods."

He sighs. Pours another pitcher of water. "Don't let him off so easily. He went to bed with her willingly enough. There's choice in that. And now there's a child. Have they posted their intent to marry?"

"Last night."

"Good."

"I can't say he was happy to do it. He went back into the tavern and soaked himself in whiskey afterward."

Ephraim shakes his head. "Our daughters are in such a hurry to marry. And our sons in no hurry at all."

"Cyrus would if he could."

"Still no luck with Sarah White?"

"No. Though I am loath to admit it, you were right. She has made her choice, and it isn't him."

"Who then?"

"That is a long story involving Rebecca Foster."

"Explain that to me."

"I will, once I tell you why Joseph North came to the mill."

I go back to my place in the story, where I was called to attend Sally. Then I tell him how I went to North Manor to give Lidia her medicine. How I found the letter that North was drafting to the Kennebec Proprietors.

"It's in my medical bag. There. In the corner."

Ephraim pauses his ministrations to dry his hands and read the letter.

"Now I understand," he says. "North's lawyer, Henry Knowland, is an agent of the Kennebec Proprietors. Or at least he was. I'd wager he loses the position after Paul delivers the documents to them."

"Documents?"

"A scheme the two of them had to take leases for themselves and gain a monopoly on the lumber trade in Kennebec County. This letter proves it. It also proves that he meant to use our property as a base of operations."

"But why take ours? Why not just build his own? There are thousands of unclaimed acres here. Most of what he's requesting in that letter is open land."

"Perhaps. But it doesn't have access to the river. Joseph North is a lazy man, Martha. He doesn't want to go to all the hard work of building a thing himself when he can take it from someone else."

See it, want it, take it, I think. *He's never changed.*

"That doesn't explain why he had our lease assigned to Burgess first."

"I think you were right about that to start with. He bought Burgess's silence with the promise of our land."

"Burgess never made any secret of wanting property with river frontage," I say.

"It's likely how he talked Burgess into going to the Fosters' that night in the first place. Burgess got what he wanted, and North got something to hold over his head. A way of controlling the property without having to do any of the work."

"That's a long game to play."

"I found his original lease request, and it was for this property."

I crane my neck to look at him. "How did we get it, then?"

Ephraim smiles. "Paul's letter of recommendation."

"Of course. *Paul.*"

We had arrived in Hallowell, in 1778, almost halfway through the

Revolutionary War, thanks to a letter of recommendation written by the famed silversmith not three years after his infamous ride through Charlestown. On a horse borrowed from my husband, no less, the same night Ephraim had taken that dirty punch and got his nose broken.

"Then I take it to mean that you have settled the issue of our eviction?"

"I have. And gained a bit of influence in the process. You are looking at the newest agent of the Kennebec Proprietors. No one can try to wrest this property away from us again. We have been on the property twelve years this month."

"So North . . ."

"Did everything he could to steal it in the limited time he had between October and April. But we have officially fulfilled all the terms of our lease. We own the land now."

"That's a relief. I am too old to start over in a new place."

Ephraim takes the soap from its basket, plunges it into the water, and begins to lather my shoulders. "Keep going," he says. "You found the letter in North's office and then what?"

"I took it. Obviously. And then he walked in. I got away by telling him that I'd only come to care for Lidia. But he figured out the letter was missing soon enough. And came looking for it later. I went to Pollard's after I left his house." I look up. "The militia is back."

"I meant to tell you that. In December. After I got back from doing that survey. They were stationed at Fort Halifax when I was there. Said they'd be coming through again this spring."

"Well, they have."

"And Sarah's man? Is he with them?"

"I'm getting to that."

I tell my husband how I came home and waited up for Jonathan after being at Pollard's, and how Doctor arrived to tell me that Rebecca was in labor. I tell him of the difficult birth. The delivery. And what Rebecca asked me to do afterward. His hands still as he waits for me to finish. They rest on my shoulders, warm and soapy.

"I took the baby to Sarah White," I tell him. "She has her for now. Until I can think of something different. Sarah also has a fiancé."

His lip curls into a smile. "Her soldier?"

"Indeed. You would have never convinced me that he'd come

back. But he did. And I have to say I'm glad to see it. He's bought
Coleman's Store, and I think he'll give her a good life."

"Hold on for a minute. I'll go get more warm water." He's back
two minutes later with a fresh kettle and a hair comb. "Go on."

I continue, telling him about how Brutus was startled by the
fox on our way home. How he threw me. And finally about finding
North at the mill. He wants to know every detail about our confrontation. Everything North said and did. He doesn't like the details, but
he listens quietly as he washes my hair with the soap.

"I've been thinking about something," he tells me.

"What?"

"That dog of North's . . ."

"Cicero?"

"He's the one that got into Percy's mews."

"I know."

"He's half mutt, half coyote, best as I can figure."

"Okay . . ."

"The thing about a half-tame dog is that it's still half-wild. That
can't be changed."

"And now you're talking about North?"

"I am making an observation, love."

Ephraim rinses my hair, then reaches for a small bottle of rosemary and lavender oil. He pours a few drops into his palm, then rubs
his hands together. He works it through my hair slowly to ease out the
tangles, and then he begins to comb, listening to me all the while. The
story ends with details he already knows. A knife and blood.

"Is he . . . ?" My voice trails off.

"Alive? Yes," Ephraim says. "You saved him."

"Did Page ask what happened?"

"He did. And I gave him the answer you suggested. North didn't
contradict a word of it."

I rest my head on my knees as Ephraim works his way upward
with the comb. We are silent for a long while once he abandons the
comb and begins to massage my neck and scalp.

"There was quite a mess at the mill," he says, thumbs rubbing
circles right behind my ears.

I mumble something that almost sounds like *I'm sorry*. Even
though I'm not.

"Three buckets of water and some scrubbing took care of the blood," he tells me. "But it took a bit of thinking to figure out what to do with the . . . rest," he says.

The thought makes me queasy. "Oh."

"I wrapped it up. Stuffed it in a box. And took it to Rebecca Foster."

I sit up straight. Gape at him. "*Why?*"

"It isn't much as far as justice goes," he says. "But it's better than nothing. And that's exactly what I told her."

"What did she do?"

"Threw the whole thing in the fire, box and all, then sat in her chair and cried."

The tears are good, I think. *That's a start, at least.*

I am cold now, and when Ephraim sees the goose flesh rise along my arms, he helps me out of the tub. Helps me dry off. Helps me into a clean dress, and onto the stool before my desk. He wraps my swollen ankle in linen bandages.

"What did you learn in Boston about Cyrus's arrest?"

"Henry Knowland paid a man to have that warrant forged. He delivered it to the court in Vassalboro himself. Obadiah Wood had no idea Knowland was representing North. They arrested Cyrus on what they believed were orders from a higher court. Knowland has been charged with bribery and corruption. He'll lose his license to practice law."

"And what of the charges against Cyrus?"

"Permanently dropped."

"Good. Because he didn't kill Burgess," I tell him.

"I know."

"Nor did Isaac Foster."

"Never thought he did."

"And it wasn't Joseph North either."

This surprises him. "You're *sure?*"

"Quite."

"Then who?"

I take a deep breath. Tell him what I've finally figured out.

DAWIN'S WHARF

THURSDAY, APRIL 22

The river is heaving. All that ice now cracked and broken into jagged blocks, a million small icebergs ready to roll downstream. We have days at most before it is moving again. It is beautiful and terrifying, this opening of the river, and on more than one occasion, the ice has heaped its fury along the riverbanks, piling up and destroying everything in its path. It's why there are no homes directly beside the river. They are all built on the other side of Water Street, safely away from the threat of flood and wreckage. The wharves, however, are in danger, and Sam Dawin stands at the end of his, checking the beams for cracks and decay.

"Will it be today?" I ask, and when he turns, startled, I point at the river. "Or tomorrow?"

He shrugs. "It will be a mess, either way. I'll likely have a good bit of rebuilding to do."

Sam has built his wharf a bit farther into the river than most. Better for fishing and for water traffic. But it's a gamble when the thaw comes. He could end up rebuilding the entire thing.

"Have you come to check on May again?" he asks.

"No. This time I came to speak with you."

"Oh? About what?"

I fold my hands together and rest them in front of me. "The rope."

"What rope?"

"The one you used to hang Joshua Burgess." I catch his gaze and do not let go. I watch his brow furrow in confusion then his eyes widen in shock. "The same rope you threw to Jonathan that night so he could pull you out of the river. Where is it?"

Sam shakes his head. But it's too quick. Too frantic. "I don't know what you're talking about."

"I would have believed that, without question, last week before I saw the lace." When Sam doesn't answer I take a step forward and point. "In your pocket."

He goes perfectly still. Says nothing.

"It reminded me of what Rebecca Foster told me, how Joshua Burgess ripped a strip of lace from the hem of her shift before he raped her. That he tied his hair back with it."

Sam jerks away with revulsion, his face contorting in horror. "It isn't . . . you can't think that I—"

"No. I don't think you had anything to do with what happened to Rebecca. But I do believe that you killed Burgess. I just can't figure out *why*. It's to do with that lace, though. I am certain of it."

I wait for Sam, having long since learned that a man who does not want to speak, won't. But I can see it there, this urge in him, bubbling up, to explain himself. He curls his fingers into fists. Releases them. Grinds his teeth together. Snorts in frustration. And still, I wait as Sam Dawin wrestles with himself.

"It was May," he says, finally. "Burgess caught her alone at the Frolic last November. She'd gone out to the privy to relieve herself. Just a few minutes before he caused that scene with Hannah. I didn't notice. I was so caught up in the fight. I had no idea she'd slipped away. But she was out there when we pitched Burgess into the snow. And he was *furious*. Poor May. *Oh God.* She had no idea what had happened. But he caught her coming back to the dance. Dragged her into the barn. He . . ."

Sam clears his throat. Shakes his head. Baffled, he blinks back hot, furious tears.

"It was so loud inside—you know how it is. No one heard her crying. But when she didn't come back, I went looking for her. And I found him, standing above her, lacing his trousers."

The look on Sam Dawin's face is nothing less than tormented.

"She was right there, weeping in the hay, pushing down her skirt. I should have noticed she was gone. I should have gone out looking for her. I should have . . ." Sam plunges his hand into his pocket and pulls out the slender piece of lace. "He took it from her. Like some kind of damned *trophy*. Took the time to tie his hair back so it wouldn't get in the way while he raped her."

"So you beat him then?"

"No. He bolted. And I had to decide whether to help May or chase him. But once I got her inside the house, safe and settled, I went after him." He continues, fast and frantic now. "I'd seen what happened to Mistress Foster when she came forward. How people whispered and took sides. How they blamed it on her even though she'd been at home, minding her business when they came. The law did nothing. It *still* hasn't. North was *acquitted* for God's sake. I wasn't as patient as Isaac Foster to see justice done. Or as naïve. I had no interest in letting it play out in a court of law."

"So you killed him?"

"Wasn't hard." He shrugs, defiant. "He'd gone through the woods on foot. We found him easy enough, what with the tracks he left behind. I'm not sorry, Mistress Ballard. And you'll never hear me claim to be."

"I'll never ask that of you, Sam."

"But are you going to tell the law?"

I shake my head. "No."

"Then why do you care?"

I think of Cyrus. Of his bruised knuckles and split lip. Of his weeks in the jail yard and the charges that have just been dropped. I need to know if my son had anything to do with that death.

"Because it matters."

"If you ever speak a word of this, I'll call you a liar. And that's a word I never want to use against you, Mistress Ballard. Please don't make me."

"I won't." I set a reassuring hand on his shoulder. "I am curious about what you did with the rope, though."

"I burned it."

"Good."

All the evidence is gone.

He exhales then, as though it's settled. "An old farmer once told me that a wolf—once it's gotten a taste for human blood—must be killed because it will never stop hunting people from that point forward. I think it's the same with men—or at least some of them—and rape. I had a *duty* to kill Burgess. It would have been someone else's wife or daughter next. Yours, perhaps. Hannah most likely. He'd already set his sights on her. What if she had gone out to use the privy instead? What would you have done? Or Ephraim?"

I know exactly what my husband would do. Because I've seen him do it.

"Ephraim is the last man on earth who would ever think less of you, Sam. You don't have to fear him either. But go on, finish your story."

"We caught him," Sam continues. "Beat him, and strung him from a tree."

"But you kept the lace. Why?"

He swallows, hard. "It's a reminder that May is mine to protect. I'll never fail her again. I *won't*."

"Does that mean May's baby is . . ."

"Possibly mine. I won't lie about that. We were . . . we did . . . go to bed last fall." By the casual way he says it, I assume it was more of a regular habit, than an isolated incident. "We were already betrothed. But when she turned up pregnant . . ."

"You married her early."

"It was the right thing to do. I had to protect her. They would *fine* her in court. You know that. They'd call her a fornicator and the baby a bastard. And if anyone ever found out about Burgess, they would never look at May the same way again. Or the child. I don't care what they think of me, Mistress Ballard, but I'll not let them disparage her. She did nothing wrong."

"I know that. And I don't blame you, Sam." I take a step closer to him. "I have said it before, but I mean it. May is lucky to have you."

"So you'll not tell?"

"Only my husband. We keep no secrets between us." We stand there watching the ice move in the river, and something else occurs to me. "Sam?"

"Yes?"

"You said *we*. 'We caught him and beat him and strung him from a tree.'" That bit of doubt is back now, scratching at the back of my mind, and I have to know for sure. "Did you take Cyrus with you that night?"

He shakes his head. Laughs at the absurdity of such an idea. "No. I took Jonathan."

POLLARD'S TAVERN

FRIDAY, APRIL 30

The Court of General Sessions meets on this last Friday of the month. It is the first warm day of spring. The sun is shining, the river is open, and what little snow remains in the Hook is hard packed and dirty, heaped in the shadows and piled at the edge of the road. Mostly there is mud.

Mud on boots and clothes and caked into horseshoes and spread across the floor of the tavern. Abigail Pollard has given up trying to keep the place clean and—judging by the scowl on her face—is tempted to toss her broom into the hearth and let it burn. Instead, she chucks it into the corner and retreats to her table. When she sees me watching, she laughs, then lifts her mug and takes a long gulp of cider.

I had not expected to find Joseph North on the bench. I had not expected to see him in public for some time, to be honest. But there he is at the table, wearing his robe and wig, sitting on a cushion, gavel in hand. If I'm being honest, he looks more than a little peaked. His skin is pale, and there is a film of sweat across his upper lip.

I've come here to do the thing required of me by my profession, and I had thought I'd be giving my testimony to Obadiah Wood. It was my understanding that he would be traveling down from Vassalboro until Judge North recovered from the strange illness that has kept him abed these last ten days. Much has been made of this in the

Hook. Rumors flitting this way and that as happens in small towns such as ours. I've heard several versions myself.

Consumption is generally agreed upon.

The croup has also been mentioned, though no one has seen him cough.

Indigestion. Humors. The ague. All of these options have taken their turn around the rumor mill.

Dropsy.

Gout.

Piles.

The putrid sore throat. Scurvy. Diarrhea.

It is boils, however, that most assume to be the cause of his affliction. Why else would he have spent ten straight days laid up in bed and now be forced to use a cushion whenever he sits? It is the logical conclusion, and one I would have taken to myself under other circumstances.

I can only assume that Dr. Page was paid handsomely for his silence because dismemberment has not once been mentioned by anyone in the Hook.

I know that North sees me at the back of the room waiting to give my testimony. I know that he sees Ephraim as well, but I get the sense that North will not make a show of me today. Or perhaps ever again.

Today's court business is typical. Petty local issues. Things of no major import to life or law. Just a great deal of ruffled feathers after a long, grueling winter. And I doubt there would have been but a handful of cases called if today had not been the day they buried Joshua Burgess. It's the first day the ground has been soft enough to dig a grave big enough and Amos insisted it was time to get Burgess out of his shed. In the end, the same seven men who cut Burgess from the ice committed him to the ground. It seemed fitting. And seeing as how there is no church, he couldn't be buried in the church yard—not that anyone would have wanted him to be. They chose the woods instead. Just a hole. No words were said. But Amos Pollard did insist upon a stone cairn.

"Last zing ve need is a leg bone getting dragged down the middle of Vater Street if ze dogs get to him," Amos had said.

No one argued.

The whole fiasco drew a crowd, however. And of course, the crowd then wandered back to Pollard's. Then proceeded to get drunk. Now everyone has a complaint, and I am ready to be home.

"Martha Ballard?" Joseph North calls my name from the front of the room. "You have business to attend?"

I stand. Make my way forward. "I have evidence to give in a legal cause."

"What manner?" he asks.

This is the call and response that we have performed for many years now. As familiar to those in this room as a nursery rhyme. Few pay attention to us.

"An unwed woman has named the father of her child, and I bring it before the court so it may be recorded."

"Name the woman," he says. "Name the father."

I have done this countless times, of course, but it feels different now. And though I hate to do it, I will not shirk my responsibilities.

"On Sunday, April eighteenth, Sally Pierce gave birth to a son."

I may as well have dropped a large stone into a small pond for all the ripples this announcement makes. Everyone listens now. Even North is surprised.

"The daughter of William Pierce?" he asks.

"Yes."

"I did not realize she was with child."

"You are not alone in that," I tell him.

"And who is the father of this child?"

It is a long breath, and I draw it slowly. But I have only opened my mouth to answer when I feel a presence at my side.

"I am," Jonathan says.

Quickly, softly, he reaches for my hand and gives it a squeeze.

"And I have come to pay her court fee. Twenty shillings. Far and above anything required by law for a first offense. You will also find that I have posted our intent to marry outside the tavern."

Jonathan pulls a coin purse from his pocket and drops it on the table before Henry Sewell. He watches as the confession and the fee are recorded, then signs his name beside both.

"Do you have any other business to attend, Mistress Ballard?" North asks.

I know that he is in pain. But I think being robbed of the chance to humiliate me before the court hurts him most.

"No," I say. But then I cannot help myself, and I add, "Though I would be remiss if I did not inquire about your health. I've been told it's taken a turn for the worse of late."

He clenches his jaw. Glares at me. "Do not concern yourself with my welfare. I am on the mend."

"A credit, no doubt, to being tended by a *trained medical professional.*"

I care not what his reaction might be, and I have turned, am halfway through the room when Jonathan catches up with me. North bangs his gavel, adjourning court, and the crowd rises, pushing back their benches. Muttering. Gossiping.

"I am not such a bad man as you might think," Jonathan says, his mouth near my ear.

"I have never thought you a bad man."

"Even now?"

"You did the right thing by Sally. And by your son."

"That's not what I mean. Sam said that you came to see him. That he told you of my part in that . . . business."

I stop as the room swirls around us. Set my hand on his cheek. I feel the stubble beneath my hands. He has Ephraim's eyes. A steely kind of blue. They are kind, but filled with a deep resolve.

"Ask your father about a man named Billy Crane," I tell him. "And you will understand why I am not angry with you."

*

Friday, April 30——Clear and warm. Joshua Burgess buried this morning. Have been to the Hook for court. Came home in the afternoon. Barnabas Lambard tarries for dinner. Moses Pollard as well. Jonathan brought Sally, along with their new son. I have been at home.

Twelve Years Ago

HALLOWELL, MAINE

APRIL 30, 1778

Ephraim pulled the three large stones from the wagon one at a time and set them on the ground.

It had been raining when we arrived the day before. A soft, warm, spring rain. But still inconvenient given we were sleeping in tents. But now the sun was out, and the children were spread across the clearing, exploring this new place. They ranged in age from Cyrus, almost twenty-two, to Young Ephraim, not quite a month.

"I have been at this a long time," I told my husband as we stood beside the wagon. I held our baby in the crook of my arm. "I am done."

"With?"

"Babies. Moving. Upheaval."

"I am happy to be done," he said, and kissed my forehead. "Now that I have finally gotten one named after me."

It took him nine years to convince me to make this move. A patient man is Ephraim Ballard. Our home was in Oxford. Our *daughters* were there. That was the hardest thing for me to reconcile. Leaving them. I could agree that Ephraim was right about the rest. We needed land and lots of it. And it made perfect sense to put his carpentry skills to use in the lumber trade. But the starting over? The living in tents while he built us another house from the ground up? I wanted no part of that.

Young Ephraim was a surprise. Born seven years after Dolly, he had arrived long after I thought my childbearing efforts complete. It was my pregnancy with him that forced me to relent. We had run out of room and opportunities in Oxford. Our compromise was to bring our daughters with us in spirit.

"Come," Ephraim said. "Let's find the right spot for our girls."

He took the baby from my arms then, and we began a slow stroll across the property. He showed me where he wanted to build the house.

"Big enough that you can have your own workroom," he said. "Hannah and Dolly can have their own bedroom. As can the boys. But upstairs."

"That's a big house."

"Yes. That's exactly what I've been trying to tell you. It will be big enough to hold us all. And all the children that our children will have one day as well. Big enough for a loud, raucous Christmas."

We wandered on.

"That's where I'll put the barn. And there"—he pointed to the swollen, gurgling creek—"is where I'll build the mill. Bigger than the barn. Big enough to store entire loads of lumber. And once I've got it finished, I'm going to make a pier that stretches out over the water so we can shove the logs directly into the current. Maybe I'll even have a waterwheel one day as well."

He had already named it Mill Creek, and, farther on, it spilled into the Kennebec, a fierce and raging river. It was broad and deep, and moved fast with spring rain and snowmelt. But that, he assured me, was exactly what you want in the lumber trade. You must transport the boards, you see. And you needed a river to do it.

Ephraim showed me pastures and gardens and paddocks that didn't yet exist. A hen house. A kitchen garden. An orchard. The woodlands were there already, of course, as was the pond. But I saw the rest clearly enough as he painted each detail with words. It took an hour, this wandering across the land, and I found that by the end we were both headed in the same direction, toward a huge, ancient live oak that grew at the top of the hill in what Ephraim was already calling the south pasture. Its canopy spread fifty feet at least, and its roots were old and gnarled. Its leaves a fresh and burgeoning green that would provide plentiful shade in summer.

He pointed to the base of the tree. "That's a fox hole. And that, love, means that we'll be watched over in this place."

I nodded but couldn't speak.

"You are tired." Ephraim wiped a tear off my cheek with his knuckle. "Sit down and rest."

He handed the baby to me and strode back to the wagon. One by one he brought the stones and placed them beneath the tree, and when it was done, he settled onto the damp grass beside me.

He reached out and brushed a thumb along my cheek. "I would not wish any companion in the world but you," he said.

"You're just full of the Bard today, aren't you?" I asked. And when he laughed, I quoted a line myself. "For which of my bad parts didst thou first fall in love with me?"

"For all of your parts. Those inward and out," he answered, pulling me closer so that he could press a kiss onto my forehead. Together we turned to survey this place where we would build a new life together.

"It feels good to be home," I said.

And it did.

OUR REVELS NOW ARE ENDED

There is screaming in the distance. Somewhere, out there, beyond the garden gate. It wakes the woman from a deep and restful sleep, and she is left kicking against the covers, reaching for the tail end of a dream that makes no sense—something about ropes and rivers—but it fades from her mind as she sets bare feet on the scuffed wood floors.

The screaming grows louder now, more intense, and two long strides bring her to the window where she pushes aside the heavy curtains. For the first time in many long months, there is no frost on the corners of each glass pane, no bits of silver filigree that catch the light. Spring has finally come to the town of Hallowell.

No, she thinks, listening closer. *Not screaming.*

The sound is that of whining and whimpering. But not a dog. Nor a wolf. Not the mean yip and snarl of a coyote. It is gentler. Softer.

So, it is my fox then, she thinks.

The woman grabs a blanket from the foot of the bed and wraps it around her shoulders. The floorboards creak with age as she moves toward the front door. Her feet are bare, pale and ghostly, but it is warmer now, and she has no need of stockings, of boots.

When the woman pulls the door open, she sees the fox immediately. "Tempest," she says, her voice little more than a breath in the cool morning breeze.

The river is open. Where once the ice lay thick and solid from bank to bank, now it moves in a molten, gurgling flow. It is still cold as death from the long winter and the snowmelt, but has become a churning, lethal wall of water, dirty and dark, flowing south. And there, in the distance, if you listen closely, is the sound of a water-wheel. It too turns freely, sending its music into the dawn. A tinkling, metallic charm.

The fox hears both river and wheel as she sits at the entrance to her den, watching the woman. She hears them and is pleased. This is a gentle season, at least until the rains begin. That always brings a different kind of trouble. For now, however, the valley is lush and verdant and filled with new life. Nuts and berries and little creatures flitting from tree to tree. There are flowers: daffodils and iris and hyacinth. The soil smells fresh and ripe, tender shoots pushing through the surface of every field. Worms and ladybugs and butterflies.

The fox also has something to offer the world this spring, and she whimpers again, urging her kits to leave the den. They are hesitant, so her mate meets her at the entrance. Presses his nose to hers. He shoves them out gently, one by one. Slowly they tumble into the grass and begin to explore the gnarled roots of the ancient, live oak tree. They investigate this new place. Scratch at the bark. Sniff the three large moss-covered stones. They climb and tumble. Hide and play.

And all the while the woman watches from her place at the door. Watches and wonders. Remembering. Wistful. Beneath her awe is a kind of grief, old and tender, like a scar. But even that cannot swallow the joy she feels at the sight before her. There are four kits. One male—big and red like his father—and three females. Slender and dark, like their mother. Silver. *Rare.*

Author's Note

If I could, I would string a line of caution tape, right here, across your path. Warning! Danger! Crime Scene Do Not Cross! All the usual descriptors apply in this situation. If you are familiar with my books, you will already know that, in the following pages, I will unpack this novel in detail. There will be revelations and explanations and spoilers aplenty. If this is the first fictional journey you have taken with me, may I say two things: thank you for trusting me with your time, and turn back now. Do not read the following pages until you have first read the novel, beginning to end.

Every story moves like a river, from source to mouth, so let this one flow, and I'll meet you back here at the end.

No doubt you'll have questions.

*

I collect people. I come by this honestly. In the same way that others collect rocks or stamps or coins, my own father collected people. To be precise, he brought home hitchhikers. In his case, it was not a dangerous pastime. My father was once a rancher. As a teenager, a friend dared him to enter a bronc-riding contest at the rodeo but, dissatisfied with the eight seconds that would win him the prize, he rode that bronco for twenty minutes straight, until it gave up altogether and stood still in the middle of the stadium, sides heaving, breathing a cloud of dust and manure. Needless to say, my father didn't technically win. But he proved his point. From there he went on to serve as a Military Police officer in the army. He could handle hitchhikers easily enough.

I mention that to say, like my father, I too am compelled to bring people home. Only I don't pick mine up on the side of the road. I find them up in libraries and newspapers and strange corners of the internet. You see, the people I invite back to my place—my office, specifically—and into my mind are long since dead: a missing judge in 1930s New York; the only woman to ever serve aboard a Zeppelin aircraft; a Russian grand duchess; the most decorated woman to serve in World War II; and now, a renowned but nearly forgotten midwife.

I collect *people*.

This one stumbled across my path in a doctor's office fifteen years ago. I was pregnant with our youngest son and my obstetrician was late for my appointment. He'd gotten tied up with a tricky delivery, and I'd gotten stranded in his waiting room as a result. I remember thinking that I should reschedule and go home. Had I done that, you would not be holding this book in your hands. I was bored and had long since finished reading the copy of *Stardust* by Neil Gaiman that I'd brought with me. I'd thumbed through every magazine, and all that was left to read was a small devotional titled *Our Daily Bread*. (For the record, I am not opposed to devotionals. This one had simply been hiding beneath a stack of alarming pamphlets and I had not seen it until then.) The entry for August 1, 2008, read "The Midwife's Tale" and proceeded to tell the story of a woman named Martha Ballard who had delivered over a thousand babies in her career and never once lost a mother in childbirth. (My own doctor—the one I was anxiously waiting to see—couldn't boast a record like that.) As happens every time I am struck by inspiration, all the little hairs stood up on the back of my neck. I tore that page out of the devotional and stuffed it in my purse. (I have it here on my desk as I write this and am laughing at the note I scribbled at the top that day: "Would make a GREAT novel!") I kid you not, my doctor walked in two minutes later. And thus began a yearslong process of research and writing and false starts. Elation and frustration and all of the things that bring a book into the world. But I never gave up.

Which brings us to a very important conversation we must have regarding Martha Ballard and this specific novel. My longtime readers know how closely I stick to historical fact. It is a point of pride for me and why many have called what I write "biographical fiction." *The Frozen River* marks my first real deviation from that track record.

The book you hold in your hands is *inspired* by real events as opposed to being *based* on them. And, as you are about to see, I took great liberties not only with dates and details but, in some cases, the historical record itself.

I did not do so lightly.

And I have good reason for it.

I would never present this novel as alternate history. Roughly 75 percent of what happens on these pages closely follows the historical record. The rest is my version of what *could* have happened. But if you are looking for the facts—and *nothing* but the facts, ma'am—I *highly* suggest you pick up a copy of Laurel Thatcher Ulrich's Pulitzer Prize–winning biography of Martha Ballard, *A Midwife's Tale*. It is, to the best of my knowledge, the only comprehensive history of her life, and is required reading if you want to understand Martha's role in history. It is an astonishing work of nonfiction.

There are numerous instances where I changed, edited, clarified, or condensed Martha's diary entries. For example, the places where Martha records that Rebecca Foster "has sworn a rape on a number of men among whom is Judge North" includes diary entries from both August 19 and December 23. I did this to give the reader a clearer, more immediate idea of what happened to Rebecca that horrible night. Not every diary entry that is included in these pages happens in the year or even on the specific date shown. A very small handful are fictional. My goal was to take many of the things that interested *me* about Martha's life and condense them into one story that takes place over a six-month period.

The court system in early America was nothing like it is today. At the time this story takes place, the Constitution had existed as the country's founding legal document for only two and a half years, and the Bill of Rights had not yet been ratified. In Martha's day there was only the Court of General Sessions (where you could sue your neighbor for petty reasons), the Court of Common Pleas (that considered more serious crimes such as assault), the Supreme Judicial Court (that handled rape, murder, and appeals from the lower courts), and the Supreme Court of the United States (there were only six justices and its first meeting was on February 1, 1790—toward the end of when this story takes place).

So when I ask you to take everything you know about due process and legal matters and throw it out the window, that is why. Honestly, the citizens of early America were lucky to have a justice system at all.

After waiting for many years, I seriously began this novel during the COVID-19 pandemic. What that meant for me, personally, is that I wrote surrounded at all times by four adolescent boys—and all the noise and chaos that entails. It is not my preferred method of writing by any stretch. But it was illuminating for one specific reason: I had to do my work right smack dab in the middle of my family life. And that is exactly how Martha Ballard lived and worked for decades. There was no separation. One phrase in her diary is repeated thousands of times over twenty-seven years: "I have been at home." When I first came across that oft-repeated remark, I thought little of it. But it took on new meaning for me during the pandemic because I too could write that in my own diary. *I have been at home.* For months and months and months. For years, in fact.

If you read Laurel Thatcher Ulrich, you will find a very different Martha Ballard than the one portrayed on these pages. In fact, you may not recognize them as the same woman. I did that on purpose. I wrote Martha as she came to me and, given that history has recorded so little of her, I will argue that my version is, at the very least, plausible. Should you endeavor to get a copy of her diary yourself, know this: it is very expensive (Picton Press published a limited number in 1992 and mine cost $350), very dry, and it's not really a diary at all. It's more a daybook. Martha does little to no editorializing. Only a handful of times in twenty-seven years does she reveal her feelings about anything she records. Instead, she gives us the date, the weather, and the facts. The longest entry she made in that time was on December 23, 1789: the date of Rebecca Foster's first legal hearing in Vassalboro. And though Martha was literate (a thing unheard-of for women in her time), few readers today would be able to decipher much of what she wrote. Here is an example of an entry I included in the book. You'll understand why I edited it as I did.

3 5 X. Birth. Charls Clearks 3d Dagt. XX Clearn morn. I was Calld by Cowen to Charls Clearks wife in travil at 2 h morn. Shee was Safe Delivrd of a Dagt (her 3d Child, all Dagts), at 4th hour. I left her Cleaverly and 8 & was Conducted to mr Pollards.

This entry is listed under the year 1789. The 3 is the day of the month and the 5 is the day of the week (I changed it to November 26 in order to open Martha's story with the birth of Betsy Clark's daughter), and the rest takes a good bit of patience to sift through. The real entry goes on for a bit longer but contained information that did not pertain to my story so I did not include it. Throughout, she makes no effort at consistency when it comes to the spelling of names or places. So I did that for her in this story. What I'm saying is: you're welcome.

A few more things because I'm sure you're curious:

A note on the various currencies mentioned throughout the novel. I use dollars and pounds interchangeably. Both were in use at this time, though the dollar (named after the Spanish dollar) was the primary coinage. However, English pounds were still in heavy circulation as well. Martha mentions receiving both forms of payment in her diary, despite the fact that the U.S. dollar was not established as the official currency until 1792—and was not minted until later that same year. It would seem that she was willing to take whatever payment she could get. Or, in many cases, chickens, coffee, sugar, or wool instead. Martha was paid in goods and services as frequently as with money.

Sally Pierce really did have Jonathan Ballard's illegitimate son, but he was born in February 1791, almost a year after this story ends. And yes, Martha did have to take her testimony in childbirth. It's the closest she comes to being gobsmacked in her diary. However the young couple might have felt about each other, they went on to have twelve more children (three were stillborn).

Cyrus Ballard never married or left home, but Martha gives no reason in her diary as to why. Ulrich notes that it was rare for a man to remain unmarried and in his parents' household in that day, and she postulates that he might have had some sort of mental or physical disability that prevented him from finding a wife. I connected those imaginary dots to a tragic time in Martha's history so that it would fit neatly within the story I wanted to tell.

Moses Pollard and Hannah Ballard did indeed get married. The wedding happened in 1792 and shortly thereafter they moved to Fort Western and opened a tavern of their own. The happy couple went on to have nine children between 1794 and 1809.

Barnabas Lambard and Dolly Ballard met a bit later than I describe in this book. They married in 1795 and were the rather prolific parents of eleven children (their first was born in 1796). As recorded in Martha's diary, Dolly, her sister, and their husbands visited often.

Sam Dawin did indeed fall through the ice trying to get to shore on a raft with Jonathan. But here is where I made a major deviation in the story: he never saw a body. Which brings us to Joshua Burgess.

Captain Joshua Burgess was one of three men accused of raping Rebecca Foster in August 1789. Yes, you read that right. *Three*. The third, a man named Elijah Davis, was cut from this story altogether. I did that in part to simplify the narrative. The harder reason, however, is that in Martha's diary, those three men sexually assaulted Rebecca Foster three different times over the course of one week. What is portrayed as horrific here was in fact a series of nine unspeakable assaults in real life.

Reader, I could not bring myself to write that.

Joshua Burgess disappears from the pages of Martha's diary somewhere around December 1789. *Poof*, he's gone. She never mentions him again. Could he have skipped town? Absolutely. Is it also possible that he died somehow or somewhere? Sure. So I went with that and used it as the bedrock for the novel. I mean, honestly, I don't feel sorry for the guy. He is dead to me!

A word about rape: it is—unfortunately—nothing new. Sexual assault and all its gradients have been with mankind from the beginning. We find records of it in every ancient text from the Bible to Shakespeare. And yes, okay, my solution to a gross injustice is severe. (Or *severing*, if you will.) And shocking. And not a little excessive. (But I would like the record to show that when Larry McMurtry made a similar choice in *Lonesome Dove*, they gave him a Pulitzer. So, you know, poetic justice, man.)

The real Joseph North walked away scot-free from his trial and was never made to account for his crimes. That is unconscionable to me. I cannot change history, but I do have control over the stories I tell, and in this instance, at least, I gave him what he deserved.

In writing that scene I could not help but think of a friend who suffered unspeakable predations for much of her childhood and adolescence until she finally took matters—and a knife—into her own hands and drove it into the thigh of her abuser. My friend, so young and brave and broken, looked at him, trembling, and said that if he ever touched her again, next time she wouldn't miss. He never did and this ending was for her. And for every other woman who hasn't seen justice in her lifetime.

It's not enough.

But it's something.

It is worth noting here that Joseph North's rape trial did not happen until July 1790. In an effort to better serve this story I condensed the time frame, but other than that, every detail is accurate, including the fact that Rebecca Foster did not attend (Martha's diary does not record a reason why). Primarily, I made that choice so that the entire story could be contained within the opening and closing of the river.

If you are familiar with Martha's life (either through the Ulrich biography or through her diary itself) you will know that she makes no mention of being a sexual assault survivor herself. Was she? According to statistics—which I do not think have changed much in the last few hundred years—there is a 33 percent chance of its being true. Of every decision I made in this book, that was the riskiest. The truth is, I don't know. But it would help explain the deep devotion she felt for Rebecca Foster.

Regarding Tempest: she burst into my life in the middle of the night on June 19, 2018. My husband and I woke up to a sound that can only be described as our most dearly beloved being slaughtered in their sleep. Turns out, after a mad dash through the house at three in the morning to make sure our children were still alive, we discovered a fox barking in our yard. (Look that up on YouTube and see if it doesn't give you the heebie-jeebies.) A few hours later, a newborn baby entered my life. It's a long story and not mine to tell, but those two things became inextricably linked in my mind. The fox and the baby. To this day, I am fiercely protective of both. So it made sense that they should each have a part in this book.

Seventeen hundred eighty-five was known as the "year of the long winter" to the residents of Hallowell, Maine. Martha Ballard's diary records that the river froze on November 25 and was still solid on April 22 of the following year. I changed it so that those events happened between November 1789 and April 1790, the year that Rebecca Foster "swore a rape against a number of men."

Martha's diary mentions the "Negro female doctor" who came to town. No first name is ever given for her, so I simply named her

Doctor. It is worth noting that there is no indication whatsoever that Martha held any kind of prejudiced feelings toward her Black neighbors. There were twelve free Black families living in Hallowell during the years her diary was written. Martha delivered their babies and interacted with them as she did everyone else in town. She wrote their full names in her diary. So it is no stretch to believe that she simply did not know the name of this female Doctor. I was personally fascinated with both the medical title and how Martha's neighbors would bypass her care and go to this other woman instead. Surely that means the woman had greater skill than Martha? Or that they had secrets to keep? Perhaps both.

I changed the name Hannah Sewell to Grace Sewell in this book. There were just too many Hannahs in Martha's journal (a very popular biblical name at the time), and it became untenable to distinguish between them on the page. *This* Hannah, not *that* Hannah. Again, you're welcome.

Because I know you're going to ask, no, I did not deliver any of my four children with a midwife. I wanted to. I believe in the work they do, and I trust the thousands of years' worth of knowledge that has been passed from one to another throughout human history. My mother had all six of her children at home with midwives. I was present for one of those births, and it quite literally changed my life. (The sister whom I witnessed coming into the world later let me witness the birth of her son. It was a perfect full-circle moment.) But my husband begged me not to. He certainly has nothing against this most noble profession either. He just couldn't stomach the idea of me being in such physical pain. And, dear reader, he was so earnest. Tormented, even, at the thought of seeing my body turned inside out without a scrap of pharmaceutical intervention. I love the man. So, I conceded. And I do not regret it. Our youngest child might well have ended up stillborn otherwise. There are times when it is wise to put your medical care in the hands of a man who knows how to use a scalpel.

Martha Ballard is the great-aunt of Clara Barton, founder of the American Red Cross. She is also the great-great-grandmother of Mary Hobart, one of the first female physicians in the United States. She left a medical legacy in this country that is unmatched. And it is all thanks to the diary she kept. Just words on paper, right? Seemingly meaningless. They're only the record of one woman's meticulous daily life. But those pages were preserved and passed to Dolly (Ballard) Lambard. She gave them to her daughter Sarah, who passed them on to Dr. Mary Hobart, who donated them to the Maine State Library, where they sat until they were organized and bound by Lucy (Lambard) Fessenden. Many years later, law librarian Edith L. Hary made those pages available to the public. And finally, Cynthia McCausland translated all six million bytes of text so that the full transcript could be published by Picton Press. Laurel Thatcher Ulrich, the Pulitzer Prize–winning historian and professor, studied the diary and wrote the definitive biography of a woman who should have vanished from history. If not for one diary and the power of words.

It bears repeating that this is a novel, a work of fiction, my version of what *could* have happened in this woman's life. It is not a biography, nor do I claim to be an historian. I'm simply a storyteller, and I have felt, for fifteen years, that Martha's story is worth telling. I want you to know her name. I want you tell your friends. I hope that you too are astonished by her life. I want the world to remember that small acts, done in love, matter every bit as much as the ones that make the newspaper and the history books.

Toward the end of Laurel Thatcher Ulrich's biography, she has this to say:

> Martha Ballard ensured that she would not be forgotten. There was nothing in Christian tradition that said a midwife ought to keep a diary. . . . For some complex of reasons, probably unknown even to her, Martha felt an intense need to re-create her own life day by day. . . . She not only documented her prayers, her lost sleep, her deeds of charity and compassion, she savored and wrote down the petty struggles and small graces of ordinary life. The diary is a selective record, shaped by her need to justify and understand her life, yet is also a remarkably honest one . . . [it] tells us that Martha was a devout Christian and humble nurse whose intelligence sometimes made it difficult for her to attend church or defer to her town's physicians, a loving mother, a gentle woman with a sense of duty and an anatomical curiosity that allowed her to observe autopsies as well as cry over the dead, a courageous woman who never quite learned to

stay on her horse, a sharp-eyed and practical woman who kept faith in ultimate justice. . . . Outside her own diary, Martha has no history. No independent record of her work survives. It is her husband's name, not hers, that appears in censuses, tax lists, and merchant accounts for her town. . . . Nor does any extant record acknowledge the testimony she took from unwed mothers in delivery. Her name appears on a list of witnesses at the North rape trial, but no one, except her, preserved a record of what was said. . . . Martha did not leave a farm, but a life, recorded patiently and consistently for twenty-seven years. No gravestone bears her name though perhaps there still grow clumps of chamomile or feverfew escaped from her garden.

During the first week of May 1812, Martha Ballard made her final diary entries:

Tuesday, May 5—Snowed and very cold. I have felt very feeble. I have been at home.

Wednesday, May 6—A very stormy day. I do not feel any better. I have been at home.

Thursday, May 7—Clear most of the day and very cold and windy. Daughter Ballard and a number of her children here . . . Reverend Mr. Tappin came and conversed sweetly and made a prayer adapted to my case. I have been at home. Very feeble.

The "Daughter Ballard" whom Martha refers to in this last entry is none other than Sally Pierce, the young woman who remained a thorn in her side for most of this book. And while I have no doubt that her own daughters were at her bedside as well in her final days, I find this last mention of Sally incredibly sweet. I like to think they made amends. I like to think that the grandson made it possible. Martha died a few days after this last entry, leaving behind her husband, Ephraim, and all six of their living children.

I love that the second-to-last phrase mentioned in her diary is the one she wrote most often, for it exemplifies the last three years of my own life as I have attempted to write her story.

I have been at home.

Me too, Martha. Me too.

Acknowledgments

I can no other answer make, but,
thanks, and thanks, and ever thanks.

—WILLIAM SHAKESPEARE

It takes a great deal of effort for an idea to become a book. Sure, the author plays a significant role in that (and I am thankful that my own brain got the job done), but not the only role. Because once I have taken that Nothing and turned it into Something, it then must go through a long, complex process to become the tangible thing that you hold in your hands. This particular book would not exist if not for the following people:

Elisabeth Weed—literary agent extraordinaire—has kept me sane and gainfully employed for over a decade. And I will never really understand how she took my dream of being published and turned it into a long and fulfilling career, but I will forever be grateful to her. I could not do this job without her. I would not want to do this job without her. She has been friend and advocate, therapist and coach. The entire team at The Book Group is a joy to work with. Other than Elisabeth, DJ Kim is the name I most love to see in my inbox. Faye Bender, Julie Barer, and Brettne Bloom have all been kinder to me than I deserve.

I had the great fortune of working with two wonderful editors on this book. Margo Shickmanter acquired Martha's story, and Carolyn

Williams got me through to the end. They are both *really* good at what they do, and I was fortunate to have them.

The team at Doubleday is unsurpassed in publishing, and I am lucky to have spent my entire career working with them. Todd Doughty, Elena Hershey, and Jillian Briglia are the best publicity team working today. Bill Thomas and Suzanne Herz have championed my work since the beginning. Judy Jacoby and Lindsay Mandel are marketing wizards. The diligence, talent, and patience of John Fontana, Nora Reichard, Lorraine Hyland, and Soonyoung Kwon are the reason that a former Word document is now a beautiful, tangible novel. I am so grateful for all they do.

The Doubleday sales team is the reason that you can buy my books wherever books are sold. Special thanks go to Jessica Pearson, Valerie Walley, Christine Weag, Ann Kingman, Emily Bates, Lynn Kovach, Beth Koehler, Beth Meister, Mallory Conder, Chris Dufault, Ruth Liebman, David Weller, Annie Schatz, Jason Gobble, and Nicholas LaRousse. Their ongoing enthusiasm means the world to me.

The support and generosity of independent bookstores has enabled me to meet readers from coast to coast. Thank you for inviting me in, for introducing me to your beloved customers, and for handselling my novels these last twelve years. I am particularly grateful for Parnassus Books, Page & Palette, Foxtale Book Shoppe, Watermark Books, Books & Company, Northshire Books, Square Books, Interabang Books, A Likely Story, Novel Bookstore, The Little Bookshop, Litchfield Books, The Poisoned Pen, and Warwick's. Thank you so, so much!

Marybeth Whalen is a rare friend: the kind who will tell you the truth. But—if necessary—I suspect she'd also help me plot revenge. For fifteen years she made me laugh and made me cry (in a good way). She has sent me snarky texts and nice purses, and I can't wait for our next adventure!

The writing community in Nashville is vast and supportive and one of the highlights of having this gig. They are the Venn diagram that combines my work life and my real life. I'm proud to call them all friends. JT Ellison feeds me queso and valuable knowledge. Lisa Patton is the reason I must seek treatment for Inappropriate Laughter Syndrome. Traci Keel serves me old-fashioneds with a healthy side of sarcasm. Blake Leyers reminds me that I am not, in fact, A Very

Dumb Person. Joy Jordan-Lake has the rare gift of encouragement. Paige Crutcher always sends the right text at the right time.

The writing community outside Nashville has also welcomed me with open arms, and I've discovered great friends in Patti Callahan Henry, Abbot Kahler, Denise Kiernan, Laura Benedict, Deanna Raybourn, Greer McAllister, Helen Ellis, and Anne Bogel.

Kristee Mays has known me longer than my husband, and let's just say that I'm not a spring chicken. She actually predicted I'd marry him! And she stood beside me at the altar when that day came. We don't see each other often enough, but can pick up right where we left off. She's seen me through it all, and I love her madly.

My uncle Will answered every question that I had about horses and cows and livestock in general while I wrote this book. Even when the text showed up at seven in the morning or ten at night. I am grateful that he was not appalled by my lack of knowledge. Given my familial history, I should know more than I do, but I'm grateful that he filled in the gaps.

Once again, Garreth Russell was a godsend in the areas of research and good humor. Many of the details about childbirth in the late eighteenth century were thanks to him. I promise to make it up to you, Garreth!

Other friends, family, and neighbors who generally kept me encouraged and fed during the writing process include Abby Belbeck, Josh Belbeck, Emily Allison, Tayler Storrs, Kaylee Storrs, Dian Belbeck, Jerry and Kay Lawhon, Blake and Tracy Lawhon, Andy and Nicole Kreiling, Jannell Barefoot, Michael and Cindy Easley, Chris Wilson, and Christine Flott.

I am thankful for Ranier Maria Rilke and his poetry collection *Rilke's Book of Hours: Love Poems to God*, and also for Mary Oliver's *Devotions*. For most of my life poetry has felt like a foreign language. Perhaps because I cannot write it? Regardless, I am learning, slowly. I read a poem from each of those books every day that I sat down to write, and I believe the spirit that I found there, that sense of wonder and worship and awe, has made its way, ever so slightly, into these pages. Thank you for teaching me this new language.

I made the best decision of my life twenty-three years ago when I married Ashley Lawhon. He has made all the difference in a life that could have gone either way. That's a gift and a mercy that cannot be explained. He's the reason for my laugh lines and also my stretch marks (hello, four children). He is the inspiration for every touching thing that Martha Ballard says about marriage in this book. He's the reason that I have no interest in writing about bad marriages. He makes me laugh every day. He lets me sleep in every day. He is my best friend, my safe place, my one and only lover. I am who I am today because he has loved me well. That is a thing I will never take for granted.

I have often talked about the children that Ashley and I made together. Those four boys could not be more different than the points on a compass. Two look like him and two look like me, and together they have added a purpose to my life that I wouldn't have thought possible in my younger years. I cannot believe that they are all grown now—or almost so. If not entirely empty, our nest is certainly quiet. I don't know how we survived the chaos this long, but London, Parker, Marshall, and Riggs are worth every bit of it. I cannot wait to watch them take the world by storm.

On the long list of things that I am thankful for, Jesus is at the top. Thirty years ago, He found a lost and broken girl in the sagebrush of nowhere New Mexico and saved her. That alone would have been enough. But He has been with me every day since. It is my greatest hope that His great love is reflected in the pages of this book.

As the Bard says above, for all that I am and all that I've been given, "I can no other answer make, but, thanks, and thanks, and ever thanks."

Ariel Lawhon is a critically acclaimed *New York Times* bestselling author of historical fiction. Her books have been translated into numerous languages and have been selections of Library Reads, One Book One County, Indie Next, Costco, Amazon Spotlight, and Book of the Month Club. She lives in the rolling hills outside Nashville, Tennessee, with her husband and four sons. Ariel splits her time between the grocery store and the baseball field.

ABOUT THE TYPE

This book was set in Adobe Garamond. Designed for the Adobe Corporation by Robert Slimbach, the fonts are based on types first cut by Claude Garamond (ca. 1480–1561). Garamond was a pupil of Geoffroy Tory and is believed to have followed the Venetian models, although he introduced a number of important differences, and it is to him that we owe the letter we now know as "old style." He gave to his letters a certain elegance and feeling of movement that won their creator an immediate reputation and the patronage of Francis I of France.

Composed by Digital Composition
Berryville, Virginia

Printed and bound by Berryville Graphics
Berryville, Virginia